MATCHMAKER'S MASQ...

When Stephanie Se... bling old mansion ... she had no idea she... the ghost of a love... Now the haunting strains of a violin disturb her sleep each night. And when she does dream, her late Great-aunt Magnolia comes to call, complaining that "someone has to deal with that man." Traveling back in time to play matchmaker, Stephanie seeks to pair up the lonely spinster with a notorious Southern rogue . . . But she soon finds herself in the arms of a devilishly charming prospectve with ideas of his own.

WALTZ IN TIME

A handsome, broad-shouldered widower, Andre Goddard is thrilled to have finally found someone like Stephanie who can match his passion and fire—and who is firm, yet loving, toward his five rambunctious children. Of course the headstrong woman's infuriating insistence that she has come from the future to unite Andre with his shy, dowdy housekeeper is a serious obstacle to his romantic plans. And Stephanie is certain she could never give her heart to such an incorrigible rascal, even one as attractive as Andre. But the unexpected tenderness she experiences in Andre's embrace tantalizes her with the sensuous promise of a love that could make time stand still for them both.

EUGENIA RILEY

WALTZ IN TIME

An Avon Romantic Treasure

AVON BOOKS ◆ NEW YORK

This is a work of fiction. Names, characters, places, and incidents either are the product of the author's imagination or are used fictitiously. This work depicts a number of actual figures from the history of the times. Although certain events and details of characterization pertaining to these figures are fictitious, whenever possible such portrayals have been done within the framework of known historical fact. All non-historical figures are imaginary, and any similarity to actual persons or events is strictly coincidental and beyond the intent of either the author or the publisher.

AVON BOOKS
A division of
The Hearst Corporation
1350 Avenue of the Americas
New York, New York 10019

Copyright © 1997 by Eugenia Riley Essenmacher
Inside cover author photograph by Lienna Essenmacher
Published by arrangement with the author
Visit our website at http://www.AvonBooks.com
Library of Congress Catalog Card Number: 97-93175
ISBN: 0-380-78910-8

First Avon Books Printing: November 1997

AVON TRADEMARK REG. U.S. PAT. OFF. AND IN OTHER COUNTRIES, MARCA REGISTRADA, HECHO EN U.S.A.

Printed in the U.S.A.

WCD 10 9 8 7 6 5 4 3 2 1

This book is dedicated
to my daughter, Lienna,
and her fiancé, Ray,
with love and congratulations
on their engagement
and upcoming marriage.

Chapter 1

Stephanie Sergeant had paused next to the stained-glass window on the old staircase landing when she first heard the eerie music. She stood watching the hazy, golden light of the fading day sift through jewel-like panels depicting a lovely spray of red roses on a background of vibrant blue. Half-mesmerized by the soft, kaleidoscopic patterns of light dancing about her, she tensed at the muted sounds of an off-key violin.

Startled, Stephanie glanced about her and listened intently, at first doubting she had even heard the faint notes. They had no close neighbors, and there was no stereo playing in Great-aunt Magnolia's old mansion.

But, yes, the music definitely was there—the squeaky, discordant strains of "The Last Rose of Summer," played in a waltz tempo. It unnerved her to realize she was hearing the tune while staring at a stained-glass portrait of roses.

She was continuing to gaze around her, trying to find the source of the unearthly refrain, when the waltz faded away, leaving her half-wondering if she had heard it at all. She shivered. Right before she'd come downstairs, a similar odd event had occurred. She'd heard a thud coming from Great-aunt Magnolia's old armoire, and opening the door, she'd observed that one of her deceased aunt's old shoes had fallen off its hook. She'd chuckled over the incident then, but now, it all seemed weird.

Hearing laughter drifting up from below, Stephanie shook her head. She recognized her sister Sam's voice, and real-

ized Sam's fiancé and his mother must have arrived for
dinner.

Stephanie brushed a wrinkle from her teal green sundress,
smoothed down her sleek blond hair, and continued down
the steps, crossing the foyer and entering the living room.
With fourteen-foot ceilings, French crystal chandeliers, and
a white-marble fireplace, the huge parlor was an airy expanse papered in gold flocked wallpaper, with elegant velvet
swags outlining the floor-to-ceiling windows, and lace panels emitting oceans of light.

Stephanie spotted Sam seated on the green-silk brocade
settee. Blond and brown-eyed, tall, and slender, Samantha
Bishop was a slightly younger version of Stephanie. Sam's
pink sundress was a fine complement for the couch, as well
as a perfect match for the Maiden's Blush roses she'd arranged in a crystal bowl on the rosewood coffee table. Next
to Sam sat Chester, in slacks and sports shirt; Mrs. Milford,
in one of her trademark flower-printed silk dresses, reposed
in a wing chair flanking them.

"Hi, Stef," called Sam. "You remember Chester and his
mom?"

"Of course."

Chester stood. "Stephanie, how good to see you again."

"And you."

"Welcome back to Natchez."

"Thanks," Stephanie murmured, shaking his hand. Tall,
mid-thirtyish, slim, and balding, Chester Milford was a
pleasant man, but he did carry baggage . . . Turning to his
mother, a hunched, wrinkled prune of a woman who was
rather deaf, Stephanie added distinctly, "Mrs. Milford."

"Hello, Stephanie," she grated out, her face screwed up
in a perpetual frown. "Sam was just telling us you're un-
employed."

Resisting an urge to roll her eyes at Sam, Stephanie sat
down beside her sister.

Chester slanted his mother an admonishing look.
"Mother, how could Stephanie move back here without first
resigning her position in Atlanta?"

"I suppose you have a point," she acknowledged sourly.

Flashing Stephanie an apologetic look, Sam handed her

a glass of white wine and a small china plate on which she'd served up a stuffed artichoke heart and two colorful canapés. "You know, Chester may have a lead on a new job for you, Stef."

"Really?" Eagerly, Stephanie turned to him.

Chester grinned. "Yes, it's true. As you may be aware, I'm president of the Adams County Historical Society, and we work closely with the Franklin Street Historic Collection, which is the most generously endowed private museum on the Old South in all of Mississippi."

"Ah, yes, I remember touring the collection with Sam a few years ago," Stephanie put in with excitement. "Such an impressive array of antebellum artifacts, and a fine library."

"How would you like to become the new curator?"

"You're kidding!" gasped Stephanie.

"Your master's in library science certainly qualifies you," Chester continued. "Sadly, our current head, Mrs. Caldwell, recently suffered a stroke, and her husband has insisted she retire. So the opening is immediate. I'm on the board, and all I would have to do is put in a word with a few of the right people—"

"Oh, would you?" Stephanie asked. "Please, tell me more."

After Chester answered Stephanie's questions, Sam patted her hand. "Isn't Chester a doll?"

"Yes, he is."

There was an awkward pause, then Mrs. Milford loudly cleared her throat. "Are you getting settled in, Stephanie?"

Stephanie laughed ruefully. "Well, my clothes are unpacked. Tomorrow the movers are bringing the furniture and belongings I couldn't bear to part with." She gestured at the room. "It was so sweet of Great-aunt Magnolia to leave me and Sam this gorgeous old house, and I do love staying in my aunt's bedroom. It's huge and has such a wonderful view of the grounds."

"Magnolia was a fine person—very active in the church," commented Mrs. Milford.

Smiling wistfully, Stephanie turned to Sam. "You know, it's odd, but I heard one of her shoes dropping upstairs."

Sam stifled a giggle. "What do you mean?"

"Don't you remember how you kept Great-aunt Magnolia's old mauve Victorian dress and those granny shoes she used to wear when she volunteered as a docent at our antebellum mansions?"

"Yes," Sam replied.

"Well, a few minutes ago, I heard one of the old shoes falling off its hook in her armoire, and it was kind of spooky."

"Forevermore!" gasped Mrs. Milford. "You've been hearing things, Stephanie?"

"No, I've not been hearing things," replied Stephanie with strained patience. "The shoe actually fell."

Chester winked at Sam. "Perhaps Harmony House is haunted, eh, sweetheart?"

Sam shuddered. "Well, I hope not! I've been living here with Great-aunt Magnolia for four years, and I've never heard or seen anything unusual." She smiled. "Besides, knowing how fussy our great-aunt was, I doubt she would have tolerated ghosts."

"What if *she's* the ghost?" he teased.

Mrs. Milford reached out to swat Chester on the arm. "Shame on you, son. Why, that's blasphemy! I'll have you know Magnolia had impeccable manners, and she would never have been so rude as to haunt anyone's home . . . especially not her own."

"Well, Stephanie, what do you say to that?" asked Chester, smiling.

"I'm not sure. You see, there's something else." Stephanie frowned at Sam. "Do any of our neighbors play the violin?"

"The violin?" Sam appeared confused. "Not that I know of. Besides, our property is so large that, even if a neighbor did play, how could we possibly hear it?"

"Perhaps so," Stephanie conceded. "But as I came down the stairs just now, I could have sworn I heard a violin playing 'The Last Rose of Summer.' In waltz time, no less."

"Isn't that the tune on Great-aunt Magnolia's old music box upstairs?" asked Sam in puzzlement.

"Yes." Stephanie gestured toward the handsome, cabinet grand piano against a far wall. "She used to play it on the piano, as well."

"So you're saying Magnolia has become a ghost and has taken up the violin?" inquired Mrs. Milford shrilly.

"Mother, really," scolded Chester.

"No, I'm just saying it all seems odd," Stephanie replied to Mrs. Milford in frustration. "I do know I heard the old waltz being played—"

"And a shoe dropping," finished Mrs. Milford. Expression formidable, she turned to Chester. "Son, do you think the Franklin Street Collection will want a curator who hears things?"

"Mother, you're making too much of this," he chided.

Mrs. Milford was about to reply when a gray-haired black woman in white uniform stepped in. "You folks ready to eat?"

"Yes, thank you, Mrs. Dawson," answered a relieved-sounding Sam. Turning to the others, she smiled brilliantly. "Shall we?"

"I think the evening went well, don't you?" Sam asked.

Sam had joined Stephanie on the front-porch swing. Beyond the sweeping, pillared front gallery of the old Greek Revival mansion, night had fallen. Spanish moss fluttered from the oaks, crickets sawed away, and a perfumed mist wafted from the rose garden.

"Dinner was wonderful," Stephanie agreed.

"I made the hors d'oeuvres and arranged the table myself," put in Sam rather defensively.

"Ah, yes," Stephanie teased back. "*Everything* was divine. I assume by now you've tucked away most of Mrs. Dawson's best recipes. You're going to make Chester a splendid wife."

Sam's look was admonishing. "Said with a hint of sarcasm."

"That's not true."

Sam sighed. "Stef, is something bugging you?"

Stephanie clamped her arms over her chest. "All right, I'll tell you. Chester's very nice, but that mother of his is a busybody, and she was ridiculing me tonight.''

Sam laughed. ''Well, you must admit you were talking strangely—about shoes going bump and imaginary violins playing von Flotow.''

''*It all happened.*''

Sam considered Stephanie's words with a frown. ''Stef, don't you think that sometimes when something weird seems to be happening, there's really a perfectly logical explanation?''

Stephanie waved a hand. ''I suppose.''

Sam eyed Stephanie curiously. ''And that's all that's bothering you?''

''Well, not really,'' Stephanie confessed. ''I'm afraid you don't know what you're getting into with Chester.''

Sam appeared taken aback. ''Stef, he's a sweet man.''

''I'm not denying that. He's very kind to help me find a job.''

''He's also rich, socially prominent, and I want him.''

''All true. But what about his mother?''

Sam smiled with secret pleasure. ''Chester and I both realize Mildred can be a stick-in-the-mud. But she and I also have an understanding. We both love Chester, and neither of us is going to ask him to choose between us. Besides, one of the things I love about Chester is that he takes responsibility for Mildred. He's really an old-style Southern gentleman in that respect. Plus, Mildred plans to move after we marry.''

''Move?''

''Yes, so Chester and I can live in Camellia Court.''

Stephanie gestured at their surroundings. ''But you've been living here with Great-aunt Magnolia ever since Mom and Dad retired to Florida. I'd assumed you'd want to continue on after your marriage.''

''When Chester and his mother own a home that rivals an antebellum masterpiece such as Longwood? You can have this house after Chester and I marry.''

Stephanie's expression was dubious. ''And where will Chester's mother live?''

''I told you she'll be moving,'' Sam retorted.

''Where?''

Telltale color stole up Sam's face. "To the guesthouse at Camellia Court."

Stephanie laughed.

Though her lips were twitching, Sam shook a finger at Stephanie. "You stop that right now! The guesthouse is twenty yards behind the main house, and besides, it has ten rooms."

"Yes, I'm sure you'll never see Mrs. Milford again."

Sam appeared troubled. "Stef, are you sure you're not just jealous because you don't have anyone?"

Stephanie flinched and glanced away.

Sam touched her hand. "I'm sorry, Stef. That was a mean thing to say. It's just that—well, ever since Jim was killed, you seem to have given up on ever loving again. And it has been five years."

"I know." Stephanie became lost in her own painful thoughts. "Maybe it's because no one can ever take my husband's place. Maybe it's because I'm grateful to have known such a precious love even once in my life."

"And maybe you're afraid of being hurt again, of losing another person who means so much to you," added Sam wisely.

Stephanie didn't reply.

"I just want you to be happy, Stef," Sam continued earnestly. "My God, you're only twenty-eight. It's not time to roll up your sidewalks yet."

Despite herself, Stephanie fought a smile.

"I want you to find someone special to spend your life with, someone like Chester."

"Spare me Chester," Stephanie teased. Before Sam could protest, she touched her sister's arm. "Look, I'm sorry if sometimes I sound like a meddler—"

"Mrs. Fix-it," amended Sam.

Stephanie smiled contritely. "But I am your older sister, and I do I worry about you." She sighed. "One thing my brief years with Jim taught me is how precious true love really is."

"Of course. You think I don't know that?"

"I know we struggled financially growing up here in Natchez, with Mom and Dad employed by the public schools." She gestured about them. "Now we've been left this beautiful estate, and once you're married to Chester, you'll never again have a financial worry—"

"So what's the problem?" Sam cut in.

Stephanie spoke passionately. "Sam, I know you want your life to be perfect, but I hope you're not just opting out for security with Chester. You see, I believe *every* woman has the right to know that one perfect love in her life, even if only briefly. And I think if Chester really was the one for you, he'd put you before his mother."

Sam's smile reflected how touched she felt by Stephanie's words. "Stef, don't worry about me. Chester really *is* the one."

"Is he?" Stephanie asked. "Even considering his unusual devotion to his mom?"

"It's Chester's nature to be generous and caring toward everyone," Sam argued back. "Do you know that when the Milfords' elderly housekeeper lost her husband last year, Chester paid for the entire funeral? Afterward, he bought Anna a retirement cottage, and he sends her a nice check every month. And you remember about my Windsor rocker, don't you?"

Stephanie frowned. "The one in your room? Didn't Chester buy it for you?"

Face lit with pleasure, Sam nodded. "Chester saw me staring at it in an antiques-store window, and the next day it arrived tied with a big red bow. He refused to allow me to pay for it, and insisted the only thank-you he wanted was a smile." Sam mischievously wiggled her eyebrows. "Well, he got a lot more."

Stephanie had to laugh. "Sam, you wicked wench! Okay, so the guy has certain talents. And if you're convinced he's worth tolerating Mildred, I guess there's no point arguing further."

Sam playfully punched Stephanie's arm. "Why do I put up with you, anyway? You're such a pain."

"Funny, I was about to say the same thing about you."

Both sisters chuckled.

Stephanie gazed thoughtfully out at the shadowy grounds.

"You know, today as I was unpacking, I was thinking about you and me . . . remembering."

"Were you?"

"I recalled the days when we were just little girls and used to visit Great-aunt Magnolia. Looking out, I could almost see us frolicking in the rose garden, chasing butterflies, while she sat nearby reading a book of Shakespearean sonnets."

An expression of wistful pleasure lit Sam's face. "Oh, Stef, what a sweet memory. I treasure those days, as well. And I miss Great-aunt Magnolia so much."

"So do I, but we still have each other." Stephanie fought back the lump in her throat. "Sam, I know we still bicker, but I want you to know I'm very glad to be back here—glad to be home."

Sam squeezed her hand. "I'm glad to have you, Stef. I've missed you a lot."

"Me too."

As the poignant moment stretched into an awkward pause, Sam glanced at her watch, then whistled. "Geez, where has the time gone? I've half a dozen calls to return. Summer is almost here, and the real-estate market is heating up again, thank goodness."

"I'm glad to hear it."

After Sam reentered the house, Stephanie lingered in the darkness, shivering as the breeze caressed her bare arms. She felt almost as if she'd been touched by human hands—unseen, sensual hands. She'd been in a funny, fanciful mood ever since she'd heard the strange music on the landing.

Was it because the wistful notes and her discussion with Sam had roused painful memories of her dead husband?

Stephanie had met Jim Sergeant while a senior at Ole Miss; Jim had been an army officer, on leave visiting his family in Oxford. Stephanie had never expected to fall in love so quickly, or so young. She and Jim had married right away; after she graduated, they'd moved to Fort Benning, Georgia, where he'd been stationed.

Their time together had been wonderful, but cruelly brief. Months before their third anniversary, Jim had been called away to fight in Desert Storm. Even now, it was agonizing for Stephanie to remember the day she'd learned of her husband's death in the scud attack on the army barracks in Saudi Arabia. She had awakened that morning full of hope, and gone to bed a widow at the tender age of twenty-three. . . .

Stephanie had brought Jim's body here to Natchez, burying him in the family plot at the Natchez Cemetery. She'd spent two months with Sam and Magnolia, healing . . . not that her heart would ever be completely whole again. She had returned to her job as a public-school librarian in Atlanta, had worked on her master's, keeping herself busy to ease the loneliness.

When Magnolia had died six months ago, Stephanie had returned for her funeral. It was then that she'd learned from Sam that their spinster great-aunt had left her estate to the two of them. The prospect of moving home, beginning a new life in this more genteel setting, had appealed to Stephanie greatly. She'd finished out the school year, then quit her job, sold her house, and moved here among the splendid antebellum mansions, the blooming camellias and intoxicating jasmine.

She sensed things were going to work out for her here. She was home, where she needed to be, where she could find peace.

Suddenly, Stephanie tensed as she heard it again—the low, discordant strains of the waltz, sad and off-key. It was as if her bittersweet thoughts had raised the maudlin tune. The refrain was so touching, so filled with unassuaged longing, that she felt her throat tightening. She glanced about, trying to detect the direction of the eerie sounds. Somehow, the notes seemed to emanate from the house itself.

"Is anyone there?" she called anxiously.

Tensely, she waited. She heard more soft, dissonant echoes, and then, she could have sworn, the low, heartbroken sound of a woman weeping. Stephanie listened, mesmerized. She had known unbearable pain herself, yet nothing like this wrenching sorrow.

That night, Stephanie's sleep was restless, her dreams strangely haunted. She heard a woman weeping, a violin playing "The Last Rose of Summer," the faint laughter of a child . . .

Then the face of an old woman loomed over her, the features pale and gaunt, the countenance haunted and desperate. The specter's hoarse voice whispered, "I can find no peace, child. That's why I brought you here . . ."

Stephanie gasped and sat up in bed. She expected to be confronted by menacing monsters, but saw only inky darkness, heard only the thrum of the air conditioner and the frantic pounding of her own heart. She pressed a hand to her chest and caught several ragged breaths. Illogically, she was both shivering and covered with sweat, slightly nauseous.

For it had been Great-aunt Magnolia's face she'd just seen. Of this she was certain. *That's why I brought you here, child.* What had the odd words meant? Was Magnolia's spirit haunting the house now?

Magnolia and who else?

Chapter 2

"**H**ow was the first board meeting, Stef?"

On a Saturday night three weeks later, Stephanie entered Harmony House to the sound of her sister's question. Watching Sam step from the parlor, Stephanie shut the door behind her and forced a smile.

"Oh, I think the meeting went fine, and the board of the Franklin Street Collection seems to like me. As the new curator, I've been asked to help out with antique costumes for the old-fashioned community fair on July 4. Chester even mentioned that I gave a good first report, and that's pretty amazing considering how little rest I've gotten lately."

Sam's expression was part sympathy, part anxiety. "You know, I'm really worried about you, Stef. Chester mentioned that you looked exhausted when he stopped by the museum yesterday. Last night, Mildred asked if you're still hearing things around here."

Stephanie laughed humorlessly. "Lord, how I wish I weren't. But don't worry, I didn't mention any more strange stuff to Chester and his mom tonight. I'm far from eager to give Mildred any more excuses to decide I'm a nutcase."

Sam groaned. "I know it must be frustrating when others don't experience what you do. I know some people believe in ghosts—I've just never been one of them."

"Neither was I," Stephanie responded cynically, gazing about her, "until all this stuff started happening. And happening."

Sam flashed her a conciliatory smile. "But I'm not un-sympathetic. I lent you my car tonight, didn't I?"

"That's another thing," Stephanie continued, waving a hand. "Things keep disappearing from my room—my sun-glasses, watch, and tonight even my car keys."

"But your keys didn't disappear, Stef," Sam assured her.

Stephanie gave a cry of disbelief. "What do you mean?"

"Surprise." Sam dug in the pocket of her slacks, then held Stephanie's keys aloft.

Stephanie's mouth fell open. "Where did you find them?"

Sam handed Stephanie the keys. "On your dresser."

"But that's impossible!" Stephanie cried. "I all but tore my dresser apart!"

"That's odd, because they were lying in plain view," Sam remarked. "Tonight, I went into your room to lay some clean laundry on your dresser, and that's when I spotted them."

"Good grief," moaned Stephanie. "Someone's trying to drive me insane."

Sam shook her head. "Who would do such a thing? Your sobbing woman with her maudlin violin?"

Stephanie waved a hand. "Sam, I really do hear her—especially around twilight. And at night I hear all sorts of weird noises—children at play, sometimes even a baby cry-ing somewhere in the house."

Sam sighed. "Stef, I'm afraid you're taking on too much. The move, your new job . . . Maybe you should go talk to someone about all these bizarre events."

"Oh, so now I'm losing it?" Stephanie asked shrilly.

"I just think you're pushing yourself too hard. Look how exhausted you are."

"If I look exhausted, it's because I haven't gotten any damn rest in three weeks."

Sam appeared perplexed.

Stephanie sighed. "Look, I'd better call it a night."

"Yes, why don't you? And don't forget that Chester and Mildred are coming for brunch in the morning, then we're all going to church together." Sam cleared her throat. "I know you're upset, Stef, but I would appreciate it if you'd continue to cool the spooky stuff around Mildred. You know what a fuddy-duddy she can be.''

Stephanie nodded. ''Sure, Sam. Good night.''

Stephanie trudged up the stairs. The last three weeks had been hell for her. Funny, how, prior to returning to Natchez, she *had* never really questioned whether she believed in ghosts.

Well, she was a believer now! Over the past weeks, even as she was trying to grasp the challenges of a new job, the weird events at home had only intensified, and no one else shared her sightings. It was bad enough to be living in a haunted house, where a woman sobbed or played her violin, laughing children mocked her from the shadows, Great-aunt Magnolia paced and fretted in her dreams, and some mysterious entity kept snatching her belongings.

What made matters worse was having no one believe her, coping with Sam's polite doubts and Mrs. Milford's snooty disdain. When dealing with such strange occurrences, a person needed bolstering; although Sam did try, Mrs. Milford had hinted more than once that Stephanie might be delusional.

Entering her room, Stephanie proceeded to the old armoire and hung up her blazer. She smiled wistfully at the sight of her great-aunt's old-fashioned, floor-length mauve velvet gown on its hanger. She ran her fingertips over the ecru lace collar and one of the long, straight sleeves. She gazed poignantly at Magnolia's old granny shoes on their hooks.

At least she hadn't heard any more shoes falling lately!

Closing the armoire doors, Stephanie went to the dresser to put away her clean laundry, only to stop in her tracks. Next to the stack of lingerie, a single, long-stemmed white rose was laid out across the crocheted dresser scarf, the bloom resting on Great-aunt Magnolia's old walnut music box. In awe, she picked up and sniffed the huge, fragrant blossom. Her first thought was that Sam must have put it there.

Then she shook her head. No, Sam was far too meticulous. She would never just lay a flower on someone's dresser; she would put it in water, in her best crystal vase.

Besides, Sam didn't care for white roses, and neither had Magnolia. There were all sorts of prize and antique roses in the Harmony House garden—but no white flowers except for the magnolias and gardenias.

What was going on? Where had the lush flower come from? Again, she sniffed the flower's sweet perfume, then opened the music box, listened to an oh-so-familiar, haunting refrain, and realized the significance.

"The Last Rose of Summer."

"Damn it!" Stephanie exclaimed.

In the middle of the night, just as she was finally drifting off into a fitful sleep, she heard it again—the poignant strains of the waltz, the weeping woman, a wailing baby. Heartbroken sobbing. Plaintive music.

Whipping off the covers, she sat up in bed, turned on the lamp, and drew her fingers through her hair. What was she to do now? After weeks of this nightly torture, she was exhausted enough to cry. She hated the thought of taking a sleeping pill, but believed she had spotted some in an old tea safe down in the kitchen. Sam had mentioned that Magnolia sometimes slept downstairs when her arthritis acted up.

Or had the ghosts driven her out of her room?

Putting on her robe and slippers, Stephanie left her bedroom and trudged down the dim hallway. She navigated the stairs guided by the moonlight spilling through the stained-glass window. The house was quiet, too quiet, and a certain eeriness hung in the air, raising an unconscious shiver, a sense of premonition. All at once, she could feel the hairs on the back of her neck beginning to stand up. She thought of turning back, then chided herself for her silliness.

Then she paused in her tracks and gasped, arrested by what appeared to be a ghost taking shape before her very eyes! A gray, hazy specter glimmered before her on the landing, the smoky apparition glowing with an uncanny light. Stephanie shook her head and blinked, but the phantom remained. It was a woman clad in an old-time nightgown. Her dark hair was pulled back in a braid, and her plain features were ghostly pale. The spirit was staring at Stephanie entreatingly, and Stephanie could only gaze back, horrified and hypnotized.

"He never loved me," the specter whispered in a frail, raspy voice. "What are you going to do about it?"

Even as Stephanie struggled to reply, the apparition vanished. . . .

Seconds later Stephanie was in the kitchen, rifling through the drawers of the old tea safe, frantically searching for medication to calm her raw nerves. Though she wasn't a pill-popper, a good dose of Valium sounded just peachy at the moment.

Yanking at a stuck drawer, she flinched as some kind of ancient card, wedged under it, fell to the floor. Thinking it was an old recipe card, she picked it up, turned it over, and was amazed to find herself staring at a scratched and faded photograph of a man.

Damn, but the picture looked old, the paper cracked and yellow. Even though the image was faint, Stephanie recognized the man's suit as being from the late nineteenth century, with the lacy shirtfront and high cravat of the day.

Much more arresting was his face, the classically handsome lines, the roguish smile, and eyes filled with so much laughing devilishness that Stephanie automatically fastened the top button on her robe.

Where on earth had this photo come from? Sam had mentioned that the tea safe was the one piece of furniture original to the house, but, heavens, the photo had to be 120 years old. How could it have escaped notice all this time?

Suddenly Stephanie began to tremble anew as the relevance hit her. She'd found the picture right after her encounter with the ghost. She'd received another message from the beyond.

Was *this* the man who had broken the sobbing woman's heart? Clearly unrequited love dwelled somewhere in this house!

Stephanie stuffed the picture into the pocket of her robe and wondered why her fingers were burning. . . .

*   *   *

"Why didn't anyone warn me that this house is haunted?"

When Stephanie charged into the dining room the following morning, Sam, Chester, and his mother all gaped at her.

Handing Mrs. Milford a plate of Eggs Sardou, Sam flashed Stephanie a strained smile. "Good morning to you, too, Stef. Won't you join us?"

Realizing how rude she must have sounded, Stephanie gave everyone an apologetic look and headed toward her chair. "Sorry. Good morning to all of you. I didn't mean to sound so abrupt—it's just that, last night, I met our resident spook."

"You're kidding!" cried Chester, popping up to pull out her chair.

"Not at all." Sitting down and muttering a thank-you, Stephanie leaned toward the others, and continued intently. "The sobbing woman woke me up, and when I headed downstairs, I saw her standing on the landing in her nightgown. She seemed to stare straight through me, and whispered, 'He never loved me . . . What are you going to do about it?' Afterward, I even found a very old photo of a man in the kitchen tea safe—and I think he must have been the one the ghost was talking about."

"My stars!" gasped Mrs. Milford. "So you're seeing things now as well as hearing them?"

Stephanie gritted her teeth. "I assure you I'm not having flights of fancy. I can even show you the picture if you're interested. And I'm wondering why no one ever warned us about the ghosts in this house."

"I think because no one else has ever seen any ghosts in this house," answered Sam patiently.

Stephanie tossed down her fork. "You people are exasperating."

Her outburst was met by stunned silence, although Mrs. Milford's haughty glance at Chester spoke volumes.

Sam cleared her throat. "Stef, may we have a word in private?"

"Of course," said Stephanie dully.

The sisters excused themselves and stepped out into the hallway. Sam glared and spoke urgently. "Stef, for heaven's sake, what's eating you? You practically bit off all our heads back there!''

"I know, and I didn't mean to be rude," Stephanie replied, wringing her hands.

Sam scowled. "So you really think you saw a ghost last night?"

"I know I did."

"Are you certain it wasn't just another bad dream?"

"I'm certain."

Sam appeared at a loss. "Lord, I don't know what to think. I'm really sorry you're having such a rough time, but didn't I ask you to watch the spooky stuff around Mildred? If you're looking for a sympathetic ear, you're not going to get it from her.''

"You're right, and I apologize," Stephanie replied humbly. "I think I'm just on edge from being so tired, and getting frustrated because none of you will believe me."

Sam groaned. "Stef, I want to believe you. But Great-aunt Magnolia lived here for sixty years and, as far as anyone knows, never saw any ghosts. I've been here a long time myself and have yet to spot so much as a suspicious shadow.''

"Just because you and she never saw them doesn't mean they don't exist," Stephanie pointed out heatedly. "Not everybody has that sort of psychic connection. And have you thought that all of this weirdness may have been stirred up by our great-aunt's death? I'm seeing her, too, you know—in my dreams."

Sam sighed. "Heavens, I hope not. I really hope she's found her peace by now. And I do think the biggest problem is that you're so exhausted. You look as if you haven't slept in weeks—"

"I haven't, thanks to the ghosts."

"Then why don't you just go back to bed?" Sam asked with forbearance. "I'll bring you up a breakfast tray before the rest of us leave for church."

"Fine," Stephanie muttered.

Sam turned and reentered the dining room. Stephanie gritted her teeth and stalked away....

Chapter 3

That night in her dreams, Stephanie heard the waltz again—"The Last Rose of Summer," this time being played on a piano. The poignant strains seemed to beckon to her.

She arose from her bed, waltzed out of her room, and floated down the hallway. She pirouetted down the stairs, frolicking among the moonbeams on the landing. She waltzed into the moonlit parlor, where she spotted Magnolia at the piano, silvery moonlight outlining her hunched figure, the shawl around her shoulders. She was wearing her old mauve dress, and her presence seemed completely natural. She was playing "The Last Rose of Summer."

Stephanie twirled about the room, a dreamy expression on her face. She turned to Magnolia, whose eyes gleamed with sorrow.

"So much unhappiness in this house," Magnolia whispered. "So many restless spirits . . . You must help us, dear . . ."

Gradually, Stephanie moved toward consciousness and became aware that she was waltzing about the parlor in the middle of the night. "Ouch," she cried as her hip collided with the piano.

Jerking back to awareness, Stephanie stopped in her tracks and stared about her, feelings of sick panic swamping her. What on earth was she doing down here, in the darkness? Heavens, she had a vague memory of dancing about the house. But that was absurd—she'd never in her life been a somnambulist! And there was no way she could have gotten downstairs without breaking her neck!

Then how could she explain her presence in the parlor? Her gaze searched the shifting shadows, coming to rest on the rosewood piano—an instrument where she could have sworn she'd spotted Magnolia seated only seconds earlier. Yet no one was there. Of course Magnolia hadn't *actually* played the piano. It was bad enough that she was sleepwalking—surely she wasn't hallucinating, as well.

To reassure herself, Stephanie tiptoed over to the piano, and that's when she spotted the old sheet music of "The Last Rose of Summer" laid out on the music stand. She was certain the music hadn't been there earlier.

Good heavens! *What* was going on in this house?

The next morning, Stephanie found a cameo brooch on her dresser. She stared at it—a woman's perfect face, etched in ivory and surrounded by antique gold filigree. It was a lovely piece, and impulsively, Stephanie pinned it on her blouse.

Downstairs at breakfast, Sam remarked on the piece. "What a pretty cameo—so Victorian."

"Thanks. I found it in my room. It belonged to Great-aunt Magnolia, didn't it?"

"No—I've never seen it before," replied Sam. "Besides, I cataloged all of Great-aunt Magnolia's belongings after she died. Are you sure you didn't buy the pin and simply forget?"

"No, I didn't buy it and forget," Stephanie retorted more irritably than she had intended.

Sam only shrugged.

Who was haunting Harmony House?

That morning, Stephanie searched the archives at work for any records on the old house. She did know that her own family had not bought the house until around the turn of the century. The file she found provided scant clues—an old sketch of the property, a brief description of how the house had been built in 1852 by one James Wilcox, a notation that Wilcox had subsequently sold the estate in 1870.

There was no mention of the new owners or of any haunt-ings . . . Stephanie replaced the folder feeling at her wit's end.

After work that day, she bought flowers and went to visit Jim's grave at the cemetery north of town. Leaving her car, she found the large, tranquil park nearly deserted, the merest breeze stirring the heavy air, filling her senses with the es-sences of honeysuckle and freshly mown grass.

Stephanie walked slowly past ornate, wrought-iron enclo-sures lined with antique roses and filled with magnificent monuments. Climbing a rise, she viewed acres of ancient headstones, statues of angels and cherubs, quaint gazebos, and, in the distance, a glistening pond surrounded by trees. At the crest of the hill, she paused at the old family plot, where a centuries-old, magnificent oak framed a view of the wide Mississippi in the distance. She opened the wrought-iron gate and slipped inside the spacious enclosure. Here, Jim was buried, as well as Great-aunt Magnolia and several others of their family.

Staring at Jim's grave, she touched the plain gold band that she still wore on the third finger of her left hand. She remembered the agonized, frantic days after she'd been in-formed of his death, how she'd come to Natchez to make arrangements, how Magnolia had sent her to the cemetery, insisting she must choose a space for Jim in the family plot. Her one moment of peace had come when she had glimpsed the gravesite, on this high rise, sheltered by the strong, com-forting oak, with the river in the distance. She had stood there sobbing, but it had been a moment of great emotional release. She'd remembered thinking, who wouldn't be peaceful, spending eternity in this place? When she died, she planned to join her sweetheart here. . . .

She knelt by the headstone, removed the withered flowers from a brass urn, and placed the fresh blooms inside. Even though the words were imprinted on her brain, she read the inscription on the marble stone: "James Arthur Sergeant, born May 8, 1964, killed in action in Saudi Arabia, Feb-ruary 25, 1991 . . . Beloved husband, friend, and hero, he died defending his country."

Stephanie's throat knotted and she wiped away a tear. Jim

had been so young, only twenty-six when he died. Yet they'd shared a lifetime of happiness during less than three years of marriage. Since his death, Stephanie hadn't even considered becoming involved with another man, even when the nights were long and her arms empty. Was it guilt? Or a feeling that no one could take his place? He'd been her first love, her only love.

Yet ever since these hauntings had begun, ever since she'd found the old photo of the roguish-looking man, something had been tugging at her, disturbing her peace, threatening her sweet memories of Jim. Was that why she'd come here today, to reaffirm her loyalty?

She picked up the dead blooms and rose to her feet. Again reflecting on the strange goings-on at Harmony House, she remembered a favorite passage from *Wuthering Heights*, in which a grief-shattered Heathcliff had beseeched Cathy's ghost to haunt him.

"Why don't you haunt me?" she whispered, wiping away a tear. "I'd like that, you know."

Yet Stephanie knew her Jim was at peace. *He* was not the one who haunted her now. . . .

That night in her dreams, Stephanie again heard the baby crying. She roamed about the house, frantically searching for an infant who kept wailing disconsolately.

She entered a darkened nursery, stole over to the Jenny Lind crib, and found a baby girl, lying on her back, holding out her arms and screaming. The child was incredibly beautiful, with dark, curly hair, a round face, a plump little body. She appeared to be about a year old and wore an exquisitely embroidered linen gown and pink crocheted booties. Her tiny legs were flailing, her button mouth quivering in indignation.

"Poor motherless thing," Stephanie murmured.

She leaned over and picked up the child, straightening and nestling her against her shoulder. Oh, such heaven! How warm the baby was, how sweet and soft!

The girl hiccoughed then quieted, curling her little arms about Stephanie's neck. Stephanie's heart twisted with tenderness at the endearing gesture. The child smelled of baby powder and milk. Stephanie patted her back and cooed to her.

"Poor, lost little angel," she murmured. "You only need love, don't you?"

She spotted a wicker rocking chair in a corner. In a pool of silvery moonlight, it beckoned her. She crossed over and sat down with the baby, and sang her the lullaby, "Sweet and Low": "Sleep, my little one, sleep."

The door opened and Great-aunt Magnolia, in her night-gown, peered inside. "So there you are, Stephanie. I was hoping someone could quiet that baby. She has no mother, you see, and her father is off carousing."

"What father?" Stephanie asked. "Why is this happening?"

Magnolia shook her head. "Too many restless spirits. They won't let me go on to heaven until their torment ends. You must help them . . . help us all."

"I'm trying to," Stephanie murmured.

"Good, child. Just rock that baby. Perhaps we can all get some rest tonight . . ."

When Stephanie awakened, her bedroom was flooded with light. She shook her head and sat up. What a bizarre dream she'd had *this* time. What had her great-aunt said? Something about restless spirits haunting the house, a man off carousing, and Stephanie being the only one who could help them.

Was the man the one whose picture she'd found? She opened the drawer on her bedside table, pulled out the old photo, and gazed at it intently. A low whistle escaped her. Yes, he had the look of a carouser, all right, and again Stephanie felt a treacherous warmth shooting through her fingers.

It was all so spooky. At least she knew her dream hadn't *really* happened; at least she hadn't sleepwalked again.

Then, as she replaced the photo, she felt her nightgown sticking to her shoulder. Pulling the fabric away, she glanced down to see a small milk stain, just where the baby's mouth had been!

Stephanie began to shiver.

Chapter 4

~~~⟡~~~

At the Fourth of July community celebration, Stephanie stood with the Reverend Carlson near a platform where the church's children's choir was singing "In the Good Old Summertime." The boys and girls were dressed in late-nineteenth-century costumes, many of which had been borrowed from the Franklin Street Collection. The park was hot but shady, and Stephanie was comfortable enough in her peach-colored sundress and sandals.

"Reverend Carlson, the children look charming," she remarked.

"Thanks to your help and generosity," replied the clergyman, a middle-aged man with thinning hair and a convivial manner.

"We at the museum were delighted to be of assistance. I needed to start sorting through our costume collection, anyway. No one has ever done a reliable inventory."

"Don't work too hard," Carlson advised, regarding her with concern. "Not to pry, Mrs. Sergeant, but you do look tired."

Stephanie flashed him a wan smile. "I'm afraid I've been suffering from insomnia ever since I arrived in Natchez."

"I'm so sorry. Folks usually find the slower pace here conducive to more rest, not less."

"Unless they live in haunted houses."

"You're joking! Harmony House is haunted?" Carlson appeared fascinated.

"You might say it's totally infested with ghosts," Ste-

24

phanie declared. "A sobbing woman playing her maudlin violin, mischievous children, a crying baby, not to mention Great-aunt Magnolia skulking about, wringing her hands . . ."

"*Magnolia* is one of the ghosts?" Carlson cried.

She cast him a sheepish glance. "You must think I'm a nut."

He patted her arm. "Not at all. Natchez is not without its legends of ghosts. Dunleith is supposedly haunted by a heartbroken spinster, King's Tavern by Richard King's murdered mistress, and I've heard that the ghost of John Jenkins can still be seen greeting visitors out at old Elgin Plantation."

Stephanie shook her head. "Well, it's comforting to know I'm not the only one who has experienced something spooky."

Carlson grinned. "And if there was anyone who would insist on becoming another 'legend' following her death, I'm quite certain it would be Magnolia."

Stephanie's expression was wistful. "She was quite a character—and a dear. Still is, as a matter of fact."

Carlson sighed. "You know, several years back, my grandmother actually had to move from an old cottage outside town. Soon after moving in, Gran swore the place was haunted by the ghost of a dead slave who was hanged by a sadistic overseer."

"How bizarre!" exclaimed Stephanie.

Carlson thoughtfully stroked his jaw. "I've heard of no history of hauntings at Harmony House, but that doesn't mean there isn't information on file. Have you done any research?"

Stephanie laughed. "I've already checked our files at work and did find some information on the house, but nothing pertaining to ghosts or anything else unusual."

"What about the local history room at the public library?"

Stephanie snapped her fingers. "That's a good idea." She smiled. "And I must tell you, Reverend Carlson, it's so refreshing to talk to someone who believes me for a change. You see, I'm the only one who has seen any ghosts at Harmony House.''

''I'm not surprised. My grandmother had a companion who never spotted anything unusual. But Gran was adamant about all the moaning and crying she heard, and I believed her.''

''You're a saint. And you've been such a comfort to me.''

He chuckled. ''I've learned to keep an open mind regarding matters of the spirit . . . especially in this town.''

Stephanie extended her hand. ''Thanks again, Reverend.''

He shook her hand. ''Take care, Mrs. Sergeant.''

Stephanie moved away, passing a line of food booths that enticed her with smells of hot dogs and pickles. In the distance, youngsters screamed with delight on the Tilt-A-Whirl and floated past on other gaudy carnival rides.

She caught a glimpse of Sam and the Milfords approaching and deliberately steered herself in the opposite direction. She had arrived with the others, but had soon drifted away. Although Sam and Chester tried their best to be sympathetic regarding the ''hauntings'' Stephanie was experiencing, she was weary of Mildred's insinuations that she was going ''around the bend.''

Stephanie was strolling back through the carnival when all at once a chill swept her as the notes of ''The Last Rose of Summer,'' played by calliope, rose to beckon her. What now?

Heart pounding, she found herself drawn toward the music and was soon standing before the old-fashioned carousel. The beautiful, painted horses bobbed up and down, gliding about to the whimsical old tune. Children laughed and waved at parents.

But *why* was the calliope playing ''The Last Rose of Summer''? The melody seemed to haunt her everywhere she went!

''Lady, will you take me for a ride on the carousel?''

Stephanie was startled by the sound of the child's voice, even more stunned to feel a small, warm hand clasp hers. She glanced down to view an enchanting little boy standing beside her. He must be one of the youngsters from the church choir, she mused, since he was dressed in old-fashioned knee pants with suspenders, a striped shirt, and a jaunty cap. Stephanie didn't remember lending this particular costume to the church, but perhaps they had acquired it elsewhere.

Handsome and slender, the boy appeared to be about five. His round face was graced by fine features, a sprinkling of freckles, and alert blue eyes.

Intrigued, Stephanie asked, "Who are you?"

Proudly, he replied, "I'm Pierre Beaufort Goddard, but everyone calls me 'Beau.' "

"Well, hello, Beau," Stephanie greeted with a smile. She gazed about the area. "Where are your parents?"

His gaze darkened. "Mama is with the angels, and Papa is busy."

Stephanie's heart went out to the motherless lad. "I'm so sorry about your mother. But surely you can't be here by yourself. Won't your father worry?"

The lad flashed her a winsome grin. "I'll go home," he promised, "but only if you'll take me on the carousel first."

Oh, he was an engaging little rascal! Hearing the merry-go-round grind to a halt, Stephanie repressed a smile. The boy was quite adept at twisting adult heartstrings, and she found she couldn't bear the prospect of disappointing him.

She grinned down at him. "Okay, you've got a deal."

The boy let out a delighted whoop, grabbed Stephanie's hand, and tugged her off. She purchased tickets, and the two entered the ride and climbed onto the platform.

The boy scrambled over to a bench. "We'll sit here!"

"But don't you want to ride a horse?" Stephanie asked.

He solemnly shook his head. "No, I want to sit with you. You're pretty."

Stephanie's lips twitched. For a five-year-old, his charm was devastating. Heaven help the girls when this junior Casanova grew up. She sat down and the boy again clutched her hand as the ride rumbled forward. She felt warmed, filled with stirrings of maternal tenderness.

She also felt entranced at the magic she spotted in his young eyes. "So, tell me more about yourself, Beau."

"I'm next to the oldest of five," he announced importantly.

"Five?" Stephanie repeated. "Gee, that's a big family."

He nodded. "Mama died last year, when baby Sarah was born."

Stephanie's mouth went dry. "Baby Sarah? Does she look like you?"

"Oh, yes," he replied. "She has my curly black hair and blue eyes. She cries all the time. She misses Mama."

"I see," Stephanie replied, heart thudding.

He regarded her wistfully. "I wish you would be my mama."

"Me?" Stephanie asked, both touched and very taken aback.

"We children need a new mother more than anything," he assured her.

Stephanie was silent, mystified.

The boy frowned. "You'd have to marry Papa, of course, but that won't be so bad. He's very handsome, and all the ladies in Natchez are in love with him. I'm sure you will be, too."

"I . . ." Stephanie remained at a loss. "I'm very flattered, Beau, but I seriously doubt your father will appreciate your trying to find him a wife—"

"We need a mother," he repeated earnestly.

"But why would you want *me* to become your mother?"

The child hesitated for a moment, then brightened. "So Papa will be happy, and maybe Miss Ebbie will quit crying all the time and playing her squeaky old violin."

Stephanie could not speak at all. She was dumbstruck, chills consuming her.

The lad eyed her with concern. "Lady, are you all right?"

She could only stare at the boy as the ride groaned to a halt. He gazed back with a look of longing that threatened to tear her heart to ribbons.

"Please come be our mother," he whispered, squeezing her hand. "We *need* you."

Then, just as abruptly he had appeared, the boy was gone,

bounding off the merry-go-round, turning, grinning at her, blowing her a kiss, and slipping off into the woods. . . .

The encounter with the boy obsessed Stephanie's thoughts. She had no explanation for an incident that defied logic.

Had the child been playing some sort of game with her? For his manner of dress and speech, and everything he'd told her, all hinted he was part of the family of ghosts that was haunting her!

Was it all a coincidence? If so, how had he managed to come up with details that so closely matched the "hauntings" at home?

Unless he, too, were a ghost! The very possibility racked Stephanie with shivers.

She was even more unsettled by the emotional pull the boy had spurred within her. During her marriage, she and Jim had badly wanted a child, and they'd tried hard in the months before he'd left for the Gulf War, without success. Stephanie had begun to suspect she was incapable of having children, but before she could go to the doctor for tests, Jim had been called to serve. After he'd been killed, all maternal instinct had seemed to die within her, as well. Years of dealing with ofttimes obstreperous students in a public-school library had only strengthened her conviction that she never wanted children of her own.

But the boy had sparked a keen emotion within her—the desire for family, for belonging, to be needed by someone. In a sense, this scared her more than did her encounters with ghosts.

That very night in her dreams, Stephanie mentioned the incident to Great-aunt Magnolia. Indeed, spending the wee hours of the morning with creatures from the afterlife had become commonplace for her.

Magnolia was in her rocking chair knitting when Stephanie waltzed by. "Who was the boy?" she asked.

Magnolia's knitting needles clicked. "One of the wraiths," came the cryptic reply. "There are five of them.

Poor, motherless mites. When are you going to come quiet this mess, child?''

''But why me?'' cried Stephanie.

Magnolia shrugged. ''Somebody has to do it, and you're Mrs. Fix-it. Besides, someone *has to deal with that man.''*

''What man?''

Magnolia shook her head and clicked away. ''Oh, my dear. My poor, poor dear . . .''

Magnolia began humming ''The Last Rose of Summer.''

In the darkness, Stephanie awakened with a start, covered in cold sweat. Quickly she turned on a lamp. Another bizarre dream: *Someone has to deal with that man.*

What man? The one whose picture she'd seen? And why had the children been referred to as wraiths? She knew a wraith was some sort of spirit, but at the moment a more specific definition eluded her.

Stephanie rushed downstairs and grabbed the dictionary, only to discover that a ''wraith'' was a living human being taking the form of a ghost. Like the boy today?

New chills danced along Stephanie's spine. Was it possible that an orphan from another century wanted a new mother so badly that he'd traveled across time to press his cause? Did his brothers and sisters join his mission at night, in her dreams?

It was all absurd! And besides, why her?

''Somebody has to do it,'' Great-aunt Magnolia had said.

Monday at noon, Stephanie sat at a table in the public library, staring at a manila folder the librarian had just placed before her. The file was labeled ''Harmony House.''

A house that was not very harmonious at the moment!

With trembling fingers, she flipped open the folder. As she might have expected, the sheaf was comprised of loose, aged papers and old photographs.

She read the first item, another history of the house, a newspaper clip from the year 1917: ''Harmony House, a most splendid example of the Greek Revival style, was built in 1852 by James Wilcox, and sold in 1870 to one Andre Goddard . . .''

The name "Goddard" wrenched a gasp from Stephanie, and she instinctively raised a hand to her thumping heart. Hadn't the little boy called himself "Pierre Beaufort Goddard"?

With mingled anticipation and dread, she continued:

> Goddard bought the house for his bride, Linnea, and over the next seven years, the couple had five children. Mrs. Goddard died in 1877 bearing their final child, Sarah Elizabeth. Linnea's devoted cousin, Ebbie, stayed on to care for Goddard and his children.

"Oh, heavens," Stephanie murmured, her gaze riveted to the names "Ebbie" and "Sarah"—two others the child had mentioned!

With deepening anxiety, she resumed reading:

> Thereafter, Goddard, a wealthy cotton broker, personified the gay widower. He never remarried, even though legend holds that Miss Ebbie fell hopelessly in love with him, and eventually died of a broken heart. Many old-time Natchezians swear that at dusk at Harmony House, Miss Ebbie can still be heard playing a maudlin tune on her violin . . .

A maudlin tune on her violin . . .

In a state of shock, Stephanie sifted through the other documents—pictures of the house, a floor plan. At last her gaze became riveted on a faded family photograph dated 1878, featuring a handsome man, five young children, and a homely woman standing in the background.

"Oh, my God!"

Stephanie began hyperventilating. For she was staring at the very little boy she had taken on the carousel ride, the baby she had rocked in her dreams, the tragic woman she had encountered on the stairs, and the man whose picture had fallen out of the tea safe.

Stephanie's hands trembled so badly, she almost dropped

the photograph. Nothing made sense, except that this was *really* happening. The house was haunted. The governess needed rescuing, and the children so desperately wanted a new mother that one of them had traveled across time to beg for her help.

This was insane! But how else could she explain all these bizarre events?

And it was all *his* fault. Stephanie stared at the handsome, dark-haired man dressed in an impeccable frock coat and dark trousers. She noted the rash confidence of his smile, and again, the mischief in those deep-set eyes.

Andre Goddard. The "gay widower," was he? Even in the faded photograph, she found that his vitality, his male magnetism, stirred something within her. Part of her was strangely fascinated by this nineteenth-century rogue. The rest of her wanted to shake him for abandoning his responsibilities.

Shoving the photo away, Stephanie buried her face in her hands. What was she going to do? She must help these people—or leave Natchez—or she'd surely lose what remained of her sanity!

Chapter 5

When she went to bed that night, Stephanie found a string of pearls on her pillow. In awe, she picked up the strand and watched the light play over the irregularly shaped, luminescent beads. The necklace was clearly both genuine and an antique.

What was going on? Whose pearls were these? She dared not ask Sam, for she had a feeling these pearls no more belonged to Great-aunt Magnolia than had the equally bizarre cameo brooch.

Who kept leaving strange gifts in her room?

She didn't even want to think about an answer.

She set the strand on her bedside table, turned off the lamp, and tried to sleep . . .

In her dreams, Stephanie walked the floor with a wailing baby, amid the clamor of the wraiths. At one point, a nightgown-clad "Miss Ebbie" sailed past overhead playing her violin.

In the distance, she spotted Great-aunt Magnolia, again in her rocker, knitting an afghan. She hastened to her side with the child.

"Please, can you help me?"

"But you must help us," Magnolia replied.

"Help you? How?"

Shaking her head, Magnolia set aside her knitting. "So many restless spirits . . . they've enlisted me in their crusade. I always was a sucker for a lost cause, you see. Now

33

I'm trapped here, and cannot go on to heaven until they're all at peace.''

''At peace? But what do they want?''

Magnolia laughed. ''Are you deaf and blind, child? Why, I've never heard such weeping and lamentation, or seen such dejected souls. They're all miserable, and they want their happiness, of course.''

''But what can I do about it?''

''Why, make them happy. You have a mission to perform.''

''A mission?''

''Indeed. There will be a sign when your journey begins ... and another when it is over...''

Stephanie bolted awake in the darkness. A mission? Signs? Was she losing her mind?

Maybe she *should* pack up and leave Natchez. She didn't know how much more of this she could take!

"Wasn't Reverend Carlson's sermon inspiring?" gushed Mrs. Milford.

"Yes, I'm all in favor of seeing the light before time runs out," replied Stephanie dryly.

The following afternoon, Sam, Stephanie, and the Milfords had just left church together. Chester and Sam sat in the front seat of Chester's posh Buick, with Stephanie and Mrs. Milford in the rear as they cruised down shady Homochitto Street, passing several of Natchez's breathtaking antebellum homes.

"The sermon was indeed thought-provoking," commented Chester, glancing at Sam. "I especially liked the part where the reverend spoke about honoring our families today. We'd be lost without our loved ones, wouldn't we?"

Watching Sam beam back at Chester, Stephanie nonetheless felt uneasy, not quite certain what Chester was hinting at.

Sam twisted about to face Stephanie and Mildred. "Well, I don't know about the two of you, but I'm going to be 'quite lost' if we don't get something to eat."

"I could use a bite," replied Mrs. Milford modestly.

"How 'bout Pearl Street Pasta?" suggested Sam. "I'm in the mood for fettuccini."

Chester called, "Does that sound good to you, Stephanie?"

"I'm really not hungry, thanks," she replied. "But I'll have a salad and keep the rest of you company."

"Are you still having a rough time at home?" Chester asked.

"Oh, yes," she replied ruefully.

Mrs. Milford patted Stephanie's hand. "Dear, you're looking so frail and run-down lately. You do need a substantial meal." Meaningfully, she added, "And perhaps to go off somewhere for a nice, *long* rest."

Annoyed by the woman's implication that she was crazy, Stephanie retorted, "What I need is an exorcist for the house! But maybe I will get some sleep tonight, if I don't have to rock the baby, or soothe Great-aunt Magnolia's histrionics."

Mrs. Milford gasped; Chester frowned confusedly, while Sam turned to roll her eyes at Stephanie, as if to plead, *Pleeeze.*

Realizing what she'd just said, Stephanie flashed Sam and Mrs. Milford a contrite smile. "I'm sorry. That must have sounded deranged, not to mention rude. Look, Chester, if you don't mind, would you drop me off at the house before the rest of you go on to lunch? I don't think I'll make very good company."

"Of course, Stephanie, whatever you want," replied Chester.

Stephanie felt bad regarding her outburst after church. She was angry at herself for again breaking her word to Sam, and dearly hoped she hadn't caused her sister more problems. Yet she was also so exhausted that she didn't waste too much time giving in to guilt. She tumbled into bed and fell deeply asleep.

Hazy hours later, her bedroom door banged open and a trembling voice demanded, "How could you do this to me?"

Stephanie sat up in bed and wiped sand from her eyes.

She stared at Sam, who stood before her with face swollen and eyes red. "Sam, what's wrong? Why have you been crying?"

"Chester and I had words."

A twinge of alarm stabbed Stephanie. "Words? You and Chester?"

"You don't have to act like it's stranger than a giraffe strutting down Silver Street."

"Sam, I'm not a mind reader," Stephanie replied patiently. "Sit down and tell me what's wrong."

Instead of complying, Sam began to pace and wave her arms. "My life is ruined, that's what's wrong!"

"What do you mean?"

Sam was still stalking about the room, her words pouring forth with turmoil. "After lunch, Chester dropped his mother off. Then we went for a ride along the bluff, and . . . Then we broke up!" She burst into sobs.

Horrified, Stephanie sprang up from the bed and rushed over to hug Sam. "Sam, I'm so sorry. My God, I had no idea—"

Sam shoved her away. "No idea? But you're responsible for this!"

Stephanie pressed a hand to her chest. "Me?"

"Yes, you!" Sam blinked at hot tears. "I know you've been through a hard time, but haven't I asked you *repeatedly* not to mention your ghosts around Mildred? Was I being so unreasonable?"

Stephanie groaned. "No, Sam, you weren't, and I've really tried. But that old biddy keeps baiting me. *Why don't you go off somewhere for a nice long rest, Stephanie, dear?* You don't have to be an Einstein to figure out she's hinting I should have myself committed."

Sam hiccoughed. "Whatever she's hinting, it's all blown up in our faces now."

Stephanie touched her arm. "Sam, please, tell me what happened."

Sam drew a convulsive breath. "Once Chester and I were alone, he told me he's having a lot of problems with Mildred. It seems she's very concerned about you, and convinced that insanity could run in our family."

"She's *what*?" cried Stephanie.

Sam laughed bitterly. "You heard me. Mildred's worried that her grandchildren may become . . . well, to put it mildly, a bunch of looney tunes."

Stephanie was outraged. "Why, that's the most outlandish thing I've ever heard!"

Sam waved a hand. "Of course it's outlandish! Yes, you've been acting eccentric, but that doesn't mean we Bishops are a bunch of loco birds. I mean, can you even imagine me with a lunatic for a child?"

"Never," Stephanie assured her.

Sam began pacing again. "Anyway, Chester asked me what we could do to calm Mildred down, perhaps try to limit contact between the two of you for a while—"

"And?"

Swinging around, Sam gritted her teeth. "Well, by then I was getting pretty steamed myself, and I made some crack about Mildred maybe having a few screws loose."

"Oh, Lord," moaned Stephanie.

Sam was wringing her hands. "Then Chester took offense, then we had words and . . . Oh, it was horrible! Now it's all over between us." Again Sam succumbed to heartbroken sobs.

Stephanie patted her sister's heaving shoulders. "Oh, God, Sam, I'm so sorry."

Sam shot her a heated glance.

Stephanie sighed. "Sam, I know you're hurt and angry, but I think you're blind to the real issue here."

"And what's the real issue?"

"The real issue is that Chester considers his mother more important than you."

"That's not true!"

"It is! Most everywhere you go, Mother Milford tags along like a cherished family pet."

"Chester is simply a responsible man and loyal son—"

"He's a mama's boy. Remember after church when he spoke of how important honoring our families is? Do you think he was talking about you? No, he was referring to 'Mama'!"

"What a hateful thing to say!"

"I'm sorry, Sam, but it's true, and you deserve better," Stephanie argued passionately. "I know you thought Mildred was on your side, but I'm convinced that woman has been lying in wait for you. Now she's using my problems as an excuse to drive a wedge between you and Chester— and it's working. As for Chester, he needs to decide once and for all who is more important—you or 'Mama.' For now, it appears 'Mama' has won."

Sam shook a finger at Stephanie. "You're just trying to cover your own guilt by blaming Chester—when he's the finest, dearest man I've ever known. And if you hadn't kept saying all that bizarre stuff, none of this would have happened."

Stephanie bit her lip. Although Sam's accusations were maddening and unfair, there was no doubt her sister was abjectly miserable, largely because of Stephanie's own conduct. She struggled to think of a way to offer Sam some comfort.

She flashed Sam an encouraging smile. "Look, I know you feel devastated now, but this sounds to me like no more than a classic lovers' tiff. I mean, don't you already regret some of the things you said?"

"Well, yes," Sam admitted grudgingly.

"I'm sure when Chester cools off, he's going to feel like a heel and come apologize. In the meantime, I'll try to put a lid on the ghost stuff."

Sam sniffed. "I'm afraid it's already too late for that." She fled the room.

Stephanie was beset by turmoil. Her conscience needled her for getting Sam in such a fix, while her pride argued that Sam had programmed herself for failure by setting her sights on Chester. Yes, he was a nice man, but he had one big flaw—his mother.

Yet in her heart, Stephanie knew how much Sam was hurting, and that Sam's blaming her was merely a by-product of her own suffering.

Still, it nagged at Stephanie that she couldn't seem to help Sam. Perhaps she should leave Natchez. Besides her job, nothing had really gone right for her since she had arrived. Perhaps Thomas Wolfe had spoken the truth when he'd said you can't go home again. Tomorrow, she would call Atlanta to see if she could get her old job back. . . .

Stephanie's anxieties made sleep practically impossible that night. When she did at last drift away, it was only to be confronted by a trailer load of hauntings that hit her with the velocity of a Mack truck.

The children were screaming, laughing, racing up and down the stairs. The woman was sobbing, sawing away on her violin. Stephanie was dashing about the house, trying to find the wailing baby. Around every corner, she seemed to encounter Magnolia.

"Do something about this!" her great-aunt implored. "This is no way to run a purgatory. I can't abide it any longer! I must find some peace!"

"I need peace!" retorted Stephanie.

Stephanie turned a corner, only to halt in her tracks as the way was barred by a devilish rogue with laughing blue eyes. . . .

Stephanie sat up with a gasp. She turned on the bedside lamp and saw from the clock that the hour was 4:00 A.M.

"Damn it," she muttered, springing out of bed and beginning to pace. "If all of you don't shut up, I'm going to travel back in time and straighten out this mess myself!"

Stephanie paused in her tracks, amazed at her own incredible words. All at once her gaze shifted to the dresser, where she spotted a small crystal goblet half-filled with red wine.

Another gift from the hereafter?

Without further thought, she crossed the room, grabbed the glass, and recklessly downed the wine in two gulps.

It tasted cool and sweet, and even before the alcohol could reach her veins, its essence somehow soothed her. Then, with the glass empty, she noticed the rose etched in the crystal . . . and she began to tremble.

Good Lord . . . *What* had she just done?

Perhaps she had just poisoned herself! But, at the moment, she was simply too tired to care. . . .

Stephanie crossed to the bed, turned off the lamp, and collapsed onto the mattress. For the first time in many weeks, she fell into a deep, deep sleep.

Chapter 6

Sometime later, Stephanie began to stir to the strains of "The Last Rose of Summer"—this time being played on a piano. Blinking, she gazed upward to view a half-tester, outlined in carved rosewood and lined with pale yellow pleated silk, stretching above her. The hanging was magnificent, with its sunburst effect radiating from a central ivory medallion etched with fleur-de-lis. Yet before, her bed had been devoid of any canopy!

Gasping, she sat up, her gaze drawn toward an antique lamp glowing on an unfamiliar bedside table. Although the wrought-iron base and pink frosted globe were lovely, Stephanie wrinkled her nose at a slight odor of kerosene. A kerosene lamp! How bizarre!

Perusing the room, she was further amazed to spot an unfamiliar, antique mahogany dresser with marble top and carved mirror above it, a mammoth cherrywood armoire she had never seen before, and a handsome dressing screen decorated with stained-glass pieces patterned after Moroccan tiles. A ponderous, beige and mauve floral medallion carpet covered the floor, where before the polished wood had been exposed. Even the walls were different, a rose-colored flocked paper replacing the former white plaster.

Where *was* she? The room in which she lay possessed the same dimensions of the one she'd left, but all the furnishings and accoutrements were different. The door to the hallway hadn't shifted from its place directly ahead of her, nor had the fireplace to her right; but a new door had appeared to her left. The windows and French doors were in the same places, but the miniblinds and modern draperies had been supplanted by gilt-edged velvet swags and lace panels. A distinctly cool night breeze was fluttering those panels—and both the opened windows and cool air seemed outlandish for sultry July.

Was this some kind of bad dream? She shook her head and blinked, yet the tableau did not shift at all. She sensed she was still in the same room, but it was a far *different* room.

How could this be?

At last Stephanie looked down at herself and was stunned to see that she was wearing Great-aunt Magnolia's dowdy mauve velvet gown, as well as her clunky old granny shoes.

Good Lord! Had she changed clothes in her sleep? From all appearances, she had changed a helluva lot more than her garments!

Even as Stephanie struggled to gain her bearings, she tensed at the sounds of women laughing out in the hallway. Feeling more anxious and mystified by the moment, she got out of bed and managed to wobble over to the door. She peered outside.

Again, the light was low, provided by two ornate wall sconces, but Stephanie hardly needed floodlights to take in the astounding scene before her. Her eyes grew enormous as she observed two "Southern belles" strolling past in lavish, floor-length ball gowns that appeared to be straight out of the late 1870s: one was a marvel of violet-colored satin, with a low neckline, fitted waist, and a skirt of three full, ruffled tiers culminating in a lavishly trimmed train; the other dress was a similar masterpiece fashioned of pink, watered silk. Both women carried nosegays, wore pearl chokers, and had arranged flowers in their upswept hair.

As the two headed for the stairs, Stephanie overheard one remark, "You know they say he'll never marry again—he's too sly a rascal," while the other giggled and replied, "Such a shame—it will break poor Ebbie's heart."

Poor Ebbie's heart?

Stephanie moved back inside, shut the door, rested against the panel, and took several deep breaths. She was utterly flabbergasted. Where *was* she and who were these two characters straight out of some sorority ball at Ole Miss? She wondered if she had somehow landed in another Natchez house during one of the annual pilgrimages—a time during which such attire would not be uncommon. But she knew of no other local mansion with this same layout.

And how could she explain the woman mentioning "Ebbie," the woman who had lived in this house over a century ago?

A *century* ago? Was she dreaming? Had she somehow landed in another time? But that was impossible!

Perhaps she was somewhere else, in a home where a masquerade ball was being staged. Perhaps someone named "Ebbie" had been invited, and she'd brought along an October breeze to titillate everyone. *Yeah, sure.*

Then Stephanie glanced at the dresser and spotted the very empty crystal goblet from which she'd drunk the wine, and she began to tremble. She rushed over and picked up the small glass, feeling its coolness in her hand, running her fingers over the etched rose. How could the glass be here if she was in another place? And it was definitely the same goblet—the inside still bore the dried residue of the red wine she'd drunk.

Perplexed, she set down the glass. Hearing another woman laugh out in the hallway, she felt a new twinge of uneasiness. What if she was discovered here? For all she knew, she was trespassing in someone else's home and might be subject to arrest. Even though she was far from dressed for the occasion, perhaps it would be best to try to sneak downstairs, slip out of the house, and return to her own home . . . wherever *that* might be!

Waiting until the woman's voice faded away, Stephanie slipped into the hallway, which, like the bedroom, was carpeted in an unfamiliar floral pattern. She tiptoed past several rococo revival chairs with tufted upholstery and cameo medallions, and a stunning pedestal side table with incised lines and marquetry panels. *Nothing* looked familiar to her, except for the dimensions of the house itself. But whoever lived here must be quite wealthy if these antiques were any indication.

Heading down the stairs, Stephanie could still hear the wistful waltz being played. On the landing she paused, perplexed to spot the same stained-glass window, etched with roses, behind her. Backlit by the moon, the jewel-like panel appeared downright eerie . . . as was her very existence at the moment!

At last she stepped into the downstairs hallway, only to spy a young couple in formal attire, kissing in the shadows near the front door and blocking her exit. For a moment she seethed in frustration, but soon realized she had no choice but to slip inside the parlor and hope she might leave quietly through the French doors.

Stephanie stepped into a scene straight out of *Gone With the Wind*. She gaped in awe. Inside the well-lit room, lovely women in breathtaking, full-skirted ball gowns waltzed in the arms of courtly gentlemen in old-fashioned formal cutaways. Sumptuous rococo revival settees and handsome wing chairs lined the walls; everywhere were vases filled with red roses. Overhead glittered a massive crystal chandelier, and in the grate a cozy fire snapped.

A *fire?* In mid-July?

The instant Stephanie's shoe touched the beautiful mauve-and-blue Persian carpet, a gasp rippled over the assemblage. Couple after couple turned to stare at her, then moved away toward the walls to get a better look.

So much for a discreet exit, Stephanie thought sinkingly. Intensely conscious of her less-than-appropriate attire, she felt as dowdy as a toadstool planted among roses. She glanced helplessly around the room, watching a silver-haired gentleman whisper to his wife, observing two young women snickering behind a peacock-feather fan. Then only the waltz was heard in the otherwise spellbinding silence.

What on earth was going on here?

Before Stephanie could contemplate her next move, a man strode toward her—a man she recognized as none other than Andre Goddard! Staggered by confusion and uncertainty, Stephanie bit her lip to keep her mouth from falling open as she took him in. His height, his wavy black hair, and his aristocratic features were familiar to her. More of a shock was the vivid blue of his deep-set eyes, and especially the intent way he was gazing at her as he approached, as if every fiber of his being was focused on her.

Heart pounding in mingled anticipation and dread, she noted that he held a small red rose in one tanned hand, and the sight of it washed her with a chill. Had he plucked the rose from one of the vases on spotting her? As if reading her thoughts, he raised the bloom and sniffed it, a wistful smile hovering on his lips.

At last he paused before her. In his formal black cutaway and pleated linen shirt, he was devastating.

He was also dead, unless memory failed her!

Even as Stephanie stared dumbfounded at him, he handed her the rose. She accepted it, regarding him quizzically as he bowed before her.

"Good evening, mam'selle," he uttered in a charming, sexy voice. "It is a pleasure to have you among us. May I have the honor of this dance?"

Stephanie could only gape at the man, who evidently accepted her silence as consent. Grinning, he pulled her into his arms and waltzed her around the room while the others watched.

Stephanie was reeling. If this man hadn't been holding her, she would have collapsed. The moment seemed so unreal, and again she wondered if she was dreaming. Yet the man waltzing her felt so alive, so warm. She could even smell his enticing scent—bay rum mingled with a slight odor of brandy. Combined with the perfume of the rose she held, the essences were potent and provocative.

But how could this man be here with her, if he had lived over a century ago? Why was she waltzing in the arms of a man who should be a ghost?

Meanwhile, all the guests were still watching them. Glancing at her host, feeling her heart hammer at the glint of mischief in his eyes, she managed to stammer, "W-why is everyone staring at us?"

Chuckling, he spun her into a turn. "Why, they're staring at you, *chérie*. You must admit you've caused quite a stir, showing up here uninvited, a beautiful stranger . . . and wearing that dowdy gown that appears to belong to another decade. Tell me, who are you and what are you doing here?''

By instinct, Stephanie countered, ''Who are you?''

He grinned in a flash of perfect white teeth. ''Why, I am Andre Goddard, owner of this house and your host for the evening. Now I must know the identity of the enchanting creature with whom I am waltzing.'' Drawing her closer, he leaned over and whispered huskily, ''You are a stranger to me, and I make it a policy *never* to allow a beautiful woman to leave my home a stranger.''

Although his words were arrogant and filled with sexual innuendo, Stephanie was too shaken to respond with the usual stirrings of indignation. Nothing was making sense to her. She glanced about the room, watching two elderly women pore over their tatting in a corner, spotting a portrait of Jefferson Davis hanging over the fireplace. Jefferson Davis, indeed! Then her gaze came to rest on none other than ''Miss Ebbie,'' who sat at the piano playing the waltz. But now the woman appeared to be anything but a specter!

''My God!'' Stephanie cried.

''What is wrong?'' asked her host, his face tensing with concern, his arm tightening at her waist.

''I . . . I'm not feeling very well,'' she stammered.

The waltz ended, mercifully relieving Stephanie of the necessity of conversing further with the man. She moved out of his embrace, and for a moment the two stared at each other. It was almost too much for Stephanie—the intensity of his gaze, the frank scrutiny of the others . . .

Stephanie was trembling badly as Miss Ebbie stepped up to join them. Stephanie restrained a flinch at being in the presence of an actual person whom she'd known previously only as a ghost. She was a plain young woman, her brown hair in a bun, her small body ensconced in a somber black silk dress. She regarded Stephanie with a mixture of curiosity and suspicion, then smiled shyly and even touched Stephanie's trembling arm.

''Andre, I believe our guest is shivering. Should I not help her find a wrap?''

''But of course,'' he gallantly replied. Blowing Stephanie a kiss, he said, ''Return soon, *chérie.*''

A shiver streaked down Stephanie's spine as the kiss eerily reminded her of one a little boy had tossed her way only days earlier. . . .

Nonetheless, she felt relieved to exit the room with Ebbie, although when she turned to spy Andre's amused gaze still focused on her, her heart skipped a beat.

Heading upstairs with Ebbie, Stephanie heaved a deep sigh. "Thank you so much for rescuing me back there. I felt very put on the spot."

On the landing, Ebbie turned to Stephanie in consternation. "Miss, whoever you are, I rescued you because I couldn't bear to see you embarrassed in front of our guests. Now I must ask, who are you? Why have you appeared here tonight, uninvited? Andre and I are well acquainted with the members of our community, and I'm certain we've never met you before."

For a moment Stephanie floundered, until a surge of bravado, mingled with inspiration, saved her. "Well, you may not have met me, but I already know all about you. I feel as if I'm intimately acquainted with every member of this household. I know you're Miss Ebbie, and that the man I just danced with is Andre Goddard. Furthermore, there are five motherless children asleep somewhere upstairs."

Ebbie's mouth fell open. "Who are you, and who told you all about us?"

Again relying on instinct, she replied, "I'm Stephanie Sergeant, and I'm here to help you."

Ebbie continued to frown, then her eyes lit with realization, and she snapped her fingers. "But of course! Did Peter Dearborn send you?"

Although Stephanie had no idea what Ebbie was talking about, she was smart enough to seize her advantage. "Yes, Peter sent me."

Ebbie clapped her hands, and with her brown eyes aglow, she actually appeared pretty. "Oh, thank heaven! Reverend Dearborn is such a thoughtful man. He realized I was under an undue burden, having to run this household and care for five young children all by myself. That's why he promised Andre and me that when he went to Jackson for his ecumenical council meetings, he would try to find another governess to assist me with my duties and dispatch her here right away. And you must be she."

"Yes, so I must be," agreed Stephanie with a frozen smile.

Ebbie hesitated. "Well, I'm glad you're prepared to help us, and I suppose if you're good enough for Peter . . . Although Andre will certainly want to interview you, go over your credentials." She brightened. "But not before tomorrow."

"Good." Ruefully, Stephanie confessed, "I've been through quite a lot tonight."

Ebbie frowned. "But you still haven't explained how you arrived here unannounced."

Stephanie thought quickly. "Well, I—er—arrived by—er—steamboat tonight . . ."

"Steamboat?" Ebbie repeated. "Then you must have traveled here from Vicksburg?"

"Exactly. And—um—when I got to the house, the young couple kissing by the front door admitted me."

"Ah, I see." Ebbie looked Stephanie over. "But where are your things?"

Stephanie sighed. "I—I'm afraid my suitcase is lost. I suspect the—er—dock person forgot to unload it before the—er—boat shoved off, and I was so tired that—well, I didn't notice it was gone until too late."

Ebbie's features twisted with sympathy. "Oh, you poor dear. Of course you're exhausted, and here I am, running on. Let's get you upstairs. We can sort out the rest tomorrow."

"Thanks. I am tired," agreed Stephanie.

Upstairs, Ebbie paused by the first door on the right. "If you'll wait for a moment, Miss Sergeant—"

"Er, Mrs. Sergeant." Taking in Ebbie's perplexed look, she held up her left hand with its gold ring. "I'm a widow."

"Ah, my sympathies. If you'll wait here, Mrs. Sergeant, I'll gather a few things."

"You're so kind," Stephanie replied.

Ebbie slipped inside. Stephanie stood holding the rose and heaving a great sigh of relief that she had passed her first test in this netherworld where she had landed. What next?

Ebbie emerged holding a white linen nightgown and a matching wrapper. "I hope these will do for tonight," she said, pressing the items into Stephanie's hands. "You're tall, and they're the largest ones I have—"

"I'm sure they'll be fine."

Ebbie smiled wistfully. "Andre made me give away all of Linnea's things after she died . . . You do know about Linnea, I presume?"

"Um . . . Andre's deceased wife?"

"Yes. It's hard to believe she's been gone a year." Ebbie crossed herself. "I didn't want to entertain tonight, but Andre insisted it was time to receive our friends again, now that our official mourning period has ended."

"Of course."

Ebbie sniffed. "At any rate, Andre doesn't hold with sentiment. He told me to give all Linnea's clothes to the church. But I did pack away her wedding gown and trousseau up in the attic—for Gwendolyn, Amy, and Sarah, you know."

Sarah! That would be the baby sister whom Beau had mentioned—the baby Stephanie had rocked in her dreams. Reeling at these realizations, she murmured, "How thoughtful of you. The girls will be happy to have keepsakes of their mother."

Ebbie nodded. "So they will. And here I am, talking away the night again, with you about to drop from exhaustion. Come along."

Stephanie was surprised when Ebbie led her back inside the same room where she had awakened. As soon as the door was closed behind them, Ebbie gasped and frowned at the bed. "Why, forevermore! Whoever crumpled the bedcovers? I swear, those boys must be into mischief again."

Appearing distressed, Ebbie quickly crossed the room, plumped the pillows in their white embroidered cases, and straightened the matching crocheted counterpane. "There."

"The room is lovely," Stephanie said.

Ebbie turned and smiled. "This was Linnea's room."

"Was it?"

Ebbie strolled to the dresser and straightened the scarf,

running her fingertips over the items set out there: a hairbrush and matching comb inset with mother-of-pearl; a pink
pleated glass basket filled with potpourri; a crystal perfume
bottle.

"Most of Linnea's gewgaws are put away for the girls,"
Ebbie explained, "but I've made up this room for guests. I
hope it will suffice."

"It's exquisite."

Ebbie turned, beaming. "I'm glad you're pleased, since
it's our only vacant room at the moment. Do make yourself
at home."

Stephanie inclined her head toward the side of the room.
"By the way, where does that door lead?"

"To Andre's room," Ebbie replied.

Stephanie blanched.

Ebbie laughed nervously. "Please don't fret. That door
is always kept locked. I don't think Andre has set foot in
this room since Linnea died."

"I see," Stephanie replied, bemused.

"Is there anything I can get for you before you retire?
Perhaps some warm milk?"

"No, thanks, I'm fine. But—is the bathroom still at the
end of the hallway?"

"Bathroom?" Ebbie repeated blankly. "Oh, we don't
have bathrooms in Natchez as yet, though I've heard they
can be found in some of the newer homes in Jackson. Did
you have one where you stayed?"

"Er—yes."

"Well, I'm afraid here we still use the old-fashioned
commode chair." Ebbie walked toward a rosewood arm-
chair with an enclosed bottom, and lifted the lid on the seat
to reveal a porcelain pot.

"You're joking."

Ebbie shook her head. "But we're doing our best to mod-
ernize. After all, it is the year 1878."

"Right," Stephanie muttered woodenly.

"Do get some rest, then. Breakfast will be served in the
dining room at eight." She started for the door.

Remembering that she was ostensibly a newly arrived

servant here, Stephanie called, "You—er—expect me to join the family?"

"But of course," Ebbie replied. "Your assistance will certainly be required at mealtimes. Tomorrow, I'll explain your duties, and introduce you to the children."

Ebbie slipped out, and Stephanie stood alone, feeling suddenly lost, helpless, and numb. She placed the rose Andre Goddard had given her on the fireplace mantel, and gazed about her in shock.

It is the year 1878, Ebbie had said. Just the memory made her shudder. Again, she wondered what on earth had happened to her. She pinched herself, trying to awaken from her outlandish dream, to no avail.

So, I am now living in a house full of dead people carrying on some bizarre nineteenth-century charade. Either that, or Andre Goddard is pretty damn sexy for a man who is 150 years old!

This is sheer lunacy!

There must be some way to make sense of it. There must.

Pacing about, she remembered her last conversation with Great-aunt Magnolia, her own rash claim that she'd travel back in time and straighten out this mess. She remembered drinking the wine . . . She glanced at the dresser and was amazed to note that the crystal goblet had vanished.

What *was* this? Magic?

All at once, Stephanie felt a sinking sensation as realization dawned. Could the wine have been the "sign" Great-aunt Magnolia had spoken of? Did her vow to "straighten out the mess" somehow propel her back in time, to meet Ebbie and the others while they were still alive, and somehow "de-spook" the mansion? It all seemed incomprehensible—yet little else was making sense. After all, she had been seeing ghosts and wraiths at will—creatures who had implored her to come help them. Was it that much of a stretch that they might eventually lure her back to their own time?

Yes, it was several thousand light-years of a stretch!

Yet Ebbie did seem to welcome her here, accepting her hastily contrived story with little suspicion, although people would be more trusting in these times—particularly naive, sheltered creatures like Ebbie. Had she truly been brought here to help the woman?

Then there was Andre Goddard—hardly naive in any way. Reliving her astounding encounter with the Frenchman, Stephanie shivered. She recalled how he had boldly crossed the room and asked her to dance. Why had he done so?

She stared at the door that led to his room. What kind of marriage could he and this Linnea have shared, if they'd slept in separate bedrooms, with a locked door between them? Still, Andre had managed to get his wife with child often enough . . .

What was it he had said? *You are a stranger to me, and I make it a policy never to allow a beautiful woman to leave my home a stranger.* Stephanie smiled cynically, suspecting that this very lusty nature was the real reason Andre Goddard had homed in on her like a stallion pursuing a newly arrived mare. *The rogue! A dead man—or a ghost, or whatever the hell he is!—should comport himself with more decorum!*

This was all too much to absorb at once. Perhaps she just needed some rest. Perhaps by morning, she'd be granted a reprieve and this nightmare would be over.

She went to the dresser, poured water from the pitcher into the basin, and washed her face. Undressing, she donned the nightgown, which was roomy and covered her to midthigh.

After an awkward introduction to the commode chair, she climbed into bed, finding the feather tick surprisingly comfortable. She felt a lump in her throat as she thought about Sam. Had she actually disappeared from the present? Was her sister worried about her? Oh, why had she been whisked away to this purgatory right after their terrible fight, with things so unresolved between them, and Sam's life in such a mess?

Maybe she'd awaken soon to discover that this *was* all just a bad dream. If not, then perhaps Great-aunt Magnolia had been right and she did have a mission to perform. In the meantime, she would not risk that mission by telling anyone here where she *really* came from—for who would believe her? Besides, she had won herself a place in this household by the skin of her teeth—and while being here had her thoroughly rattled, she was far from eager to go dashing off alone into a world that she already suspected might be totally alien to her. . . .

After the last guest departed, Andre Goddard stood on the front gallery, smoking a cheroot in the darkness, his lips curled in a bemused smile, his thoughts centered on the strange, enchanting creature who had arrived unannounced at his soiree tonight.

How lovely the woman was! In his mind's eye, he pictured her now: the tall, willowy form, the sleek, shoulder-length blond hair, the long, exquisitely featured face—most particularly, that full, kissable mouth!—and her gorgeous, honey brown eyes. Even as he remembered holding her lush curves against him, the sweet scent of her and the endearing bewilderment in her eyes, he felt his senses stirring for her.

Who was this captivating mystery lady who had appeared at his home so unexpectedly, wearing such a dowdy costume? As he and Ebbie had bidden their guests good night, she had mentioned that the visitor would be staying overnight, that Peter Dearborn had dispatched her to help them. Ebbie had also promised a fuller explanation in the morning.

Taking a draw on his cheroot, he mused that he could not wait to hear more about their intriguing visitor. Yet his thoughts also brought a stab of guilt and wrenching memories of Linnea . . . his dear, departed wife.

Funny, how most everyone in this town thought of him as a jaded widower, cruel breaker of feminine hearts. Yes, he possessed an eye for the ladies, a thirst for fine liquor, a love of cards. But beyond such surface pleasures, Andre knew he hid his true feelings well. No one really knew of his private anguish and despair, especially a year ago after he had lost his wife. He had married a woman he hadn't loved. He'd been true to her in a physical sense, though his heart had never really been in the marriage. Then he had watched her die bearing his child. . . . At times his regret was still overwhelming. Yet love and concern for his children kept him from wallowing in remorse—at least, that's what he told himself in his nobler moments.

He sighed. He did worry about his children. They deserved more than a mother in her grave and a father who was a profligate. With great tenderness, he thought of his youngest, baby Sarah, remembering the day she was born, the same day that Linnea had left them, and how his wife had insisted that bearing their last child made all her suffering worthwhile. Linnea had left this life with a smile on her lips, whispering of her love for him.

The memory filled him with self-recrimination. He glanced up at the starry skies. Perhaps Linnea was better off up there with the angels, and he in this earthly realm where he could suffer for his sins. . . .

Chapter 7

Stephanie awakened with a smile and yawned lazily. Such a pleasant dream she'd had, of being transported to the Old South and waltzing in the arms of a handsome rogue . . .

Only it wasn't a dream! With a gasp, she jerked upright and gaped at her surroundings. Feelings of unreality engulfed her at being in this room which was at once the same yet so different from the one she'd left behind. She was filled with a sense of wonder at having apparently landed in an earlier time, but with an equally intense feeling of dread to be wrenched away from all she held near and dear.

She gazed at the lacy bed linens, watched flickers of light dance about on the Victorian carpet, and observed the breeze rippling the lace panels at the windows. There was clearly no electricity or air-conditioning in this house. A glance at the walls and ceiling confirmed the absence of outlets or vents.

There was no plumbing, either, she recalled ruefully.

Getting up, she put on the lace-trimmed linen wrapper that Ebbie had lent her, opened the French doors, and stole out onto the veranda. At the railing she did a double take, staring ahead at an amazing, foreign curtain of fall greenery—elms and pecans with golden leaves fluttering in the dappled light, sycamores and sweet gum trees decked out in reddish gold glory.

What were those trees doing here, and why were they

dropping leaves so soon? It was supposed to be summer, not fall!

The only familiar aspect of the lawn was the massive oaks. Although the trees appeared mature, and were dripping with Spanish moss, they were nowhere near as gnarled and ancient as they'd been in the present. The landscaping was strange, as well, with scattered rose plantings replacing the formal garden, and foreign clumps of crepe myrtle, camellias, and azaleas spilling from several round beds.

Turning to examine the facade of the house, Stephanie found it appeared the same, but newer; the red brick looked much fresher and brighter, without the timeworn crustiness she remembered. The shutters that had been white in the present were a forest green now.

Hearing a clip-clop sound, Stephanie glanced toward the street and was astounded to glimpse an antique box buggy rattling along, carrying a couple in old-fashioned attire, the man driving the large bay-colored horse. Even the street was different, with dirt replacing the former asphalt and clouds of dust rising from the buggy wheels.

Stephanie shook her head and tried to make sense of the mind-boggling contradiction of her existence at the moment. How on earth could a woman from the 1990s be standing amid a late-nineteenth-century world? But, from all indications, she truly had traveled back in time to the Old South. Either that, or she was having one doozy of an hallucination! What *had* been in the wine she'd drunk last night? Whatever magical ingredient the brew had contained, it had led her on one grand adventure through time—though she was still too mystified to enjoy her trip.

With a sigh, Stephanie returned inside. If she truly had been transported through time, then, as Ebbie had mentioned last night, she must now be living in the year 1878. That's right—for the photo she'd seen back in the present, depicting Andre Goddard and his family looking much as they did now, had been dated 1878!

Impossible! Yet at the moment, Stephanie Sergeant seemed to be *living* the impossible. . . .

*   *   *

Stephanie brushed her hair and donned Great-aunt Magnolia's old clothes. She felt dowdy in the tacky frock and silly granny shoes, but they were her only suitable garments at the moment. And surely her wardrobe was the least of her worries.

Heading for the stairs, she could hear the sounds of children's exuberant voices, accompanied by a loud banging, drifting up from the first floor. She frowned, all her instincts offended by the clamor. The ruckus was so jarring that she flinched several times while going down the steps.

In the downstairs hallway she hesitated. The banging was much louder now, the children's voices reaching a rowdy crescendo. The din clearly emanated from the dining room, and was totally incongruous in these genteel surroundings.

Indeed, the downstairs hallway, awash in sunlight, appeared even more elegant than it had last night. Stephanie took in the Oriental runner on the floor, the gleaming rosewood tables with their priceless Ming vases and crystal bowls filled with roses, the gilt-edged mirrors and crystal chandeliers.

Grimacing at a particularly loud bang, Stephanie realized she was stalling and decided she might as well face the lions. She took a deep breath and smoothed down her hair. Squaring her shoulders, she entered the dining room.

She paused in her tracks at the astonishing scene. The elegant Queen Anne table was set with snowy white linen, blue Staffordshire china, and gleaming crystal. A polished walnut punkah fan hung over the table, and on the gilt-edged French sideboard were several brilliantly painted Bristol figurines of beautiful ladies and handsome children, as well as a striking salmon, ivory, and gold Sèvres vase painted with cherubs.

But there all semblance of gentility ceased. At one end of the long table was seated a very flustered Ebbie, who was trying to feed oatmeal to a baby girl in a high chair. Eyes wide, Stephanie recognized the baby from her dreams. The child was being most uncooperative, squirming and waving her plump little arms. Judging from the amount of food spattered all over the baby and Ebbie, more of the cereal had landed on them than in the child's stomach!

Toward the middle of the table sat a little girl of about three; with long, curly black hair and china-doll features, she was an adorable older version of the baby. She was sucking her thumb and staring solemnly at Stephanie.

At the other end of the table sat Andre Goddard with another girl, who appeared to be about four, seated in his lap. Andre was scowling, attempting to read *The Natchez Sun*, while the child was cheerfully carving up the pages with embroidery scissors. The imp was precious, with her long mane of curly, red-gold hair, and when she glanced up at Stephanie in curiosity, Stephanie caught an image of a long, exquisitely shaped face, a strong, proud chin, and huge green eyes. The girl stared at Stephanie for a moment, then shrugged and resumed cutting up the newspaper.

Under the table was crouched a boy who appeared to be about seven. Dressed in short pants and a jacket, he squatted amid boards, nails, and a hammer; he was pounding away, apparently trying to construct a crude birdhouse. Next to him, a small, champagne-colored Pomeranian was lapping up spilled milk.

On the far wall, Stephanie spotted none other than the five-year-old boy she had met in the present, the one who called himself Beau. Dressed in attire similar to his brother's, he was standing on his head and pounding his heels against the gold flocked wallpaper, his antics rattling a painting of a Pomeranian similar to the dog under the table. With awe, Stephanie recognized the work as a Gainsborough—a masterpiece that might soon crash down on the boy's head.

Was this a home or a circus? As the boy continued his insufferable kicking, Stephanie watched the Sèvres vase dance precariously close to the edge of the sideboard. She dashed over and managed to grab it just in time.

"You stop that, right now, young man!" she ordered, replacing the vase on the sideboard, then carefully adjusting the Gainsborough.

At Stephanie's loud command, the noise in the room gradually faded away. Face red from exertion, the boy tumbled down from the wall and grinned up at her. Thinking he was quite a charming monster, Stephanie nonetheless cast him a stern glance before daring a look at the table. When she did, she almost recoiled at the sight of seven sets of eyes, including the dog's, intently focused on her. From utter pandemonium seconds earlier, the room had grown so quiet that even the little dog's soft growl sounded like a lion's roar.

Then Stephanie caught Andre Goddard staring at her with amusement glinting in his bright blue eyes. She fought the treacherous excitement his look stirred. Lifting her chin, she deliberately turned toward Ebbie, who wiped cereal from the baby's face and smiled brightly.

"Why, Mrs. Sergeant. Good morning. Won't you join us?"

"Thank you, I'd be happy to."

"Indeed, Madame Sergeant, you *must* join us," agreed Andre. "Ebbie was just telling us—er—all about you."

With these words, the master of the house set aside his newspaper, carefully retrieved the scissors from his daughter's hands, then stood with the child. Kissing the little girl's cheek, he set her in her own chair and quickly strode to Stephanie's side.

As he took her hand and kissed it, the others watched, and Stephanie felt a new flutter of excitement at the scoundrel's brazenness.

He straightened and grinned at her, only enhancing her agitation. He did look quite dashing in a dove gray frock coat, charcoal-colored satin waistcoat, and tan trousers. Oh, why was her heart suddenly pounding so frantically? She was hardly some dizzy debutante swooning over her first glimpse of a handsome male, but an experienced, mature woman—a widow.

"Good morning, Mr. Goddard," she replied stiffly.

He gestured expansively toward the table. "Come, come, Madame Sergeant. You must have a chair, and some breakfast."

He made a great show of taking her arm and escorting her to the table, then pulling out a chair. As Stephanie sat down, she heard the little dog let out another menacing growl and prayed that her ankles would be safe from those sharp little teeth. She was soon distracted from this anxiety as Andre pushed in her chair and deliberately leaned close. Catching a tantalizing whiff of his shaving soap, she restrained a shiver.

"Welcome to our humble abode, Madame Sergeant," he murmured.

Humble abode, my foot! she thought. Aloud, she smoothly replied, "Thank you."

As he moved away, Stephanie calmly unfolded her napkin. She glanced up to see that the three girls were all still staring at her; indeed, the child Andre had set down appeared to be furious, a female whose territory had been invaded. Taking their places, the boys also studied Stephanie frankly.

Resuming his seat, Andre flashed Ebbie a grin. "Ebbie, be a darling and ring for some breakfast for our guest."

"Y-yes, Andre," Ebbie answered, clearly flustered by his endearment as she reached for a small brass bell. She managed to ring it—then promptly dropped it on the floor. "Sorry, Andre," she muttered, blushing.

His expression was magnanimous. "No matter, dear."

Andre was once again gazing at Stephanie when a tall, middle-aged mulatto woman entered the room. Stephanie found her lovely with her smoothly featured, honey gold face, the colorful tignon on her head, her fine linen shirt and full, flower-printed skirt.

"Yes, sir?" she asked Andre.

Andre gestured at Stephanie. "Lilac, this is Madame Sergeant, who has come to assist Miss Ebbie with her duties. Kindly bring Madame some breakfast."

The woman nodded shyly at Stephanie. "Yes, sir." After retrieving the bell Ebbie had dropped, she left the room.

All at once, the room grew quiet again, too quiet, and Stephanie became conscious that Ebbie and all of the children were still watching her intently.

Then the oldest girl, the one who'd been cutting up Andre's paper, turned to her father, and demanded imperiously, "Who is she, Papa? Our new teacher? And why was she so mean to Beau?"

"I don't think she was mean," interjected Beau, grinning at Stephanie.

Andre chuckled. "Now, Gwen darling, as you can hear, Beau isn't offended. And is this any way to greet our visitor? Why don't you let Papa—er—deal with Madame Sergeant?"

The girl hurled a rebellious look at Stephanie, then informed her father, "*Only* if you punish her for being so mean to Beau."

Andre was obviously fighting amusement as he glanced at Stephanie, who sat in outraged silence. "If I—er—punish Madame Sergeant, she may get angry and leave."

"Good. Give her a spanking and make her leave."

All four of the older children hooted at Gwen's outrageous comment, while Stephanie wished she could give the little termagant a piece of her mind.

Andre was regarding his daughter with amused indulgence. "Gwen, whenever have I spanked *anyone* in this house?"

Gwen frowned, while Ebbie, her features aghast, scolded, "Really, Gwen! You're being quite rude to our guest."

Andre held up a hand to Ebbie. "The child means no harm, dear."

Appearing miserable at his admonishment, Ebbie hung her head. "Yes, Andre."

Stephanie was appalled at the way Andre was humoring a spoiled child at Ebbie's expense and almost protested, then thought better of it.

Gwen shot Stephanie another contemptuous look. "I bet she doesn't even know any good stories."

"Oh, on the contrary, pet, I have a feeling Madame Sergeant knows *lots* of good stories," Andre replied cynically. "Why, from what I hear, she's already told Ebbie quite a fascinating tale."

Gwen shrugged and began playing with the food on her plate. Stephanie's spirits sank. So Andre already questioned her cover story—as most any intelligent person should.

Andre leaned toward Stephanie. "Madame Sergeant, Ebbie was just describing to us your unfortunate circumstances, how you were dispatched here by Reverend Dearborn, only to lose all of your belongings at the landing."

Stephanie met his eye, still indignant over the way he had condoned his children's mischief, and even more anxious because he obviously doubted her concocted story. Would he expose her as an imposter and send her on her way? From his avid gaze, she somehow doubted this.

Never easily daunted, Stephanie replied forthrightly, "Yes, that is precisely what happened. I am here at the—er—behest of your Reverend Dearborn, but unfortunately my belongings are somewhere in Louisiana by now."

"I see," Andre murmured, thoughtfully stirring his coffee. "And thus you arrived here in this"—he eyed her slowly—"peculiar traveling costume?"

"Exactly," Stephanie answered through gritted teeth.

"If you are to remain in this home, we simply *must* do something about your wardrobe," he went on ruefully, shaking his head. "Don't you agree, Ebbie?"

"Yes, Andre." Ebbie flashed Stephanie a shy smile. "I'll see to it right away."

"Also, Madame Sergeant, I take it you have a letter from Reverend Dearborn recommending your employment here?" Andre continued mildly.

Stephanie blanched. Why hadn't she thought of this? Andre Goddard might be an outrageously permissive father, but of course he would question the credentials of any potential new governess.

"Er-no," she stammered. Thinking quickly, she added, "The letter was also lost with my luggage."

"Lost with your luggage." Andre raised an eyebrow at Ebbie. "How convenient."

Chewing her lower lip, Ebbie appeared the epitome of frayed nerves. "Andre, I've no doubt Madame Sergeant is here—er—legitimately." Flashing Stephanie a wan smile, Ebbie explained, "You see, last night when she arrived, Madame Sergeant informed me that Peter had sent her here to us. And she knew all about us—our names, even about—er—Linnea. It was clear to me that Peter must have told her all about us."

"Good point." Stirring his coffee, Andre continued off-handedly, "And Peter Dearborn will doubtless clear up this little discrepancy as soon as he returns from Jackson, *n'est-ce pas*, Madame Sergeant?''

Stephanie lifted her chin bravely, even as her stomach churned. "Of course he will."

Andre chuckled. "In the meantime, we are eager to learn more about you. From whence do you hail?"

"From Atlanta." Watching his eyebrows shoot up, she hastily added, "I was in Jackson visiting friends when I met your Reverend Dearborn."

"But your people are from Atlanta?" he pursued.

Stephanie decided that the truth—or a reasonable facsimile—would suffice. "My parents recently retired to Florida."

"To live among the swamps and alligators?" he inquired. "How singular."

"They like it well enough."

Andre stared pointedly at her left hand with its gold wedding band. "I understand you are a widow?"

Would this grilling ever end? "Yes."

"My sympathies. Was your loss recent?"

"Five years ago." *More like 115!*

Andre appeared rather pleased. "Ah, so you have been five years without your dear husband to—er—care for you?"

Stephanie marshaled her patience at a statement oozing male chauvinism. "I've managed to care for myself quite nicely, thank you."

Although Stephanie thought she detected a glint of ire in his eyes, he leaned lazily back in his chair. "You're certainly a creature of spirit. I do admire that."

Stephanie smiled sweetly.

"And however have you been occupying yourself these—er—past five years?"

"Well, I've been—um—working with children," she replied. "I've been a governess for various families, and I've also—er—volunteered at the library and at church, that sort of thing."

"Ah, so you're self-sacrificing, as well," he drawled.

His sarcasm was more than apparent, and Stephanie battled an urge to hurl a spoon at him. She was relieved of the necessity to respond as Lilac reentered the room carrying a tray. In front of Stephanie she placed a plate filled with sausages, eggs, and grits, a napkin and silverware, and a cup of steaming coffee.

"Thank you," Stephanie murmured.

Nodding, Lilac left the room.

Stephanie was picking up her fork when Ebbie spoke up. Flashing Andre a shy smile, she asked, "Andre, should you introduce Mrs. Sergeant to the children?"

"But of course," he answered. "How thoughtless of me." He turned to Stephanie. "Madame Sergeant, I take it you do like children?"

As the silky words rolled off his tongue, Stephanie dropped her fork. Why was it that this rogue could turn the simplest question into something illicit-sounding?

"Of course I do," she replied with strained patience.

Andre nodded toward his younger son. "Your rather sharp comment to Beau would seem to indicate otherwise, but perhaps the children who frequent your libraries are not so well bred?"

Seething at Andre's criticism and watching Beau pull a face at her, Stephanie evenly replied, "If I was sharp with Beau, it was because he was about to destroy a priceless vase—and knock a Gainsborough off the wall."

"Ah, so you acted due to your own offended artistic sensibilities?" Andre asked.

"I acted, sir, because I don't find it proper for young children to stand on their heads kicking walls during breakfast—nor to play with dangerous hammers or sharp scissors."

He smiled patiently. "But how else can they learn? They're just having harmless fun."

"If you find hammers or scissors harmless in the hands of young children, sir, then obviously you have need of my services."

"Obviously, I do," he agreed smoothly.

Feeling her face flame, Stephanie clamped her mouth shut. She had walked right into that one!

Andre dabbed at his mouth with his napkin to hide a self-satisfied grin. "Then of course I must introduce you to my brood." He gestured toward the nearest boy. "Madame Sergeant, meet my oldest son, Paul Andre Goddard."

Stephanie nodded to the boy. "How do you do, Paul?"

The child smiled back shyly. "You're pretty. You kind of look like my mother—only her hair was more red."

"Thank you, Paul," Stephanie murmured. "What a nice compliment."

"Yes, Madame Sergeant is quite a lovely woman," agreed Andre. He extended a hand toward the younger boy. "I believe you and Beau have already become somewhat acquainted?"

"We have." Stephanie slanted the lad a chiding glance.

Undaunted, the boy reached down and picked up the little dog. It snarled, baring its sharp teeth at Stephanie. "And this is Pompom. Papa bought her for us in England. Pompom's the great-great—well, an *ancestor*—of Queen Charlotte."

As Stephanie wondered at this odd tidbit, the girl named Gwen whooped a laugh. "No, silly, Pompom's *not* an ancestor—she's a disaster—I mean, a dissenter—"

"A *descendant*, darling," provided her father.

"A *descendant* of the queen's *dog*," finished Gwen with an imperious jerk of her chin.

"Well, she's royalty!" Beau snapped back. "Isn't that true, Papa?"

"Yes, indeed." As the dog again snapped at Stephanie, Andre coughed. "I think you can put her down now, son."

"Yes, sir."

"Next, I want you to meet my beautiful daughters," continued Andre. Gesturing around the table, he announced, "Gwendolyn, who is four; Amy, my three-year-old; and the baby, Sarah."

Stephanie smiled at each girl in turn. Sarah gurgled back and waved her arms. Amy stared. Gwendolyn tossed her curls, glowered at Stephanie, and stated, "I can tell Papa likes you, and I don't want a new mother."

At this outspoken remark, Andre burst out laughing, and Stephanie could have crawled under the table. The boys began to tease their sister.

"Gwen, you're silly," chided Paul.

"And besides, Papa doesn't want a new lady," added Beau. "He wants *all* the ladies."

Both boys all but split their sides laughing.

"Boys, boys, let's not scare Madame Sergeant away on her first day," Andre admonished, his expression all secret amusement.

At last Ebbie, whose countenance appeared stricken, dared to speak up again. "Andre is right, boys. You must display better manners. And Gwendolyn, you were rude to greet Madame Sergeant that way."

Watching Gwen's little face tighten in mutiny, Stephanie turned to the child and spoke soberly. "That's quite all right. Gwen, I want you to know that I came here to help out . . . not to become anyone's mother."

The child hesitated, her expression wavering. She turned to Andre. "Is that true, Papa?"

He nodded to the child, then thoughtfully regarded Stephanie. "I assure you, pet, that when I look at Madame Sergeant, my impression of her is *anything* but maternal."

The child beamed, while Stephanie turned her attention to the food on her plate to hide the deepening blush on her face.

Chapter 8

⟨═══ ୬୧ ═══⟩

Following breakfast, Andre announced he must head off to town and drop Paul off at school, then made a great show of hugging and kissing his four younger children. At last he paused by Stephanie's chair, grinned at her, and again took her hand.

"Madame Sergeant, I shall leave you in Ebbie's capable hands until I return. I'm sure she can more than adequately explain your new duties."

"I'm sure she can," Stephanie agreed, flashing him a polite smile, while wishing she were free to throttle him for continuing to fawn over her.

"Andre, we must discuss a suitable salary for Madame Sergeant," put in Ebbie.

"Of course we will." After placing another lingering kiss on Stephanie's hand, Andre turned to his oldest son. "Come along, Paul, we'll be late."

Father and son left, taking with them all semblance of order in the room. At once Beau decided to finish his brother's birdhouse, and disappeared beneath the table to pound nails. Gwen started skipping about the room while loudly calling out a nursery rhyme, the little dog yapping at her heels. As before, Amy merely sucked her thumb and stared.

Stephanie turned to Ebbie, who had removed Sarah from her high chair and was struggling to keep the squirmy baby in her arms. "You really have your hands full here, don't you?" Stephanie commented.

Ebbie forced a smile. "Indeed, but it's a little easier with Paul in school during the day. I used to try to tutor him, but Andre and I decided that he'd be better off with children his own age at the Natchez Institute."

Stephanie glanced at Ebbie's plate. "You never got to finish your breakfast. Why don't I take the baby so you can eat?"

"Oh, I'm really not hungry," Ebbie demurred, grimacing as Sarah yanked on her hair.

Stephanie stood and walked over to Ebbie's chair. "Come on. With this brood, you need your nourishment."

Throwing Stephanie a grateful smile, Ebbie handed over the child, and Stephanie sat down with her. At once the baby quieted and stared up at her. A moment later, Sarah began cooing to herself and wrapped a strand of Stephanie's long blond hair around a chubby finger.

Her fork in midair, Ebbie regarded Stephanie in pleasant surprise. "Why, she seems to take to you. It's almost as if she already knows you."

"Maybe she's just worn-out," Stephanie replied diplomatically as Ebbie's words brought an unconscious shiver.

"No, I think not." Ebbie sighed heavily. "I'm afraid I don't have much of a way with children."

"Oh, I'm sure that's not true," Stephanie reassured her.

Gwen came up to eye Stephanie and the baby suspiciously, while Pompom growled by her side. "Sarah likes you," she accused.

"Well, I am here to help," Stephanie replied, ignoring the snarling dog.

With a flounce of her red-gold curls, Gwen turned to Ebbie. "I don't like Madame Sergeant."

Ebbie slanted the child a chiding glance. "Gwen, you're being rude again."

Gwen stamped her foot and pouted. "I don't care! I don't like her, and I don't want her here!"

Although her voice trembled badly, Ebbie stood her ground. "Gwen, I shall not listen to this impertinent talk."

While Stephanie admired Ebbie's show of courage, the child glared back, then burst out, "I want my doll!"

Ebbie set down her fork. "I'll take you upstairs to get it."

Stephanie spoke up. "Gwen, Miss Ebbie hasn't finished her breakfast yet. Can't you wait a moment?"

The child turned on Stephanie. "I don't have to mind you!"

Before either woman could respond, Beau popped up from beneath the table. "I'll take Gwen upstairs."

Stephanie turned to Ebbie. "Is that all right?"

Ebbie glanced dubiously at Beau. "If you'll promise to go straight upstairs to the playroom and come right back."

"Sure."

The two children danced out of the room, the barking dog following, the threesome almost knocking over an elderly black woman, her back bent, who stepped across the threshold.

Approaching the table, the old woman, in a plain blue muslin gown and housecap, glanced curiously from Stephanie to Ebbie. "Miss Ebbie, you wants I put that baby down now?"

"Yes, thank you, Martha."

The gray-haired woman took the baby from Stephanie, then glanced at Amy. "You wants to come?"

Nodding solemnly, the three-year-old slid off her chair, walked around the table, and took the old woman's hand.

Watching the children leave with their nurse, Stephanie released a sigh and turned to Ebbie. "At last, a moment of relative peace."

"Relative is correct," Ebbie replied. "If Gwen and Beau aren't back soon, we'll have to go searching for them." She flashed Stephanie an apologetic smile. "I'm so sorry about Gwen's behavior, Madame Sergeant. You see, she's very possessive of her father—you know, after losing her mother and all."

Stephanie felt a surge of sympathy for the defiant little minx. "I understand, and please call me Stephanie."

"Very well, Stephanie." Ebbie drew a deep breath. "I swear, though, Gwen and Beau are into more mischief than a colony of ants with spilled honey. At least Martha helps out with the wee ones, though I worry about her. She's getting so old, and some days she's crippled by rheumatism. Still, Sarah and Amy aren't quite the handfuls the older ones are.''

"And Amy is so different from the others . . . so quiet.''

Ebbie nodded. "So you noticed.''

"Does she speak?''

"Oh, yes, when she wants to,'' Ebbie replied. "She's just more interested in sucking her thumb and watching everyone else. I do believe she took Linnea's passage the hardest.''

"As did you?'' Stephanie asked wisely.

Emotion choked Ebbie's voice. "My cousin and I . . . were very close.''

"I'm so sorry.'' Sensing she'd best not press the subject, she asked, "So, is Mr. Goddard gone for the day?''

Ebbie brightened. "Most likely. Andre's a cotton factor and he usually has . . . well, important meetings with other gentleman in town.''

"I see,'' Stephanie murmured as an image sprang to mind of the rogue spending his "important meetings'' gambling and drinking mint juleps.

Ebbie rushed on. "I'm glad things went so well at breakfast. Andre seems to like you.''

"So I noticed,'' Stephanie muttered dryly.

"I want to tell you how grateful I am to have you here, Madame—er, Stephanie. It's going to be so wonderful having help with the children. Perhaps I'll be able to spend more time assisting at church, or practicing with my string quartet.''

"You belong to a string quartet?''

"Yes, I'm a member of the Natchez Quartet, along with Mr. Trumble, Mr. Fortier, and Mr. Wister,'' Ebbie related self-consciously. "We practice at least twice weekly and perform at a number of a social events each season.'' She blushed. "Andre constantly teases me because the three gentlemen in the quartet are all bachelors. He is certain one of them will steal me away from Harmony House.''

Taking in Ebbie's flustered demeanor, Stephanie asked, "Pardon my frankness, but you're quite fond of Andre, aren't you?''

Ebbie's face turned scarlet. "I—well, in the year since Linnea's death, I have devoted my life to him and his children."

"And it didn't bother you when he undermined your authority with the children at breakfast?"

Ebbie shook her head. "Stephanie, I have no real authority with the children. Like you, I'm only here to help."

"Only?" she pursued. "Then, pardon my bluntness, but why are you so agitated around Andre?"

Ebbie twisted her napkin in her hands. "Well, he is quite a masterful man."

"Do you find him masterful?" Watching Ebbie's squirm anew, Stephanie reached out to touch her hand. "I'm sorry. You'll have to excuse me, but I'm inclined to speak my mind."

Ebbie laughed nervously. "Well, I suppose since Linnea died, it's pretty much been assumed hereabouts that Andre and I will eventually—er—wed."

"And how do you feel about that?"

"Feel?" Ebbie's hand fluttered to her throat. "Why, what woman wouldn't be thrilled to marry Andre Goddard? He's quite a prince, isn't he?"

Lost in her thoughts, Stephanie didn't answer. Gwen and Beau burst back into the room, with Gwen holding a large rag doll. She skipped over to Ebbie.

"Ebbie, I brought you dessert!" she announced brightly.

And before Stephanie's horrified eyes, Gwen pulled a large garter snake from the pocket of her pinafore and tossed it onto Ebbie's plate. Her eyes enormous at the sight of the writhing reptile, Ebbie shot to her feet and screamed; the dog yapped loudly, and the children howled with laughter.

Stephanie surged to her feet. "That is enough!"

At her forceful words, Gwen and Beau froze like a couple of statues, both staring at Stephanie in disbelief. Even the little dog flinched and hunkered down. Grimacing, Stephanie grabbed the snake off Ebbie's plate. With the children and dog following her, she strode to the opened window and tossed the creature out into the bushes.

"Hey!" protested Beau. "That snake was my pet."

"Not anymore, young man!" Stephanie shook a finger at him. "You should have thought of that before you used it to terrorize Miss Ebbie." Returning to Ebbie's side, she touched the woman's arm. "Are you all right?"

Ebbie shuddered. "I just n-never liked snakes."

"I'm not overly fond of them myself, but I can handle the harmless varieties if I have to." She whirled on the children. "However, *any* snake can be terrifying to a person who is afraid of them. How would you two like it if someone tried deliberately to frighten you?"

"Oh, it wasn't that bad," Ebbie interjected.

"I disagree." Stephanie continued to face down the mutinous youngsters. "Well? Don't you think you both owe Miss Ebbie an apology?"

Gwen defiantly lifted her chin. "We don't have to listen to you—or mind you."

"Oh, but you do," replied Stephanie softly.

Blinking rapidly in betrayal of her agitation, Gwen turned to Ebbie. "We don't have to mind her, do we?"

"Well, dear, I'm afraid you do," Ebbie answered. "I am in charge of you, and Mrs. Sergeant is here to help me. So you have to listen to her, as well."

Gwen tossed her hair at Stephanie. "I'm telling Papa on you, and he's gonna throw you out faster than that squirmy old snake."

Stephanie fought amusement at the child's bravado. "We'll see about that."

The girl grabbed Beau's arm. "Come on, let's go play."

Watching the two speed toward the door with the dog following, Stephanie called out, "Wait just a minute, young lady."

Her expression rebellious, Gwen turned to Stephanie.

"As long as I'm a member of this household," Stephanie said firmly, "there will be no young children playing with embroidery scissors"—she paused, staring meaningfully at Beau—"or with a hammer and nails."

With Gwen glaring and Beau grinning, the two left the room.

Stephanie turned to Ebbie. "I'm sorry I couldn't get them to apologize, but it did seem a bit much right off the bat."

Ebbie beamed. ''Why, you were wonderful with them. I'm so thankful you're here. I only wish I had your back-bone with the children.''

Stephanie felt warmed by Ebbie's praise. ''Thank you, but I think you give me too much credit. After all, you stood up to Gwen, too—at least, after Andre left.''

''But not like you did.'' Ebbie glanced out the window and grimaced. ''Oh, dear, I see Gwen and Beau outside already. I'll get my knitting. I expect we'd best go keep an eye on those two . . .''

Chapter 9

Moments later, Ebbie and Stephanie sat on a bench together, Ebbie knitting a baby blanket, while beyond them, Beau and Gwen took turns pushing each other on the swing suspended from a sturdy oak. Nearby, the little Pomeranian was racing about, barking and chasing squirrels.

Remembering breakfast and Gwen's defiance, Stephanie restrained a sigh. Obviously Ebbie had little control over these youngsters—and Andre, the overindulgent father, wasn't helping matters. The children needed a much firmer hand; indeed, Gwen already appeared to be daunted enough by Stephanie that she had unleashed her resentments on poor Ebbie instead—although Stephanie didn't doubt for an instant that the children would try to make her the object of their wrath before long.

How could she help Ebbie take charge of this household? Glancing at the young woman, Stephanie noted the pleasing oval of her face, her dainty upturned nose, delicately pointed chin, and large brown eyes. She looked to be no older than her mid-twenties. With wonder, Stephanie realized that Ebbie was actually rather pretty—yet her drab black clothing, her unbecoming hairstyle, and her tense, anxious expression, masked her youth and comely looks behind a veil of plainness.

Ebbie caught Stephanie staring at her and smiled shyly.

Stephanie cleared her throat. "That blanket is charming," she commented, nodding toward Ebbie's handiwork. "I love the pink and blue together."

"Thank you, Stephanie. I do try."

"You're very talented."

"Well, I've learned the rudiments of seamstry. Tonight we'll have to get out my sewing basket and start thinking about a new wardrobe for you."

"You don't mean to sew me a wardrobe, along with everything else you must do?"

"Oh, no," Ebbie replied. "But I do have a few designs and fabric samples. I thought it might be fun to do some planning. Then tomorrow if Martha thinks she can handle the children for a couple of hours, we'll go into town to see Mrs. Hodge, our dressmaker."

Stephanie was craning her neck to get a better look at the children, who had left the swing and were now playing near the fishpond. "That sounds wonderful, but I must reimburse you as soon as I'm paid."

"Oh, don't worry about that now. Besides, it's always a joy to work on a wardrobe for a beautiful woman like you." Ebbie sighed. "I feel that my garments are lost on me."

"Why, that's not so at all!" insisted Stephanie. "I was just thinking that you're quite lovely. If only you would wear something besides black, I think you'd look great."

Ebbie had paled. "Oh, but my wearing colors is out of the question. I'm still in mourning . . . for Linnea."

Hesitating, Stephanie asked, "But didn't you say a year has passed?"

"Yes, but these decisions are very individual." Ebbie returned her attention to her knitting.

Sensing she was again making Ebbie uncomfortable, Stephanie tried another tact. "Ebbie, tell me more about yourself."

Ebbie glanced up. "What do you mean?"

"Where you come from, your childhood, that sort of thing."

Ebbie smiled shyly. "Well, both Linnea and I hailed from Vicksburg. My father was killed early in the war, at Wilson's Creek, and my mother never did quite recover from that, or . . . from the siege."

Remembering the accounts she'd read in history books,

Stephanie nodded with keen compassion. "Those times were truly horrible, weren't they?"

"Oh, yes," Ebbie murmured, her eyes darkening with anguish. "I was just a child at the time, but I remember all the deprivations, the fear, and especially the roar of the Yankees' cannons, a din that never seemed to cease." She sighed. "My poor mother didn't last out the war, and my family lost everything—our land, our money."

"As did so many people in the South. I'm so sorry, Ebbie."

Ebbie nodded, her knitting needles clicking. "Afterward, I spent the remainder of my youth at Linnea's home."

"No wonder the two of you were so close."

Ebbie smiled wistfully. "We were like sisters, almost exactly alike, except that Linnea was the beauty, not I. Though the house was large, we shared the same room, just because we wanted to."

Stephanie swallowed a lump in her throat. "It's wonderful having a sister, isn't it?"

"Do you have one?"

"Yes." Stephanie spoke hoarsely.

Ebbie patted Stephanie's hand. "Then you must know how I felt when Linnea married Andre and left."

"Were you jealous? I mean, because she had a husband and you—"

"Oh, heavens, no," Ebbie interrupted, laughing. "But I missed her dearly. And I knew my aunt and uncle were disappointed in me for not making a fine match as she had. Thus, a year and a half ago, when Linnea wrote to say she was expecting again and desperately needed my help, I couldn't wait to leave. By then, I was considered an old maid, anyway."

"An old maid?" Stephanie repeated. "How old are you?"

"Twenty-six."

"Twenty-six? Why, you're still young. I'm twenty-eight myself—"

"No!" Ebbie cut in, gazing at Stephanie, aghast. "With that beautiful skin of yours? Why, you don't look a day over twenty-one!"

"I'm twenty-eight, all right, and hardly consider myself a spinster."

Ebbie fought a smile. "I should hope not, since you're a widow."

Both women burst out laughing. "Aptly put," agreed Stephanie.

Ebbie touched her arm. "We're being terrible, aren't we? I must have sounded so insensitive regarding your own loss."

"Please, don't apologize," Stephanie reassured her. "I firmly believe in the old adage that sometimes if we don't laugh, we'll cry."

Ebbie nodded.

Stephanie frowned thoughtfully. "So, after you came here to Natchez . . ."

"At first it was so wonderful, like old times between Linnea and me," Ebbie continued. "Of course we both had problems with the children—Beau and Gwen could be obstreperous even then. And Linnea's condition was troublesome. She spent many a day in bed. Still, I took such comfort in being with her. I never thought . . ." Ebbie paused, mouth trembling and shoulders heaving. "That I'd lose her . . ."

Stephanie felt wretched as the other woman began to cry. Helplessly, she patted Ebbie's shoulders. "I'm so sorry. I shouldn't have made you speak about all this."

Ebbie sniffed and shook her head. "No, Stephanie, it actually helps to talk about it. I can't discuss Linnea with Andre. Why, he hardly even visits her grave. I go every Sunday."

Stephanie fell silent. "You mentioned last night that he doesn't hold with sentiment. Did you mean he doesn't care—"

Ebbie's emotional gaze shot up to Stephanie's. "Of course he *cares*. I think that poor man is eaten up with guilt."

"Guilt? But why?"

Ebbie glanced away. "I—I really can't explain further. I've already said too much."

Stephanie mulled over Ebbie's odd words. Was there

more to the cavalier rogue, Andre Goddard, than she had first assumed?

She flashed Ebbie a contrite glance. "Look, I'm really sorry for bringing up such a painful subject. But since I'm a member of the household now, I am curious."

"Of course you are."

"And I must say I think you're a saint to devote yourself to Andre and his family this past year."

"Oh, I'm hardly a saint," said Ebbie ruefully as she took up her knitting again.

Stephanie frowned. What did she mean by *that* comment?

Despite her confusion over Ebbie's cryptic remarks, Stephanie realized she'd learned a lot this morning. First of all, she had reconfirmed that Andre Goddard was a scoundrel with an eye for the women. Ebbie was obviously in love with the man, and also incapable of exercising any real control over his children. Ebbie was clearly well on her way toward her legendary fate of pining away from a broken heart and haunting Harmony House forever. Having known the joys of true love herself, Stephanie found her heartstrings twisting at the thought of Ebbie's being denied the miracle every woman should know.

Yet, if Great-aunt Magnolia's message was correct, wasn't that why she was here—to alter Ebbie's dire fate, to become her guardian angel, to resolve the dowdy woman's life so that, hopefully, she herself could then return to her own time and find peace? Clearly, she had her work cut out for her as Ebbie seemed incapable of doing much to aid her own cause.

All at once, Beau and Gwen rushed up. Both children were flushed and laughing—and Stephanie's suspicions rose as she spotted the mischief in their bright eyes.

"Miss Ebbie, we've come to apologize," Gwen announced importantly. "We're sorry about the snake."

Clearly pleasantly surprised, Ebbie murmured back, "Well, thank you, dear."

"Yes, Miss Ebbie, we're sorry," added Beau. As Gwen giggled, he hugged her neck and smacked her cheek.

A split-second later, Stephanie was bemused to hear both children squeal and watch them tear off toward the house like a couple of thieves fleeing the scene of the crime. Glancing at Ebbie, she soon discerned the reason for their flight. The poor woman had gone ghostly pale. She bolted to her feet, dropped her knitting, and began to squirm and scream.

"Ebbie, what is it?" Stephanie cried. "What did they do to you?"

After several seconds spent writhing like an eel, Ebbie leapt sideways and pointed at the ground. "Stephanie, please help!"

Stephanie stared down at a tiny, squirming bit of life. "A goldfish? You mean Beau put that down your dress? Of all the rotten—"

"Stephanie, help!" Ebbie pleaded.

Stephanie patted her arm. "There, there, the fish can't hurt you anymore."

Ebbie violently shook her head. "No, no, you don't understand! I can't abide touching squirmy things, and if you don't put the fish back in the pond, it will die."

Stephanie's mouth fell open. "Those brats are terrorizing you, and you're worried about a goldfish?"

"*Please,* Stephanie!" Frantically, Ebbie pointed. "Just look—the poor little thing is gasping for air."

Rolling her eyes, Stephanie scooped up the fish, and headed for the pond. Returning, she dusted off her hands, retrieved Ebbie's knitting, and handed it to her. "There, you sit down and collect yourself. I'm going back to the house to have a word with those two terrors."

Ebbie's grateful smile followed Stephanie as she marched back toward the house. . . .

Chapter 10

B y dinnertime, Stephanie was exhausted. And no wonder. Neither Gwen nor Beau had shown Stephanie or Ebbie any mercy for the balance of the day. Despite the scolding they'd received following the goldfish incident, the unrepentant partners in crime had promptly stolen a pie from the kitchen window and taken it out back as a "feast" for the squirrels. Later the youngsters had turned against each other, getting into a screaming row over a favorite kite, ripping it to bits, and chasing each other around the house.

In both cases, Ebbie could only wring her hands and Stephanie's sternness had been required to restore order, although Gwen in particular had become more sullen and resistant with each reprimand. Just when there was finally some peace in the household, the baby had awakened cranky from her nap, and only Stephanie had been able to quiet her.

Ebbie did try, but she seemed to lack the strength of will and intestinal fortitude needed to do her job well. Stephanie could again see why the poor woman's life was headed toward disaster and heartache.

How could she stop this runaway train?

When Stephanie returned to her room to freshen up for dinner, she was intrigued to see a rose laid out across the dresser. A chill washed over her. She'd found a similar rose on her dresser back in the present, and Andre had handed her a rose last night.

She picked up the flower. The bloom was exquisite; huge and a dusky pink, it appeared to be of the Queen Victoria variety. She sniffed its fragrance and couldn't repress a sigh at the tantalizing aroma.

Who had placed the flower there? She smiled cynically. Andre had, no doubt.

She felt disarmed by the sweet gesture, but disquieted by the likelihood that he'd been in her bedroom today. Did he have the key to the locked door that separated their rooms? Or had he come in from the hallway, the veranda?

Still holding the rose, Stephanie opened the French doors and stepped out onto the upper gallery, taking a deep breath of the cool evening breeze. She noted the closed doors to Andre's room next to hers. On the lawn beneath her, an old black man in workman's clothes and straw hat was trimming the azaleas, and the rhythmic clipping of the shears was soothing to her weary nerves.

Hearing hoofbeats, Stephanie glanced toward the street and observed Andre Goddard galloping toward the house on a magnificent brown stallion, the setting sun outlining rider and mount. How exuberantly the man rode.

Near the hitching post, he reined in the animal and vaulted off its back. The old black gardener ambled toward him; the two men spoke for a minute, and Stephanie heard Andre laughing. Then the gardener led the horse away, and Andre strode briskly toward the house, whistling, "Camptown Races" under his breath, as if he hadn't a care in the world.

She supposed he hadn't.

Mere feet from the front steps, he glanced up and spotted her. Grinning and removing his hat, he dipped into a courtly bow.

"Ah, Madame Sergeant. You make such a pretty picture standing there. How was your first day with my children?"

Though Stephanie fought a smile at his charming banter, she replied ruefully, "You don't want to know."

He chuckled. "I was just out admiring the sunset as I rode along the bluff." He gestured about him. "This time of day is so invigorating. You must come down and sit for a while in the garden."

Though again she was tempted, she replied primly, "Sir, I have other duties."

"Do you?" He stepped a bit closer. "I see you're holding a rose. So perhaps you've already sampled the pleasures of our lovely grounds?"

Fighting her amusement, Stephanie raised the bloom and sniffed it. "Someone has."

He appeared bemused. "Indeed?"

"You see, some mysterious person left this rose on my dresser."

Andre slowly shook his head. "I wonder who that could have been?"

Stephanie didn't answer him.

"Will we see you at dinner, madame?" he asked.

"I'll be there."

Andre replaced his hat, and Stephanie heard his low chuckle as he sprinted up the stairs and entered the house . . .

That night as Stephanie sat at the candlelit dinner table with Andre, Ebbie, and the four oldest children, she was dismayed to note that a carnival atmosphere again prevailed. Although Amy was being her usual reticent self, sucking on her thumb and watching intently, her three other siblings more than compensated for her placidity. Beau was playing with a wrought-iron toy train locomotive, making loud chugging noises as he rolled it up and down his end of the table, repeatedly hitting the porcelain gravy boat and sloshing gravy all over the fine linen tablecloth. Nearby, Paul was feeding scraps of roast beef to a yapping Pompom. Gwen was being particularly perverse, grinning as she used her spoon as a catapult, pelting everyone with small bursts of peas and carrots.

Stephanie was appalled that neither Andre nor Ebbie was correcting the children. Andre was sipping his wine and gazing thoughtfully at Stephanie, and Stephanie had to admit that his concentration was commendable under the circumstances; Ebbie appeared too exhausted for words, her coiffure disarranged, her features blank as she nibbled at her food and stared at her plate.

Even as Stephanie tried to think of some way to help the poor woman, a pea bounced off the tip of her nose, and Gwen chortled. Setting down her fork, Stephanie regarded the child frigidly. "Young lady, you will stop that immediately."

Though she did not set down her spoon, Gwen hesitated, her expression petulant.

Stephanie turned to Beau. "As for you, young man, hit that gravy boat again with your toy, and you'll *personally* lap up the mess off the tablecloth."

Beau had the grace to appear chagrined; he hastily removed the locomotive from the tabletop.

Expression mutinous, Gwen turned to her father. "Do we have to mind Madame Sergeant?"

Andre chuckled. "Well, pet, it is not so nice to shower all of us with your vegetables—nor for your brother to slosh gravy about."

Gwen pouted. "I don't like Madame Sergeant. Today she called Beau and me a bunch of hooey."

"A bunch of *what?*" Andre laughed.

"Gwen, you're wrong on both counts," corrected Stephanie. "First of all, it takes more than two to make a 'bunch.' Secondly, I never used the word 'hooey.' I called you and your brother a *couple of hooligans.*"

Even as Andre lifted an eyebrow in bemusement, Gwen announced, "Papa, I want you to put her out."

Andre shook his head at the child's spirit. The boys grinned, while Ebbie gasped. "Really, Gwendolyn!"

"Now, now, Gwen," cajoled Andre. "If we put out Madame Sergeant, where will she go?" He glanced devilishly at Stephanie. "The poor woman has no one else to care for her."

"Indeed, I'm utterly helpless," Stephanie retorted, her pride bristling.

"I don't care," the girl declared, defiantly lifting her chin. "Madame Sergeant is mean, and I want her to leave."

Andre frowned. "In what way has she been mean?"

Gwen began to appear uneasy. "Well, she scolded us today—"

"And why was that?" Andre pursued patiently.

The child hesitated.

"Yes, Gwen, why was that?" prodded Stephanie sweetly.

The girl tossed her spoon down onto her plate with a loud clang. "I don't want her here."

"Oh, Andre," put in an obviously distressed Ebbie. "You must do something about Gwen! She's been quite impossible all day."

Andre held up a hand and glanced about the table. "How do the rest of you children feel about Madame Sergeant?"

There was a moment of uneasy silence as the boys glanced at each other. Stephanie might have known Andre would let the inmates run the jail.

Then Beau grinned, and announced, "I like her!"

"Me too!" added Paul.

Andre turned to his youngest daughter. "Amy?"

Surprising everyone, the child wiggled off her chair and walked around the table toward Stephanie. Without removing her thumb from her mouth, she solemnly linked her free arm through Stephanie's. At the sweet gesture, Stephanie smiled down at the child, and Amy glanced up at her with large, adorable brown eyes. Stephanie felt very touched.

Andre turned regretfully to Gwen. "Well, pet, I'm afraid you're outvoted."

As Amy moved back toward her own chair, Stephanie watched a struggle cross Gwen's face—wounded pride, followed by gritty determination. Crossing her arms over her chest, she commanded, "Then you must tell Madame Sergeant not to be so mean to us."

Andre turned to Stephanie. "Madame, you might wish to consider that these are only children—"

"Children who will grow up one day," cut in Stephanie crisply. "And, by all appearances, with atrocious manners."

A flicker of steel glinted in Andre's blue eyes. "Madame, my children do not have atrocious manners—"

"They don't?" she cried in disbelief, gesturing about her. "Have you looked at the wreck they've made of this table? It looks like cows have been grazing in this dining room."

At the blunt description, Ebbie chortled a laugh, then covered her mouth with her napkin. "Madame Sergeant does have a point, Andre."

But Andre's features had tightened in indignation, and his gaze was boring into Stephanie's. "Madame just made a most unfair comparison. Furthermore, I believe children learn from the example of their elders—"

"You're referring to yourself?" Stephanie inquired.

Andre's voice was rising. "You might consider what sort of example *you're* providing, madame, by going on harangues like a shrew and calling my children names!"

Stephanie was shocked to silence, while Gwen giggled and clapped. "Good for you, Papa!"

For a moment Stephanie sat smoldering, wishing she could shake some sense into this maddening man. Then she calmly folded her napkin. "Very well, sir. If I'm not wanted here, I'll leave."

"Stephanie, no," gasped Ebbie.

Stephanie was already on her feet; even Ebbie's distraught, pleading look did not sway her. Head held high, she marched out of the room, only to stop in her tracks in the hallway. What on earth was she doing, allowing the exasperating rogue to ruffle her feathers this way, and venting her pride at the risk of her mission?

Besides, she had nowhere to go! Much as she hated to admit the scamp Andre Goddard was right, it was all too true that she'd likely be destitute without his protection.

A split second later, a firm hand grabbed her arm and she was pulled around to face Andre's forbidding countenance. To her further agitation, he appeared both angry and determined. For a moment they faced each other down. The strength of his grip, the intent way he was gazing at her, made her pulse race and her cheeks flush.

"You are wanted here, Stephanie," he said at last.

Caught off guard by his tantalizing words, Stephanie could barely force a response off her own tongue. "I—I haven't given you permission to call me Stephanie, sir."

He smiled. "Nor did I give you permission to storm out of my dining room."

"You may have not given me permission, but you gave me ample cause."

He smiled. "Madame, have you thought it might be best if we not bicker in front of the children?"

Pulling her arm free from his grip, she gathered her fortitude. "Sir, why are we having this conversation? I was under the impression that my services are not required here."

He gazed heavenward. "Stephanie, be reasonable."

"I said don't call me Stephanie."

"I was merely trying to maintain peace in this household—"

"By indulging your children's misbehavior? Mr. Goddard, children need discipline and limitations. You may keep peace in the household tonight by bowing to their whims, but you won't help them in the long run by allowing them to be cruel toward others."

He appeared taken aback. "They were cruel to you?"

"They run all over poor Ebbie, and you don't help her at all."

"But they are just children."

"They are junior juvenile delinquents, and they need a firmer hand."

Frowning, he stroked his jaw. "I'm not saying I completely agree with your methods, but I do think we need you here, madame. I've noticed Ebbie seems under an undue burden—"

"Ah, so you've noticed Ebbie?" she cut in sarcastically.

He squared his shoulders. "Both she and I would appreciate your staying to help. Well? Will you?"

His tone was commanding, and she responded with equal firmness. "Will you cease undermining my, and Ebbie's, authority with the children?"

"I'll bear your request in mind, but I make no promises," he replied. "If I think either of you is wrong, I'll intervene."

Stephanie hesitated.

He drew closer, regarding her with amusement and triumph, as his voice took on a cajoling note. "Think carefully before you say no. As I mentioned in the dining room, you have nowhere else to go, *n'est-ce pas*? That's is, unless there's more about your situation that you're not telling us."

She bristled at his accurate assessment of her plight. "You are infuriating, sir."

He raised an eyebrow. "Stephanie, I didn't mean to make you angry. But you know if you leave, you'll only hurt Ebbie."

She groaned. He was right—and they both knew it.

His gaze strayed to her mouth. "What does it take to make you change your mind?"

Irked by his brazenness, she retorted, "Don't even think about it!"

"Think about what, Stephanie?" he teased.

"You know darn well what."

He threw back his head and laughed. "Ah, such spirit. You needn't fear I'll resort to desperate measures. But come, now. Relent."

Grudgingly placated, Stephanie expelled a heavy sigh. Under the circumstances, she knew she had little choice but to submit with grace. "Very well. I'll stay."

"Splendid." Smoothly, he took her arm and linked it through his. Its warmth and weight made her heart pound. "Shall we return to the dining room and see if we can all conclude our meal with a modicum of congeniality?"

As he escorted her through the elaborate archway, Stephanie gritted her teeth. To hear the rogue talk, one would think *she* had caused all the chaos at the dinner table!

Chapter 11

The group was just finishing dinner when the butler, a slightly built, middle-aged black man, stepped inside the dining room. "Sir, Miss Elizabeth Stanton's come a'callin'."

Andre beamed. "By all means, Daniel, show Miss Elizabeth in."

A moment later, a statuesque brunette stepped inside the room. Pretty, pink-cheeked, and bright-eyed, the young woman appeared to be only about eighteen. Nonetheless, she possessed the serene smile and regal bearing of a queen.

Eyeing the visitor's extravagant attire, Stephanie was reminded of a Centennial gown she'd once seen in a costume book. The frock was fashioned of royal blue serge, with a long, lace-trimmed jacket and fitted waist. The skirt, with both modest hoops and a lace-trimmed bustle, was a clever melding of antebellum and postbellum styles. Blue gloves, a jaunty red bow tie, and a wide straw hat trimmed with a bower of miniature red silk roses completed the colorful ensemble. With a silk fan fluttering in one hand, the young woman appeared as if she'd just stepped off a Victorian fashion plate.

As she glided toward Andre, he stood and grinned. Stephanie glanced at Ebbie, to find her expression tense and bemused.

"Why, Andre, you handsome old fox, it's so good to see you," the woman crooned in a soft Southern drawl.

"Elizabeth, dear." Andre took the woman's gloved hand

and kissed it. "What a pleasant surprise. How is everyone out at Windy Hill Manor? Your lovely sisters are thriving, I hope?"

"Oh, yes. Bea and Maude were just saying you must come out and hear us recite Keats and Wordsworth."

"Sounds enchanting."

Elizabeth flashed her queenly smile around the table. "There are those darlin' little angels. And hello, Ebbie, dear. And—" Her gaze paused on Stephanie. "Who have we here, Andre?"

Andre gestured toward Stephanie. "Mam'selle Elizabeth Stanton, I would like you to meet Madame Stephanie Sergeant, who has come here from Jackson to assist Ebbie with the children."

"Ah—a new governess?" Elizabeth asked pleasantly.

As Stephanie gazed coolly at the newcomer, Andre merely chuckled. "In a manner of speaking. Madame Sergeant is actually a widow whom we are welcoming as a new member of our family."

"I see," murmured Elizabeth. "Nice to meet you."

"And you," Stephanie replied, conscious that the woman hadn't offered her hand.

"Well, Elizabeth, what can we do for you?" Andre asked. "Will you join us for an after-dinner cordial, perhaps?"

"Oh, no, no." She tapped Andre's arm with her folded fan. "I really must apologize for interrupting your—er—cozy family dinner. It's just that I'm the assistant program chairman for the Magnolia Art League, and we were all so hoping that you would speak at our January meeting."

"Me?" He laughed. "But I'm no expert on art."

"Why, Andre, you're far too modest!" she cajoled. "You've visited the finest museums in the world—the Louvre, the Victoria and Albert." She gestured toward the far wall. "Why, you can talk about your Gainsborough."

"I suppose," he murmured, scratching his jaw.

"Then you'll do it?" she asked raptly.

He winked at her. "Who am I to turn down an evening with two dozen of Natchez's most ravishing ladies?"

She clapped her hands. "Everyone will be thrilled!"

Andre nodded toward Stephanie. "Have you considered inviting Madame Sergeant to one of your meetings? She impresses me as a highly educated young woman, and I'm sure she would be interested in art."

Elizabeth smiled stiffly. "Some of us ladies will have to call on her."

"Perhaps Ebbie might be interested in attending," Stephanie volunteered.

Elizabeth waved her off with her fan. "Oh, my dear. You must know that Ebbie is not a joiner, except for church and that string quartet of hers. Isn't that right, Ebbie?"

"I . . ." Appearing quite self-conscious before the dazzling brunette, Ebbie stammered, " 'Tis true I don't belong to many organizations."

Elizabeth preened to Andre. "See me out?"

He offered his arm and grinned. "But of course."

As the two swept out, laughing gaily, Stephanie again glimpsed the sadness in Ebbie's deep, dark eyes. Her heart welled with sympathy for the plain young woman. How devastating it must be for her to love Andre, yet feel incapable of attracting his attention.

Devastating, indeed. If she couldn't help Ebbie, this situation could prove *deadly* for the poor woman.

Getting all the children ready for bed was quite a job. While Ebbie helped Martha settle the baby, Stephanie took charge of the older children. She left Beau and Paul to amuse themselves in the upstairs playroom, and accompanied Amy and Gwen to their bedroom.

While Stephanie sat on the girls' double bed, changing Amy into her nightdress, Gwen squatted on the floor playing with a rag doll, her lovely face caught in a fierce struggle. "I'm not going to dress for bed!" she announced.

Stephanie shrugged as she pulled Amy onto her lap and began brushing the child's thick, curly raven hair. "Suit yourself. But I'll bet that dress and pinafore will be uncomfortable to sleep in."

Gwen considered this for a moment in brooding silence. "Well, I don't care. And you can't brush my hair, either!"

"Well, gee, that's a shame," Stephanie murmured, gently

pulling the brush through Amy's gleaming tresses. "Then it will never look as pretty as Amy's, will it?"

Though Gwen looked mad enough to pop her cork, she held her tongue. Amy glanced up at Stephanie and grinned shyly. Stephanie pulled a face, then tweaked Amy's cute little nose. "What's so funny, silly?"

Amy chortled and kicked her feet.

Gwen rushed over and grabbed a handful of Stephanie's skirt, yanking hard. "Stop that! You can't have fun with my baby sister!"

"Wanna bet?" Stephanie countered.

Again Gwen was reduced to murderous silence.

Stephanie set Amy on her feet and smoothed down her gown. "You've been so good, why don't we go to the playroom for a few minutes and see what the boys are doing?"

"Yes!" cried Amy in a sweet little voice.

Thrilled that the shy girl had at last spoken to her, Stephanie led Amy from the room. Gwen sullenly followed. They stepped inside a huge room that Stephanie remembered poignantly as Sam's bedroom back in the present. Yet this space bore no resemblance to Sam's haven of ruffles and laces. Here, virtually every inch of the floor was cluttered with toys—building blocks, wrought-iron train sets, and toy boats for the boys; dolls, tea sets, and doll furniture for the girls. In a far corner, children's books overflowed a bookcase, spilling onto an overturned wicker doll carriage that had seen better days.

Stephanie shook her head at all the clutter. Yet her ears were even more insulted than her eyes were as, near the front windows, Paul vigorously pounded a toy drum. Nearby, Beau laughed and wrestled with Pompom. The two played tug-of-war with a ratty cotton shawl, the little dog snarling and clawing the rug as she yanked at the prize with her teeth.

Stephanie held up a hand. "Boys, please! Isn't it time to go to bed?"

Paul stopped hammering, while Beau let Pompom have the rag. Both boys gazed at Stephanie in amazement.

"Bed!" Paul protested. "We never go to bed this early."

"That's right!" seconded Beau.

"I rather doubt that, but regardless, you're going to bed early tonight," Stephanie announced.

The boys groaned.

Stephanie gestured about the room. "But first, you all need to straighten up this pigsty."

"No!" protested Gwen. "We never pick up our toys. We have maids for that."

"Why should they clean up this mess, when you made it?"

"I don't care, we don't have to!" exclaimed Gwen.

Stephanie was about to pursue the matter when she felt a tug at her skirt and looked down to see Amy. The child was extending a storybook to her and smiling wistfully. Her heart melting, Stephanie scooped the child up into her arms, book and all.

"So you want a story, do you, darling?"

Amy nodded.

Stephanie glanced about the room and spotted a rocker in one corner. "You know what, I'd like a nice story, too." She turned to the others, surprised to see all three of the older children watching her with interest. "Why don't the rest of you just go on to bed?"

"No!" Paul protested. "Beau and I want to hear a story, too! No one ever reads to us, not since . . ." The boy's voice trailed off, and he gulped.

Although Paul's poignant expression tugged at Stephanie's heartstrings, she held her ground. "I'd be happy to read to you, Paul, but I never read bedtime stories to children who aren't in their nightclothes." She shrugged. "And Amy's the only one who has her nightie on."

"We'll change!" declared Beau.

Stephanie fought a smile. "And I never read to children who haven't put their toys away."

"What about Amy?" demanded Gwen with a pout. "She hasn't put her toys away."

"She's too young to know better—and besides, I don't think she's the one who made all this mess."

Gwen bit her lip, obviously struggling within herself.

Paul popped up, tugging at Beau's sleeve. "Come on, let's change and put away our toys." He grinned at Stephanie. "Promise you won't start the story till we're through, madame?"

"Promise."

The boys dashed out, the dog yipping after them, while Gwen lingered, glaring at Stephanie. "Well?" Stephanie pursued. "Do you want to join us or not?'

Gwen threw down her doll. "Who cares about your stupid old story?"

But Stephanie had the distinct impression that Gwen did care, for her eyes were suspiciously bright as she marched out. Stephanie sat down and rocked Amy, reading her some nursery rhymes to pass the time. Within minutes the boys returned, looking adorable in striped nightshirts and bed caps. The two dashed about putting the room to rights. Stephanie laughed over their antics as they tripped over toys and even developed a relay system, Beau tossing blocks to Paul, who neatly stacked them.

The brothers finished in record time, then bolted across the room and slid into place at Stephanie's feet, reminding her of a couple of batters scoring home runs.

"Now, read to us, madame!" ordered Paul.

"Yes, read!" seconded Beau.

Stephanie was delighted by the rapt anticipation she spotted in their young eyes. Laughing, she opened the book and read the children "Jack and the Beanstalk." As a veteran of many storybook hours back in the present, she knew how to read in a dramatic manner that kept the children enthralled.

Indeed, all three listened in fascination; even the little dog soon squeezed between the boys, looked up at Stephanie breathlessly, perked her ears, and appeared to be listening.

Stephanie felt deeply touched by this first small triumph with the children. Yet the best was yet to come. Halfway through the story, Gwen appeared in the doorway wearing her nightgown—even if it was put on backwards and inside out. Her expression was pouty and her chin thrust high, as if she were daring Stephanie to evict her. The girl hesitated a moment, and, when Stephanie made no move toward her, she quickly crossed the room, grabbed her doll, and seated herself a few feet away from the others, glowering at Stephanie all the while.

Stephanie glanced up at Gwen calmly, fought a smile, then turned the page and continued reading. . . .

Andre stood at the doorway to the playroom, covertly watching Stephanie read to his children. The woman was utterly charming, her face so expressive, her voice so dramatic. His normally rowdy brood sat entranced by her storytelling. With a lump in his throat, he realized no one had read to his children in a very long time. Ebbie had tried, but she lacked Stephanie's vitality and had been unable to hold his offspring's attention.

Although he still had doubts concerning who this woman really was, he was glad he had accepted her into his household. Perhaps she was too strict, but she did have a way with his brood—a way with him, for that matter.

Opening his pocket watch, he smiled. He was late for a poker game with some gentlemen friends at the Pollock House, but he might make an early evening of it, just so he could come home and see what else the enchanting Madame Sergeant might be up to.

He'd had a mistress until recently—a saucy little vixen he'd kept in a cottage over on Clifton Street. Daphne had arrived in Natchez tainted by a less than pristine past. They'd had great fun together until she'd set her sights on him, without success. Only two months ago, the little baggage had shocked him by running off to marry a showboat tenor. What some of these women would do to snare a husband!

Of course Stephanie was no Daphne, but, considering the dubious circumstances of her arrival at his home, he couldn't help but wonder if she might be hiding something. After all, there was a strong chance she had lied to him, as a woman would do when trying to conceal any hint of scandal. And although she was clearly well educated, she could also be outspoken, even impudent, and didn't hesitate to castigate him verbally or boldly meet his eye—a brazenness he was unaccustomed to in the ladies he knew. Yet even her pertness he found refreshing and engaging.

Would she welcome his attentions?

Perhaps he was a wicked fellow to entertain such thoughts of her, but the mystery of her had him thoroughly intrigued. Was she really as straitlaced as she seemed to be claiming? Or did she harbor some secret, buried beneath all that tantalizing beauty, spirit, and pride?

Chapter 12

❦

"**B**oy, were those children a handful!" declared Stephanie to Ebbie. "But I finally got them all settled."

"I just don't know what I would have done without you today," Ebbie replied feelingly.

Half an hour later, Stephanie and Ebbie were in the sewing room, sitting side by side on cushioned white wicker chairs. Stephanie was perusing a stack of *Godey's Lady's Book* magazines, marveling at the quaint illustrations, while Ebbie was going through a box filled with fabric swatches.

"What does His Highness do while we're chasing down the little monsters and trying to corral them into bed?" Stephanie inquired.

Ebbie laughed, appearing perplexed. "Are you referring to Andre?"

"Of course."

"Why, I think he had a card game planned with some gentlemen in town."

"How lovely to be a man," Stephanie mused cynically.

"He might well be home in time to kiss the children good night," Ebbie added.

"How princely of him."

The two fell silent, Stephanie flipping through pages of the fashion book while Ebbie held various fabric swatches to the light.

Ebbie pointed at an illustration Stephanie had paused on. "That's the latest rage—a 'Dolly Varden.' "

Stephanie grimaced. "Well, I think it's silly, with that grossly exaggerated bustle. And that ridiculous hat looks rather like an inverted flour scoop with feathers."

Ebbie giggled, watching Stephanie turn a page. "That one is elegant."

Stephanie gazed at the smart day dress with exquisite tailoring and a beautifully flared overskirt. "Yes, I like the lines."

"You'd look quite good in it," Ebbie continued, "in a nice lime green." Frowning, she sifted through the many swatches in her lap, then held one up. "Like this one."

"The color is vibrant," Stephanie agreed.

"We'll show Mrs. Hodge the picture and swatch tomorrow."

Stephanie continued leafing through the magazine, pausing on a jacketed dress fashioned of soft rose wool. "And you'd be lovely in this."

"Oh, no," protested Ebbie, laughing.

"You would," Stephanie insisted. "The color would be perfect to bring out your hair, your lovely dark eyes."

Ebbie averted her gaze. "'Twould look better on you."

"I don't think so. Why don't we ask Mrs. Hodge tomorrow?"

"I . . . you know I'm more comfortable in my black."

With a sigh, Stephanie dropped the matter. "That was some costume Scarlett O'Hara wore tonight."

Ebbie scowled. "I beg your pardon? I don't believe I've had the pleasure of meeting Miss O'Hara."

Stephanie laughed. "I was referring to Miss Elizabeth Stanton."

"Ah, yes, Miss Elizabeth. Well, some of the ladies hereabouts are still wearing the centennial style two years after the vogue has died down. But then, many of us still have to make do here in the South. Our household is much more fortunate."

"Then the Stantons are not as well fixed as Andre is?"

"I believe times are hard out at Windy Hill Manor."

"You'd never know it from the way Miss Elizabeth carried herself tonight. One would think she's an empress."

"Well, in her defense, she traces her bloodlines back to

royalty. And the Stantons are one of the most socially prominent families in Natchez. Why, 'twas out at Windy Hill Manor that Aaron Burr once courted Madeline Price. The Stanton sisters have preserved the path where they walked as our local lovers' lane.''

''That is impressive,'' agreed Stephanie. ''And I suppose Miss Elizabeth needs to marry well?''

''Perhaps.''

''What do you think of her?''

Ebbie sighed. ''She and I have little in common. She's more of an old-style Southern belle.''

''You mean she's a flirt?''

Ebbie colored. ''That is a rather unladylike way to put it.''

''Andre doesn't seem to mind her coquettishness,'' Stephanie said, hoping to learn something from Ebbie's response. ''In fact, he seemed flattered by her attentions tonight.''

Ebbie's expression grew perturbed. ''Andre is merely friendly. He means nothing by it. He's that way with all the ladies.''

But not with you. Although Stephanie dared not voice the thought aloud, she did find Andre's conduct troubling. And, studying Ebbie closely, she could again see a telltale sadness in her gaze.

After a moment, she ventured, ''You know, when Andre was flirting with Miss Stanton, I must say you looked— well, in low spirits. Were you disappointed in him?''

Ebbie grew extremely discomfited, nervously replacing swatches in her box. ''Disappointed? Why, never.''

''Really?''

Ebbie hesitated for a long moment, then confessed, ''I suppose I did feel some regret—for Linnea's sake. It has only been a year, after all. And I felt . . .'' Her voice trailed off miserably.

''Yes? You felt?'' Stephanie prodded.

Ebbie coughed. ''I really can't say any more, Stephanie. I've gone too far already.''

''I apologize for prying,'' Stephanie said. To herself, she added, *And I've really heard all I need to know. . . .*

* * *

Well, scratch day one back in time, Stephanie thought as she undressed for bed. She still halfway felt as if she were living a dream—or, a nightmare!—far removed from her dear sister, her parents, her job, the very life she'd known back in the present. More than that, however, she felt bone-weary, exhausted from her confrontations with the children and Andre. Her feet throbbed after being cramped in the granny shoes all day.

Hanging her dress in the wardrobe, she thought of the tremendous challenges facing her. How could she bring the children around? And Ebbie—so helpless and unassuming. How could she teach the mousy woman to take charge of the youngsters?

Sweet little Ebbie. She was clearly in love with Andre. How could she get the two of them together? Talk about an odd couple. From his audacious behavior toward both herself and Elizabeth Stanton, Andre obviously did not hesitate to flirt with anything in a skirt. How could she possibly hope to get the rogue's mind on matrimony—much less with the lackluster Ebbie?

In her nightgown, Stephanie slid into bed and stuck a foot beneath the covers. She promptly screamed as something cold and clammy flipped about on her foot.

Wide-eyed, she bolted out of bed and threw back the covers. The ugliest brown toad she had ever seen croaked back at her—and it had made a horrible mess of her sheets!

"That does it!" she cried.

Stephanie tore back into her clothes, not even pausing to comb her tousled hair. Grabbing a lantern, she charged out of her room and down the hallway, flinging open the door to Paul and Beau's room.

"Beau, you get out of bed this instant and get dressed!" she ordered.

From the darkness, a sleepy voice called, "What's wrong?"

"You know exactly what's wrong, young man. You're in big trouble."

Wide-eyed, Beau popped out of bed. "It wasn't me! Gwen put the frog in your bed!"

"Oh, really?" Stephanie retorted. "If you didn't help her, how could you know about it?"

The boy gulped.

Across the room, Paul chortled. "You put your foot in your mouth now! Madame's going to give you the business!"

"That's quite enough from you, young man," Stephanie scolded. She shook a finger at Beau. "As for you, you will meet me in the hallway in one minute—fully dressed—or else!"

Stephanie left the room, and, in similar manner, went to rouse Gwen. Within two minutes, both children met her in the hallway, clothing crookedly buttoned, hair mussed, eyes still slightly dazed, and countenances guilty.

"What do you want?" Gwen asked sulkily.

"Why, I'm going to take the two of you on an adventure," Stephanie replied. "We're all going to take Mr. Toad back to his home in the garden, then you're going to change my sheets, which he conveniently used as his outhouse."

Both children were aghast.

"We don't change sheets!" cried Beau.

"Not with froggy do all over them!" seconded Gwen. "We have servants for that."

"Do you actually think I'm going to awaken them to clean up your disaster? Not on your lives!"

Although both children continued to protest, in the end Stephanie prevailed. The three took the toad back to the garden, and within moments, four-year-old Gwen and five-year-old Beau were in Stephanie's room struggling to make up her bed, while she stood at the sidelines giving brisk instructions.

All the time, Stephanie fought not to laugh, for the youngsters were downright comical as they wrestled with the bedclothes, trying to tug the bottom sheet over the huge feather tick, when neither child was as tall as the bed. Stephanie ended up helping more than she gave instructions, while telling herself that it was the lesson that counted.

Just as the children were finishing up, Andre, still in evening clothes, strolled through the open door and eyed the scene in mystification. "What is going on here?"

As both children turned to face their father with suitably guilty expressions, Stephanie took pity on them. "Beau and Gwen couldn't sleep, and I thought that this was as good a time as any to teach them how to make a bed."

He appeared incredulous. "You are jesting, *n'est-ce pas*, madame? Are you not aware that we have maids for such menial pursuits?"

Stephanie faced him forthrightly, arms crossed over her bosom. "Sir, my mother always told me that *every* child must learn how to make a bed."

"I see," he murmured. "One must know how to make one's bed so one may lie in it, no?"

"Precisely."

Stepping further into the room, he drawled, "What else did your mother teach you?"

"That vigorous physical activity is conducive to good rest."

Wicked amusement glinted in his eyes. "Ah . . . Perhaps I'd best not comment there."

Stephanie had already realized her error—and her face was scarlet.

"Madame, why is your face red?" asked Beau.

Hearing Andre's insufferable laughter, Stephanie could have kicked him. "From exertion," she snapped back to Beau. "Now hurry up, both of you. I'm tired."

Andre winked at Gwen. "Carry on, children. Madame is eager to lie in her bed," he murmured, and strode out.

Stephanie heaved a tremulous sigh. How could she have said something so inane, so filled with sexual double meaning, to Andre? As if the rogue needed any encouragement!

"Madame Sergeant, are we finished now?" whined Gwen.

Stephanie glanced at the bed and almost burst out laughing. The sheet was hanging halfway off it, and the pillowcase was inside out. But the children had tried, and they did appear both exhausted and contrite.

"Very well. If you'll both promise to get into no more mischief—"

Her words were halted by a woman's piercing scream, coming from the direction of Ebbie's room. At the sound,

Beau and Gwen both went wide-eyed, then bolted for the door.

Stephanie neatly caught them both, grabbing each child by an arm. "Hold it right there, you two! What did you do to Ebbie?"

Miserably guilty expressions were her only answer.

"Don't tell me you put a toad in her bed, as well?"

The children exchanged a frantic look.

"Well?"

"No, ma'am," confessed Beau. " 'Twas a snapping turtle."

"Oh, God!" cried Stephanie, in a full-fledged panic, tugging both children into the hallway. "Let's go rescue poor Ebbie before she has a heart attack. And, Beau, I swear, if that turtle has bitten her toe, I'm going to bite *your* head off!"

Chapter 13

S tephanie was awakened in the middle of the night by a baby's cry. She stumbled about, lit a lamp and put on her wrapper, then went down the hallway to the nursery.

Stepping inside the dark, cool room, she heard both the baby's wail and the sound of soft snores. She peered inside the anteroom to see the elderly nurse, Martha, deeply asleep on her cot. The poor woman likely couldn't even hear the baby.

"There, there," Stephanie whispered to the child, setting her lamp on the dresser and closing the door to the anteroom.

By the time she reached the crib, little Sarah had already quieted somewhat at the sound of her voice. Spotting Stephanie, she managed a hiccoughy smile, and was utterly adorable with her pink cheeks and bright eyes.

Heart melting, Stephanie picked up the baby. "My, my, you're soaking wet."

She took the child to a daybed stacked with diapers and gowns, and quickly powdered and changed her. Sarah enjoyed the attention, kicking her little feet and babbling to Stephanie in a baby's nonsensical way. Standing with the child, Stephanie spotted a nursing bottle, half-filled with water, on the dresser. No doubt the nurse hesitated to give the child milk at night and thus encourage her to get up more frequently.

She had just grabbed the bottle and settled with the child in a rocker when the door swung open and Andre strode in wearing a burgundy brocaded dressing gown.

Despite herself, Stephanie heard a little gasp escape her at the sight of him. She knew her response was owing to much more than her shock at his unexpected entrance. For the man appeared incredibly sexy—his dark hair rumpled yet gleaming in the light of her lantern, his handsome face darkened by a shadow of whiskers, the V of his robe revealing a tantalizing glimpse of a muscled chest covered by crisp black hair. The robe covered him only to mid-calf, and, judging from his bare legs and feet, he wore nothing underneath.

Even as her heart hammered at this titillating realization, he murmured sleepily, "I heard the baby crying. Is everything all right, madame?"

Oh, he was too damn appealing, the husky, sleepy timbre of his voice tantalizing her, especially as his gaze was fixed on the child with such concern and tenderness. She heard her voice quiver on her reply. "Sarah is fine. She just needed changing, and I guess Martha must not have heard her cries."

"*Oui*, her hearing is no longer so good."

Andre pulled up a wicker chair and sat down next to Stephanie, and the sexy scent of him wafted over her. She thought of protesting at their scandalous proximity, but soon realized that, as the baby's father, he had a right to be close to her.

What Andre Goddard's rash proximity was doing to Stephanie was another matter altogether, especially as he leaned over and kissed the baby's mop of curls, inundating Stephanie with his seductive nearness.

Sarah cooed happily at her father, and cried, "Papa!"

Andre grinned with an unabashed pride that touched Stephanie's heart. "See, madame, she knows who I am," he murmured with delight.

"So she does."

"Papa, Papa, Papa!" chortled Sarah.

As both Stephanie and Andre laughed, he kissed one of Sarah's little feet, then tweaked her nose, prompting her to squeal with glee. Stephanie watched and struggled to keep her breathing even.

Straightening, he eyed her with perplexity. "Are you all right, madame? You sound rather . . . breathless."

Stephanie felt telltale color stealing up her face. "Well, of course I was distressed and rushed when I heard Sarah crying."

"Ah, yes. It was good of you to come to her aid."

"Isn't that my job?"

"You could have awakened Martha."

"I'm sure she needs her rest."

"And you do not?" he teased.

"Martha suffers from rheumatism, and I'm quite a bit younger," Stephanie asserted.

His gaze flicked over her. "So you are. And very kind."

Stephanie laughed ruefully. "I'm not sure Gwen and Beau see me in that light."

He sighed. "Again, I do regret our little misunderstanding at dinner. I hope you're planning to stay on, madame."

Stephanie lifted her chin. "We don't exactly see child-rearing in the same light."

"True. But you know how much Ebbie needs you . . . how much we *all* need you."

Stephanie lowered her gaze, her heart fluttering at the silken inflection in Andre's voice. Why did she strongly sense that when he said "all," he really meant himself?

Smoothly, he continued, "And it can also be great fun to work out these—er—differences, no?"

"I suppose."

He frowned. "Before you judge my parenting style too harshly, you must understand that things have been very difficult around here ever since we lost Linnea."

She glanced at him contritely. "Yes, and that was only a year ago, wasn't it? I'm sure it has been a tremendous strain, and I'm sorry."

He nodded. "The children are . . . doing well under the circumstances, I suppose. But I still fret over them." He reached out to straighten the collar on the baby's gown, stroking her soft chin with a fingertip, then grinning as she pushed away the bottle to gurgle at him. "You're right that Gwen and Beau are likely into more mischief than they should be. Paul, as the oldest, puts up a good front, but in some ways I think he misses his mother the most. The baby cries too much, and Amy—well, she's so withdrawn. I try to pay attention to her, but still, I worry. Ebbie does her best to help, but her hands are full.''

Stephanie studied his anxious face and felt warmed to realize he was a loving and concerned father, however permissive he might act toward his brood. Coaxing Sarah to take more water, she murmured, ''It's traumatic for a child to lose a parent. Children are bound to express their needs in different ways.''

''But extra attention from you could help, no?''

''Yes, I think so. But parameters are also important to children. When they're left to their own devices too often, and don't know what's expected of them, they tend to founder.''

He considered her comment with a scowl. ''Isn't it enough that they lost their mother? Must they be corrected and scolded all the time, as well?''

''Do you mean you're indulging their whims out of guilt? Will that help them cope with life?''

He smiled. ''You are an outspoken woman, madame. Do you always challenge men in this manner?''

''Only when they're wrong.''

''Touché,'' he acknowledged. ''My point is, however, that more than anything else, my children need love. Especially Amy and Sarah. I would like to ask you to pay particular attention to them.''

''I'll certainly be happy to,'' Stephanie replied solemnly, smoothing the baby's gown. ''And I'll do my best to help Ebbie. At least for a time.''

His jaw tightened. ''I wish you would see yourself as a permanent member of this household.''

She laughed. ''You seem to adopt family members rather recklessly, when only this morning you were questioning my credentials. You really know nothing about me.''

His gaze slid indolently over her, raising a new blush. ''Oh, but that is not true. I saw you reading to my brood tonight—''

''You did?'' she interjected, taken aback.

He nodded. ''And I'm already convinced that you have

my children's best interests at heart. I know you're a woman of both strength and compassion—else why would you be sitting here, rocking the baby rather than waking the nurse?''

"I might like rocking the baby," she ventured.

A teasing light glinted in his eyes. "Indeed. I rather like the sight of you holding *my* baby."

"Why, Mr. Goddard," she couldn't resist taunting back, "I thought you didn't see me in any maternal way."

He grinned. "Are you hinting that you would like to become a mother, and are desirous of some—assistance?"

Stephanie felt utterly rattled. How did the conversation take this dangerous turn, and how had she managed to paint herself into such a corner?

Nonetheless, she lifted her chin and countered smoothly, "Are you desirous of having your ears boxed?"

Andre chuckled. "I see my chivalrous offer has been declined."

"It's been declined—and it wasn't chivalrous."

Acknowledging her point with a self-deprecating smile, he glanced devotedly at the baby. "Whatever ill you may think of me, madame, I do love children."

"I've rather gathered that."

Reflectively, he added, "I'd like to have another one . . . even several more."

"You're thinking of remarrying?" she asked, struggling to keep her tone impersonal.

"Not right away—but in time. It would be good for the other children, no?"

"They could use a mother's influence."

"Five is an odd number." He broke into a wistful smile. "I'd rather like another boy someday. Actually, Linnea and I lost one son—"

"You did? How heartbreaking."

He drew a heavy breath. "Jean Louis Goddard, born between Paul and Beau. He came to us in the dead of winter— and was so tiny, and soon so sick with the ague. It broke our hearts to bury him."

"I'm sure it did," Stephanie murmured.

He regarded her thoughtfully. "You and Mr. Sergeant, you had no children?"

"No children."

"But you wanted them, no?"

She cleared her throat. "We weren't blessed."

He nodded. "Perhaps it is just as well. In bearing new life, sometimes a woman must give up her own, as did my dear wife. I feel guilty about that ofttimes."

His unexpected admission made Stephanie look at him with new interest, feeling disarmed that he had revealed such a sensitive side of himself. As he noted her perusal, she hastily glanced away.

She leaned over to kiss Sarah's forehead, and watched her little mouth pause on a grin before she continued sucking from the bottle. "I doubt your wife would want you to feel guilty," she murmured.

As she straightened, Andre's long forefinger touched her chin, tilting her face toward his. "You are quite taken with my children, no?"

"Oh, yes," she breathed, disarmed by his touch.

His voice lowered a sexy notch. "And how about their father?"

Despite her hot cheeks, Stephanie shot him a scolding glance. "You're not the one who needs me here, sir."

"Are you so sure?" he countered, dropping his hand.

Heart thundering in her ears, Stephanie dared not answer him. The look in his eyes already spoke volumes.

Her agitation only increased as Andre reached across her, brushing her bare forearm with his warm hand before he patted the baby's head. "She's asleep now, the little angel. Shall I put her in bed?"

Stephanie reeled at the thought of being alone with this captivating man once the baby was safely tucked in bed. "Er—no, I think I'll rock her a while longer," she stammered.

Andre stood, leaned over, and kissed the baby's cheek. His hot gaze riveted Stephanie's. He was so close, too close! She could see the sexy whiskers along his jaw and smell brandy on his breath. Everything about him intoxicated her. She felt pinned to the spot; she could not think or breathe with him staring at her as if he couldn't resist her.

Then, with infinite tenderness, he leaned closer and just brushed his warm mouth over hers. Stephanie gasped, her heart racing. Somehow, she couldn't bring herself to protest. The kiss was so sweet and innocent, yet she felt as if Andre had seized her in the most passionate embrace.

Straightening, he smiled into her flushed face. "Are you so sure, madame?" he repeated softly.

Stephanie wasn't certain of anything! But before she could answer, Andre slipped out of the room. . . .

Returning to his room, Andre grinned. Stephanie had looked adorable rocking his baby, making him yearn to take her back to bed with him. Of course she was not ready for such brash intimacies—and might never be, depending on what kind of woman she really was. This enigma of her kept him guessing, and wondering whether his thoughts of her were merely wayward or downright wicked.

He *was* sure he had affected Stephanie tonight, judging from the blushes staining her cheeks and the breathless way she'd stared at him after he'd briefly kissed her warm, sweet mouth. Oh, she was intoxicating, so beautiful and soft! Fleeting kisses would never be enough with her. Never. He found himself wanting *all* of her, this woman who already captivated him on much more than a physical level. He admired her outspoken spirit, her forthrightness, her way with his children.

Remembering how she'd verbally "boxed his ears," he grinned. She was a spunky one, all right, and great fun. Was she really a staid widow, or was she leading him on a merry chase?

The more he got to know her, the more he yearned to solve the mystery of her.

After Stephanie put Sarah down, she returned to bed, only to toss and turn, her encounter with Andre still churning in her mind.

The man was far too sexy! He had the ability to reduce her, a grown, mature woman, to a quivering debutante. She groaned as she remembered how deliciously male and rumpled he'd looked, his teasing little remarks, the way his bright eyes had seduced her, how heavenly his mouth had felt on hers . . .

Get a grip! she scolded herself. She was here to help Ebbie, *not* to indulge her own errant libido. After losing Jim, she had thought herself beyond the carnal, and even now her feelings for this cavalier rogue stirred her guilt. Yet somehow, Andre Goddard had unleashed five years of secret yearnings bottled up inside her. She had never dreamed that holding a man's baby, while the two of them sat in their nightclothes without even touching, could incite such wicked, wicked cravings. It was unsettling, to say the least, to realize this virile man held such power over her, that he could rattle her and make her vulnerable, make her *want* him . . .

She was finally drifting off to sleep when she started at a clicking sound coming from the left side of her room. Alarmed, she sat up and drew the covers up to her neck.

Someone was trying to open the door between her and Andre's room! Was the rogue attempting to join her in her bed? Again, she wondered if he possessed the key to that door.

Then, as abruptly as the sound began, it ended, and all Stephanie could hear was the roar of her own frantic heartbeat. Lying back down, she seethed in the darkness. She dared not get up and try the door. If it was unlocked, she might find herself face-to-face with a sexy scoundrel, who would be only too eager to view her action as an open invitation. She hastily shoved away the scandalous, tempting images that thought provoked.

One thing was certain: Andre Goddard was toying with her, and playing a game he intended to win. . . .

Chapter 14

The following morning found Stephanie sitting next to Ebbie in a stylish open barouche. A black coachman drove the two women down the narrow dirt road toward town. Around them on the gently rolling landscape, the leaves of elm and sycamore trees had turned a deep gold, and appeared glorious in the soft light; a crisp autumn breeze blew the scents of waning greenery over them.

"Isn't that Dunleith over there?" Stephanie cried. "Why, we must be on Homochitto Street!"

Ebbie glanced at the pillared, Greek temple–style mansion situated on a rise beneath stately oaks. "Yes, that is Dunleith, so named by Alfred Davis, who lived there during the war. How did you know of it?"

Remembering that she had supposedly just arrived here from Jackson, Stephanie mentally kicked herself. Offhandedly, she replied, "Oh, I think the driver pointed it out when I was en route to the house from the landing."

Although Ebbie appeared skeptical, she murmured politely, "I see. Well, the man was wrong about the street. We are traveling along Woodville Road. I know of no street hereabouts named 'Homochitto.'"

Stephanie smiled to herself. Considering that she had traveled back in time over a hundred years, of course some of the street names would be different. She gazed at the lovely grounds of the estate, the gleaming magnolias and still blooming crepe myrtle, and watched a gardener clip the front hedges.

"Dunleith is supposedly haunted, you know," Ebbie remarked.

"Really?"

Ebbie's gaze darkened. "Yes, by the ghost of Miss Percy, who was a governess to the children of the Dahlgrens, the original owners. Legend holds that Miss Percy was jilted by a lover in France, then came to Dunleith as a governess and pined away from a broken heart. Some say she still plays her harp at sunset."

"How fascinating." Although Stephanie already knew of the legend, hearing Ebbie speak of it raised more than a few shivers. Would Miss Percy's ghost someday offer advice on "hauntings" to Ebbie's ghost? she wondered with whimsical humor.

"Dunleith has a colorful history," Ebbie went on. "During the war, the Yankees wanted to requisition some of Mr. Davis's best horses, but when the officers came to call, Davis cleverly hid his thoroughbreds in a cellar beneath the dining room—while overhead he plied the Yankees with his best bourbon. The horses must have sensed their pending fate, for they made not a sound. The Yankees left without recruiting a single mount."

Stephanie laughed. "Who lives there now?"

"The Hiram Baldwins. Mr. Baldwin died some years back, but his family, especially his daughter Kate, still entertains lavishly. Why, the Baldwins are the ones who sponsored Miss Consuelo del Valle."

"Did they?"

Ebbie smiled conspiratorially. "There was quite a stir in our town two years ago, when Consuelo caught the eye of George Montagu of the British nobility. Now she's Lady Mandeville, living with her husband in New York and hobnobbing with the Vanderbilts. In time she'll become duchess of Manchester."

"I'm impressed."

Ebbie nodded with pride. "People may call us provincial here in the South, but we do have our claims to fame."

"Indeed."

They continued down the rather bumpy lane, the driver maneuvering the barouche to the far right so that a dray crammed with cotton bales could squeeze by. They glided past more Greek Revival– and Victorian-style homes that Stephanie didn't recognize. Sheltered beneath oaks dripping Spanish moss, the mansions gleamed with fresh whitewash; windowpanes sparkled in the sun, and hanging baskets spilled lush blooms from the eaves.

"The town does appear prosperous," Stephanie remarked.

"The wounds of the war are still healing, but Natchez is rebounding," Ebbie explained. "Thank heaven for the river trade, although Under-the-Hill is a blight. Still, with the recovery of the cotton industry, the Old Guard have been able to rebuild an economy based on agriculture and the mercantile trade. As for our landowners, whereas once they owned slaves, now they employ sharecroppers."

Stephanie nodded, thinking that Ebbie was no mental slouch. They had now turned into town and were heading down Commerce Street. As they passed Trinity Episcopal Church, Stephanie remembered the site from the present, although this building, a square arcaded structure with a huge tin dome, appeared alien to her. Across the street, she recognized the more familiar landmark of Glen Auburn, a Second Empire Victorian masterpiece. The huge mansion gleamed, from its jaunty, columned front porch, to its fanciful cornices and brackets, to its high dormers and widow's walk. Stephanie realized in awe that the grand house appeared no more than a few years old—which made sense, of course.

They continued along a wide commercial thoroughfare lined by trees and old-fashioned storefronts with railed awnings. A passing black man on a mule tipped his straw hat, and a flashy gentlemen speeding by in a cabriolet acknowledged them with a flutter of his whip. Stephanie spotted mainly the male of the species about: old-timers playing checkers on the porch of J.C. Schwartz Hardware; young boys shooting dice in an alleyway; younger men in shirtsleeves, vests, and bowler hats discussing the events of the day outside the offices of *The Natchez Sun*. She did spot a couple of more familiar landmarks—the dome of the Adams County Courthouse to her west, the high steeple of St.

Mary's Cathedral to the east. The mixture of old and new convinced her she was still in Natchez—though it was a far different town.

As they turned onto High Street, Ebbie remarked, "It's only a few more blocks to Mrs. Hodge's cottage." She blushed slightly. "By the way, Andre reminded me again this morning that we are to spare no expense in outfitting you."

Stephanie frowned. "I can't allow you to do that. Heavens, you're already planning to pay me a salary—"

"As we should. Besides, you're a part of our family now—"

"No, I'm not."

Ebbie was aghast. "Stephanie, why would you say such a thing?"

Stephanie shook her head. "I'm sorry, I don't mean to be rude. But have you considered how oddly you and Andre treat me?"

"What do you mean, 'oddly'?"

"Well, think about it for a minute," Stephanie reasoned. "I came here to Natchez only two days ago, a complete stranger, and no more than a servant in your home. Yet you have welcomed me with open arms, and elevated me to family-member status. You insist I eat with you, and you clearly plan to include me in your social activities—"

"And why wouldn't we?" Ebbie cut in stoutly. "You're obviously a well-educated young woman, of good family, and we would not dream of excluding you. Why, for that matter, if you should be treated as a servant, then so should I. After all, I came to this family as no more than a 'poor relation.'"

"I suppose you have a point . . ."

"Andre and I wouldn't dream of doing less than to make you part of our lives, our family."

"I wish you wouldn't," Stephanie repeated ruefully.

Ebbie appeared crestfallen. "Why would you say that?"

Contrite, Stephanie touched Ebbie's hand. "Forgive me, I don't mean to sound ungrateful. You and Andre have been good to me. It's only—well, I've obligations, family back in—er—Atlanta. I have a sister who needs me, as well as elderly parents, and I can't stay here permanently.''

"You can't?" Ebbie lamented. "But you're so so good with the children. I was hoping I could count on your help.''

"You can—but not indefinitely," Stephanie replied gently. "I do plan to stay long enough to—well, to help you take charge of things on your own.''

Ebbie shook her head. "Oh, Stephanie! I'll never manage things as you do—''

"Of course you can." Stephanie patted her arm. "I'll give you some pointers soon, and I'm sure you'll carry on just fine.''

"Oh, I think not," Ebbie insisted. "The children clearly need your firm touch. And . . . well, I must confess to wanting you to stay for a selfish reason, too.''

Stephanie slanted the other woman a disbelieving glance. "Ebbie, I may not know you well, but I can't imagine you having a selfish bone in your body.''

Ebbie colored slightly. "You think far too highly of me, Stephanie. The truth is, Linnea was like a sister to me, and I've felt so lost without her." She regarded Stephanie wistfully, and spoke in a small voice. "I know you and I haven't known each other long, but I feel as if I've found a new sister in you.''

Stephanie's heart melted, especially as Ebbie's words stirred up her own fond memories of Sam. "Oh, Ebbie. That's the sweetest thing anyone has ever said to me.''

Ebbie brightened. "Are they so pressing . . . these obligations back in Atlanta?''

Stephanie squeezed Ebbie's hand. "Let's not worry about them now.''

Ebbie clapped her hands. "Good. Well, my dear, we are going to order you a splendid wardrobe. You see, here in Natchez each season, there are endless soirees, especially from Thanksgiving through New Years Day, and you must be prepared. After we visit Mrs. Hodge, we'll stop by A. Bahin on Main and get you a few basics to wear until the rest of your new things are ready—''

"Ebbie, I can't let you do so much—''

"But we must," Ebbie cut in. "Andre can certainly afford it, and furthermore, he'll be furious at me if we scrimp in the least.'' She winked. ''You don't want to get me into trouble with Andre, now do you?''

Stephanie smiled grudgingly. The *last* thing she wanted was to stir up trouble between Ebbie and Andre.

Chapter 15

After completing their business in town, Stephanie, Ebbie, and the coachman arrived home to the sounds of a full-blown crisis. They were no sooner inside the door than Beau and Gwen skidded across the hallway, both yelling "Sarah!" at the top of their lungs, with Pompom yapping between them. Stephanie watched in confusion as the threesome scampered into the dining room without even taking note of the adults near the door.

A split second later, Martha lumbered into view, holding Amy by the hand. Spying the others, she spoke frantically. "Oh, Miz Ebbie, I so glad you back. We lost the baby."

"Lost the baby?" Ebbie cried. "However could you have done that?"

The old black woman's lower lip began to quiver. "The baby was in her cradle in the parlor. I turn away just for a minute to tie Miss Amy's shoes. When I turn around, that baby was gone."

"Why, forevermore!" Ebbie gasped.

"This is terrible!" declared Stephanie.

With a distraught-looking Ebbie leading the way, the group hurried into the parlor. "A baby can't just disappear," fretted Ebbie, rushing over to the settee and moving about throw pillows.

"Indeed," seconded Stephanie, already at the cradle rummaging through the bedding.

The coachman cleared his throat. "You want I help, Miz Ebbie?"

She turned to the servant, who was juggling a huge stack of boxes. "Willie, kindly take those boxes upstairs to Mrs. Sergeant's room, and see if you spy Sarah up there."

"Yes, miss."

Stephanie and Ebbie dashed about the room searching under cushions and behind chairs, while Martha stood to one side wringing her hands, and poor little Amy appeared close to tears.

Soon Stephanie moved to the open window nearest the cradle. Leaning over the sill and gazing at the azalea hedge below, she asked fretfully, "You don't suppose she could have crawled out here and landed in the bushes?"

"Oh, my!" exclaimed Ebbie.

Ebbie was tearing across the room to join Stephanie when a loud crash sounded from the dining room. Stephanie popped back up. Wide-eyed, she rushed with Ebbie out of the room and across the hallway.

Gwen and Beau, both guilty-faced, stood next to the open sideboard. On the floor near their feet were the shards of a smashed Meissen vase.

"What are you two doing?" Stephanie demanded.

Beau gulped. "Sarah isn't in the sideboard."

"How refreshing of you to discover that for us," Stephanie replied.

As Beau chewed his lower lip and stared at the floor, an astonished male voice inquired, "What in God's name is going on here?"

Four sets of eyes turned to view Andre, in frock coat and top hat, standing there with Paul at his side.

"Oh, Andre," replied Ebbie, rushing toward him. "We're so glad to see you."

"We've lost Sarah!" added Stephanie.

"You've lost her?" he demanded, wild-eyed. "How could three adults lose one baby?"

Ebbie flung her hands outward. "Well, you see, Stephanie and I went in to town to see the dressmaker, and Martha turned her back only for a moment—"

"Never mind," he cut in impatiently. "We're wasting time—we must find her."

"But we've already scoured the downstairs," protested Stephanie.

"Then we'll do so again—and expand the search," Andre responded.

Taking charge with the brisk efficiency of a general, he ordered Martha and Amy to inspect the dining room carefully, Ebbie to comb the back of the house, Paul to search outside beneath the windows and at the fishpond, and Beau and Gwen to explore the crawl space under the stairs.

As the group dispersed, Andre grabbed Stephanie's arm. "You, madame, shall come with me. We'll have another look at the parlor. I'm betting Sarah is still in the house."

"Of course," said Stephanie, hurrying off with him.

She watched him make a beeline for the cradle. "Don't bother—I've already looked."

He whirled and began to prowl the room, scratching his jaw and examining the furniture from different angles.

"What are you doing?"

"I can't believe a one-year-old could have strayed so far—"

"Then you underestimate one-year-olds, sir," Stephanie finished.

Andre continued to search, looking more uneasy by the moment. All at once, he paused in his tracks and snapped his fingers.

"What is it?" she asked breathlessly, rushing to his side.

He grinned. "Either the settee has sprouted two additional, chubby little feet, or we've just found our lost lamb."

As Stephanie watched in amazement, Andre strode over to the settee and began pushing it away from the wall. With a protesting squeak of ball-and-claw feet, the heavy sofa moved, and Andre squatted down behind it. Next, Stephanie heard a baby squeal, "Papa!", and Andre declaring, "There you are, minx!"

To Stephanie's amazement, Andre stood with the baby in his arms. Sarah was gurgling, playing with her father's cravat, as if she hadn't a care in the world.

"Why, she looks no worse for wear!" Stephanie exclaimed.

Andre stepped over to the archway and called out, "All

right, everyone, you can stop! The prodigal is found.''

Within seconds, Ebbie, Martha, Amy, Paul, Beau, and Gwen had all converged inside the parlor.

''Sarah's all right!'' Gwen cried, clapping her hands and jumping up and down in glee.

''Where did you find her?'' Ebbie asked.

''Behind the settee,'' Andre replied. He glanced meaningfully at Beau and Gwen. ''I'm curious about something. Sarah was tightly wedged behind the settee. I don't see how she could have gotten in that fix all by herself.''

Beau and Gwen exchanged guilty glances.

''Well, children?'' prompted Stephanie.

Both began squirming and staring at their toes.

''Beau! Gwen! Surely you couldn't have!'' cried Ebbie, aghast.

After a moment of charged silence, Beau glanced about in panic, then burst out, ''But Sarah likes being hidden!''

Stephanie waved her arms. ''I can't believe this! They hid the baby!''

''We didn't hurt her!'' added a frantic Gwen. ''We were careful.''

''That isn't the point,'' stated Andre, for once acting the stern father. ''You two put everyone—including poor Martha—in a panic. I think some apologies are in order. Don't you?''

Reluctantly, Beau muttered, ''I'm sorry, Martha.''

''Me too,'' added Gwen sullenly.

''Well, thank heaven Sarah's all right,'' put in Ebbie.

Andre held the baby over his head; she chortled and kicked her little feet. ''I suppose all's well that ends well.''

''Providing it doesn't happen again,'' pronounced Stephanie.

Andre glanced at Beau and Gwen. ''It won't. Right, children?''

Both nodded.

Ebbie glanced at the mantel clock, and gasped. ''Oh, my heavens, the gentlemen are due in half an hour for string quartet practice. Perhaps, given all the excitement, I should cancel it.''

''Nonsense,'' affirmed Andre. He winked at Stephanie.

"Mrs. Sergeant can handle the children during your practice. That is why she is here, no?"

"Absolutely," replied Stephanie. "In fact, with all this excitement, I do think Beau and Gwen should go down for a nap with the younger girls."

"But we're too old for a nap!" protested Beau.

"That's right—we're not babies!" added Gwen, flipping her hair defiantly.

"Then you should act accordingly," stated their father. "This time I must agree with Madame—a nap is definitely in order."

Beau hung his head, and even Gwen appeared contrite.

Ebbie clapped her hands. "Well, then, children, let's all go grab a quick luncheon before my misters arrive."

As Ebbie and Martha led the older children off, Andre turned and placed Sarah in Stephanie's arms. "Keep a good eye on her now."

"You bet I will." Kissing the baby's hair, she flashed Andre a grateful smile. "Thank you for backing me up just now."

He chuckled. "Madame Sergeant, I fully intend to keep on outrageously spoiling my children. However, I draw the line at allowing them to endanger themselves or others. And hiding the baby is totally unacceptable."

"I agree, and thank heaven you were so skilled at finding Sarah."

He stepped closer to her and drew a teasing fingertip along her jawline. His passionate gaze held her breathless. "You'll find I'm not an easy man to hide from, *chérie*."

Chapter 16

◦━━◦◯◯◦━━◦

The children were unusually subdued as the group shared luncheon, then Andre left to take Paul back to school. After settling the younger children for their naps, Stephanie viewed Ebbie below in the hallway with three gentlemen, all of whom were holding instrument cases. The group was chatting merrily.

"Stephanie!" Ebbie called up. "Come meet my misters—the members of my string quartet."

Stephanie lifted her hem and walked briskly down the stairs.

As she arrived in the hallway, Ebbie gestured first toward a robust man with florid cheeks, a heavy mustache, and a mischievous twinkle in his dark eyes. "Mrs. Sergeant, I'd like you to meet Mr. Abner Trumble, our cellist—and the true leader of our group."

Stephanie extended her hand. "Pleased to meet you, sir."

Beaming, Trumble firmly shook her hand. "And you, madame. But I must say our dear Miss Ebbie is too modest. She's the true genius of our group."

"Oh, Abner, how you do run on," Ebbie teased back. "Your vibrato is truly the best, and no one performs such masterful hammer strokes."

While Stephanie fought her secret amusement, Abner appeared eminently pleased, twirling his lacy cravat. "Well, dear, if you insist, who am I to argue with a lady?"

"Mr. Trumble is also one of the best hunters in this region,'' Ebbie went on. "Indeed, he just brought us several plump quail from his Vidalia plantation."

"I must thank my bird dogs," Abner bragged to Ebbie. "I've the best hounds and retrievers in all Louisiana."

"How fortunate for us," Stephanie remarked.

Trumble wagged a finger at her. "Tell Andre he must come hunting with me."

"We'll be sure to."

Next, Ebbie gestured toward a tall, pale man with curly fair hair and light green eyes. Wearing a fussy-looking black suit with velvet lapels, along with a silver brocaded vest, and a lacy white shirt, he appeared handsome, if rather effeminate. "And this is Mr. Charles Fortier, our other violinist."

"How do you do?" Stephanie shook his hand, finding his grip cool and limp.

"Good to meet you, Madame Sergeant," he responded in a high, cultured voice with a slight French inflection. "Mam'selle Ebbie was just telling us what a great help you are to her."

"Thank you, Ebbie," Stephanie said.

Ebbie winked at Stephanie. "Our Mr. Fortier is a genius at pizzicato."

"Pizza—*what*?" Stephanie asked blankly.

As the gentlemen laughed, Ebbie explained, "String plucking."

"Ah, yes."

Ebbie eyed Fortier fondly. "Charles is also quite a genius at scoring."

"Scoring, eh?" Stephanie quipped.

"Why, yes, he does all our transcribing. He studied at the Paris Conservatory."

"My, I'm impressed." She turned to him. "Do you miss France?"

He frowned. "Not much of my family is left there, I'm sad to say, madame. Our men tend to accept commissions in the French Foreign Legion . . . then get lost somewhere in Algeria."

"How terrible," gasped Stephanie.

"But Charles is different," Ebbie declared with an admiring smile. "So much more civilized."

Fortier grinned.

Ebbie turned toward a tiny man with curly black hair, delicate hands, and small, beady eyes, pince-nez adding a hint of erudition. "Last but not least, here is our viola player, Mr. Walter Wister."

Stephanie offered her hand, which the little man shook vigorously. He spoke with a clipped British accent. "Madame, I am most pleased to make your acquaintance."

"Walter is truly unparalleled in the arts of fingering, tuning, and scale playing," Ebbie remarked.

Lips twitching, Stephanie nodded. "Isn't it wonderful that you all have your special talents to contribute?"

"Indeed, madame," Walter replied.

Ebbie gestured effusively. "We're so excited, because Mr. Trumble has brought us the score to Mr. Tchaikovsky's new string quartet, which will be on our agenda today." She regarded Trumble with pride. "Abner was fortunate enough to hear the musician perform his composition in New York in '76."

"And to hear Mr. Samuel Clemens on his lecture tour," Trumble added, fingering his mustache.

"We're all so envious," gushed Ebbie.

Trumble boomed out a laugh. "Well, if you would come along with me on my travels, Miss Ebbie, you could hear Tchaikovsky, as well."

Ebbie blushed, appearing secretly pleased as she lifted a hand to her cheek. "Why, Mr. Trumble! What a scandalous suggestion."

He wiggled his eyebrows. " 'Twould not be scandalous were we wed, my dear girl."

Stephanie fought giggles.

"Abner, really!" Ebbie demurred. "You are a rascal, and during our sacred practice hour, no less."

Chuckling, Trumble slanted his roguish gaze toward Stephanie. "Do you play an instrument, Madame Sergeant?"

"Only the piano—and rather badly."

" 'Twould be an honor to have you join us, madame," suggested Mr. Wister. "There's a part for piano in the Schubert Quintet.'' He glanced at Fortier. ''Isn't that true, Charles?''

Charles nodded solemnly. *''Oui,* Walter.''

''You are both so kind,'' replied Stephanie, ''but believe me, I'm doing you a great service by declining.''

The men chuckled.

Stephanie flashed them all a breezy smile. ''Well, I must keep an eye out for the children. However, I'm sure I'll be able to hear your lovely music.''

With nods and farewells the group moved off into the parlor, closed the double doors, and began rehearsing. Lingering in the hallway to listen, Stephanie felt amused by her encounter with the eccentric group. Trumble in particular seemed fond of Ebbie, though Ebbie's most obvious passion was for the music itself. As for herself, terms like ''stroking'' and ''scoring'' did not necessarily raise images of Mozart.

Oh, Stephanie, you wicked wench, she scolded herself.

Although she enjoyed her wayward thoughts more than she should have, she soon came to regret her remark about the ''lovely music'' as the most god-awful squawking poured forth from the parlor. Despite Ebbie's praise of everyone, the quartet seemed to know nothing about playing in harmony, much less in tune. With each member sawing away at his or her own discordant pace, they proceeded to butcher Schubert and annihilate Brahms, leaving Stephanie to grimace and wince.

Within moments she was retreating upstairs to avoid the ruckus. She checked on the children, and that's when she noticed another one was missing—this time Amy!

Stephanie quickly searched the upstairs rooms, wondering where the child could have gone. Amy was the most obedient of the five children and the last one Stephanie would have expected to run off.

Coming downstairs, Stephanie cringed at the squeaky sounds of the Tchaikovsky quartet pouring forth from the parlor. And it wasn't as if the music were cheerful to begin with. Indeed, the off-key sawing only added more funereal overtones to the dirgelike main theme. Even the lighter, more wistful passages sounded downright gruesome when performed with such unrelenting discord.

In the downstairs hallway, Stephanie glanced about her. Where *was* Amy? Surely she hadn't gone in to hear the quartet—the child hadn't seemed to possess masochistic tendencies.

Then she heard it, a child's low, heartbroken sobbing. She dashed behind the staircase to spy Amy sitting in a corner. Dressed in her lacy nightie and holding a stuffed bear, looking adorable and forlorn, the child was sobbing her eyes out.

Stephanie squatted down beside her. "Darling—what's wrong?"

Amy tilted her tearful little face up toward Stephanie. "Music hurts my ears," she said with a sniff.

"Oh, poor baby!"

Quashing a secret smile, Stephanie scooped the child into her arms. She carried Amy over to the staircase and sat down with her. Wiping Amy's tears, she soothed, "Really, darling, they don't mean to make it sound so dreadful."

"Makes me sad," Amy said, hiccoughing.

"I know, sweetie. Me, too."

Amy glanced up at Stephanie, her button mouth trembling. "I miss my mama," she whispered.

"Oh, darling."

Stephanie cuddled the child close, and as Amy's body shuddered against her, she felt a deep, elemental tenderness twisting inside her. "It's all right, precious."

Amy's thin arms curled about Stephanie's neck, and she gazed up at Stephanie with exquisite yearning. "Will you be my mama?"

At the child's plaintive words, Stephanie died a little inside. What could she say? She knew these children needed love desperately, but she wasn't even sure how long she'd be allowed to stay here. According to Great-aunt Magnolia, she was only here on a mission which would have both a beginning . . . and an end.

"Will you?" the child repeated.

"I—I'll try to stay as long as I can, dear."

Amy's arms tightened about Stephanie's neck, and Stephanie felt warm tears welling. For just a moment, she dared to let herself dream, to remember that idyllic time when she and Jim had been together and so deeply in love, when they had wanted a child so badly. What if this precious little girl could be hers? The prospect filled her with unbearable longing.

All at once Stephanie stiffened as the front door swung open, and Andre Goddard strode inside. He cut quite a masterful figure in his black suit, his tall figure outlined by the soft light spilling through the door's side panels.

Stephanie averted her gaze as he approached, feeling embarrassed that he had caught her in this very private moment, when she felt so vulnerable. Amy twisted about in her arms to stare up at her father.

Andre gazed down at the two in bemusement. "What is this?" Leaning over, he lifted Amy's chin with a finger. "Why these tears, pet?"

Stephanie regarded Andre bravely. "The music upset Amy."

"No doubt," he murmured, pulling a face as a new shriek emanated from a violin in the parlor. "I'm surprised the chandeliers aren't rattling." He brushed a tear from Amy's cheek. "May I have a smile, pet?"

"Yes, Papa." Her grin was downright cherubic.

"Bien." Appearing pleased, he glanced at Stephanie. "Madame, I asked you to be especially mindful of Amy, and I'm pleased to see that you already are."

Feeling rattled by the appreciative and too-intimate gleam in his eyes, Stephanie heard a defensive edge creep into her voice. "Mr. Goddard, Amy is a precious child, and I'd be delighted to do anything for her—regardless of whether or not you asked me to."

"Would you, now?" He winked at Amy. "Pet, it seems you've captured Madame Sergeant's heart." Leaning over, he kissed Amy's cheek. "All better now?"

Amy nodded solemnly.

Andre drew his face up toward Stephanie's, his lips hovering recklessly close to her own. "And how about you, madame? Do you need a kiss, too?"

Stephanie floundered. Andre was too close, and far too

sexy. She could feel the heat of his breath on her lips, could smell the sandalwood soap he'd bathed with, could see the vibrant blue of his eyes, and was quickly losing herself there . . .

Before she could stop herself, she retorted, "Why don't you just leave us alone?"

He flinched as if she'd struck him, then backed away, a mask closing over his features. "But of course," he uttered coldly.

Watching him turn and stride away, Stephanie could have kicked herself. Perhaps his motives in offering the kiss had not been entirely noble, but whatever had possessed her to act like such a shrew? Andre's devastating effect on her libido, that's what! The man had totally undone her with just a burning look and a few tempting words—though it was no excuse for her atrocious behavior.

Feeling wretchedly guilty, Stephanie carried Amy upstairs, hugged her, and left her with Martha. Then she rushed back down and searched for Andre. When she found the door to his study closed, she did not hesitate to fling it open.

"I'm sorry," she said.

He looked up, scowling, from his desk. "You have not heard of knocking, madame?"

Stephanie almost retreated, for his glare was formidable, his tone frigid. She bucked up her courage and started toward him. "Let's not play games now. I was rude, and I owe you an apology."

Andre appeared mildly shocked. He stood and approached her. "The perfect Madame Sergeant has come to apologize?"

"Yes, and your sarcasm isn't helping much."

He set his arms akimbo and regarded her arrogantly. "You don't deserve help."

"Quite true," she admitted.

He grinned, clearly enjoying his advantage. "Ah, such a commendable display of humility from the spirited madame. So tell me—why were you so rude?"

She gulped. "B-because—well, you interrupted a very special moment between Amy and me—"

"*I* interrupted?" he cut in, his soft voice raising shivers along her spine. "Have you forgotten, madame, that Amy is *my* child? That her welfare is very much my business?"

"You're right." Stephanie was appalled to realize she was wringing her hands. "I'm not talking about Amy, but about me. I was thinking about myself alone when I—er—spoke so discourteously, and that was wrong."

He was silent for a long moment. "Why did my presence upset you so?"

Uneasily, she glanced away. "I'd rather not say. Isn't my apology enough?"

He took her arm, turning her toward him. "No. You owe me a full explanation."

She groaned. "You're not going to make this easy, are you?"

He eyes gleamed with triumph. "I thought we'd already established that."

Oh, the rogue! He was making her squirm like a worm on the hook, and enjoying every second!

"Very well," she conceded heavily. "You see, when you came in, you—well, caught me off guard."

"Off guard?"

Stephanie tried to force down the hard knot of emotion in her throat. "As I mentioned last night, when I was married, my husband and I never had children, even though we wanted them very much. Holding Amy raised maternal feelings in me. Then you came along and you seemed to be—well, manipulating the situation, trying to turn it into something . . ."

"Something cheap?" he provided in a steely tone. "Is that why you think I offered you a kiss?"

Stephanie lowered her gaze. "I didn't say that."

"But you were thinking it, no?" He moved closer, placing his hands on her shoulders, and spoke intensely. "Is it so difficult to believe that I may have been as moved as you were in that moment? Do you think I am incapable of feeling those special feelings you just spoke of?"

Stephanie was drowning in his nearness. "I . . . No. It's obvious you love your children—"

He lifted her chin and stared down into her turbulent eyes. "What else is obvious, Stephanie?"

She gulped. His intent gaze, his warm touch, were devastating her. Never had she so longed to run away.

"What else is obvious?" he repeated softly.

Her voice trembled badly. "That you're out to seduce every fair belle in Natchez."

He dropped his hand, and his expression went cold. "You persist in trying to turn my motives into something tawdry."

"So you weren't pressing your advantage at all when you offered that kiss?" she asked.

"And you weren't feeling anything for me?" Andre began to toy with the lace at her collar, further agitating her. "If you're honest, Stephanie, you'll admit that you know what's happening between us. And the real reason you got so angry is because I caught you at your most vulnerable, when you held my child in your arms, when you saw me and felt all your well-ordered emotions coming apart—"

"You are a pompous cad!" she cut in.

He seized her face in his hands. "When you wanted to kiss me as much as I wanted to kiss you."

Heart hammering, she whirled away. "That's not true."

He caught her arm and continued ruthlessly. "Well, you took your careless jab at me, trying to deny what you feel, and it didn't work. Now the piper must be paid."

"You're wrong! I have no such feelings!" she declared with bravado.

"Really?"

Stephanie's own tears proved her a liar as Andre pulled her into his arms and claimed her lips with fierce tenderness. At once, a riot of sweet feeling turned her blood to fire. Yes, she *had* wanted this, she realized sinkingly, had wanted it so badly. The tender moment with Amy had affected her as much as it had affected him. She had wanted to touch Andre, to taste him, to feel his strong, warm arms holding her.

Nonetheless, she tried to fight him, tried to squirm away, but her own incoherent sounds gave her away. When he only nestled her closer, pressing a hand to the small of her back and splaying his fingers over her hips, when she could feel the beckoning heat of his desire, she was lost.

He knew it, too. Where before he had claimed, now he coaxed, seducing her with his skilled lips and tender flicks of his tongue. A shudder shook Stephanie as her mouth seemed to melt beneath his persuasive heat. Her breasts tingled against the pressure and warmth of his chest. Hot desire penetrated her, twisting and spiraling deep in her belly.

Stephanie clung to him, absorbing his heat, feeling his tongue cajoling between her lips, opening her to him, then plunging deeply, immersing her in raw delight. Oh, how tempting it would be to give in, to let him have his way. She felt unnerved, exhilarated, and she desired him so much that it scared her to death. What frightened her even more was that he knew of her weakness, and exulted in it.

At last he released her. "Stephanie . . ." he whispered, his voice a plea.

Not daring even to look at him, she turned and walked dazedly out of his study.

Andre stood there, overwhelmed by his own emotions. Why had he become so angry with Stephanie? To be brutally honest, she'd only treated him like the scamp he likely was.

Except that he had not *felt* like a scamp when he'd watched her hold Amy. Seeing her comforting his child had roused such tenderness within him—and her rejection had stung, unexpectedly and cruelly. When she had apologized, he'd relentlessly pressed his advantage.

Such passions she stirred in him. His mistress, Daphne, had been an eager little baggage, skilled in the art of seduction. Their relationship had been physical and diverting. But this was different. Everything about this woman intrigued and tantalized him. She stimulated his thoughts and roused his emotions in ways he was unaccustomed to. She could melt him with those lovely eyes of hers, or wound him with just a few sharp words.

He remained stunned that she had railed at him in the hallway, then had turned about and apologized. That had shocked and disarmed him most of all, for it had proved she was affected by him as much as he was by her. Before it was over, they had both lost control to a degree. He wasn't accustomed to feeling this way around women—not quite as in charge of his own emotions as he'd like to be.

And he wanted more, so much more with her. To learn all her secrets. To kiss the soft breasts he had felt pressing into him. To explore every inch of her with his mouth. To feel those long legs wrapped around him as he possessed her so deeply that, when he gazed into her eyes, she could hide nothing from him. *Nothing.*

Was he wicked to feel this way? Wicked or not, he felt it. She fascinated him, and he knew he would not be satisfied until he discovered everything about her. . . .

Chapter 17

~~~⊃⊂~~~

Stephanie retreated to her room, trying to impose order on her chaotic emotions. For the second time, Andre Goddard had penetrated her defenses both physically and emotionally, making her ache with desire for him.

You know what's happening between us, he'd said. Oh, she did know! Never had she dreamed that a man so different from her could affect her so much—and so quickly. For that matter, she didn't really know him well at all—but she knew she wanted him. Not even with Jim had she felt such irresistible cravings.

Dear Jim. Memories of her husband's handsome face, his familiar smile, brought feelings of guilt and a lump to her throat. How would he have felt if he'd known she wanted another man? The two of them had never discussed it, for neither had dreamed he'd be killed in the Middle East. Remembering his kind and generous spirit, Stephanie doubted he would ever have expected her to pine away for him. He would have wanted her to carry on with her life, to love again—though surely not a scamp like Andre!

She supposed she'd assumed she would never love again mainly out of a conviction that she could never again find a man as wonderful as Jim. How ironic, then, to realize she was lusting after the *wrong* man—a libertine with an eye for the ladies. She must take charge of herself, or her mission here would be in ruins! How could she hope to help dear Ebbie if she succumbed to Andre herself?

After pacing for a time, Stephanie took note of the large

stack of boxes on her bed and began unpacking the clothes Ebbie had insisted on buying her: a pair of old-fashioned, button-topped shoes; silk stockings and sturdy garters; lace-trimmed pantaloons, chemises, and petticoats; and two ready-made, "serviceable" day dresses of magenta and blue broadcloth—both cut a bit short and tight in the waist, in keeping with the smaller girth of most women living in this age. Ebbie had also bought her a rather silly straw hat with egret feathers, and a whalebone corset that resembled something from the Spanish Inquisition. Fingering a rigid stay, Stephanie grimaced; she resolved she would forgo the torture device if she could manage to squeeze into her dresses without it. At least the frocks were high-necked and long-sleeved, modest enough not to give Andre more ideas—she hoped. Within the week, Mrs. Hodge had promised to have at least three more dresses sewn for her.

After putting everything away, Stephanie checked on the children again, then napped, wakening later to hear the youngsters laughing out in the yard. The sounds of music had faded away, and she wondered if Ebbie was outside with the kids.

Stephanie donned her new undergarments, stockings, and shoes, then squeezed into her new blue dress. Venturing out onto the veranda, she was surprised to see Andre in the yard giving the older children, and some friends from the neighborhood, rides on a Shetland pony. The buff-colored animal was precious, with its shaggy coat, its gray mane and tail. Beau was perched on the Shetland's back as Andre led the pony about in a circle.

Stephanie could not help but admire him as he entertained the youngsters. After giving two more children rides, with broad gestures he ordered the boys to bring water and oats, the girls to fetch a currycomb and body brush. He showed the youngsters how to unsaddle, brush, and feed the animal.

Stephanie shook her head. He was a good father, she had to admit. Indeed, the rogue had many talents.

She went hunting for Ebbie, knocking on her bedroom door, and was pleased to hear her friend call, "Come in!" Entering, she spotted Ebbie seated at her dressing table, pinning errant strands of hair back into her bun. Remembering her earlier, shameful conduct with Andre, Stephanie felt a stab of guilt, and redoubled her determination to help Ebbie win him over.

"Well, hello, Stephanie, have you had a pleasant afternoon?" Ebbie greeted her.

Stephanie laughed. "Actually, I took a nap, and it looks like Andre took charge of the children."

Ebbie nodded. "He loves to entertain them."

"That's good of him. How was your practice?"

Ebbie beamed. "Just wonderful. I do believe we're mastering the Schubert. And with the holidays coming, we must have our repertoire in order."

"You really seem to love your group."

"Oh, I do," Ebbie declared.

"How often do you practice?"

"Well, sometimes all of us get together only once a fortnight, but with the season nearing, we'll have to gather at least twice weekly. Of course there are less formal rehearsals. Mr. Fortier and Mr. Wister are able to practice together often, since they live next door to one another, at the old Spanish officers' quarters down near the plaza."

"How convenient," murmured Stephanie.

"And Mr. Trumble is coming by for a special session with me tomorrow. He needs some help with his bowing."

"His bowing and a lot else," Stephanie muttered.

Ebbie appeared confused. "I beg your pardon?"

Stephanie winked. "I think he likes you."

Ebbie waved her off. "Oh, Abner is a hopeless flirt. Besides, I have . . . other obligations."

Observing the tension on Ebbie's face, Stephanie moved closer. "Do you consider Andre an obligation?"

Ebbie blushed. "Why, of course not. 'Tis a joy to care for him and his family."

"And eventually you'll make that your permanent job?" Stephanie suggested.

Ebbie's smile was shy. "As I've explained, I think that is pretty much expected."

Standing behind Ebbie, Stephanie eyed her friend's reflection in the dressing table mirror. "If, as you say, you and Andre will eventually wed, you might move things along a bit if you made yourself more colorful.''

Ebbie turned toward Stephanie. ''Colorful?''

Stephanie gave Ebbie an admonishing look. ''I was disappointed today when you did not order yourself a new wardrobe.''

''But I'm in mourning—''

''You've already explained that, though we both know your year is up. I must wonder—are you trying deliberately not to draw attention to yourself?''

Ebbie blanched. ''Isn't it immodest for a woman to make a spectacle of herself?''

''I'm not saying you have to put on feathers and a red dress.''

A smile hovered on Ebbie's lips. ''True, but I think I'd feel almost naked without my black.''

Stephanie mulled this over. ''Hmmmm . . . Why don't we take this step by step?''

''What do you mean?''

Stephanie strode over to Ebbie's armoire. ''May I?''

Ebbie nodded.

Stephanie flung open the doors and examined the dresses hanging there, most of them drab black like the one Ebbie wore. Then she laughed and drew out a vibrant burgundy-colored shawl.

''Why, this is lovely!''

''That?'' Ebbie inquired. ''Katie Banks knitted that shawl for me, though I never did feel quite right wearing it.''

''But it's perfect for you.'' Stephanie crossed the room and draped the shawl around Ebbie's shoulders. ''Look how it brings out the pink in your cheeks.''

Ebbie smiled. ''You do have a point.''

Stephanie eyed the dressing table. ''Where is your jewelry, your gewgaws?''

''Put away in the drawers.''

''Let's get everything out.''

Ebbie actually became caught up in the fun as Stephanie studied her accessories, selecting a string of pearls for her neck, and adorning her bun with several small, mauve-colored silk flowers that complemented the shawl.

"There!" Stephanie said, admiring her handiwork. "You look so much better."

"True." But Ebbie's smile faded as she studied her reflection in the mirror. "Though I feel as if I'm—well, showing off."

"And why shouldn't you?" Stephanie demanded. "Have you thought of how a few dashes of color might improve your relationship with the children?"

"Why, no."

"Where I come from, I volunteered at the library a lot, and I can tell you, young children respond to bright colors. Even when it comes to disciplining the children, a more striking and youthful appearance will help you assert yourself."

Ebbie laughed. "Oh, Stephanie, I'll never be able to command the respect that you do."

"Of course you can. It's all a matter of confidence and projecting the proper image. Here, I'll show you." Stephanie touched Ebbie's arms. "Now, straighten those shoulders."

Ebbie actually grinned. "Yes, ma'am."

"Next, stare forbiddingly into the mirror."

Ebbie made an attempt, then convulsed into giggles.

"*Ebbie*," Stephanie scolded.

"Very well."

Ebbie attempted a harsh look, but managed only to look vaguely pained.

Stephanie sighed. "Well, that's a beginning. Now repeat after me: 'Young man, stop that at once!' "

"Young man, stop that at once," Ebbie muttered.

"Ebbie!" Stephanie wailed. "You don't sound assertive at all!"

"That's because I'm not you," lamented Ebbie with a crestfallen expression.

"Well, I refuse to give up," Stephanie declared. "So we shall go over this over and over . . . until you get it right!"

Chapter 18

S topping off at her room, Stephanie found a small Victorian tin container, painted with flowers and cherubs, on her dresser. On its lid was the outline of a heart, the words "With Fondest Regard" inscribed in the middle.

A treacherous tenderness tugged at her emotions. She lifted the lovely lid and stared at the rich bonbons inside. Was this the work of Andre again? Was it a peace offering following their spat? If so, how had he known she had a weakness for chocolates?

If she didn't watch herself, she'd develop a weakness for *him*.

She picked up a candy, took a nibble, and sighed at the scrumptious taste. Gazing about her, she shivered at the realization that he'd likely been in her room again. Carefully sniffing the air, she thought she detected the faintest essence of his bay rum still lingering.

Or was it only her imagination, a fancy Andre Goddard stirred much more than she should allow?

An unexpected guest dropped in for dinner. Ebbie, Stephanie, and the children had already gathered in the dining room, and Lilac had just brought in a platter filled with several mouth-watering stuffed quail, when Andre strode in with a tall, fair-haired gentleman wearing a white suit with a string cravat and a planter's style white hat. Stephanie noted that he was attractive in his way, with a thin, angular face and well-drawn male features, the unlit cigar he chewed on suggesting a hint of flamboyance.

At once the newcomer was mobbed by the four older children, who, like eager puppies, inundated him with cries of, "Mr. Robillard, where is our treat?" Grinning, he dug in his pockets and handed out wrapped toffee candy to all four.

While he was busy with the children, Andre stepped up to the table, his gaze first pausing curiously on Ebbie. "Why, Ebbie, dear, how lovely you look. I like those flowers in your hair, the jewelry, and that colorful shawl."

Ebbie blushed, fluttering a hand at her throat. "Thank you, Andre. Stephanie insisted I add a bit of color."

"I'm pleased to hear it." With amusement, Andre's gaze flicked to her. "And that's quite a comely dress, Madame Sergeant. I'm happy to see you and Ebbie have started working on your new wardrobe. Blue is a fine color for you."

"Thank you, Mr. Goddard," Stephanie replied, uncomfortable at his compliments, but glad he had noted the improvements to Ebbie's appearance.

Andre gestured toward the guest. "Ebbie, I hope you don't mind, but I came across Henry in town and persuaded him to come home and have dinner with us."

"But, of course, Henry is always welcome," Ebbie replied. She gestured toward a large platter at the center of the table. "Mr. Trumble brought us several plump quail, so there is ample food."

"Good for Abner."

Frowning at the children, who by now were unwrapping their second and third candies, Ebbie scolded, "Children, please resume your seats and place the remaining candies under your plates for dessert."

At once a chorus of protests rose from the youngsters, but Andre quelled the rebellion with a raised hand. "Ebbie is right," he concurred. Gazing at Stephanie, he grinned. "Too much candy can spoil the appetite, eh, Madame Sergeant?"

Though she felt a telltale heat moving up her face, Stephanie calmly nodded.

In the meantime, their guest was also imploring the children. "If you youngsters will just mind Miss Ebbie, I promise there'll be more sweets later."

These last words did the trick. Watching the children rush dutifully for the table, Ebbie smiled at the men. "Thank you, gentlemen. But, Henry, you do spoil the children terribly."

He chuckled. "Thank you for having me, Miss Ebbie." Removing his hat to reveal a head of curly light brown hair, he bowed elegantly to Stephanie. "Actually, I just had to accept Andre's invitation, after hearing from Miss Elizabeth Stanton that you have a lovely new addition to the household."

"Indeed," put in Andre. "Madame Stephanie Sergeant, meet my business partner, Henry Robillard."

Stephanie offered her hand. "How do you do, Mr. Robillard?"

With a flash of white teeth, he firmly shook her hand. "Just splendid, thank you, ma'am."

"Well," piped in Ebbie, "shall we eat?"

"Yes, ma'am!" agreed Henry.

Once they were all seated, Andre began pouring wine for the adults while Ebbie served oyster soup. Handing Henry his bowl, she asked, "How is your dear aunt?"

Murmuring a thank-you, he replied, "Aunt Katie is doing right fine."

"It's such a coincidence that you've dropped by," Ebbie continued, "since Stephanie just persuaded me to wear the lovely shawl Katie knitted for me."

Henry snapped his fingers. "I thought it looked familiar. Aunt Katie will be pleased to hear you're wearing it."

As the conversation lagged, Stephanie asked Henry, "Have you and Andre known each other long?"

"Oh, Andre and I go way back," Henry replied. "As young men, we attended Jefferson Military College together, then went on to the university. We've been business partners for over seven years." He winked at Stephanie. "Actually, I was right pleased to come across this old rascal in town. He's been spending far too much time gambling or at the racetrack, and he needs to give me a hand at the office.''

While Stephanie stifled at snicker at this not-surprising revelation, the older children laughed. Gwen turned imperiously to her father. ''Papa, have you been bad?''

Andre solemnly shook his head. ''Certainly not, angel.'' He glowered at Henry. ''Shame on you, my friend. You are telling tales out of school, in the presence of my children and these two lovely ladies, no less. Besides, I do not spend an inordinate amount of time gambling. Why, I dropped in at the office only last week—''

''For all of ten minutes,'' Henry finished drolly. ''It's fall, Andre, our busiest time. Have some mercy on your old friend, won't you? During your recent excursions to Silver Street, have you taken a look at the docks? Cotton is pouring in from up and down the river, and we can barely fill the orders for Rufus Learned's mill, much less those from the Eastern factories. I could use your fine eye to help grade the cotton.''

Andre only laughed. ''I'm sure our firm will prosper under your able leadership, Henry.''

He rolled his eyes. ''I'm not so confident. The plantation owners like to be paid, and when their product is left rotting in warehouses on Water Street, there's little incentive for them not to take their business farther downriver to one of the able factors in the Exchange in New Orleans.''

''Henry, Henry, you are like a mother hen,'' Andre chided. ''Now I must insist you cease boring the ladies to tears with this talk of business.''

Henry colored. ''Ladies, I do apologize.''

''Oh, please don't.'' Stirring her soup, Stephanie flashed a saccharine smile at Andre. ''Actually, I find Mr. Robillard's discourse fascinating.''

Andre frowned. ''More wine, Henry? It's an excellent Chablis.''

''Certainly.'' He held out his glass.

Pouring the wine, Andre shot a heated look at Stephanie. ''It may interest you to know, Madame Sergeant, that when Henry and I began our business, it was with the understanding that I was to provide the capital, while he took on most of the administrative duties. Isn't that so, Henry?''

"Of course, Andre, but that was seven years ago, and I do feel I've made enough of a contribution that it's not unseemly of me to ask for your assistance. Besides, we're swamped—''

"Enough," cut in Andre, replacing the wine decanter on the table with an emphatic thud. "You have made your point, *mon ami*, and I'll be delighted to discuss the matter further—*after* dinner.''

"As you wish," acquiesced Henry.

During the remainder of the meal, the group chatted about the children, the mild weather, and the latest gossip concerning which local young gentleman had been seen with what young lady, and which families were off "visiting," or touring Europe. Frequently Stephanie caught Henry staring at her, and she felt certain she had attracted his attention.

This was confirmed after dessert, when Andre and Henry excused themselves to adjourn to his study for brandy and cigars. On his way out of the room, Henry thanked Ebbie for supper, then paused next to Stephanie's chair and kissed her hand. "Madame Sergeant, it has been such a true pleasure getting to know you. I was wondering . . . might I have the honor of calling on you?''

Stephanie was about to answer in the affirmative when Andre replied coldly, "You may not.''

Stephanie gasped in outrage.

Expression perplexed, Henry turned to his friend. "Andre, have you some prior claim over Madame Sergeant?''

"She is a member of my household," stated Andre. "That is ample claim.''

Stephanie stood. "I disagree," she informed Andre coolly. "I may be in your employ, sir, but that gives you no right to dictate my decisions." Before he could respond, she turned to Henry. "Sir, I'd be delighted to receive you.''

Henry winked at Andre. "Well, old friend, it seems the lady has spoken.''

Andre eyed Stephanie meaningfully. "So she has . . . though she may not have had the final word.'' He flashed Henry a stiff smile. "Shall we adjourn, then?''

"Indeed. Thanks again, ladies.''

They left, and Stephanie and Ebbie ushered the children upstairs to the playroom. The youngsters were exuberant, Paul and Beau chasing each other, playing cowboys and Indians, while Gwen pulled Amy around the room in a small wooden wagon.

Ebbie and Stephanie sat down on a window seat together. "It was good to see Henry," Ebbie remarked.

"Yes. I enjoyed meeting him."

"And he appears to have taken a shine to you."

"So he does."

Ebbie bit her lip. "Stephanie . . . I hope you're not angry with Andre."

"Why would I be angry?"

"Because he tried to forbid your seeing Henry. You must understand that he's very protective of everyone in this family."

"Is he protective of you?"

Ebbie laughed nervously. "But of course. I don't know what I'd do without him and the children."

Stephanie smiled. "He seemed to like the bits of color we added to your outfit."

Ebbie's countenance brightened. "Yes, it seemed he did."

Stephanie raised an eyebrow meaningfully. "We're going to have to get you some prettier dresses."

"Well . . . we'll see." Ebbie grimaced as Beau emitted a particularly loud Indian yell. "My, but the children are rowdy."

"I'm sure it's all that candy Henry gave them."

"Really?"

"Oh, yes. Sugar can have an almost narcotic effect on some children."

"Why, I had no idea."

Stephanie snapped her fingers. "You know, this would be a good time for you to practice our lesson."

"What do you mean?"

"Well, get the children to calm down, pick up their toys, then read them a story."

Ebbie waved her off. "Oh, they won't mind me."

"Come on, Ebbie, don't be a wimp," Stephanie scolded.

"A what?"

"What I'm saying is, show some spunk. You'll never know unless you try."

Ebbie forced a brave expression. "Yes, I suppose you're right." She got up, went to the center of the room, held up a hand, and spoke softly. "Children, it's time to calm down."

Stephanie groaned. Ebbie sounded about as forceful as a church mouse. The children ignored her—Gwen careening past with Amy dangling from the wagon, Beau chasing a whooping Paul around Ebbie's skirts, the boys almost knocking the woman over with their antics.

Ebbie glanced helplessly at Stephanie.

"Try again," she suggested.

Ebbie made a second attempt, speaking louder this time, but still the children ignored her. Desperate, Stephanie fetched a small brass bell from the bookshelf and took it to Ebbie. "Here, ring this."

Ebbie tinkled the bell and waited hopefully. Still, no response. "Stephanie, please," she implored.

Gwen raced past with Amy again, running the wagon's wheels over Stephanie's toes. "Ouch!" she yelled. "That does it!"

She grabbed the bell from Ebbie and rang it loudly. When she, too, was ignored, she stuffed two fingers in her mouth and shrilled out an ear-piercing whistle, not stopping until the children froze in place with grimaces and hands over their ears.

"There—finally!" she declared, shaking a finger at them. "Now we're going to clean up this playroom. Then Miss Ebbie will read you a story."

"Do we have to?" wailed Gwen.

"Absolutely!"

After a little more resistance, the children complied. In due course, the room was straightened, the children dutifully seated around the rocker where Ebbie sat.

Stephanie thrust a storybook into Ebbie's hands. "Now read," she commanded.

Ebbie began a dry reading of "Cinderella," and soon the

children were fidgeting again. In less than a minute, Gwen turned to glare at Stephanie.

"Why don't you read to us, madame?" she demanded.

Stephanie raised a finger to her mouth. "Shhhhh! You're being rude. Miss Ebbie is doing a fine job—"

"No, she's not," cut in Beau. "She's boring!"

Gwen and Paul howled with laughter at Beau's unabashed comment. Noting that Ebbie had set down the book and looked miserable, Stephanie could have shaken the little monsters.

Ebbie cast her an imploring look. "Stephanie, would you kindly finish the story? The children are right. I'm not a good storyteller like you."

Stephanie crossed over to Ebbie's side. "Well, they're wrong for not giving you a chance." She shot an admonishing look at the youngsters. "And how would they feel if someone laughed at them while they tried to read?"

This comment subdued the group at once; Gwen, Paul and Beau all grew quiet and guilty-faced.

Ebbie stood and handed Stephanie the book. "Please, Stephanie. I need to check on Martha and the baby, anyway."

Stephanie waved a hand in defeat. "Very well."

Stephanie read to the oldest four, then dispatched them to bed. After tucking in the girls, she went to check on the boys, and found them already under the covers. She was surprised when Paul sat up and regarded her contritely.

"Madame, we are sorry about Miss Ebbie," he murmured. "We didn't mean to hurt her feelings."

Both surprised and warmed by the sensitivity of the boy's comment, Stephanie sat down on his bed and ruffled his dark hair. It occurred to her that he looked just like his father, with his black hair and bright blue eyes. Yet the child had an innocence and guilelessness that the father lacked.

"That's a fine thing to say, Paul, but have you apologized to Miss Ebbie?"

He hung his head.

"She doesn't like us like you do," Beau chimed in.

Stunned, Stephanie turned to the lad. "Why would you say such a thing?"

As Beau averted his gaze, Paul answered, " 'Tis true, madame. I think Miss Ebbie finds us tiresome. She prefers her Bible, or her violin and her gentlemen friends with their squeaky instruments. But you . . ." He grinned shyly. "You like children."

Stephanie couldn't resist smiling back. "Of course I do, darling, but Miss Ebbie likes you, too. She's just much shier than I am. The four of you scare her with your rambunctious behavior. You have to give her more of a chance."

"Why?" asked Beau.

"Because she's committed to you, and this family. And she'll always be here for you."

"And you won't?" asked Paul, frowning.

Stephanie shook her head. "I'm only staying until Miss Ebbie can handle things on her own."

"I wish you would stay, and she would go!" burst out Beau.

Stephanie bit her lip. Beau was only a child who was being honest about his feelings. It wouldn't be right to make him feel guilty. Gently, she replied, "Beau, you don't really want Miss Ebbie to leave, do you? Why, this is her home. Where else would she go?"

While Beau wavered, obviously confused, Paul piped up. "I know. Both of you must stay—forever! Miss Ebbie can help mind the babies, and you must read us more stories."

"Yes, thousands of stories," agreed Beau, performing exuberant somersaults on his bed.

Much as the boys' words tugged at Stephanie's heartstrings, making her sad because she couldn't grant their wish, she forced a pleasant look. "Well, we don't have to solve this tonight, do we?"

Though neither boy appeared pleased, both shook their heads.

"Good night, then." Stephanie kissed each boy on the forehead and made her escape while she could.

She had just closed their door when she encountered Andre in the hallway. His determined gaze was riveted on her, his features tense, his arms set akimbo.

"Madame, I shall have a word with you."

Stephanie ground her jaw. She was in no mood for another confrontation with this arrogant man. "I don't think we have anything to discuss."

Anger gleamed in his eyes. "You dare to defy me and see Henry?"

"You do not own me, sir."

"You are in my employ. I could discharge you."

"Why don't you?" Head held high, she started away.

Andre grabbed her arm and pulled her around to face him. His voice trembled with anger. "Madame, if you will receive Henry Robillard, you will damn well *receive* me, as well."

Furious, she shoved him away. "You cad! Don't you give any thought to Ebbie's feelings?"

He appeared incredulous. "Ebbie? What has she to do with it?"

Stephanie slowly shook her head. "You are a self-centered, egotistical fool," she said and stalked away.

Andre stood watching her. Much as her words had bemused him, he couldn't help but admire the sway of her hips as she slipped inside her room and slammed the door. Lord, but she had looked splendid in that new blue dress— so snug across her nicely shaped bosom and trim waist— and how she fired his blood! She also defied him at every turn, only increasing his fascination with her . . . and his desire.

Why had she scorned him today, then encouraged Henry tonight? He was all but furious enough to call out his best friend. Of course, he doubted a man like Robillard could really attract a spirited creature like Stephanie. Though he could affect a charming drawl with the ladies, Henry was basically the salt of the earth, about as exciting as the cotton he graded.

On the other hand, he *was* sure Stephanie had responded ardently to him in his office this afternoon. Was she simply a tease, playing up to Henry to stoke his own passions?

Even that possibility excited him. For Andre Goddard knew just how to deal with a coquette.

Then, remembering her parting words, he frowned. What had she meant when she'd said he had no regard for Ebbie's feelings? How did Ebbie enter in?

"Andre?"

As if his musings had summoned her, he glanced up to watch Ebbie approach. "Are the children all in bed?" he asked.

She nodded. "I just tucked Sarah in. Did you see Henry off?"

He scowled. "Yes, though I have a feeling we'll be seeing much more of Robillard now that he's gotten an eyeful of Madame Sergeant."

Ebbie regarded him quizzically. "You seemed displeased when Henry asked to call on Stephanie. Did you consider her conduct—well, improper for a governess?"

His expression turned grim. "It doesn't speak well of her that she's already inviting men to come calling only days after joining our household."

"Oh, but Andre, she's not like that at all," Ebbie hastily assured him. "I've already found Stephanie to be devoted to the children—and to me. Do you not like having her around?"

He smiled. "You need the help, and I'm glad she's here for your sake." Ruefully, he added, "And for mine."

Ebbie appeared uncertain, twisting her fingers together. "I'm glad you're pleased, then. There's only one thing . . ."

"Yes?" Andre prodded. "Out with it, Ebbie—"

"I don't think Stephanie's planning to stay very long," she fretted. "Today, she mentioned that she intends to leave once I can carry on without her."

His gaze narrowed. "Did she?"

Ebbie nodded soberly.

He fell silent for a long moment. "Then we'll have to change her mind, won't we?"

Ebbie nodded. "I hope we can, Andre. I do find I depend on her already. She's wonderful with the children, so dynamic and firm, without being the least bit unkind. Truly, I wonder how I've managed so far without her."

Hearing the anxiety in her tone, Andre stepped forward and took her hand. "You poor dear," he said contritely. "I'm a cad not to give more thought to your situation. How great the burden must have been on you this past year, losing Linnea, whom you loved so much, then taking on my rowdy brood—not to mention, me.''

Shyly, she confided, "It's truly been a labor of love, Andre."

"Has it, dear?" He raised her hand and kissed it. "Thank you, Ebbie."

Coloring, she lowered her lashes. "You're welcome, Andre."

Down the hallway, Stephanie stood peering out her just-cracked door. The sound of voices had drawn her there to watch, though she couldn't quite make out what Andre and Ebbie were saying.

Still, she saw the tenderness in his gaze as he took Ebbie's hand, and the demure pleasure on her face. She watched him raise and kiss Ebbie's hand, saw her avert her gaze while appearing secretly thrilled.

Feeling like an interloper, she clicked shut the door and leaned heavily against it. Heavens, she was trembling!

What was the meaning of the vignette she had just witnessed? Was Andre such a rogue that he was out to seduce *every* woman in Natchez, Ebbie included? Or, was her own scheme beginning to work? Had Ebbie's improved appearance truly caught Andre's eye, and was he finally pursuing her?

Pursuing her for what purpose? Lord, Stephanie hoped a noble one! Would she be able to accomplish her goals, to secure Ebbie's happiness, then return to the present, to Sam, to her parents, her *life*?

The very possibility should have elated her. Then why did she suddenly feel so depressed?

Chapter 19

⁓ෙ⟲⟳ෙ⁓

Soon after Stephanie spotted Andre and Ebbie in the hallway, she heard Sarah crying, and went to rock the baby to sleep. By the time she returned to her room, she was tired enough to drop.

But she found a new surprise awaiting her, this time a little gray mouse cowering in the shadows by the foot of her bed.

Stephanie gasped as the little invader eyed her warily and perked its ears. For a moment the two opponents sized one another up, the mouse appearing ready to take flight, and Stephanie wondering frantically how she would get rid of her unwelcome guest.

Gazing about her for something to use to combat the intruder, she spotted the small fireplace broom next to the hearth. She rushed over to grab it, but by the time she had turned, the mouse was on the run, racing under her armoire.

"Oh, no you don't!"

Expression grim, Stephanie dashed over and poked around beneath the wardrobe. In no time the pest skidded away again. Stephanie gave chase, catching up with the critter by the French doors. As the cornered rodent scurried about in confusion, Stephanie flung open a door and swept the mouse outside.

But the creature had a mind of its own, brazenly trying to make a run past Stephanie's skirts to get back inside the room.

"No way!" she cried.

150

Again, she whisked the pest back onto the veranda, and, for good measure, chased it several feet down the gallery. Then she froze at the sound of male laughter . . .

Andre had been standing in the shadows of the veranda, sipping brandy, when he heard the clamor in Stephanie's room. Seconds later, one of her French doors had banged open, and he observed Stephanie doing a silly little dance with a fireplace broom before bursting outside. In amazement, he'd watched her wriggle her way down the veranda, all the while bent over thrashing with her ridiculous little broom, her derriere bobbing becomingly.

He watched her straighten and turn at the sound of his laughter, regarding him in shock, wisps of hair trailing enticingly about her face. "Are you practicing some quaint new housekeeping technique, Madame Sergeant?" he called.

Stephanie was taken aback by the sight of him in the moonlight, his shirt partially unbuttoned, a snifter of brandy in his hand, and merriment glinting in his eyes. Embarrassed, she stammered, "I—I didn't see you standing there, sir."

"Obviously not," he drawled, "or you doubtless would have swept me out of your way, too."

Stephanie couldn't help herself. She had to laugh.

Andre drew several steps closer, eyeing her in mingled amusement and perplexity. "Madame, you are forever delighting me with new aspects of your character." He nodded toward the broom she held. "Tell me, are you so obsessed with cleanliness that you would resort to such absurd measures? I'm sure we've a full-size broom somewhere down in the butler's pantry."

Stephanie chortled. "I guess I must have looked pretty silly."

He eyed her intently. "Silly is not the word I would have chosen, but you definitely intrigued me."

"You don't understand," she protested. "I was sweeping a mouse out of my room."

"Ah," he murmured. "Heaven help the poor rodent that crosses the path of the formidable Madame Sergeant."

She cast him a scolding look.

He offered her his snifter. "Here, have a drink to calm yourself."

Propping her broom against the house, she waved him off. "I assure you, sir, I'm no swooning woman with a bad case of nerves."

"On the contrary, you appeared on the verge of apoplexy just now, so I insist." He pressed the snifter into her hands. "Besides, this is quite an excellent French brandy."

After slanting him another chiding glance, Stephanie lifted the snifter and took a slow sip, feeling a decadent thrill to be sharing the same glass with him. "You're right—it's wonderful." She handed the snifter back, feeling a new twinge of excitement as their fingers brushed. "Now if you'll excuse me . . ."

"But I don't excuse you," he replied.

Stephanie felt her hackles rising. "Look, sir, if you're planning to lecture me again regarding Henry Robillard, you can just forget it."

Andre whistled. "Why would you assume I was going to lecture you again?"

"Because you're always trying to interfere in matters that are none of your concern."

Andre shook his head in disbelief. "Those who live under my roof are none of my concern? From whence do you hail, madame, that you've acquired such peculiar notions?"

Stephanie fought a grudging smile; she supposed that, from the perspective of the typical nineteenth-century male, he had a point. "I guess in some ways, I must seem odd to you."

He offered her a conciliatory smile. "Why don't we try to call a truce for now?"

"A truce?" Unable to resist, she flashed him a superior look. "If you're so anxious to establish peace, is that why you left the tin of bonbons in my room?"

He chuckled. "You seem to be suffering from the delusion that some mysterious person keeps visiting your room."

"I know you have."

He regarded her sheepishly. "Madame, as I've stated previously, I do regret our disagreements. I'd like you to realize I'm really not so terrible a fellow.''

''Yes, you've convinced me you're a saint,'' she quipped back. ''But now I must go in.''

He touched her arm. ''No, please stay for a while.''

''Why?'' she asked, intrigued and disarmed.

He shook his head wonderingly. ''You really don't know, do you?''

''No, but I could guess.''

''If you guessed, you'd be wrong,'' he stated.

''Would I?'' Stephanie crossed her arms over her bosom. ''You know, I'd love to be wrong about you for a change. So tell me why I should stay.''

Turning toward the railing, he made a sweeping gesture. ''Because it's a sin to turn one's back on so beautiful a night.''

Caught off guard by his words, Stephanie stared out at the picturesque moonlit grounds. She watched the foliage stir in the breeze. The light was exquisite, and the scent of the air was intoxicating. The night was incredible, she had to admit it. And he was right—she hadn't even noticed.

Andre moved closer to her. ''Look, madame. See how beautiful the moon is, and watch the light dance on the Spanish moss. Hear the whistle of the wind and the sawing of the crickets. Smell the jasmine, the roses.''

Stephanie felt her senses stirring at his words, along with an unexpected tenderness, and twinges of regret. How long had it been since she'd taken the time to gaze out at a beautiful night?

But could she afford to do so with him so temptingly close? Remembering how they'd both almost lost control in his office earlier that day, she didn't think so.

''Yes, the night is lovely,'' she acknowledged, her voice quivering slightly. ''But I mustn't linger.''

''Why?'' he asked. ''Does a night like this bring memories of your husband? Does it make you sad?''

Amazed by his insight, and feeling a rush of bittersweet emotion, Stephanie nonetheless shook her head. ''My husband would never have wanted me to look at a beautiful night and feel sad.''

Andre nodded. "Then he was quite a noble fellow."

"Yes, he was."

He edged closer still, regarding her wistfully. "The night can bring out secret yearnings, you know."

His words, while tantalizing, put Stephanie in a half panic. "Look, I can't be having this conversation with you."

He touched her shoulder. "Wait. You have no real idea what I'm talking about, do you?"

Bewildered, she could only stare at him.

Once again, he gestured out at the grounds. "When I was young, my family lived in a big house south of town. In the evenings, all of us used to gather on the front gallery, and Mama would read to us children."

"How charming," she murmured.

"She'd also tell stories of our family history, of her and Papa's travels. On spring or summer nights, we children used to play on the front lawn. We'd lie in the grass on our backs, smell the magnolia blossoms, and look up at the stars, even dream of how we might visit the heavens."

Stephanie found her gaze drawn up to the sky. The images he spun were entrancing.

"I hear you read to my children now," he went on. "Did anyone read to you when you were young?"

"Of course," she replied tightly. "My parents did."

Gently, he teased, "And what was the stern Madame Sergeant reared on? Perhaps lectures on household efficiency, or mastering one's schedule?"

She rolled her eyes at him. "Certainly not. My parents read me Perrault and Hans Christian Andersen, the *Arabian Nights*."

"Ah, fairy tales. Then we shared some of the same stories."

"I suppose we did."

"And there was also a time when madame was more fanciful, no? That is, before you became preoccupied with agendas and rules, and silly little brooms."

Stephanie couldn't answer him. She was fighting an unexpected lump in her throat.

Andre looked toward the sky. "As a boy, I used to gaze

up at those heavens and imagine myself gathering stars in a big basket.''

"What a beautiful image.''

"And you? Did you have such yearnings?''

Stephanie hesitated, realizing this conversation could stray easily into dangerous territory. She looked up at the sky, and felt poignant memories welling up. "I've never gotten to travel much. Sometimes when I was young, I used to stare up at the night sky and wonder what it would be like to see the moon and those stars from another perspective—like standing in the Piazza San Marco in Venice, or on the Left Bank in Paris, or in the Strand in London.''

He reached out to touch her cheek. "I've been to all those places, Stephanie. I could take you there.''

She shut her eyes. She dared not answer him.

"Stephanie, look at me.''

She opened her eyes to see him gazing at her soulfully. The night swirled about them, like a sensual blanket enfolding them, pulling them closer.

"What do you yearn for now?'' he whispered.

Oh, he could be devastating! Even as her heart thrummed out a passionate response, she knew she dared not answer honestly.

"I—I think it's time for us to call it a night.''

Surprising her, he only smiled and sipped his brandy. "Pleasant dreams, Stephanie.''

Unsteadily, she turned and reentered her bedroom. Already she very much feared her dreams would be of him. . . .

Chapter 20

❧ ◦❀◦ ❧

The weekend was soon upon them. On Sunday morning, when Sarah awakened cranky because she was
teething, Stephanie volunteered to stay home with her while
the rest of the family attended mass at the Episcopal church.
Ebbie mentioned that a visiting minister would be conduct-
ing the service, since Reverend Dearborn was still away in
Jackson. Remembering that the reverend had allegedly dispatched her here, Stephanie prayed he would stay gone
much longer, since she had no excuse to offer for having
lied about his sending her here.

Stephanie was grateful for the respite. She wasn't ready
for her first real foray into Natchez society—especially
since she still lacked a dress that fit well—and she hoped
the outing would give Andre and Ebbie more time alone.
Plus, following the poignant moments she'd spent with Andre on the veranda the other night, she found her emotions
all too threatened by him; his musings had revealed a
thoughtfulness and possible depth of character that disarmed
her even more than his sexy banter. She couldn't afford to
let down her guard with him again, or to forget that right
before he'd charmed her on the veranda, she'd spied him
playing up to Ebbie in the hallway. Assuming he did possess a more sensitive side, he seemed generous about sharing it.

The days flowed smoothly until Tuesday afternoon. Stephanie was sitting outside in the brisk air, watching the
older children play and Pompom chase a brightly colored

ball, when Martha lumbered out to join her, carrying Sarah. "I come to watch these children," she informed Stephanie. "They's company in the house. Mr. Goddard says you gots to come in."

"Thank you, Martha," Stephanie murmured.

Walking across the leaf-strewn lawn, she removed her straw hat and smoothed down her hair, then brushed wrinkles from her burgundy frock. She wondered why Andre had called her inside. "Company" seemed a regular occurrence here in the Goddard household, but then, these were the days of the graceful Old South, with no marvels of technological entertainment available, when whole families would often pack up and go "visiting" for days or even weeks. Still, being summoned in this peremptory fashion made her uneasy.

When Stephanie stepped into the parlor, it was only to stop in her tracks. Ebbie, looking pale and confused, sat wringing her hands on the settee. Andre, appearing both suspicious and intrigued, occupied one wing chair. In another wing chair sat a handsome thirtyish man in priest's garb.

Stephanie's stomach did a nosedive. Oh, heavens! Ebbie had mentioned that an older Presbyterian minister had conducted the service on Sunday, and she had a sinking feeling this man must be the Reverend Dearborn. Had her secret already been exposed?

Even as the unsettling prospect pushed her teeming mind toward panic, both men spotted her and rose. Wearing a cynical expression, Andre approached her. "Madame Sergeant, I believe you already know Reverend Dearborn. Ebbie and I were just thanking the man for sending you to us—but he seems curiously lacking in an appropriate response."

Ebbie toyed with the lace on her collar and laughed nervously. "Oh, Andre, I'm sure Reverend Dearborn is simply too modest to take credit for sending us a jewel like Stephanie."

Raising a brow, Andre turned to Dearborn. "Is that the case, Peter? Or do you even know this woman?"

Dearborn gulped and seemed at sea. As the silence

stretched on until it screamed, Stephanie knew she must act. She hurried toward Dearborn, quickly assessing his face—the dark brown, compassionate eyes, the blade-shaped nose, the finely drawn, sensitive mouth. Although the man appeared to be modest and unassuming, he also radiated kindness and an inner strength.

Stephanie pumped his hand. "Reverend Dearborn, how good to see you again! Surely you must remember meeting me at—er—the home of my dear friends in Jackson? I know our time together was brief, but I can't thank you enough for sending me here to the Goddard home."

"Er—you're welcome," he stammered back.

Stephanie could have shouted her relief. At least Dearborn wasn't exposing her lie outright—though she was far from out of the woods.

"Then you do know this woman?" Andre inquired.

As Dearborn began to stammer, Stephanie could have kicked Andre.

Ebbie popped up and rushed to Stephanie's side. "Of course Peter knows Stephanie."

Andre's skeptical gaze was still focused on the reverend. "If your meeting with Madame Sergeant was so brief, how could you have determined that she could be a proper governess for us?"

Dearborn blushed.

Ebbie turned to Andre. "Andre, really, must you interrogate our guest so?"

He chuckled. "But these are simple questions, and I think Peter can answer for himself, no?"

Dearborn glanced uneasily at Stephanie, then carefully replied, "Being a clergyman, I do consider myself to be a good judge of character. Surely I would have known just by looking at—er—this woman that she's a worthwhile person."

"Well put, Reverend," Andre mocked. "Ebbie, where is Lilac with our tea? Kindly ring again, will you? Shall we all sit down and have a cozy little chat?"

As everyone complied, Ebbie jingled her bell and brightly asked, "Peter, how is your dear mother, and the sweetheart she writes to in South Carolina?"

He sighed. "Mother's still working on the General's new uniform, I'm afraid. She hopes to send it off to Charleston before Christmas."

"Ah yes, so the General may lead the charge against Sherman?" Ebbie inquired sadly.

"Unfortunately, yes," he confirmed.

Bemused, Stephanie dared a glance at Andre, and he pointed meaningfully at his head.

"And how is the General faring?" Ebbie continued.

Dearborn sighed. "According to Mother, he's still holed up at the Citadel, though he swears that after Sherman is routed from South Carolina, he'll come get her and carry her off on his white horse."

"How lovely," Ebbie replied.

Stephanie felt compelled to say something. "Excuse me, Reverend, but wasn't the Civil War concluded over a decade ago?"

Dearborn coughed. "Not in the minds of some people."

"Ah," murmured Stephanie.

The conversation momentarily lagged as Lilac brought in the silver tea service, setting it on a small table in front of Ebbie. After she left, Andre drawled, "Reverend, tell us more about your fascinating meeting with Madame Sergeant, and how you decided to send her to us."

While the man hesitated, blinking in obvious discomfort, Ebbie declared, "Tell us about your ecclesiastical training!"

Dearborn heaved a great sigh, his eyes gleaming with zeal. "My pleasure, Ebbie. I can't tell you how rejuvenated I feel after the council meetings in Jackson. Bishop Green came in to give some of the sessions, and his interpretation of the Sermon on the Mount has renewed my faith in God . . . and man." He turned to the others. "Indeed, one reason I've come by today is to tell you about my personal epiphany."

"How fascinating," drawled Andre.

"Just this morning, I was thanking my friend Reverend Stratton for filling in for me while I was away, and I remarked that there is too much separation among the Christians here in Natchez. He agreed, and we've decided to host an impromptu picnic and revival meeting on the Old Spanish Parade Grounds this Saturday—and the entire community of churches is invited.''

Ebbie beamed as she passed Dearborn a cup of tea. ''Why, that sounds splendid.''

''I was hoping you and your quartet might provide background music,'' Dearborn ventured.

Clapping her hands, Ebbie appeared as delighted as a child at the prospect of Christmas presents. ''We'd be honored, of course. Although our repertoire is rather secular, I'm afraid.''

''I'm sure it will be just fine.''

Ebbie turned to Stephanie. ''Peter plays a fine violin himself.''

''Does he, now?''

''I wish he could join our group,'' Ebbie remarked wistfully, ''but alas, his duties preclude it.''

''And if I joined up, you wouldn't be a quartet anymore,'' Peter teased.

''Oh, Peter, you're so clever.'' Ebbie laughed. ''Perhaps I could bring you a list of our planned program before Saturday?''

''That would be wonderful.''

''The misters will be so thrilled,'' she gushed. ''I can't wait to tell Mr. Trumble when he comes by for our session later today.''

''Good.'' Dearborn smiled at Andre, then Stephanie. ''All of you, please help spread the word, and ask each family to bring a covered dish.''

''We'll be happy to,'' put in Stephanie.

The group continued to chat for a while longer. Each minute ticked past like an excruciating eon for Stephanie, especially when, several more times, Andre attempted to grill the reverend regarding her. Mercifully, each time, Ebbie or Stephanie managed to detour the conversation to more neutral territory. She did find it ironic to see how comfortable Ebbie seemed around Peter, so unlike her flustered behavior around Andre. She suspected Ebbie and the reverend were long-standing friends.

At last Dearborn noisily cleared his throat. ''Well, I really must be going, since I've several more families to call on this afternoon. Our housekeeper is sitting with Mother, and I mustn't prevail on her patience too long."

"Will we see your mother on Saturday?" Ebbie asked.

"I rather doubt it, I'm afraid."

"Then give dear Alice our best," replied Ebbie.

He stood. "I will. And thank you for the tea."

Andre also rose. "May I see you out, Reverend?" he inquired meaningfully.

Stephanie bolted up. "I'll see the reverend out," she declared.

Ebbie popped up, as well. "Yes, Stephanie, do see the reverend out." She turned and gripped Andre's arm, speaking with unaccustomed firmness. "Andre, I really must speak with you regarding Sarah's teething . . ."

Although his expression burned with resentment, Andre deferred to Ebbie, and Stephanie escorted the minister out the front door with all due haste. She walked with him down the front steps, then paused beside a crepe myrtle to touch his arm, biting her lip as she caught his reproachful expression.

"Thank you so much," she told Dearborn feelingly. "You saved me a great deal of grief back there."

He frowned and stroked his jaw. "That wasn't a very nice thing you did, Mrs. Sergeant."

"You're absolutely right," she readily admitted.

"Care to explain your situation to me?"

"Yes." Stephanie bit her lip. "You must understand, Reverend, that I'm essentially a good person—"

His laughter interrupted her. "Mrs. Sergeant, if I hadn't immediately sensed that you are a good—albeit misguided— young lady, you'd be packing your bags by now."

Stephanie nodded. "I understand. Thank you again."

A half smile sculpted his lips. "And I must confess that the main reason I hadn't the heart to expose you is that Ebbie seems so fond of you. She's been through an utter trial during the last year, especially at losing Linnea, and I was loath to bring her another disappointment. However, what you did—hoodwinking Andre and his family—was reprehensible, and I must know your circumstances before

I can judge for myself whether or not Andre and Ebbie should be informed of your deceit.''

Stephanie gulped. ''I don't blame you at all. The truth is, I'm a widow, and down on my luck. When I arrived in Natchez, I heard the Goddard household needed a new governess, and when I arrived here and Ebbie assumed you had sent me . . .''

''You seized your advantage?'' he finished.

''Yes.'' In a rush, she added, ''It was despicable of me, but I was destitute, without a penny.''

He was silent, scowling.

Stephanie's expression beseeched him. ''Reverend Dearborn, I know you have no reason to trust me. But please try to believe that I have this family's best interests at heart. If you'll give me a chance, I promise I'll do everything in my power to help Ebbie and the children.''

He shook his head. ''I suspect I may be mad, but I'm inclined to trust you.''

''Oh, bless you!''

''I suppose I have something of a whimsical streak from my mother,'' he confessed. ''Very well, your secret is safe with me for now.'' He shook a finger at her. ''But I'll be watching you carefully, young lady. And if there's ever any hint that my faith is misplaced—''

''It isn't. I promise.''

''We shall see.''

Giving Stephanie a last, admonishing look, Dearborn strode off toward his buggy.

Stephanie heaved a great sigh and returned inside. But she had no sooner closed the door than she collided with Andre.

His flinty gaze seemed to bore holes in her, and his voice rang with steel. ''Come with me, Madame Sergeant.'' And he seized her arm.

Realizing she was in deep trouble, Stephanie dug in her heels. Heedless of her protests, Andre pulled her down the hallway, into his study, and closed the door. When she tried to leave, he pressed his solid back against the panel.

''Now, tell me who you really are,'' he commanded.

By now too maddened by his arrogance to feel afraid,

Stephanie retorted, "What? Sir, I have no idea what you're talking about."

"Oh, yes you do," he retorted. "I'm talking about the fact that Reverend Dearborn never laid eyes on you before today."

Stephanie crossed her arms over her bosom and faced him down. "You must be jesting. Reverend Dearborn knows me well."

"He doesn't know you from Eve, my dear," Andre mocked. "Peter may have found much ecclesiastical fire in Jackson, but it's obvious he never found you."

She raised her chin. "It's not obvious to me."

An incredulous laugh escaped him. "I can't believe what a cool little liar you are! Who are you really, Stephanie? A woman with a shady past?"

"Certainly not!"

"For all your sanctimonious pretensions, I suspect otherwise." He reached out and toyed with a button at her throat. "But that could make things simpler between us, no?"

She shoved his fingers away. "Of all the gall! How dare you insinuate I'm hiding something tawdry. Move out of my way and let me out of here."

"You are going nowhere." Suddenly, he smiled. "Except, perhaps, to the church picnic with me on Saturday."

"In your dreams!" she scoffed. "What about Ebbie?"

He appeared exasperated. "What about her? And why are we talking about Ebbie again when you're the one in deep trouble?"

"Well, we are talking about Ebbie—talking about her *right now*—or I'm leaving this office."

Andre stepped closer, his eyes blazing into hers. "Leave this office, and you may leave my home."

She faced him down defiantly. "Fine."

"Damn it," he muttered, backing away. "You are maddeningly stubborn, woman, and full of more mettle than should be lawful. Very well. *What* about Ebbie?"

Stephanie rolled her eyes. "You don't know?"

"Know what?"

"I can't believe what a self-absorbed cad you are."

"What are you ranting about now, woman?"

She stepped closer to confront him. "Don't tell me you've never noticed the way she looks at you, how flustered she is around you. She's in love with you."

He laughed. "Don't be ridiculous."

"Don't *you* be ridiculous!" she shot back. "Furthermore, I don't for a minute believe your pretense of innocence where she's concerned. You must be aware of her feelings. Why, last week I saw you fawning over her."

He appeared both insulted and delighted. "You little eavesdropper. So you watched us, did you? Tell me, were you jealous?"

"Jealous? No, I wasn't jealous, only keenly disappointed to see you toying with the affections of a woman who genuinely cares for you and your family. But then, *every* woman is fair game to you, isn't she?"

While she had spoken, something about Andre's expression had changed, hardened. When he spoke, the deceptive softness of his tone sent a shiver down her spine. "*You* certainly are, love."

Stephanie resisted an urge to stamp her foot. "Will you get your mind off your lusts for a moment and listen to me? Can't you see that when you flirt with me or Elizabeth Stanton or whoever, you only hurt Ebbie?"

He fell silent, then spoke in measured tones. "Stephanie, not that it's any of your business, but what you witnessed last week was a moment of tenderness between two friends. I am not in love with Ebbie, nor is she in love with me—"

"You're wrong!"

He held up a hand. "Assuming for the sake of argument that she is in love with me, I'm afraid there's still nothing that can be done about it."

"Oh, yes, there is," Stephanie retorted. "You could court her."

"What?" he cried. "That's out of the question."

"Have you given any thought to all she's sacrificed for you and your family?"

He sighed. "Of course I have."

"Have you really?" she pursued. "Ebbie's a saint, hard-working, devoted to your children, loyal to you—to a fault. Do you know she refuses ever to criticize you?"

He smiled. "You might take a lesson from that."

Stephanie ground her teeth. "Stop being so cocky and listen to me. Don't you feel any sense of responsibility toward her after she's given up her life, her own dreams, for the sake of you and your family?"

"I've given her a home."

"You've given your dog a home."

He had the grace to appear guilty.

She touched his arm. "Andre, Ebbie told me that pretty much everyone in town expects the two of you to eventually marry."

His features tightened. "That's only silly gossip."

"Well, silly gossip can ruin people."

"What do you mean?"

Stephanie waved a hand. "Must you be so thickheaded? The woman lives in your home while you're off playing the Lothario. On the very night I arrived here, I heard two ladies gossiping about how Ebbie was making a fool of herself over you. Then, the instant I arrived in your parlor, you danced with me, with Ebbie right there. The following evening, you drooled over Elizabeth Stanton. Has it never occurred to you that you might be hurting her feelings, not to mention making a laughingstock out of her?"

By now, he was scowling fiercely. "Just what are you suggesting I do?"

"You could start by taking her to the church picnic."

He ground his jaw. "Stephanie, I've already told you I'm not going to court Ebbie."

"Why? Will you please tell me why?"

"Why don't you tell me why you're so determined to push us together?" he demanded.

"Very well." She stared him in the eye and spoke vehemently. "Whether you believe me or not, Andre, I happen to know that Ebbie is *desperately* in love with you. And she will die of a broken heart if you don't court her—and marry her."

For once the audacious rogue actually appeared taken aback. He paced about the room, muttering to himself.

"Well, Andre?"

Resolutely, he turned to her. "If you are telling the truth—which I doubt—that is unfortunate. For I've no intention of marrying another woman I don't love."

Stephanie was exasperated enough to shake him. "Yes, it's obvious you never loved your wife."

She was unprepared for his fury as he strode forward, grabbed her by the shoulders, and pushed her against the door, forcing her to face his impassioned visage. "Yes, I never loved my wife," he uttered in a chilling whisper. "Ours was an arranged marriage, and Linnea was a sweet and retiring creature, like Ebbie, who worshiped me but was never woman enough to hold me. Don't you know it torments me that she died without ever knowing true love in her life? I shall not subject Ebbie to that same fate."

Staring up at him, Stephanie couldn't doubt his sincerity, especially given his guilt over not having returned Linnea's feelings. Still, she managed to argue back, "But you don't mind subjecting me to your attentions."

With her words, his anger faded, and his voice took on a tantalizing huskiness as he drew a teasing finger along her jawline. "That is different. You have the spirit and the passion to satisfy a man like me."

Too late, Stephanie glimpsed the desire burning in Andre's bright eyes. Even as she tried to duck away, he caught her face in his hands and ardently kissed her. His mouth coaxed and seduced; his body pressed hers into the wall. His hand slid down her dress, his thumb caressing the underside of her breast.

Stephanie was appalled by the excitement that unwittingly stormed her. Sinking fast, she pressed her palms against his shoulders and pushed him away. "Andre, stop it. Please, you must at least give Ebbie a chance. Take her to the picnic."

He hesitated for a long moment, staring down at her. Then a devilish smile lit his face. "Very well. I'll take her to the picnic on one condition—"

"Which is?"

"If you'll become my mistress."

Stephanie was too flabbergasted to speak. Then she furiously shoved him away. "You scoundrel! Why would you even make such a ludicrous proposal? You hardly even know me."

His gaze flicked over her. "That's something we can remedy—in my bed."

"Spoken like a typical, egotistical male." Trembling, Stephanie drew herself up with pride. "Well, I want you to know something about me—and know it well. I spent three glorious years with a man none other can ever compare to. And I won't ever love again."

Although a glimmer of pain crossed his face, Andre drawled a reply. "You don't have to love me, *chérie*. Just come to my bed."

Something snapped in Stephanie then, and she started flailing at Andre with her fists, calling him every despicable name she could think of. He quickly restrained her, laughing the whole time, exacerbating her fury.

"I take it that's a no?" he teased, still struggling with her.

"You may take it and shove it, sir!"

"Then perhaps I'll have to settle for another kiss."

She froze, regarding him suspiciously. "What do you mean?"

"I mean I want another kiss."

She hesitated, regarding him fiercely. "Are you saying you'll take Ebbie to the picnic if I—er—comply?"

He groaned. *"Oui."*

Stephanie gave a great sigh. "Very well."

But as she waited, the kiss did not come, and Andre only regarded her with amusement.

"Well?" she demanded.

He slid a finger over her underlip. "I think I'll let you do the honors, love."

Oh, he had her, and he knew it. Just one kiss—and he would take Ebbie to the picnic. But could she bear to pay his price? Or would she risk giving all?

Drawing a shaky breath, Stephanie stretched on tiptoe and just brushed her mouth against Andre's. She hadn't expected the fleeting contact to ignite such explosive feelings. A moment later their lips collided with fiery hunger. Andre drew her close and slid his tongue inside her mouth slowly, tantalizingly. Stephanie moaned, feeling her resistance melting in a puddle of lassitude. Her arms coiled about his neck. She ached for him all over—her nipples tingling, yearning for the wet heat of his mouth, her womanhood throbbing to feel him inside her.

He whispered at her ear. "Tell me who you really are, love. Then come to my bed."

That remark at last brought her to her senses. She pressed him away and spoke breathlessly, though she dared not meet his eye. "I—I've met your terms and I expect you to keep your word."

Stephanie was amazed that her shaky limbs bore her out of his office. Retreating up the stairs, she found she felt vulnerable and confused, close to tears. She wanted to get Andre and Ebbie together so that she could return to the present, make amends with Sam, and find her own badly needed peace. Yet she kept feeling more drawn toward the irascible Frenchman, her own feelings threatening to derail all her fine plans. For she *couldn't* love a man like Andre, a man she could never trust, a man whose profligate outlook on life was totally at odds with her own.

A man who, by all rights, belonged to another . . .

Andre sat in his office smoking a cigar. He felt the strangest combination of emotions—excitement, exhilaration, confusion, frustration. He would like to throttle the maddening woman who had just fled his arms, even as he burned to hold her again.

Who *was* Stephanie really? And why was she pushing him toward Ebbie? Following Peter Dearborn's visit, there was little doubt in Andre's mind that Peter and Stephanie had never met before. Then why had she shown up in Natchez, giving them such a contrived story? Why did she resist him so, when he knew she wanted him, too?

He smiled. Whoever this woman was, she was clearly no easy conquest. Remembering how she'd stoutly refused his scandalous proposal, he had to grin. He'd been left feeling new respect for her . . . and wanting her more than ever. At the same time, her spirit, her pride, her inner strength, all convinced him that it wasn't just her delightful body he craved. Never before had he met a woman who could hold her ground with him like this one, giving him tit for tat. She was fun and a challenge, and they played off each other well.

But where would this lead them? He wanted Stephanie, but wasn't prepared to offer marriage. Perhaps he should leave her alone, but he couldn't seem to stop himself. He grew more intrigued by her with each passing day.

He was making progress with her, but at a cost. He was flabbergasted over her insistence that he court Ebbie. It seemed crazy, yet playing along also seemed to be his only hope of winning Stephanie over.

Now he was compelled to take Ebbie to the church picnic, and this did bother him. For what if Stephanie were right and the sad little woman truly was in love with him? Though he doubted this, he also hated the prospect of encouraging Ebbie, giving her false hope. Of course, it was not uncommon for him and Ebbie to step out together in public. If he walked a fine line, he might be able to humor Stephanie without risking Ebbie's feelings.

Chapter 21

~~~❍❍~~~

The house had grown quiet, except for the grate of a cello drifting up from the first floor. Realizing that Abner Trumble must have arrived for his "private lesson" with Ebbie, Stephanie looked around upstairs for the children and, finding no trace of them or Martha, returned to her room. Finally, she ventured downstairs to find the place deserted. She strolled onto the gallery and spied Ebbie on the side porch.

Oblivious of Stephanie's approach, Ebbie sat sorting through a tin containing old letters. Intrigued, Stephanie wondered who had sent them. But what stunned her most was the look of wistful pleasure on Ebbie's face as she carefully arranged the yellowed envelopes inside the box and hummed a theme from Tchaikovsky.

Why was Ebbie so happy? Had Andre been true to his word and asked her to the picnic?

"You look cheery," Stephanie called.

Glancing up and appearing rattled, Ebbie hastily replaced the lid on the tin and shoved it aside. "Oh, Stephanie. Do come join me."

Stephanie sat down next to Ebbie on the porch bench and nodded toward the tin. "So what were you doing, Ebbie?" she teased. "Rereading old love letters?"

Ebbie blushed and pushed the tin farther away. "Stephanie, really! I was just sorting through some correspondence from—er—an old friend."

"Uh-huh," Stephanie murmured, bemused. "So, where

is everyone? I haven't heard a peep out of the children, so I figured they must be off somewhere."

Ebbie nodded. "Andre took all of them into town for ice-cream sodas."

"All by himself?" Stephanie asked with a laugh.

"Well, Martha went with him."

"I see. How was your practice session with Mr. Trumble?"

"Oh, splendid. Abner is so excited about Saturday."

"Great." Stephanie hesitated a moment, then cleared her throat. "Ebbie, about Reverend Dearborn's visit—"

Ebbie touched Stephanie's arm. "Hush, now."

"But I owe you an explanation."

"You owe me nothing of the kind."

"How can you say that?"

Ebbie eyed her soberly. "Stephanie, I don't care where you come from."

"You don't?" Stephanie was astounded.

Ebbie laughed. "Well, I do care. Of course I do. My point is, I trust you, and I need you. If you're here under some—er—contrived circumstance, I must assume you have a valid reason for keeping your true situation to yourself. Otherwise, I don't want you to leave."

Stephanie's heart melted. "Oh, Ebbie. You're being far more generous to me than I deserve."

Ebbie's eyes were moist as she smiled back. "Didn't I tell you I already think of you as a sister?"

Stephanie shook her head wonderingly. "I'm truly blessed to have you regard me so highly. Actually, you think more of me than my own sister does."

"Indeed?"

Stephanie felt a lump rising in her throat. "My sister, Samantha, and I have always been close. But she's hardly blind to my faults."

Ebbie appeared incensed. "Why, I wasn't aware you had any."

Stephanie laughed. "Sam's a perfectionist, and very in charge of her own life. She thinks I tend to be an interfering older sister—you know, Mrs. Fix-it."

Ebbie frowned. "Mrs. Fix-it? Is she someone I should know?"

Stephanie laughed. "No, not at all. Actually, Sam and I are a lot alike—both fussy and fastidious. Only, she doesn't want to admit it."

"I wish I could meet her. Could she come for a visit?"

Stephanie's visage turned sober. "I'm afraid not."

"I'm sorry."

Stephanie shrugged. "Enough about me. Let's talk more about the picnic on Saturday."

"Yes, isn't it exciting?" Ebbie asked brightly.

Stephanie eyed her quizzically. "Has Andre asked you to go with him?"

Ebbie colored slightly. "Why, yes, he mentioned it before he and the children left. You'll come with us, of course?"

"Well, I hadn't thought about it." She playfully tapped Ebbie's arm. "Is that why you appeared so happy when I walked up—because Andre asked you?"

Ebbie hesitated, demurely lowering her gaze. "Well, yes, I suppose. It was also so nice to see Peter Dearborn again . . . and to practice with dear Abner. His bowing is becoming truly masterful. And I've also been thinking about the music—"

"The music?"

Ebbie slanted Stephanie an apologetic look. "I do hope you'll pamper yourself today, Stephanie, because I must prevail upon your generosity for the remainder of the week. I've already dispatched a servant with notes for Mr. Fortier and Mr. Wister, as we'll need to practice extensively before Saturday. So, if you don't mind watching the children—"

"Certainly not. That's why I'm here."

Ebbie beamed. "You're so good to me. We'll try not to impose on your kindness too often. Then, later in the week, we'll go into town for your fitting. I do hope Mrs. Hodge will have one of those lovely frocks ready for you to wear to the picnic. And we can drop off the quartet's repertoire with Reverend Dearborn."

"Of course."

"Oh, Saturday is going to be such fun!" Ebbie declared.

As Ebbie went on chatting, Stephanie frowned to herself. If she didn't know better, she'd suspect it was not the prospect of going out with Andre that excited Ebbie so much, but the thought of butchering Schubert.

Or was it the tin of old letters that had put Ebbie in such a buoyant frame of mind?

For the remainder of the week, the house rang with the grate of a cello, the squeak of violins, and the squawk of a viola. Stephanie kept busy with the children and didn't see Andre as much during those days, except at mealtimes. Once, when she remarked to Ebbie on his more frequent absences, Ebbie mentioned he was at Pharsalia Track racing his French trotter. On a couple of other occasions late at night, she heard Andre stumbling about in the next room, and wondered if he were drunk. His antics made her despair of his ever becoming a proper husband for Ebbie.

It must be nice to live such a life of excess and debauchery, she often cynically mused. Or perhaps he was wisely avoiding the din of Ebbie's practice sessions. Indeed, the noise grew so nerve-fraying that Stephanie soon began taking the older children outside into the delightful fall air, where she started tutoring them in earnest. Of course, she wished it were Ebbie spending this sort of "quality time" with the youngsters, but she supposed it made sense to try to tame the urchins a bit before she turned them over to the woman.

Stephanie spread out a blanket beneath the sheltering arms of an oak, and gathered Beau, Gwen, and Amy around her with their primers, McGuffey's readers, and storybooks. Although Amy was too young to learn much, she proved far more attentive than Beau and Gwen, who were easily distracted by squirrels chasing each other up trees, or hummingbirds feeding at trumpet vines, or Pompom barking at the neighbor's cat. While not discouraging the children's appreciation of the outdoors, Stephanie did insist they attend to their studies, and soon resorted to bribing them with promises that she would read to them once they completed their lessons and recited their sums. There she met with success, since all three children adored being read to. Even the normally belligerent Gwen screamed with glee the day Stephanie read "The Emperor's New Clothes."

When Stephanie closed her book, Gwen asked excitedly, "You mean only a child could see the truth, that the emperor was . . . *naked*?"

As the children chuckled, Stephanie restrained a smile. "That's right. But I'm surprised you're not familiar with the story."

Gwen lowered her gaze. "Our mother read to us, but Miss Ebbie hardly ever does. Even when you asked her to, she made me want to take a nap."

Stephanie's reaction was one of both sympathy and bemusement. "I'm sure Miss Ebbie would read to you more if you'd encourage her."

Gwen shook her head. "She doesn't like us."

"I don't think she likes us, either," seconded Beau.

"Children, that's just not fair—or true," argued Stephanie.

"Do you like us, madame?" Gwen asked wistfully.

Stephanie felt a twinge of emotion at this evidence of vulnerability in the normally willful child. "Of course I do, dear. But have you thought that Miss Ebbie may not *seem* to like you because you play so many tricks on her, because maybe you scare her a little?"

Both children averted their gazes, then Beau brightened. "We haven't played any tricks on her since we hid the baby!"

"Well, thank heaven for that," Stephanie declared. "I shudder to think of what you two monsters might have done to top that little stunt."

For a moment both children eyed her warily, then they burst out giggling. Despite herself, Stephanie smiled as well.

"Will you read us another story, Mrs. Sergeant?" pleaded Gwen. "Pretty please?"

"I'd be happy to," answered Stephanie.

As the days passed, Stephanie found the children responded to her teaching and discipline like roses to sunshine. They hardly became cherubs, but they were less rowdy; even mealtimes grew much more pleasant now that someone had finally imposed limitations on the brood. Stephanie rewarded their successes with more stories, which they loved.

She was outside reading to the children on Thursday afternoon when Henry Robillard drove up in his buggy and strode toward her. Once again, he wore his white suit and planter's hat. But when Stephanie started to set down her book to greet him, he shook his head and motioned for her to continue reading. Lighting a cheroot, he lounged against a nearby oak tree while she concluded the story.

The instant Stephanie finished, Gwen, Beau, and Amy all bolted up, rushing to Henry and demanding toffee. Chuckling, he handed out the candies. "Hey," he told the children, "I saw Martha in the butler's pantry, mixing up a huge pitcher of lemonade. Why don't you youngsters go have some?"

Gwen turned plaintively to Stephanie. "May we, madame?"

Stephanie nodded. "Take Amy by the hand, and go straight in the back door. I'll be watching."

"Yes, ma'am!"

Squealing with glee, the threesome started off.

Stephanie stood and watched the children until they were safely inside the back door. Henry approached her, removing his hat.

"Well, ma'am, I don't think I've ever heard such a charming recitation of 'Puss in Boots.' "

Stephanie laughed. "You're lying, I'm sure."

He placed a hand over his heart and feigned a wounded look. "On my honor, ma'am. And to see how you're bringing those rascals of Andre's around. No insult intended, but Beau and Gwen can be little terrors."

"I've noticed."

He drew on his cheroot. "It's no wonder, with that father of theirs. Don't get me wrong—I'm fond of Andre, but he's a right undisciplined fellow."

"I've noticed that, as well," she muttered.

"Well, someone has to keep the grogshops and gambling dens in business, I reckon." Grinning, Henry touched her arm. "But I'm forgetting why I came."

"And why did you come today, Mr. Robillard?"

Charm oozed off his tongue. "Why, to see your lovely face again, Mrs. Sergeant. Actually, I was wondering if you'd do me the honor of accompanying me to the community picnic on Saturday."

Stephanie hesitated only briefly, quickly realizing she couldn't afford to decline Henry's invitation. If she went with him to the picnic, she wouldn't have to attend with Ebbie and Andre, and she'd also be able to observe the couple together, and make sure Andre was honoring his word. And by dating someone else, she'd also make clear to Andre that a romantic involvement between the two of them was out of the question. She reveled at the prospect of driving *that* particular message home. Yes, Henry's invitation was perfect.

Stephanie noted his anxious expression and smiled. "Why, Mr. Robillard, I'd be honored to accompany you on Saturday."

Henry grinned and kissed her hand. . . .

That night, Stephanie was rocking Sarah in the nursery when Andre burst in. "You are attending the picnic with Henry?"

"Shhh!" Stephanie scolded, raising her forefinger to her lips. "You'll awaken Sarah."

He sat down on the chair next to her and repeated fiercely, "You are going with Henry?"

Stephanie gulped. The man sitting beside her radiated intensity, from the fire burning in his blue eyes to the menace oozing from every pore of his taut, muscled body. The fact that he was less than perfectly groomed, and smelled of tobacco and brandy, only added to his potent allure. He'd removed his jacket, vest, and cravat, and with his shirt partially unbuttoned and a rakish curl dangling over his forehead, he appeared earthy, sexy, and dangerous.

She raised her chin and struggled to keep her voice steady. "Yes, I am going out with Henry."

"*Mon Dieu!*" Scowling fearsomely, he got up and began to pace. "That is out of the question."

"Not at all," she retorted. "I'm a grown woman and

quite capable of making my own decisions, thank you.''

''You will have no chaperon—''

''So, big deal. What do you think this is, the nineteenth century?''

He eyed her askance. ''What century do *you* think it is?''

Stephanie shrugged.

''And why would you even want to go out with Robillard?''

''That's none of your business.''

He shot her a fuming look. ''You certainly don't mind thwarting *me* at every turn.''

''Well, perhaps I like Henry's manners a lot better than I like yours,'' she responded saucily.

He made a growling sound. ''Are you trying to make me jealous?''

''Be serious!'' she scoffed.

''I am serious.''

''Well, I couldn't care less if you're jealous, sir. Furthermore, you're a fine one to tell me I can't go to the picnic, when you're taking Ebbie—''

''At *your* insistence. For that matter, we'll have the children along, as well as Martha.''

''The children and Martha?'' Stephanie cried. ''But they weren't in our agreement at all—''

''What was the agreement?'' he cut in nastily.

''That you take Ebbie out alone.''

Appearing smug, he crossed his arms over his chest. ''I recall no such agreement.''

Stephanie could feel her blood pressure surging. ''Oh, you sneaky rascal! I wanted you to take Ebbie out alone! This way, you're sacrificing nothing. Not with Martha and five children along—''

''And you, Stephanie,'' he finished obdurately. ''You're forgetting that we expect you to accompany us, as well.''

''Well, you can expect until you turn to stone, Mr. Goddard.''

''Has it occurred to you that your help may be required with the youngsters?'' he inquired coldly. ''I have not granted you the day off, madame.''

''Oh, of all the . . .'' Stephanie churned in frustration,

then smiled triumphantly as inspiration dawned. "I know. Henry and I will be happy to take the children, so you and Ebbie can be alone."

"That's not what I had in mind," he snarled, thrusting his fingers through his hair.

"Obviously," she taunted back. "You had in mind thwarting me—and it's not going to work."

"Why are you being so difficult?" he demanded.

"Why? You're really romancing Ebbie, aren't you?"

"I have no intention of romancing her."

"Then you're a lying cad!" she declared, blinking rapidly. "Damn it, I paid your price, and you promised me you would take Ebbie out—"

"Take her out I shall. And you will accompany us like a good girl—"

"A good . . . !" Feeling the baby squirm against her, Stephanie lowered her voice. "I will do nothing of the kind, and you will leave this room immediately before you awaken Sarah."

Far from doing her bidding, he leaned close to her, so close that she could feel the heat of his anger, smell his scent, so close there was no escaping the fire burning in his eyes.

"You're very agitated, Stephanie," he murmured. "Near tears, I'd say. What can be the matter? Haven't you realized yet that it will be much more fun if you stop playing these silly games with Henry and simply give in to me?"

"You—go to hell!" she whispered savagely. "And it will be one *cold day in hell* before you finagle any more kisses from me!"

Stephanie hadn't meant for her words to be an invitation, but Andre's sudden, ruthless smile left no doubt as to how he interpreted them. Before she could even gasp, he leaned over and briefly, passionately claimed her lips.

Leaving her trembling, he turned and strode from the room.

Chapter 22

Friday afternoon found Ebbie and Stephanie being
driven away from Mrs. Hodge's house with three new
gowns packed in the boot of the barouche. Both women
were exhausted yet exuberant following Stephanie's fitting
at the dressmaker's. Earlier, they'd shopped, and Stephanie
had spent most of her first wages on jewelry to wear on
Saturday, as well as on a couple of everyday blouses and a
skirt.

"Oh, I simply love your new lavender coatdress with the
open collar and lace trim," Ebbie declared. "My dear, you
simply must wear it to the picnic!"

"It is quite lovely," Stephanie agreed.

"And I adore the hat Mrs. Hodge picked out for you—
the high-brimmed one with the ribbon streamers."

Stephanie touched one of the small silk flowers on the
quaint silk bonnet she wore. "Yes, it certainly beats this
one—though, of course, I'm grateful you found it for me
in the attic."

"Well, you're fixed up quite smartly now. I must help
you dress tomorrow—"

"I must help you."

Ebbie waved her off. "Oh, I need no assistance."

"On the contrary, I want to fix your hair. Furthermore, I
wish you'd wear something besides black—"

"My dear, we've been over this before."

"But you're going out with Andre!"

Primly, Ebbie responded, "If Andre didn't like what I wear, I'm sure he would say so."

Rolling her eyes, Stephanie fell silent. A moment later the carriage lurched to a stop.

"Here we are!" announced Ebbie.

Stephanie stared at a cozy cottage with a railed gallery where late-blooming jasmine curled. "Why are we stopping?"

Ebbie pulled a piece of parchment from her reticule. "This is the Episcopal rectory. We're stopping to give Reverend Dearborn the quartet's repertoire for tomorrow."

"Ah, yes—I recall your mentioning that."

Willie assisted the two ladies out of the carriage, and they strolled through the yard and up the steps. Their knock was answered by Dearborn; his eyes lit with pleasure at the sight of Ebbie, then he smiled at Stephanie.

"Why, ladies, this is a pleasure."

"Peter, it's always a joy to see you," Ebbie replied, shaking his hand.

Dearborn ushered them inside a ponderously decorated parlor, complete with wrought-iron chandeliers and a black marble fireplace. Stephanie stared at a rococo revival settee festooned with fringed throw pillows and fussy antimacassars, and upholstered with enough burgundy roses to fill the Harmony House garden. The dark walls were decorated with religious prints, and everywhere were displayed pots of blooming flowers. Fussy velvet bows were tied around many of the containers, and the room had the creepy feel of a funeral parlor.

"How lovely," Stephanie murmured, toying nervously with the collar of her dress.

"Won't you have a seat?" Dearborn offered, gesturing at the settee.

"Only for a moment," answered Ebbie. "We dropped by, as promised, to give you a list of the quartet's repertoire."

Dearborn took the list and scanned it as the three sat down. "Schubert, Brahms, Tchaikovsky . . . why this sounds marvelous! The townsfolk will feel so blessed."

They'll wish they had stayed home with a bad case of

food poisoning, Stephanie mused ruefully, although she was too polite to comment.

"Yes, and it's too bad you can't join us for the Schumann quintet," Ebbie continued to Peter. "I think another violin would sound wonderful."

He sighed. "I would enjoy that, dear, but duty calls . . . that and my—er—other obligations."

Ebbie nodded sadly.

Sensing an awkward undercurrent in the room, Stephanie asked, "Well, Reverend, how are the plans for the picnic coming along?"

"Oh, just splendidly. We're expecting a very good turn-out—the Methodists, Baptists, and Presbyterians will all be joining in . . ."

Dearborn's voice trailed off at the sounds of a woman's faltering soprano out in the hallway. Stephanie grimaced, listening to an off-key rendition of Foster's "Under the Willow She's Sleeping." She glanced at Ebbie, who responded with a long-suffering look.

A moment later an elderly woman waltzed into the room. Observing her, Stephanie clenched her jaw to keep her mouth from falling open. Appearing to be in her early seventies, the woman had flowing silver hair, was dressed in a lacy white nightgown and matching wrapper, wore several large blue satin ribbons in her hair, and carried a large tin watering can. As Stephanie and Ebbie looked on in amazement, she went from pot to pot sprinkling water on the blooms and trolling away in her quavery voice.

Meanwhile, poor Dearborn had flushed scarlet. "Er-Mother?"

His only response was a croaky chorus of, " 'Fair, fair with golden hair . . . Under the willow she's sleeping,' " as the woman continued her rounds.

Dearborn turned apologetically to his guests. "I'm sorry, ladies."

Leaning toward Stephanie, Ebbie confided, "That is the reverend's mother. She's quite hard of hearing."

And short a few marbles, as well, Stephanie thought.

The old woman crept about toward the settee, only to recoil as she spotted the visitors. Her gaze darted from Stephanie and Ebbie to Peter. Stephanie attempted to smile at the woman, then froze at the sight of her eyes—which were large, light blue, and gleaming with madness.

"Son, we have visitors!" she shouted.

"Yes, Mother, I know."

"We must offer them tea."

"I've done so, Mother."

Ebbie waved gaily to the woman. "Hello, Mother Dearborn!"

The old woman's gaze darted suspiciously to Stephanie. "Who is she?"

"A dear friend who's come to Harmony House to help me with the children."

The old woman snorted. "Then you'd best hide your silver in the cellar, missy. You can't trust hired help these days. She's likely a scalawag or a carpetbagger, to boot."

"Oh, no, Mother Dearborn, she's from Jackson," Ebbie replied earnestly.

The old woman harrumped.

"How is the General?" Ebbie continued.

The old woman preened with pleasure, adjusting a ribbon in her hair. "Oh, my darling Milton will be coming to fetch me soon, after he kicks that scoundrel Sherman out of South Carolina. But there's been another delay—the General's horse has the colic—"

"I'm so sorry."

"You know how touchy these Thoroughbreds are," the old woman confided. "Always getting the wind. And they do need the General so badly at the Citadel. Why, they're under siege, the last I heard." She fluffed her hair. "So, I must wait and write my letters."

"You're so noble and self-sacrificing," commented Ebbie.

She brightened. "Well, I must finish my watering."

And she continued to waltz about the room, singing her maudlin song. Once she had anointed all the flowers, Stephanie was stunned to watch the woman sprinkle water over the upholstered roses on the arms of the settee. Stephanie glanced at Peter to see him groaning and burying his face in his hands—then she was further amazed when his mother waltzed into place before her and watered the flowers on her hat!

Face dripping, Stephanie was too perplexed to respond. Ebbie also appeared dumbstruck, and poor Peter mortified.

"Mother, please!" he implored, rushing to her side and grabbing the watering can.

At once the old lady snatched it back. "All done now, sonny boy."

And, as the others watched in stupefied silence, Mother Dearborn glided out of the room, singing another chorus of " 'Fair, fair, with golden hair . . . ' "

At last Stephanie and Ebbie glanced at each other, only to struggle to contain their laughter. Dearborn still appeared stricken as he dabbed at Stephanie's hat with his handkerchief. "Mrs. Sergeant, I'm so sorry. Your poor hat—"

"Has seen much better days," Stephanie finished, pulling it off and shaking off the moisture.

"Well, I just don't know what to say," fretted Dearborn.

Ebbie reached upward to clutch his hands. "Peter, dear, we quite understand."

He heaved a great sigh and smiled back at Ebbie. "You're a saint." With a hasty glance at Stephanie, he added, "You, too, Madame Sergeant."

Once they were in the carriage being driven away, Stephanie glanced askance at Ebbie. "About Mrs. Dearborn . . ."

"She's quite mad," finished Ebbie.

"You noticed, too, eh?" Stephanie asked, and both women burst out laughing.

Ebbie touched Stephanie's hand. "We're being terrible."

"Perhaps, but you know she really was a breath of fresh air. And she seems happy enough."

"Yes, but poor Peter."

"He can't have much of a life being responsible for her, can he?"

"No," Ebbie confirmed heavily. "He never knows when she may go wandering off, and he hasn't the heart to put her in an asylum—"

"Like the General?" Stephanie suggested wisely.

Ebbie nodded. "So you guessed that the General isn't really at the Citadel, but is locked away at the Charleston Hospital for the Mentally Infirm?"

"It wasn't much of a leap that he must be committed somewhere."

"I feel so sorry for Peter," Ebbie continued. "He has a housekeeper who watches his mother during the day, but otherwise—well, the poor man is under quite a burden."

"You know, I think he likes you," Stephanie remarked.

"I beg your pardon?" Ebbie asked, tensing.

"You mean you didn't see the way he lit up when he spotted you on the porch? And I can't help but notice how comfortable the two of you are together."

Ebbie nervously tugged at her gloves. "Well, we've been friends for years. And I'm very active in the church and in our prayer circle."

Stephanie's eyes widened. "That's what it was on his face—religious zeal!"

Ebbie giggled. "Stephanie, you're wicked! Besides, with Peter's mother . . ."

Nodding, Stephanie fell thoughtfully silent. "This may sound odd, but in a way I envy Mother Dearborn."

"You envy her?" Ebbie asked, surprised.

"She was just—so unpredictable and refreshing. Sometimes I feel as if my life is so ordered, so regimented, that I've lost all sense of fun, spontaneity, creativity. Even with my coming to Harmony House, I feel I have a mission to perform, then it's back to my old life . . . I hope."

Ebbie slanted her a chiding glance. "I wish you wouldn't say such things."

"I'm sorry." She squeezed Ebbie's hand. "But to return to the subject at hand, take a child, for instance. The other day, I helped Gwen and Amy have a tea party, and Amy took a tiny cup of tea to the dog. It was so funny—the dog just stared at it, looking very confused. An adult would surely know that a dog has no use for a cup of tea, but children don't have those preconceived notions. That's why they're always doing quirky things that so amuse us."

"What is your point?" asked Ebbie.

"Well, it never would have occurred to me to water the

flowers on the sofa, much less on anyone's hat. And that makes me kind of sad, as if I've lost something.''

Ebbie could only regard Stephanie in consternation.

That night when Stephanie went to bed, she felt an object beneath her pillow. Moving the pillow aside, she was astonished to see a book lying there. The handsome, slim leather volume was Elizabeth Barrett Browning's *Sonnets from the Portuguese.* Opening it, she found a man's bold script on the flyleaf, and the message, ''Forget me not. A.''

Forget me not. Stephanie had to admit the sentiment was touchingly romantic. Andre's charm could be devastating. Was this another peace offering, following his fit of temper over her planned outing with Henry?

If so, could he read her mind? For how could he have known that the sonnets were a favorite of hers from her college British lit course, and that the poems had brought her much comfort following Jim's death?

Stephanie closed the volume and pressed it to her bosom. Having this precious gift made her feel more at home here than she'd felt since she'd arrived. . . . and made her feel closer to Andre than she wanted to. Even the fact that he had placed the book beneath her pillow, touching the very bed where she slept, warmed her rather than causing affront. It was far easier to think of him as a cad than to realize he possessed this level of sensitivity. And how ironic that she'd found his gift now, mere hours after she'd remarked to Ebbie on the lack of spontaneity in her own life. Andre was nothing if not spontaneous.

Oh, he could be treacherous, storming and blustering one moment, cajoling the next. She could handle his tempers, but when he charmed her like this . . . there she *was* vulnerable.

Forget me not. Whatever the outcome of her adventure here, how would she *ever* forget him?

Chapter 23

Late the following morning, Stephanie, garbed in underclothes and a heavy wrapper, was in Ebbie's room putting the final touches on her coiffure. "There, you look divine. Andre will be charmed."

Sitting in front of Stephanie, wearing a black silk dress, Ebbie peered into the dressing-table mirror, studying the curls arranged about her face, then turning to view the length of her hair, which was gathered with a turquoise ribbon at her nape.

"I've never worn my hair quite this way before," she fretted.

"Well, you should," Stephanie declared. "You have a lovely oval face, and those ringlets are the perfect highlight." She turned to a nearby chair draped with accessories. "Now for the finishing touches."

Stephanie arranged a turquoise shawl about Ebbie's shoulders and placed a strand of multicolored beads around her neck. "There, you look much more vibrant—"

"But I feel a traitor for brightening up my black—"

"Well, enjoy your black while you can," advised Stephanie, "for I'm determined to see you shedding it."

Ebbie chuckled. "Stephanie, you're a martinet! And you really must go dress now. I realize Andre and I are leaving early, since he wants to take the pony out to the bluff for the children to ride, but if you don't watch out, you'll still be in your nightclothes when Henry calls for you."

Stephanie nodded. "Are you excited about the outing with Andre?"

Ebbie nervously adjusted her beads. "Of course I am."

Stephanie hesitated a moment. "Ebbie, have you thought about, well, trying to entice his interest more?"

"What do you mean?"

"Well, haven't you said you hope you and Andre will eventually marry?"

"Yes."

"Then you must get your message across to him." Stephanie picked up a perfume bottle and dabbed Ebbie's temples. "And here's a start."

Ebbie smiled.

"You could also try some feminine wiles."

"Indeed?" Ebbie appeared shocked.

"Yes. I'll demonstrate." Stephanie backed away and assumed a tragic pose. Pressing the back of her hand to her forehead, she began playacting. " 'Oh, Andre, darling, I believe I've lost my handkerchief, and I do feel a monstrous sneeze coming on.' "

Ebbie burst out laughing. "Stephanie, really!"

"Or try this." Stephanie wavered on her feet and went bug-eyed. " 'Oh, my dear Andre, I feel faint. May I hang on to big, strong old you?' "

Ebbie was doubled over with mirth. "Stephanie, you silly goose! I can't believe you'd suggest I stoop to such tactics."

"Why not? Men love to feel needed, to come to the aid of a damsel in distress. Haven't such methods worked quite well for the female gender ever since the dawn of time?"

"Well, if I can't win a beau unless I condescend to playing the simpering Southern belle, I'm just not interested," Ebbie declared primly.

Stephanie felt troubled. "Ebbie, don't you want to win over Andre?"

Ebbie turned away. "Certainly I do."

Yet Stephanie felt far from reassured. Stepping closer and gazing into the mirror, she studied Ebbie's image and again saw the sadness reflected in her dark eyes. Though she put on a good front, was Ebbie disheartened because she was secretly aware of the tremendous challenge she was up against with the rogue Andre?

An hour later, Stephanie opened the front door to see Henry Robillard standing on the porch, looking dashing in his white suit and hat. "Good day, Henry."

Grinning, he removed his hat and perused Stephanie in her lavender muslin coatdress with striped sleeves, enticingly low neckline, full bustle, and lace trim, pearl jewelry, and stylish ribboned hat. "Mrs. Sergeant, you look divine. I'll be the envy of every gentleman at the picnic."

Hiding a secret smile, Stephanie stepped out onto the porch with a picnic basket in hand. "You exaggerate, I'm sure, Mr. Robillard."

He took her basket with one hand and offered her his free arm. "Not at all. And what have we in the basket?"

"Chess pie—an old family recipe."

"My mouth is watering already."

Stephanie laughed.

Escorting her down the steps, he cleared his throat and added, "I hope you don't mind, but I've brought along my spinster aunt. I didn't feel it would be proper for us to go out unchaperoned—at least not our first time."

Stephanie glanced ahead to view in the buggy a little old lady in burgundy silk, with a matching, feathered bonnet on her head. "Why, Mr. Robillard, I assure you I'd be charmed to meet your aunt. And how kind of you to consider my reputation."

"Well, actually," he admitted sheepishly, "Andre threatened to call me out if I took you to the picnic unescorted."

"He . . . *what*?" She stopped in her tracks.

"But I'm sure you'll like Aunt Katie," he added hastily.

"Oh, of course I will," she muttered.

Henry beamed and led her to the buggy, placing her basket in the boot and assisting her inside.

At once the elderly woman, whose lined, pixie face showed traces of a youthful beauty, thrust her gloved hand into Stephanie's. "Hello, dear, I'm Miss Katie Banks, this fine lad's aunt. And you're Stephanie, are you?"

"Yes, I am."

"My Henry has been talking about you all week."

"Aunt, please," Henry pleaded, red-faced.

"Oh, hush," she scolded, turning back to Stephanie. "You any kin to the Sargents of Gloucester?"

Stephanie quickly remembered her Natchez history. "No, I believe their name is spelled differently from mine."

The woman nodded. "A pure shame about poor George Washington Sargent, killed by a Yankee marauder while standing at his own back door. Pretty much ruined his day, I'd say, and that was the end of the Sargents hereabouts. Good to have another amongst us."

"Thank you," Stephanie replied, enjoying the woman's droll remarks.

By now Henry had climbed in beside Stephanie and was working the reins. "Now, Aunt Katie, please don't talk Stephanie's ear off with Natchez history. You'll scare her away."

As Stephanie giggled, Katie waved at her nephew with a lace hankie. "Bah! She doesn't look like a timid woman to me."

"Indeed I'm not," agreed Stephanie.

"Now, tell me all about yourself," Katie ordered.

"Aunt, have some pity on Mrs. Sergeant," implored Henry.

"Don't worry, Henry, it'll be my pleasure," Stephanie reassured him. She proceeded to give Katie an account of the same contrived background she'd furnished to Andre and his family, while the old lady listened with interest.

"I'm just so glad to see my Henry taking you out," Katie pronounced afterward. " 'Bout time he settled down with a respectable widow lady—"

"Aunt," cut in Henry, rolling his eyes, "this is only my first outing with Madame Sergeant. You'll send her running away with thoughts that you've already married us off!"

"Oh, fiddle," scoffed Katie. "I'm not scaring you, am I, my girl?"

"No, indeed."

"Now drive this buggy and let us women talk!" ordered Katie.

With a groan, Henry complied, while Stephanie again fought laughter.

"Now as I was saying, I want my boy settled," Katie continued. "He's been my responsibility ever since his dear parents passed on. Andre is a frightful influence on him—too many excursions to Under-the-Hill and the racetrack."

Henry shot his aunt a menacing look, which she ignored.

"Andre Goddard is one devil of a charmer, all right." Katie whispered at Stephanie's ear. "You've heard about his mistress, of course?"

Eyes wide, Stephanie shook her head. "He has a mistress?"

"Had one."

"Oh!"

Behind her hand, Katie confided, "That hussy Daphne Ravel came to town last winter hunting for a husband, and didn't mind giving out samples to the gentlemen, if you know what I mean. Andre set her up way out on Clifton Street, not far from Cemetery Road, with poor Linnea barely in her grave nearby."

"No!" gasped Stephanie, fuming as she recalled Andre's outrageous proposal to her only days earlier.

"Of course no one received the trashy little trollop," Katie continued grimly. "It's well-known her aunt is a madam in a New Orleans brothel. Can't blame Andre for not making another dash to the altar—he had his children to consider, after all."

"What happened?" Stephanie asked.

Katie grinned. "When the little Jezebel couldn't persuade Andre to wed her, she ran off with a tenor from a showboat. Showed him up but good, didn't she?"

Despite herself, Stephanie chuckled.

As the women moved apart, Henry glowered at his aunt. "What are you two gossiping about?"

Katie tapped his arm. "Just drive. I was only warning Stephanie about Andre." She winked at Stephanie. "You're not going to allow the scoundrel to beguile you, are you?"

"Certainly not."

"She is out with me, is she not?" added Henry sourly.

"Yes, indeed." Katie patted Stephanie's hand. "I can tell

you're one smart girl, and you'll never join the ranks of poor Ebbie Rice.''

Stephanie stiffened. ''I'm Ebbie's friend, you know.''

''Of course you are,'' Katie sympathized. ''Ebbie's a sweetheart, and I'd never think ill of her. But the fact is, the whole town knows she's in love with that rake Andre, and making a fool of herself over him. If that poor girl doesn't watch herself, she'll die of a broken heart and join the ranks of Miss Percy, the resident ghost at Dunleith.''

Stephanie was amazed at Katie's wisdom, and she already liked this charming, forthright lady. ''Andre has taken Ebbie to the picnic today,'' she pointed out, ''and she *is* above reproach as a prospective wife. Who knows? Maybe he'll come around and marry her.''

Katie hooted a laugh. ''And the South shall rise again, my girl. The South shall rise again!''

Chapter 24

$\sim$ ✺ $\sim$

Out on the Old Spanish Parade Grounds, Andre stood with Ebbie amid a throng of humanity. The historic ground, dating back to the days of the town's founding, was one of his favorite spots. Huge, mossy oaks sheltered the clearing, with the town proper stretching to the east of the park and the bluff facing the west. Beneath the bluff flowed the wide, silvery river; roustabouts could be seen loading cotton onto a sternwheeler at the landing Under-the-Hill.

Dozens of Natchez families milled about: ladies in their finest silk, satin, or muslin; men in Sunday suits; gaily dressed children who darted about, rolling hoops or tossing balls. The air rang with laughter and happy conversation; the aromas of fried chicken, boiled hams, and other delectables wafted over to them from the long picnic tables where numerous baskets had been laid out.

Not far from the couple, the coachman, Willie, was giving Shetland pony rides to a long line of children, including Andre's, who awaited their turns. Martha stood supervising Andre's brood; Sarah had remained at home with Lilac.

But where were Stephanie and Henry?

"Andre, it was so kind of you to bring us all out here today," Ebbie remarked with a quavery smile.

Distracted, he turned to her. "My pleasure, dear. It's good to see the community coming together this way. And a joy to see you stepping out and dressing more colorfully."

Ebbie self-consciously adjusted her shawl. "Once again, Stephanie insisted I spice up my outfit."

"Good for Stephanie," he muttered.

She bit her lip. "You look perturbed, Andre. Did I say something wrong?"

"Oh, no," he quickly reassured her, glancing about. "I was just wondering where the devil she and Henry are."

"I'm sure they'll be along soon." She brightened. "You're kind to worry about her. You're so devoted to us all."

He laughed. "My dear, you think far too highly of me. I'm really quite a blackguard."

Ebbie appeared stunned. "Why, Andre, whatever would possess you to say such a thing about yourself? I'll not hear that kind of talk. I just won't!"

He grinned sheepishly, while inwardly feeling bemused. Ebbie was such a good person, like Linnea, and he'd been thoroughly self-absorbed over the last year, giving her feelings, her future, her very life, little thought. The woman refused ever to think ill of him—indeed, she placed him on a pedestal—and it made him even more uneasy. For what if Stephanie were right and Ebbie was in love with him? He shuddered at the possibility. Had Stephanie no idea of the dangerous game she could be playing in trying to force the two of them together?

He sighed. His instincts argued that Ebbie couldn't really be enamored of him, but, assuming she was, what would be the greater cruelty—marrying her or spurning her?

"Oh, look, there Stephanie is now!"

At the sound of Ebbie's voice, Andre pivoted to spy Henry in the distance, helping Stephanie and his aunt out of his buggy. "Yes, there she is," he muttered. "If you'll keep an eye on the children, I'll go say hello."

"Of course, Andre." She craned her neck in another direction and waved. "Oh, I think I see Mr. Wister and Mr. Fortier approaching."

Andre was just striding away when he all but collided with Elizabeth Stanton, who looked very much the Southern belle in a full-skirted dress of white muslin sprigged with tiny blue flowers, and a wide hat garnished with numerous matching silk blooms.

"Why, Andre, you old rascal, how good to see you

again,'' she greeted, grabbing his arm. ''You simply must come say hello to my sisters. And several ladies from the Magnolia Art League are just dying to hear a preview of your January lecture.''

Andre could only groan as Elizabeth led him away. . . .

Katie was talking nonstop as the threesome moved onto the parade grounds, while Stephanie glanced about her in awe.

''This area is where the old Spanish fort used to stand,'' Katie explained, ''and that's Rosalie over there.'' She pointed at a redbrick, pillared mansion to the south. ''General Grant slept there during the war—the blackguard. The place was built over fifty years ago by Peter Little. Peter married Eliza Low when she was an orphaned child and immediately sent her East to be educated properly. What poor Peter didn't know was that Lorenzo Dow had already fired that child's soul with the old time religion. Years later when he and Eliza began their marriage in earnest, Peter had to build the parsonage yonder''—she pointed at a smaller bungalow to the east—''to accommodate all the circuit riders Eliza kept taking in. Of course, they're both dead and gone now.''

At Katie's account, Stephanie shook her head and smiled at Henry, who winked back, raising one of two picnic baskets he carried. ''If you'll excuse me, ladies, I'll place our baskets on a table. And I think I see Rufus Learned over there. I've been meaning to have a word with him—''

''Take your time, nephew,'' put in Katie. ''I'll make the rounds with Stephanie.''

As Katie led her away, Stephanie continued to gape in amazement. Although some of the surrounding landmarks, such as Rosalie, were familiar, the people astounded her. She was enchanted by the Natchez Old Guard in their elegant, old-fashioned attire—the ladies with their bustles, feathers, fans, and jewelry; the men with their lacy shirtfronts, silk top hats, and jeweled walking sticks; the little girls in their pinafores and lacy pantaloons; the boys in their knee pants, jackets, and straw hats. The grand scene fascinated her, as did Katie's stories, and she felt as if she were truly living a moment of history, experiencing a way of life she had only dreamed about before. She was in the Old South, all right.

"Now where shall we begin?" Katie was musing aloud. She pointed at a gazebo near the edge of the bluff. "See that fine-looking gentleman standing yonder on the steps? That's Colonel Balfour, one of our finest officers during the war. He's good friends with the Waverlys, who are hosting a reception for the Jefferson Davises tomorrow when they pass through."

"Really?" asked Stephanie, greatly intrigued.

"Now Jeff Davis and Varina Howell, theirs was one grand romance," Katie related with an ecstatic sigh. "We're invited to the gathering, of course, and you must come along and meet them."

"Why, it sounds charming," she agreed.

All at once, Katie gave a cry of delight as an elderly couple in black paused before them. "Ah, Mr. and Mrs. Junkin, how good to see you. I want you to meet my new friend, Mrs. Stephanie Sergeant."

Mrs. Junkin offered a gloved hand. "How do you do, dear?"

"Fine, thank you," Stephanie replied, shaking her hand, then turning to shake hands with her husband.

Proudly touching Stephanie's arm, Katie announced, "Mrs. Sergeant is a widow from Atlanta who has just joined the Goddard household as a companion to Ebbie Rice."

Mrs. Junkin nodded. "How nice. Welcome to Natchez."

"Thank you."

Behind her hand, Katie confided to the couple, "Stephanie is my Henry's new flame, and I expect her to receive *all* the right invitations."

"Why, of course," declared Mrs. Junkin.

"We must be on our rounds, then," Katie continued brightly. "See you folks later."

As Katie again tugged her off, Stephanie was shaking her head. "Katie, you astound me. Henry's new flame, indeed! And all the right invitations. You're some operator."

The old woman scowled. "An operator? What is that?"

Stephanie thought for a moment. "A mover and shaker."

Katie chortled. "That I am, my dear. That I am. Now step lively. We've many others to meet."

Continuing to stroll with her new friend, Stephanie craned her neck and spotted Andre, Ebbie, and the children in the distance. Although the youngsters were happily at play or awaiting pony rides, she was disappointed to note that Andre and Ebbie stood far apart; Ebbie was visiting with Mr. Wister and Mr. Fortier while Andre flirted with a rapt Elizabeth Stanton and two other young women whom Stephanie assumed must be her sisters.

The rogue! Remembering Katie's appalling story about his former mistress, she felt her blood boiling. The event had only just begun, and already the cad had deserted Ebbie. Even as she glared at him, he glanced her way, seeming to sense her scrutiny. She turned hastily back to Katie.

Katie pointed ahead. "Come along, now. I want you to meet my dear friends, the Joseph Carpenters. Real pillars of our community. And I see the Allison Fosters over there, as well. A lovely home, their Cottage Gardens . . ."

True to her word, Katie introduced "Henry's new lady" to the scions of Natchez society, keeping up a running commentary as they went along. Stephanie was thrilled to be graciously greeted by all, and amazed to meet members of families she'd only read about in history books: the Davises of Melrose; the Baldwins of Dunleith; the Boyds of Arlington; the Marshalls of Lansdowne.

When the Reverend Dearborn called everyone to come eat, Henry joined them at an oilcloth-draped table. After Dearborn intoned the grace, Henry smiled apologetically at Stephanie. "Sorry, dear, I didn't mean to desert you. Guess Rufus and I got carried away discussing the order for his factory."

"Oh, I'm fine. Your aunt has kept me amply entertained."

As they began their meal of fried chicken, potato salad, and biscuits, Stephanie was dismayed to watch Ebbie and her "misters" take seats in a small gazebo at the edge of the bluff, then draw out and begin tuning their instruments. Gazing about, she spotted Andre at a far table, surrounded by beautiful, tittering females—including the Stanton sisters. Nearby, Martha was serving the children.

Even as Stephanie seethed over this frustrating turn, the musicians began a squeaky version of the Brahms quartet.

"My land, bring me my smelling salts!" declared Katie, raising a hand to her brow. "I swear I shall swoon if we have to listen to that abominable quartet again!"

"Now, aunt," implored Henry, "be charitable."

She eyed him askance. "Henry, those ninnies perform everywhere we go, totally oblivious to the fact that they have no more musical sense than poor Alice Dearborn has a hold on reality." Glancing at Stephanie she added, "I'm sorry, dear. I know Ebbie is your friend—"

"Well, I agree the quartet could use some help—"

"Help?" She waved a hand. "They all need to be put out of their misery!"

Stephanie stifled a laugh.

Katie gazed sternly at Henry. "Nephew, when I die, lock them up, and don't let them anywhere near my funeral. If Saint Peter should ever hear that infernal racket, he'll lock the Pearly Gates and it'll be the devil's pitchfork for me for sure!"

Chapter 25

❧⌒⌒✑⌒✑

Following the meal and concert, there were religious speeches by the various Natchez clergy, all aimed at bringing the community closer together. Several times during the oration, Stephanie caught Andre staring at her from across the way. The rascal was still surrounded by adoring belles, while Ebbie was seated some distance away with her "misters."

Once the sermons ended, Stephanie excused herself and went in search of Ebbie. She caught up with her by the trees at the edge of the clearing.

"Ebbie, why aren't you with Andre?"

Appearing embarrassed, Ebbie avoided Stephanie's eye. "Should I be?"

"You came here with him."

She toyed with the ties on her reticule. "Yes, of course I did, but I did not put a leash around the man's neck. Besides, I have been busy performing with my misters. As for Andre, he is very friendly and always visits with everyone whenever we attend a social."

Stephanie gazed heavenward. "Ebbie, he's been flirting with every female here!"

Ebbie laughed. "Oh, my dear, I'm sure you exaggerate."

Stephanie was about to comment further when the Reverend Dearborn stepped up. "Well, hello, Mrs. Sergeant. Ebbie."

"Reverend," Stephanie greeted. "That was one fine sermon."

"Thank you." He smiled at Ebbie. "And your music was simply divine."

Stephanie glanced away to hide an incredulous expression.

"Why, thank you, Peter," Ebbie replied, touching his arm. "Like Stephanie, I too was so intrigued by your discourse on the meek inheriting the earth. We must discuss the Sermon on the Mount more at our next prayer circle."

"We must," he concurred. "Actually, Bishop Green inspired my subject matter . . ."

Stephanie slipped away, leaving the two to their religious discussion. She wondered why Ebbie seemed so at home around Peter Dearborn and the men in her quartet, yet so awkward around Andre. That was an easy one to answer, she quickly decided. Andre was the one Ebbie really loved, the one who kept her emotions off-kilter—much as he did with Stephanie.

Well, the meek may inherit the earth, she thought, almost muttering to herself, *but Ebbie is never going to win over Andre unless she cleans up her act. And if Reverend Dearborn thinks that quartet plays divine music, then he's as nutty as his mother!*

She was heading back toward Katie and Henry when abruptly her arm was seized and she was pulled into the woods—to face a grinning Andre.

"Talking to yourself, Stephanie?" he teased. "Does Henry bore you so much?"

"You!" she cried, trying to pull her arm free. "You let me go this instant!"

But he firmly tugged her on, down a twisting, dappled trail, past scarlet sweet gum and golden elm. "On the contrary, we shall take a little constitutional, you and I."

Stephanie continued to argue and dig in her heels, to no avail. Finally, about twenty yards from the clearing, Andre released her arm.

She glowered. "Just what is the meaning of this abduction?"

He eyed her tenderly. "I missed you, Stephanie. God, you look so lovely in that pretty frock—like such a lady."

Although her heart raced, she set her arms akimbo and

faced him mutinously. "It's good of you to notice I'm a lady."

He slanted her a woebegone look. "Why are you so angry?"

"Why?" She gave a disbelieving laugh. "I'm afraid my reasons are too numerous to count, sir. But we can start with your threatening to call Henry out unless he brought along a chaperon today."

"That?" Grinning, Andre shook his head. "I did you a favor, Stephanie. Have you thought of the gossip if you arrived here unchaperoned? Even though Henry has got to be one of the dullest men I know—"

"He is not! He's perfectly affable."

"Oh, he can drawl, 'My, ma'am, you look charmin',' 'th the best of us, but beyond that, he hasn't got much use for women," Andre teased. "No staying power. Unlike myself—"

"Spare me the details of your uses for women."

He chuckled. "My, you are in a temper. My point is, I did you a favor by insisting Katie come along. Am I wrong?"

Stephanie restrained a guilty smile. "She is fascinating."

"That woman knows more about Natchez history than the Mississippi does."

Stephanie harrumphed. "Well, she certainly knows plenty about *your* history."

His gaze narrowed. "What do you mean by that?"

She flashed him a poisonous smile. "Have you so quickly forgotten dear Daphne?"

He uttered a blistering curse. "I'll strangle her!"

"Strangle who? Daphne?"

"No, Katie Banks!"

"For telling the truth?" Stephanie scoffed. "And it *is* the truth, isn't it, Andre?"

He was silent, glowering.

Contemptuously, she continued, "You are such a scamp. I can see now why you so quickly propositioned me, since your mistress jilted you, leaving the position conveniently vacant. Tell me, were there many before her?"

His eyes blazed with anger. "I was never unfaithful to my wife."

She laughed cynically. "Oh, yes, you're a real hero among men. You even set up your mistress out on Clifton Street—presumably so you could visit her and your wife's grave in the same afternoon."

Stephanie did not realize how cruel her words sounded until they had already spilled out. She watched Andre flinch and back away, his features white.

She stepped toward him and touched his arm. "I'm sorry."

He laughed bitterly. "God, you can be a shrew sometimes."

"I don't condone your actions, Andre," she replied, lifting her chin, "but my comment was . . . unseemly."

He hesitated, the anger fading slowly from his face. Then he stepped toward her and ran a fingertip teasingly along her jaw. She gasped.

"Does that hurt?" he asked.

Taken aback, she stammered, "Y-you mean when you touched me?"

He edged closer. "No, I mean, does your jaw hurt? You are clenching it so fiercely that surely you must be in pain. Is that what the thought of my being with another woman does to you?"

"No!" she denied.

He smiled. "No?"

Stephanie fought a smile, too. "Actually, I suppose I'm one of those people who has pretty much gone through life with a clenched jaw. At one point, my dentist scolded that if I didn't stop grinding down my enamel, he'd have to fit me with an appliance."

Andre appeared amazed. "*Mon Dieu!* That sounds serious!"

Stephanie had to laugh. Andre was so mystified that he was downright comical.

Her amusement encouraged him; he placed a warm hand at her waist. "If you spent your time kissing me, you wouldn't be able to clench your jaw."

"Oh!" Even as his words titillated her recklessly, she

pushed him away. "You are a shameless scoundrel."

"Now what have I done?" he cried.

"What haven't you done?"

"Stephanie, please—"

Heedless, she began striding away from him, glancing about in confusion. Unfortunately, the walk had disoriented her, and she wasn't sure how to get back to the clearing.

Over her shoulder, she called, "You're supposed to be attending this gathering with Ebbie, yet you flirt with every woman here, then you try to take me on—"

His wicked chuckle cut short her words. "Stephanie, I've been dying to take you on since the moment you arrived in Natchez."

"I've noticed!"

He caught her hand and pulled her toward him. "Sweetheart, you can have me, anytime."

She tugged free. "And you can go jump in the river."

She was hurrying away when he cried, "Stephanie, wait!"

Not recognizing the words as a warning, Stephanie stormed through a tangle of vines to find herself suddenly, terrifyingly tottering at the edge of the bluff, her shoes slipping in the red mud, the Mississippi a dizzying hundred feet below!

"Stephanie!"

She heard Andre shouting her name, then she was pulled back against him, crushed against the safety and strength of his hard body, cocooned between him and the smooth bark of a sycamore tree, looking up into his turbulent eyes. For a moment time stood still as her heart crashed in her chest, and she was conscious only of this moment, his scent and heat, her own ragged breathing, the whisper of the wind, the plaintive song of a cardinal.

"Darling, be careful," he whispered at last. "It's treacherous here."

All at once Stephanie could not breathe as the word "darling" sent a traitorous ache twisting inside her. "I know," she whispered helplessly. "Damn treacherous."

Suddenly, he was kissing her, and she him. For Stephanie, it was like spontaneous combustion, as if she were starved, and had waited forever for this moment. How could this man incite such fierce, uncontrollable urges in her?

She only knew he did, that as much as he maddened her, he still moved her and touched her as no man ever had before. She clung to him, letting his tongue have its wicked way with her. She was trembling, she wanted him so much. Her brush with danger only intensified her excitement. *He* was danger, and something wild and shocking inside her readily embraced the risk, forsaking her usual, safe existence.

His hot mouth slid down her throat. "Stephanie, darling . . . How I ache to be alone with you."

His tone left no doubt as to his intent, and wrenched Stephanie back to reality. Somehow she gathered the strength of will to press him away. Her anguished eyes met his confused countenance. "Andre, no."

"Why?"

"Because of Ebbie," she said miserably. "Andre, she's in love with you—"

"She is not."

"Damn it, she was all aglow after you asked her to the picnic."

He fell silent, appearing torn.

"And Katie has been telling me how the whole town knows she's in love with you. Yet you've forsaken her today, playing the Lothario."

He groaned. "Stephanie, you're trying to fan a spark that isn't there—"

"And you're not trying at all."

He waved a hand. "Should I give her false hope, set her up for heartache?"

"Why must you assume it won't work?"

He appeared incredulous. "How can you ask such a question after you just kissed me the way you did? Can you envision that kind of passion ever developing between Ebbie and me?"

"Is passion all you ever think about?" she countered. "My God, you hardly know me."

He smiled and touched a finger to the taut tip of her breast, tracing a circle around the small, turgid nipple visible through the heavy fabric of her dress. She winced help-lessly.

"I know you excite and fascinate me," he whispered in-tensely. "And I intend to get to know you much better."

Face crimson, Stephanie backed away from his touch. "This is not going anywhere, Andre. You must believe that."

"Damn it, what do you expect of me?"

"To make a real effort to court Ebbie."

"You can't be serious."

"I *am* serious."

"Have you given any thought to Ebbie's feelings in this?"

"That's precisely what I'm thinking of."

"And you still want me to court her?"

"Yes."

"And what if I do? What will you give me in return?"

She flushed deeply. "I won't become your mistress." She regarded him with pride. "Don't expect me to become an-other Daphne."

He whistled. "Very well." He placed his hands on her shoulders. "Now, my dear, hear *my* terms: For every minute I spend with Ebbie, you shall grant me equal time."

Stephanie's mind spun with his outrageous proposal and its various implications. "Equal time where?" she scoffed. "In your bed?"

"Wherever I choose," came the cocky reply.

"That's absurd!"

"*Whenever* I choose," he added adamantly.

Stephanie made a sound of frustration. "Andre, no, you're being unreasonable. I cannot possibly agree to what you ask—and especially if there are no ground rules."

He pulled her close. "There will be only one: I won't force myself on you. Otherwise, there will be no rules."

"Then forget it."

"Fine." He turned and started back toward the clearing.

She rushed after him, grabbing his arm. "Damn it, wait a minute!"

"Well?"

Exasperated, she exclaimed, "You hold all the cards!"

Maddeningly, he grinned. "So you've finally realized that? Have you also realized, dear Stephanie, that I intend to win?"

"So do I!" she blustered.

He actually appeared sympathetic. "You won't last long, poor dear."

"Don't bet on it."

"Do we have a deal then?"

She hesitated, scowling.

"Do we?"

"Yes," she hissed at last. "A devil's bargain."

He chuckled. "I'm glad you fully recognize your opponent. I suppose we can even start tomorrow, since John Waverly just invited us all to attend a reception at Auburn to honor Jefferson Davis."

"I know," she replied, straightening her cuffs. "Katie has already asked me to attend the gathering with her and Henry."

Something dangerous flashed in his eyes. "Has she?"

"Yes."

He glowered. "Then I shall ask Ebbie."

"Fine."

His gaze flicked over her. "But first you're mine."

"What?" she cried.

"Payment in advance, Stephanie."

"Payment in . . . But what if I pay up and you don't keep your promise?"

Crossing his arms over his chest, he appeared supremely confident. "You'll just have to trust me."

"Trust the devil, you mean."

"As I said, first you're mine. Do you accept or reject my terms?"

"*I accept.*"

"Good. Do you ride?"

"Just what do you mean by that crack?"

He grinned. "I thought we'd ride horses in the moonlight."

"How romantic."

Her anger only seemed to amuse him. "Meet me at the stable at midnight."

She glared.

Grinning, he touched her tight jaw. "And Stephanie . . . You can clench that pretty jaw all you want now, but you won't get away with it tonight. And *that*, my dear, is a promise."

Just the way he said it made her blush crimson again as he turned and strode away. . . .

Chapter 26

You belong to me at midnight . . .

Andre's possessive words haunted Stephanie for the remainder of the day, leaving her giddy with anticipation. Sneaking out of the house that night, she couldn't believe she was actually meeting him. Since she didn't own a riding habit or boots, she had dressed in a plain, full skirt and long-sleeved white blouse, and wore button-top shoes that would at least offer her ankles some protection from the stirrups. On her head was tied a wide-brimmed straw hat.

While outwardly she was prepared, inwardly she was a mess. She felt guilty, and disloyal toward Ebbie, for attending the rendezvous. But what choice did she have, when the scoundrel Andre had refused to continue taking Ebbie out unless she granted him equal time?

The problem was, that equal time was getting Stephanie in deep, deep trouble. She was a woman accustomed to being in full charge of her life, her emotions; but from the moment she'd met Andre Goddard, she'd been battling an out-of-control libido. Every moment she spent with the irrepressible rogue, every time he charmed her with a gift or a clever remark, every time he raked his devilish gaze over her or kissed her, she became more bewitched by him, caught deeper in his spell.

She had come across time as a matchmaker, yet now she seemed to be falling for the prospective groom! Where had everything gone so wrong? Somehow, she must keep Andre at arm's length until she could convince him Ebbie was the right woman for him. Yet she wasn't even certain she could convince herself anymore. Nor was she convinced—especially after learning about the scandalous Daphne—that he could ever become a proper husband for Ebbie. Sometimes, she wondered fatalistically if Ebbie was destined for tragedy no matter what she did, for the little spinster and Andre seemed the original odd couple. What if she was only making matters worse?

Perish the thought! Stephanie realized she had to operate on what she knew, and she knew only what Great-aunt Magnolia had told her, that she had a mission to perform, a mission to secure Ebbie's happiness. She had to go about it the only way she knew how—and that meant getting Andre and Ebbie together.

As Stephanie approached the stable, she spied a puddle of light spilling from the front window. She opened the crude door and stepped inside.

Appearing dapper and hard-muscled in his English riding suit, Andre stood beside two breathtaking horses—a magnificent brown Thoroughbred with a white star, a flowing black mane and tail; and a stunning Arabian with a coat of dappled cream, with a champagne-colored mane and tail. The brown was bridled and saddled, and Andre was adjusting its cinch; the Arabian wore only a bridle.

"Good evening," she called.

He turned and smiled. "Good evening to you."

"The horses are magnificent."

"Thank you." Andre stroked the gleaming flank of the brown. "This is Prince Albert. I bought him on my last trip to London, and I have papers tracing his bloodline back to the days of Queen Anne. I race him often, and he always beats out the competition at Pharsalia Track." He gestured toward two other horses in nearby stalls. "We also run the chestnut trotter over there and the gray Irish Thoroughbred."

She cleared her throat. "I do hope you're not planning a race tonight."

"No, only a ride in the moonlight." He strode toward the Arabian. "I thought of this little Arab mare, Empress, for you. She's spirited but hardly ungovernable.''

Stephanie moved over and stroked the mare's muzzle. The horse neighed, moving her head against Stephanie's hand. ''She seems friendly enough—and she's drop dead gorgeous.''

He raised a brow. '' 'Drop-dead gorgeous'? Don't believe I've heard that term before.''

Stephanie was tempted to reply, *You should have, for it suits you well*, but thought better of the rash impulse.

Andre gestured toward some tack on a wall. ''I was about to place a sidesaddle on her—''

''Don't you dare!'' cut in Stephanie.

He glanced dubiously at her attire. ''You wish to ride bareback?''

''No, I want a regular saddle, like yours. I've precious little riding experience, and I'm not about to ride sidesaddle and get pitched off the bluff in the darkness.''

His eyes glittered with amusement. ''We aren't going anywhere near the bluff.''

''Then into the nearest ditch.''

He dipped into an exaggerated bow. ''As you wish, madame. And I must say how I admire a woman who dares to defy convention, riding astride her horse.''

''I just aim to keep my neck intact.''

He moved a step closer and teased, ''Do you enjoy riding astride, Stephanie?''

She groaned. ''Saddle the horse, and let's get out of here.''

He touched her arm. ''A moment first. We have some unfinished business to discuss.''

''What?''

He shot her a chiding glance. ''Before we embark on our first adventure alone, is there something you wish to tell me?''

''Like what?''

''Like who you really are, and how you arrived at my home?''

She laughed in disbelief. ''Are we back to that again? I thought we'd already established that I'm exactly who I say I am.''

He made a clucking sound. "Stephanie, Stephanie. Are you certain that's how you want to leave it? Tell you what—confess the truth now, and there will be no dire consequences."

She harrumphed. "You're just hoping I'll divulge something really scandalous to justify *your* outrageous behavior."

With a self-deprecating chuckle, he reached out to toy with her collar. "Stephanie, you think of me as such a rascal."

"So I do," she readily agreed.

"Just because I want to know more about you?" he reproved.

She eyed him skeptically. "Setting aside the issue of your motives, let me respond this way: There's nothing more I can tell you now that you'd believe—or that would justify your acting like such a scamp."

He groaned. "Ah, woman, you torment me so."

"If my company offends you, I'll be happy to leave," she offered sweetly.

"Not a chance in hell."

He saddled her mare and within minutes they were off, trotting their horses beneath the oaks to the street, then riding south on Woodville Road. As Andre had promised, Stephanie liked the feel of her mare; there was spirit in her gait, but she was steady, restrained, trustworthy. Stephanie enjoyed the freedom of riding through the trees in the darkness, the powerful horse moving beneath her, the cool wind in her face—and, much as she hated to admit it, Andre by her side. The aura the night spun about them was so sensual—the rustle of the leaves, the scent of earth and dew, the moon glimmering overhead through the clouds.

"Where are we going?" she called to him.

"I thought I'd take you out to Elgin Plantation."

Stephanie paused, remembering her conversation with the Reverend Carlson back in the present. Hadn't he told her the plantation was haunted?

Shifting uneasily in her saddle, she cleared her throat. "Are—um—the owners expecting us?"

"I'm a friend of the family, but I did hear Elizabeth Stanton mention at the picnic that the younger Jenkinses are in Europe at the moment.''

"There could still be a caretaker about to shoot us for trespassing.''

Andre howled with laughter. "The things you fret about.''

They continued riding in silence. Stephanie watched silvery tree limbs draped with Spanish moss float past overhead, and listened to the hooting of owls, the sawing of cicadas. At a fork in the road, they continued east and rode on for more than a mile over gently rolling hills.

As they crested a rise, Stephanie shivered as a house seemed to materialize on a rise in the distance—it was a stately two-story plantation house with narrow columns spanning the front. Standing deserted, its galleries cloaked in shadows, its roof framed by tall trees and backlit by dark, silver-tipped clouds, the house reminded Stephanie eerily of the moment in the movie *Gone With the Wind* when Scarlett went home to discover that Tara was still standing.

"It's spooky,'' she murmured to Andre.

"Come on—don't be afraid.''

Trotting her mare toward the plantation entrance, Stephanie gasped as a funny light flickered near the gates. As she watched in awe, a specter seemed to take shape there—a silver-haired gentleman in a rocking chair, waving his hand at them. The presence seemed so natural, so at home, that initially Stephanie wasn't sure how to respond. Then, as abruptly as the phantom had appeared, it was gone!

"Are you all right?'' asked Andre.

Wary of telling him what she'd seen, she stammered, "I—I think so.''

Inside the gates, they trotted up the rise, halted their horses near the front steps of the house, and dismounted. Both horses blew and stamped as Andre tied the animals to the hitching post.

Stephanie gazed warily at the eerie house, half-afraid of seeing more ghosts, shivering as a shutter creaked in the wind. "Why did you bring me here?''

Andre took her hand. "To show you the Jenkinses' gardens.''

"Gardens?"

He gestured toward an area down the hill, on the other side of the road. "Dr. John Jenkins was quite a horticulturalist. Since his death in '55, his gardens have fallen into decay, but are still worth seeing."

Stephanie shuddered. "I still don't think we should have come here."

Andre wrapped an arm around her shoulders and chuckled. "Why not? When we have permission from the owner himself?"

She dug in her heels. "What do you mean? I thought the Jenkinses were away in Europe."

"John Jr. and Louise are," he replied. "But that was John Sr.'s ghost that just admitted us."

She jerked away from him. "My God!"

"You did not see him?" he teased. "He's quite a legend in these parts."

She gulped. "I did see him. But I assumed that you . . ."

"Come on, silly," he coaxed, taking her hand. "I'll protect you."

He led her down the hillside through a lavish formal area where camellias, gardenias, and azaleas were arranged about lacy summerhouses. Although the shrubs were choked with undergrowth, Stephanie could see the beauty of the original layout.

"Annis Jenkins loved growing flowers," Andre explained, "and John loved cultivating various fruits." He pointed ahead. "Yonder between the cedars are his old laboratory and greenhouse, his orchards."

"What happened to the elder Jenkinses?" she asked.

Andre sighed. "Both died during the yellow fever epidemic in '55. But four of their children survived, thank heaven. John Jr. has been happily wed to Louise Winchester for six years now."

They proceeded down a path choked with creepers and vines and lined with rosebushes gone to seed. Stephanie was pleased to note some favorite antique varieties—Souvenir, Old Blush, Hermosa. The night air was thick with the perfume of blossoms.

"I can see how beautiful this must have been," she remarked.

"At one time the Jenkins gardens rivaled the Tuilleries in Paris."

"I've always wanted to see the Tuilleries," she murmured.

"I took Linnea to Paris on our honeymoon. I'd like to take you there." He reached out and stroked her cheek.

Though treacherously excited, she stiffened. "You should take Ebbie."

He put his hands on her arms and turned her toward him. "No, Stephanie," he said sternly. "Tonight is just about you and me. We will not discuss Ebbie tonight."

"If you insist," she conceded.

He clutched her hand and tugged her onward. "Are you enjoying our excursion? Did I surprise you by bringing you here?"

"You're very impetuous, Andre."

"So I am."

"What was your family like?"

"Impetuous."

She laughed.

"And loving," he added wistfully. "Indeed, Father's favorite game was to pack the entire family off to Europe on a whim—to London to find just the right painting for the parlor, to Munich to purchase a piano, to Venice to hunt up figurines. One time my older brother and I got lost in Paris as my mother was hunting for chairs in the Faubourg Saint-Antoine. The *gendarmes* finally found us playing with an organ grinder's monkey in the Palais Royale."

She giggled. "Sounds like you."

"And of course we traveled extensively in this country, and visited with all the grand families of Natchez. Those times were good, especially before the war." He sighed. "Nothing has been quite the same since then, but we make do."

"I'll say," she muttered.

They had paused by a greenhouse covered with creepers. "John Jenkins created quite a stir by grafting various fruits," Andre told her. "He also preserved pears in his cellar by hanging them from strings, and shipped them north at a handsome profit.''

''How fascinating,'' she murmured.

''Then too soon, it was all gone,'' he finished.

''I know. Life can be cruelly short sometimes.''

Beneath an apple tree, he turned to her. She caught a sharp breath at the sight of his face, exquisitely beautiful etched in moonlight.

''How did you lose your husband?'' he asked.

Caught off guard, she replied, ''In the war.''

He frowned. ''Which war? The only war in recent memory is the Franco-Prussian affair. Unless you mean the Indian wars—''

''Yes,'' she hastily cut in. ''My husband was a major in the army—that is, the cavalry—and he died out West, er, fighting Geronimo.''

''I'm sorry. You loved him very much?''

''Yes,'' she replied tightly. ''Ours was the kind of love that comes only once in a lifetime.''

His features tightened. ''Are you so certain?''

Though she wondered at the tension in his voice, she nodded. ''It's something you can know only if you experience it.''

He glanced away.

''I'm sorry. Are you thinking about your wife?''

''Yes. We have something in common in our loss, no?''

''We do.''

He flashed her a rueful smile. ''I do feel guilty for never having loved Linnea. Our families wanted the match, you see. Originally, my father owned several vineyards in the south of France, and he had already accumulated a fortune by the time he came to America and settled in Georgia. He married to increase his wealth, choosing a bride whose family had extensive holdings here in Natchez. When I came of age, he expected me to follow in his footsteps. I was only twenty-two—what did I know of life? Months later, I finally realized I had married a woman with whom I had nothing in common—neither temperament, nor passion for life. But by then it was too late—Linnea was pregnant.''

''I'm sorry.''

He sighed. "I am the one who has regrets—that our years together weren't happier ones. How I lament the times I spent at the track, the nights gambling . . . If only I could have known our days together would be so brief, I would have tried harder, for her sake."

Touched by his admission, Stephanie blinked at a tear. "But you had your children. You were both so fortunate there."

"They brought Linnea great joy." With a sigh, he touched her cheek. "Stephanie . . ."

"Yes?"

"I know you badly wanted a child with your husband, but at least you appreciated what you had together."

"Jim always used to say that when I got blue. 'We have each other, Stef.' "

Andre gazed at her tenderly. "He called you Stef?"

She nodded.

He scowled pensively. "Stef . . . I'm not sure that sounds quite right for me. Perhaps I'll call you 'Steffie.' "

"I'm not sure that sounds quite right to *me*."

"Why? Is it too intimate, too soft?"

"Perhaps I just don't like your presumption in calling me by a pet name."

He chuckled. "Forever the spirited one, aren't you? I like that about you."

"Don't like me too much," she chided.

"But I do. I even appreciate your fussiness."

"What fussiness?" she inquired piously.

He rolled his eyes. "Don't try to claim you're not fussy, Madame Sergeant. I've watched you with my children, and have seen the vengeance you've unleashed on unsuspecting mice. We must have order, discipline, everything in its place. A life of schedules, goals, a bell for this and a whistle for that. It all tempts a wayward fellow like me to wreak havoc in your orderly life."

She smiled guiltily. "I do come from a fussy family. My parents were both educators."

"Ah, yes. No impetuous background for Madame Sergeant."

"They were strict, but kind," she continued. "Lots of

books in our home, lots of classical music. And no impetuous trips to Europe—nor any money for such extravagances.''

He turned more thoughtful. "Do you miss your family?"

She nodded. "I particularly miss my younger sister. My parents—well, they're quite a bit older, and they have a good life in Florida. We haven't been as close since I became an adult. Of course I look forward to seeing them from time to time." *Will I ever again?* she added to herself.

They continued walking, passing pear trees tangled with raspberry vines, ducking beneath the limbs of plum and apricot trees. Andre stopped Stephanie next to a twisted tree not much bigger than a large shrub.

"Look, Steffie, ripe cherries."

She eyed the glistening fruit. "I'm surprised there are any left this late in the season. I do love cherries."

He plucked off a shiny fruit and plopped it into her mouth. She bit in, devouring the sweet juices.

"It's divine, but what do I do with the pits?"

"Spit them in my hand."

"You must be joking. I'm not spitting *anything* in your hand!"

Stephanie leaned over, depositing the pits in some weeds, and when she straightened, Andre plopped another fruit in her mouth, then leaned over and seized her lips.

An incredible thrill shot through her as he kissed her amid the crush of the fruit and the bursting of its nectar. Oh, he was depraved. Juice trickled out of her mouth as he shared the decadent sweetness with her.

More thrilled than she cared to admit, she pushed him away just to breathe, and turned to spit out more seeds. "You are wicked! Now the juice has dribbled into my blouse—and one of the pits, too, I think!"

"And such a tempting path to follow," he murmured.

An unwitting sound of pleasure escaped Stephanie as Andre ran his tongue from the corner of her mouth, to her chin, and slowly down her throat . . . It did not take her long to figure out where his lips were heading.

"Andre, no!"

"Steffie, please don't fight me," he coaxed.

Already his sexy voice and seductive mouth were shattering her defenses. She tried to squirm away, too late, as her own feelings overwhelmed her, as Andre's hand at the small of her back pressed her close, as he unbuttoned her blouse and nudged his lips inside. The scent and heat of him inflamed her. He pushed aside her camisole, and then his tongue found her nipple—taunting, teasing, barely tasting her, yet Stephanie was on fire.

"Oh, God!"

He pulled her down on her knees, beside him on the ripe earth, leaned over and sucked the tip of her breast deeply into his mouth. Stephanie reeled, tossing her head back, watching the silvery clouds float by. Andre's tongue was wicked, his mouth so wet and hot that she could feel the pleasure searing through her. She knew this was wrong, yet she was in heaven, out-of-control. She had never expected to feel so giddy, so ecstatic. She might be lost in time, but she was totally at home in this man's arms. She could not control her runaway heartbeat, her frantic breathing, as his intimate stroking touched her deep inside. Her fingers dug into his shoulders, her hands helplessly clenching and unclenching.

He straightened, his eyes burning into hers, while in the distance a mockingbird sang a plaintive song. "Steffie, love me. You know you want me as much as I want you."

"This is crazy," she replied breathlessly. "We can't."

"Why not?"

"Because there are a world of barriers in our way."

"Such as?" he pressed.

"Your children, your obligations, Ebbie—"

"Your memories of your first husband?" he cut in.

"Yes, that, too," she admitted in a small voice.

His passionate gaze beseeched her as he raised and kissed her hand. "Steffie, perhaps together we can ease your pain—"

"Please don't say that," she said, reeling.

"Think about it, dearest," he implored. "We've both known loss, and we're far from starry-eyed innocents. You've sworn never to love again. And I'm not ready for remarriage yet. Why don't we explore these delicious feelings and see where they lead us?''

"Lord, you're such a sweet talker," she chided in trembling tones. "But I know you really don't respect me."

"Not true, darling." He lifted her hand and solemnly kissed each finger. "I respect you. I just can't resist you."

Stephanie could only moan as Andre proved his words with another ardent kiss. For long moments they clung together.

Afterward, he pressed his mouth to her ear and spoke soulfully. "Steffie, six years ago, my father kissed my mother good-bye, went out for a ride, and was discovered dead after his horse threw him. My mother went to her bed and never recovered. Life is so fleeting—why not enjoy what pleasures, what comfort we can?"

"Gather rosebuds while we may, to paraphrase the poet?"

"And such darling buds." He leaned over, gently kissing each breast through her camisole as she moaned shamelessly. "Steffie, please, love me now."

As much as Stephanie was drowning in his skilled seduction, she managed to pull herself back to reality and pushed him away. "Andre, no."

"Don't you want me?"

With trembling fingers, she began buttoning her blouse. "Yes, I'll admit that I feel some of the same lust you feel."

"Only lust?"

"Forgive me if I happen to place honor and loyalty above carnal needs," she said hoarsely. "Forgive me if I don't share your profligate, hedonistic outlook on life."

"Why must you see me as such a cad?" he demanded. "Am I not devoted to my children?"

"You are—but equally devoted to seeking your own pleasure."

"And that is a crime?"

Her troubled gaze met his. "Has it occurred to you that a man who is truly concerned about his children might marry Ebbie to give them a mother?"

"Stephanie, I will not discuss her tonight," he reiterated.

Stephanie groaned. "I'm trying to get you to do what's right. I think your values are misplaced, that you need to reassess your goals, consider what you're doing with your life."

"Do you? Well, since you're so inclined to discuss goals and philosophy, Madame Sergeant, why *do* you think we're here in this world?"

"To be useful," Stephanie readily replied. "To make a contribution. We are here to help others—"

"You would help me so much if you came to my bed—"

"And *not* to pursue our own selfish desires," she finished in quavery tones.

"Why do you think I am being selfish?"

Stephanie felt as if she were arguing with a post. "Because there's a woman who's in love with you, who's devoted to you and your family, and you're blind to her."

He regarded her sadly. "And you, my dear, are blind to what you really feel. Stephanie, you are here to love me. You just do not know it yet."

He did not allow her to deny his words, kissing her instead.

Riding home beside Andre, Stephanie was immersed in turmoil. She had come out with him tonight hoping to convince him to court Ebbie in earnest. She had come away in deeper trouble than before.

For the rogue was determined to beguile her, and she was far from immune to his charms. Should she have a love affair with him, hoping he'd quickly tire of her and then, finally, turn his attentions to Ebbie?

A dangerous tactic, indeed, and Stephanie dismissed the traitorous prospect at once. Already, getting to know Andre better had dramatically undermined her own defenses. She was finding out that he was a man of true feeling, more than just a hedonistic cad. She not only wanted him, she liked him more with each passing day. If anything, his faults endeared him to her.

He was also tempting her with a different way of life, a life devoted to living in the moment and glorying in sensual pleasure. Steeped as she was in the Protestant work ethic, she still found she had never felt as alive as she did when seeing the world through *his* eyes.

How could she stop from falling in love with him?

Chapter 27

Sunday afternoon found Stephanie again wedged between Henry and Katie in Henry's carriage, the conveyance clipping down a narrow road cut deep in the red earth. On either side rose steep banks covered in thick creepers; above them stretched mossy oaks and sycamores decked out in striking scarlet foliage.

Stephanie was dressed for the fall day, wearing a gold silk gown and matching bonnet, the same outfit she'd worn to church that morning with Andre, Ebbie, and the children. Thank heaven, Andre had behaved himself during the service, though several times she'd caught him staring at her with a look of secret pleasure.

"You know, 'tis truly an irony that this reception for the Davises is being held at Auburn," Katie was remarking.

"And why is that?" Stephanie asked.

Katie snorted a laugh. "Why, the previous owner, Dr. Stephen Duncan, was a unionist, my dear girl!"

"Oh, Aunt, haven't you forgotten about the Ross affair by now?" Henry scolded. "It was settled more than thirty years ago."

She harrumphed. "If not for traitors like Ike Ross, John Ker and Stephen Duncan joining the American Colonization Society, we never would have had to fight the war!"

Henry slanted his aunt a reproachful glance. "Ross, Ker, and Duncan weren't abolitionists. They merely wanted to help freed slaves return to their homeland." He turned to Stephanie. "Way back in 1829 when Ike Ross died, he left the balance of his estate to be used to resettle his upwards of two hundred slaves as free men back in Africa. His daughter, Margaret, and his friends, Duncan and Ker, were determined to carry out his final wishes. But there was a tremendous public outcry over Ross's will, and Margaret and the others had to fight every step of the way—their friends, the state legislature, even the supreme court of Mississippi. Although eventually the court ruled in their favor, still further resistance was encountered. The dispute was the death of Margaret, as well as John Ker; finally, Stephen Duncan spirited most of the slaves away to Africa.''

''How fascinating—and how sad,'' murmured Stephanie.

Katie glanced askance at her. ''If you ask me, 'twas a pointless fight. And look where we are now, with the negroes freed and the South crippled beyond repair.''

Stephanie was tempted to pounce on Katie's last comment, but, hearing the bitterness in the old woman's voice, she held her tongue. Although the very thought of slavery was anathema to her, she had to remember she was now living in a different time, during which an entire economy had been built on the wrongful and doomed system. Those old wounds would heal slowly, and it was too much to expect Katie Banks to accept today that the South was now headed in the right direction.

As if in testimony to the deprivations of war, Auburn rose before them, its redbrick Georgian beauty somehow unmarred by the paint peeling on its huge round columns or the mold on its carved capitals and ornate pediment. The mansion stood on a rise carpeted in fallen leaves, its yard teeming with carriages and buggies. Stephanie remembered seeing the mansion in the present—where it was better maintained, though it seemed grander now.

''What a fabulous home,'' she murmured.

''The house has faded a bit since the days when Stephen Duncan entertained Henry Clay and Edward Everett Hale,'' Katie remarked. ''And by the way, Hale's *The Man Without a Country* was a total fabrication. Hale never should have used an actual person's name in a fictitious story. The real Philip Nolan was married to one of our local belles, Fannie

Lintot of Concord. Nolan may have been an adventurer, but he was *never* a man without a country.''

Fighting laughter, Stephanie glanced at Henry, who winked back. ''Do the Waverlys own the house now?'' she asked Katie.

''Oh, the Duncans still technically own the place. Stephen went north when the war broke out. He's long gone now, and his son only rarely returns. However, the Waverlys are good tenants. Colonel Balfour was telling me yesterday that they've been making some repairs in exchange for lower rents.''

Henry parked the buggy and helped both ladies out. Climbing the front steps, Stephanie heard laughter and music spilling out. She marveled at the front door, with its exquisite glass sidelights and the fanlight overheard, framed by a masterfully fluted arc of wood.

A smiling butler admitted them. Stepping inside the wide, cypress-floored hallway, Stephanie's gaze was drawn at once to her left, to the stunning spiral staircase that hung as if suspended in midair, with no visible supports along its swirling sweep to the second story.

The butler escorted them inside a huge parlor filled with elegantly dressed Natchezians, many of them older couples. The guests moved about visiting with one another, amid the clink of punch cups and the rustle of the ''dust ruffles'' which cascaded off the ladies' voluminous silk and taffeta bustles.

Stephanie noted that the crush of humanity rather obscured the frayed setting—the thinning upholstery on the fine Belter chairs, the holes in the Aubusson rug, the water stains on the high plaster ceiling. At a stunning gold grand piano, an elderly black man was playing a soft, soulful rendition of ''Silver Threads Among the Gold,'' embellishing the poignant old melody with runs and trills more lavish than the lace on a Southern belle's crinoline.

At the far end of the room, she spotted the Davises; the gray-haired former president of the Confederacy towered over most of the other men. At his side stood a tall, stately woman grown plump with middle age. The two were surrounded by a throng of admirers. Stephanie felt a surge of excitement, a little catch in her throat upon seeing these two actual figures from history.

But Henry sounded nonchalant enough as he murmured, "Excuse me, ladies, I'll get you some punch."

After he sauntered off, Stephanie continued to scan the room, and spotted Andre and Ebbie near the French doors. Wearing her black dress and a beige shawl, Ebbie was chatting with the Reverend Dearborn; Andre stood scowling nearby, arms akimbo, obviously bored. Then he spotted her, bowed, and grinned, his manner far more avid than in church. Torrid memories of last night flooded her, and she hastily turned away.

"Come along, dear," ordered Katie. "There are so many people you must meet today." She tapped Stephanie's arm with her fan. "Then, by the time we're ready to announce your and Henry's engagement, you'll be received in all the right homes."

"Oh, Katie, you're such a rascal," Stephanie teased back. "You barely know me, and I don't think Henry even likes me. And already you're talking marriage for me and your nephew."

The old woman's mouth dropped open. "I'll have you know, my dear girl, that my Henry speaks of nothing but you." Behind her hand, she confided, "You don't know how thrilled I am to see my Henry seriously interested in a woman—not to mention a pretty jewel like you. Henry's my nephew, and I love him, but the boy's a bit stuffy. All he thinks about is his cotton. He needs to relax and have more fun."

Spoken like Andre Goddard, Stephanie thought ruefully.

Katie made her rounds with Stephanie. Again, the scions of Natchez society swirled past Stephanie in a maze of introductions, to Bisland, Postelwaite, Dunbar, Hunt. The vivacious Stanton sisters were present again, and she met the pretty daughters of the late Haller Nutt of Longwood fame, as well as their hosts, Anne and John Waverly.

In due course Katie presented Stephanie to the Davises. "President Davis, it's truly an honor to see you again," gushed Katie. "And dear Varina, you look lovely, as always."

"Why, Miss Banks, what a pleasure to see you," replied Davis, shaking the old woman's hand. "It's been much too long."

"Indeed," concurred Varina as she, too, shook Katie's hand.

Katie motioned to Stephanie. "President and Mrs. Davis, I want you to meet my dear Henry's new friend, Mrs. Stephanie Sergeant, who has recently joined the Goddard household."

Exchanging pleasantries and shaking hands with each Davis, Stephanie noted how gaunt and lined Jefferson's face was, how sad Varina's eyes. About both hung a defeated air buttressed by an unmistakable dignity. Yet Varina's round face still showed hints of her youthful loveliness; while her dress was black, a red camellia corsage—surely hothouse blooms for an out-of-season flower—showed a hint of spirit. Again Stephanie felt a surge of awe and excitement to be in the presence of the former royalty of the Old South. What would those she'd left behind say if they could see her now?

Not long after the introductions were finished, John Waverly took Davis aside, and Stephanie and Katie were left alone with Varina.

"I hear you and the President have returned to Mississippi and he plans to write his memoirs," commented Katie.

"Yes, we are so fortunate to be living with our dear friend, Mrs. Samuel Dorsey, at Beauvoir down on the coast," answered Varina. "Sarah Ann has been so good to us."

Katie lifted an eyebrow. "I suppose that's only just, after her stepfather, our own Charles Dahlgren, gave Jefferson such hell during the war."

"What do you hear of Mr. Dahlgren?" asked Varina. "He and Sarah Ann have been estranged for so many years now. I suppose he never forgave her for marrying Judge Dorsey."

"Last I heard, Mr. Dahlgren left Natchez and went back East somewhere," replied Katie. "And the Yanks can have him."

Repressing a smile, Varina turned to Stephanie. "Mrs. Sergeant, have you been in Natchez long?"

"I came only recently to Harmony House."

"You'll love it here," said Varina, a wistfulness stealing over her face. "Natchez is such a special place for me and Mr. Davis. You know, Jefferson and I married here at my family's home, the Briars."

"Yes, Katie has told me that you and President Davis had one of the grandest romances in Natchez history."

"I actually met Mr. Davis at Diamond Place upriver from here. I'll never forget that Christmas, the first time I watched him ride up to the house. I have never seen a man command a horse with such grace, even if he was a Democrat. Ah, those were the days . . ."

As Katie asked Varina another question, Stephanie again gazed about the room. Not seeing Andre or Ebbie, she craned her neck and finally spotted Andre out on the back porch. He was smoking a cheroot, visiting with John Waverly, Jefferson Davis, and several other gentlemen. She watched the men stride away toward a cottage next door.

Frustrated, she looked around again for Ebbie, and finally spotted her next to the marble fireplace. She was standing beside Mr. Trumble, who was obviously flirting with her. Even from here Stephanie could hear his booming laugh and see him twirling his mustache.

But it wasn't Abner Trumble Ebbie wanted! Even as Stephanie thought this, she spied Ebbie looking about the room, her expression fraught with anxiety and disappointment. She was obviously searching for someone else . . .

Andre—the cad!

"Oh, there you are!"

Stephanie turned as Henry stepped up and handed her a cup of punch. "Thank you."

As Varina busied herself greeting another guest, Katie turned to take her cup of punch from Henry. "You two children enjoying yourselves?" she asked.

"Of course," answered Stephanie, trying to sound cheerful.

"Indeed," agreed Henry.

"I can't remember when I've had so much fun," Katie

declared. "Now I want us all to keep stepping out, and I shall tolerate no arguments. Why, the season is upon us, and everyone's all astir because that fine troupe is coming through from New Orleans and performing *Camille* on Wednesday night. We have seasons tickets to the Natchez Theatre, so you must come with us, Stephanie, dear. Then on Saturday night, there's the annual harvest ball at the Jefferson Hotel, and Henry and I are hosting a dinner party afterward. We always entertain all of Andre and Henry's best customers and friends. . . ."

As Katie went on cheerfully making plans for the three of them, Stephanie smiled and nodded. Inwardly, however, she was feeling frustrated and demoralized, especially as she glanced across the room again at Ebbie, now alone and appearing despondent. Her role as a matchmaker was not going well at all, and Andre Goddard was about to get one big piece of her mind!

Chapter 28

~~~~~~

At home, Stephanie came upon Ebbie on the upstairs veranda. Oblivious of Stephanie's approach, the little woman sat with an open Bible in her lap, and was contemplating a dried rose that had obviously been pressed between its pages. In this unguarded moment, Stephanie could see the sadness in Ebbie's visage.

But who had given her the faded bloom? Of course, Andre liked to tantalize ladies by leaving stray roses, Stephanie recalled with a twinge of unease. Had he given Ebbie the flower some time ago? That might explain why Ebbie now appeared so forlorn. She must be so disappointed with him.

Stephanie was ready to shake the rascal herself. She felt so torn. She really liked Ebbie Rice and wanted to help resolve her life, yet in so many ways the woman was still a mystery to her. What was Ebbie *really* thinking? Stephanie didn't know, since Ebbie was so often vague about her feelings, and even spoke in riddles. But at moments like this, Stephanie could only remember the anguished plea of Ebbie's ghost—*He never loved me . . . What are you going to do about it?*—and she could see in Ebbie's dark, morose eyes the tragedy that would haunt her entire existence.

The quandary was, could Stephanie do anything about it? At the moment, she didn't feel like a very effective guardian angel!

Even as Stephanie struggled with her doubts, Ebbie glanced up, then stuffed the rose in her Bible and closed it. "Why, Stephanie, I didn't see you standing there."

"I hope I didn't startle you."

"Not at all. I'm just preparing for prayer meeting on Tuesday night. Peter has asked me to lead the discussion. Do join me. We must relax while the children are still napping."

Stephanie sat down in a rocker next to Ebbie's. "Did you have a good time with Andre?"

"Oh, yes," Ebbie murmured. "It was lovely to see the Davises, and to know they're doing well with dear Sarah Ann Dorsey."

"What about you and Andre? How did it go?"

Ebbie blushed. "He was a perfect gentleman, of course."

"I did not like it when he deserted you," Stephanie put in.

"To speak with the former president of the Confederacy?" Ebbie countered. "Why, I would have been appalled had Andre not paid his respects. Poor President Davis gave his all for the Cause, performing brilliantly, yet he has been heartlessly vilified ever since the war began."

"I suppose you have a point. Still, I think Andre could have been more attentive—"

"He invited me to the theater on Wednesday," Ebbie added tremulously.

"Did he?" Stephanie grinned. "Are you happy about that?"

Ebbie lowered her gaze. "Why, of course."

Stephanie's smile faded. "Ebbie, you do want Andre, don't you?"

Ebbie laughed nervously. "Didn't I tell you it's assumed we'll wed?"

"Yes, but do *you* want him?"

Ebbie fell silent, then nodded. "I believe it's my destiny to become Andre's second wife, and care for his children."

"I see."

Yet Stephanie felt even more perplexed, as once again Ebbie gave answers that didn't quite satisfy. Of course Ebbie seemed giddy and uncertain around Andre, and she must be kept constantly off guard by his outlandish behavior, and must also wonder if the rogue would ever truly love her.

As for Ebbie's reticence, it must be too humiliating for her to voice her true fears, even to a friend.

Ebbie reached out to pat Stephanie's hand. "Won't you come with Andre and me to the theater?"

"Thank you, but Henry invited me."

Ebbie winked. "Is there a romance developing between you and the handsome Mr. Robillard?"

Stephanie chuckled. "Actually, I think I go out with him mainly because I enjoy his aunt so much. Katie Banks's stories of old Natchez are enthralling."

"Oh, I know. One night when she and Henry were over for dinner, she kept us all riveted with tales of the days when murderers and thieves used to rove the Natchez Trace." Ebbie crossed herself. "I swear I couldn't sleep a wink that night. At any rate, you would do well to marry into that family."

Stephanie chuckled. "To tell you the truth, I think it's Katie Banks who wants to find Henry a wife much more than Henry himself wants to marry. And for some reason, Katie's taken a real shine to me."

"Why wouldn't she?" demanded Ebbie, irate. "You're a delight, Stephanie."

She fought a smile. "Enough about me. Let's talk more about you, and what you're going to wear to captivate Andre on Wednesday."

Ebbie colored. "Stephanie, really!"

Stephanie wagged a finger. "Oh, no you don't! This time, Ebbie Rice, I forbid you to wear black, even if I have to burn all those old shrouds of yours!"

Ebbie fell into gales of mirth, and Stephanie felt proud for having finally cheered her friend.

The following afternoon, Stephanie sat on a blanket on the lawn with the children. Ebbie was away for the afternoon, her quartet playing at a tea hosted by the Fosters.

With Amy in her lap and Gwen, Beau, and Pompom gathered about her, Stephanie was reading "Rip Van Winkle." The children sat motionless and riveted, and even Pompon again appeared entranced by Stephanie's storytelling. On a nearby bench Martha sat holding the baby; although Sarah couldn't possibly understand all the words, she, too, was rapt at the sound of Stephanie's voice.

"Did he really sleep for twenty years?" asked Gwen when Stephanie finished.

Stephanie winked back. "He did in Washington Irving's imagination."

"Sometimes I'm tired enough to sleep for twenty years," declared Beau with a grin. He popped up, grabbed a stick and threw it for Pompom. The two dashed away, the dog barking shrilly and Beau laughing.

Gwen was regarding Amy thoughtfully. "She likes you," she said to Stephanie. "She always wants to sit in your lap."

Stephanie smiled down at Amy. "Do you like me, little one?"

The child grinned shyly. "Yes!"

Stephanie hugged Amy close. "I sure like you."

Gwen still wore a pensive expression. "She needs a mother."

Stephanie looked up sharply. "You all have Ebbie."

Gwen's mouth tightened. "We had a *real* mother and she died. No one can take her place."

Stephanie touched the child's stiff shoulder. "Of course not, darling. No one will ever expect you to forget your mother."

The girl visibly relaxed. "But Amy is younger. Maybe she doesn't remember Mama, and needs a mother more."

"Oh, she may remember more than you know."

Gwen's earnest face lit up. "Do you really think so, madame?"

Stephanie nodded.

Gwen popped up. "Know what?"

"What?"

Gwen leaned over and quickly kissed Stephanie's cheek. "I like you, too!" she declared, then waltzed off.

Stephanie was caught totally unaware by Gwen's endearing gesture. Gradually the child had been warming to her, and this small victory was especially satisfying, yet also disturbing. Stephanie had come here to help Ebbie successfully bond with this family. Yet instead, each day she was here, both the children and Andre were gravitating toward *her*, not Ebbie.

Ebbie wasn't helping matters much, either. She was sweet, but she remained almost painfully shy around Andre, as well as emotionally distant, nervous, and ineffective around his children; indeed, Ebbie seemed to prefer that Stephanie supervise Andre's youngsters while she knitted, read her Bible, or practiced with her misters. It was only during these pursuits that Ebbie seemed truly comfortable. Ebbie did seem to yearn for more—but also seemed powerless to secure what she really wanted.

Stephanie sighed deeply. Why couldn't she bring this family together?

She was pondering this thought when a masculine voice murmured, "My, but you're making an impression on my children, Madame Sergeant."

She turned to watch Andre stride toward her from a nearby oak tree, looking too handsome for words in a brown frock coat, buff-colored trousers, and a black planter's hat. "How long have you been standing there?"

"Long enough to know you've become Gwen's favorite." Stepping closer, he tossed his hat on the blanket, then leaned over and scooped Amy up out of Stephanie's arms. The child chortled with glee, hugging her father's neck as he kissed her cheek.

Stephanie rose beside him. "I was about to take the children inside."

Setting Amy down, Andre turned to the nurse, who still held the baby. When little Sarah waved her arms and squirmed to get down, Martha set her on her feet. The baby toddled a step toward Andre, then fell on her bottom and giggled. Stephanie smiled at the sight; she'd seen Sarah attempting to walk several times lately.

Andre scooped Sarah up into his arms and kissed her. "Ah, minx, you'll be walking in no time," he murmured with pride, handing her back to her nurse. "Martha, dear, kindly take this brood inside, and Madame Sergeant will join you shortly."

Martha stood with the baby. "Yes, sir."

Amy skipped over to take Martha's hand, and the nurse

led the children away. Suddenly Stephanie was alone with Andre, and unnerved by the intent way he was gazing at her.

"I really should help Martha—" she began.

Andre held up a forefinger. "Martha can manage for five minutes. I will have a word with you."

"A word?"

He leaned over and kissed her cheek. "Lord, but you look lovely today."

She shot him a scolding look. "Andre, really."

He retrieved his hat and grabbed her hand. "Walk with me to the stables."

"The stables? If you're planning to try to spirit me off again—"

"Come along," he interrupted, already tugging her away.

Stephanie lurched into motion to keep up with his long-legged strides. "Thanks for giving me a choice."

"You'll find, Stephanie, that I'll not give you many choices," he teased back. "You're going to spend time with me whether you like it or not."

She groaned. "Andre, I can't keep spending time with you."

"Why not?"

Because I'm afraid I'm falling in love with you, she thought sinkingly. Aloud, she muttered, "I just can't."

"You're seeing Henry," he pointed out irritably.

"That's different."

"Why?"

"Because he doesn't want—"

"Yes?" Andre prodded.

She felt her face heating. "To seduce me."

He laughed. "Stephanie, you're either hopelessly naive or not very smart."

She ground her jaw. "You're just too much of a scoundrel to believe Henry could be a gentleman."

"In public, I'm sure Henry's a gentleman," Andre replied. "Alone with you, I wouldn't trust him for five seconds."

"Well, I do."

"Did you have fun with him yesterday?"

She held her head high. "I had a grand time."

He scowled. "If Katie Banks weren't along, I'd be putting a stop to your relationship with him now."

"Never!" she retorted.

He chuckled. "Well, we'll see if we can't blot the inimitable Mr. Robillard from your mind tonight."

She dug in her heels. "What do you mean, tonight?"

Appearing smug, Andre pulled her inside the dank stable and into a small storeroom off to one side. Opening a scarred trunk, he pulled out a stack of clothing and handed it to her.

Stephanie gazed at a pair of dark trousers, a brown broadcloth shirt, suspenders, and a brown cap. "What on earth are these?"

"Your disguise."

"My what? Whose clothes *are* these?"

Andre lounged against a scarred desk and crossed his arms over his chest. "Oh, they belonged to one of our stableboys, who left to seek his fortunes in New Orleans. Since he was about your size, I had the garments laundered just for you."

Stephanie was flabbergasted. "Why? Why have you brought me here under a veil of secrecy, and given me a disguise?"

His eyes gleamed with repressed merriment. "Because we are going on another adventure tonight, you and I."

"We are doing nothing of the sort!"

"Indeed? Then I won't be taking Ebbie to the theater."

"You scoundrel."

"We have a deal, Stephanie," he reminded her sternly. "For each moment I spend with Ebbie, you spend equal time with me. Payment in advance. No rules."

"No rules?"

"Well, only one," he murmured meaningfully.

She tossed the clothing down on top of the trunk. "Oh, you are just maddening! You're playing this situation up for all it's worth—"

"Of course I am," he cut in smoothly. "And you have no choice but to comply, Stephanie, if you want my cooperation in exchange."

"I don't know why I don't just throw in the towel," she shot back. "You're giving only token service to courting Ebbie. You deserted her again yesterday."

"I deserted her?" he shot back, incredulous. "She was so busy chatting with Peter Dearborn about prayer circle and discussing today's repertoire with her misters that I was quite left out."

"Were you offended?"

"What do you think?"

"I know she's taken with you, Andre," Stephanie continued earnestly. "But you make her nervous. If only you would try to put her at her ease—"

He stepped very close. "How should I do that? Should I kiss her?"

Disconcerted, Stephanie backed away. "Andre, please—"

"Should I?" he repeated softly, pursuing her.

She looked helplessly up at him, and he leaned over and gently touched her lips with his own.

That fleeting kiss seared her, raising a moan, and more feelings of vulnerability. "Damn it, Andre, you could try harder with Ebbie, instead of abandoning her like you did—"

"I only went outside to pay my respects to Jefferson Davis, and several of us smoked in Stephen Duncan's old billiard parlor. Would you prefer I had simply ignored Davis?"

"No. Even Ebbie insisted you were obligated there."

"Then what do you expect of me?"

Exasperated, she demanded, "Why don't you try to charm Ebbie as you do me?"

Grinning, he wrapped an arm around her waist. "You know why, Stephanie. Ebbie doesn't excite me, or challenge me, as you do." He gave an elegant shrug. "But perhaps I will try harder at the theater on Wednesday—*if* you'll meet me tonight, love."

"Oh, you are ruthless. Andre, she *really* cares for you."

A glint of anger flashed in his eyes. "I'm fond of her as well, and the last thing I want is to cause her any pain. You're the one who has insisted on this absurd ruse. So if Ebbie ends up hurt, it's on your head."

Stephanie flung a hand outward. ''There you go again, twisting things around and trying to blame me!''

Rather than respond, Andre calmly retrieved the stack of clothing. Shoving the items into her arms, he reached out and toyed with a strand of her hair. ''Be sure to pin up that glorious hair—and hide it under the cap.''

''But—why would you want me to go out with you dressed like a boy?''

He threw his head back and laughed. ''Stephanie, darling, where I'm taking you, you *won't* want to be recognized as a woman.''

Intrigued, Stephanie tried to pry details from him, but Andre refused to say more.

Chapter 29

Stephanie felt illogically both silly and rather decadent as she sneaked out of the house that night in stableboy garb, her hair pinned under her cap. She'd also left her wedding ring in her room, much as doing so had spurred her guilt. Still, wearing the band could have easily given her away as a woman.

What did Andre have in mind for them tonight anyway?

She headed for the appointed place where she was to meet him, at an oak near the stable. She soon spotted the bright blot of a lantern. Drawing closer, she realized the lamp was hanging from the front board of a racing gig, to which the chestnut trotter was harnessed, blowing and snorting. She spied Andre standing nearby wearing the same suit and hat he'd had on earlier.

"Good evening, *chérie*," he greeted in husky tones. "How fetching you look."

She gestured toward the gig. "We're going on another ride?"

"That will be only the first part of our sojourn."

"But there won't be room for us both on that narrow seat."

"Want to bet?"

Before she could protest, Andre caught her beneath the arms and hoisted her onto the narrow bench, then strode around the conveyance to squeeze in beside her. They did both fit, Stephanie had to admit, though it was disconcerting, to say the least, to have Andre's hard hip and muscular thigh pressing so intimately against her.

"Where are you taking me?" she asked breathlessly.

Rather than answer, he lightly tapped the trotter's back with a whip, and the conveyance lurched forward. Stephanie grabbed her hat and then Andre's arm and gave an exuberant laugh.

That's when the fun really began, as they flew across the lawn and into the street. When they hit a bump, Stephanie could not help herself; she stole an arm around Andre's waist, and heard his contented sigh.

Oh, it was treacherous being close to him this way, as the trotter raced toward town, her stride fleet and magnificent. Stephanie had never been in a racing gig before, and the sensation was exhilarating. She was captivated as they sprinted over the rolling terrain, past darkened mansions and moss-hung trees. They soon careened out onto the bluff by the Old Parade Grounds, spectacularly awash in silver, then proceeded north into a quiet neighborhood filled with quaint Victorian homes. With the wind in her face and Andre beside her, Stephanie for once dropped her guard and succumbed to the thrill of the moment.

But as they headed out of town, still following the bluff, she gasped. "Don't tell me you're taking me to the cemetery! Last night was scary enough."

"No, silly goose. Don't worry, we'll stop soon."

True to his word, he soon pulled the conveyance to a halt before a graying shack that stood outlined in moonlight. As the trotter stamped and puffed, Stephanie eyed Andre in perplexity.

Then she spotted another light, as an old black man in dungarees emerged from the sagging porch. His lantern swinging, he ambled toward them. "Eve'nin', Mr. Goddard," he called.

"Evening, George." Handing the man the reins, Andre hopped out and assisted Stephanie to the ground. "Keep a good eye on my trotter, now. And you'll be waiting for us later, at the appointed spot?"

"Yes, sir."

Andre gave the man a gold coin. "Is everything else ready?"

"Yes, sir, just like you wanted." He handed Andre his lantern and pocketed the coin. "Much obliged. You folks have a good time."

"We will. See you later."

As Andre led her off, Stephanie glanced back at the old man, who still stood holding the trotter's reins. If George had found it odd to see Andre Goddard showing up late at night with a "boy" in tow, he'd made no comment.

She turned back to Andre. "Do you mind telling me what's going on? And what's this cloak-and-dagger business about us meeting later at the 'appointed spot'?"

"All in good time," came his smooth reply.

Chuckling, Andre led her behind the house and down an embankment. To her astonishment, they soon arrived on the shores of a quiet bayou, cut deep into the earth and lined by trees. Mist hung along the waterway and silvery light danced on the foliage. Stephanie couldn't restrain a sigh of delight at the romantic scene.

Andre gestured toward a small craft moored to a stump. "Madame, your chariot awaits."

"A rowboat?"

"I want you to see our bayous at night," he explained. "They're truly enchanting."

Stephanie didn't protest. The setting was wondrous, and at least there was little chance Andre would ravish her in a rowboat. She accepted his assistance into the craft and held the lantern, as he pushed off and worked the oars.

They glided down the smooth, gleaming strip of water. Stephanie gazed above her at the gray, interlocking limbs of oaks and elms, the cascades of Spanish moss, the full moon peeking through the clouds overhead. She listened to the hum of cicadas, the muted cries of swamp birds; the night thrummed with life. She breathed deeply of air scented with earth and the dank, murky waters. She gasped at the loud hooting of an owl, then ducked as the bird made a dive from a nearby tree, curving over their heads before flying off, a spectral image in the night. Hearing Andre's chuckle, she pulled a face at him.

"You're right, it is quite lovely here," she murmured.

He grinned. "So what do you think of our little town here on the Hill, Madame Sergeant?"

"I'm impressed—particularly by the fortitude of your people in recovering from the war. Yesterday, I found Jefferson Davis and Varina Howell Davis truly remarkable in their dignity and spirit."

His visage darkened.

"Did I say something wrong?"

"No, it's just I always felt rather guilty about the war, and the reception at Auburn brought back those memories."

"Guilty in what way?"

"Torn might be a better word," he explained. "My loyalty has always been with the South, but I never approved of slavery."

"I'm pleased to hear that, Andre," she murmured. "I never approved, either."

"You know, old George, whom you just met, is one of my family's former slaves."

"He is?"

"My father once owned a vast plantation in Vidalia. After the war, Papa sold off some of it, but also gave away many tracts to our former slaves. I was proud of him for not trying to force our negroes into the bondage of sharecropping, and I still try to help out some of the old families."

Stephanie felt herself softening toward Andre; the mounting evidence that he was more than an empty-headed profligate was disarming. "You're a remarkable man, then, a better man than many of your contemporaries."

He laughed. "Don't make me out as too noble. My parents left me so much better off than many of my peers. Thank God Papa never put much faith in Confederate currency. And many of our men sacrificed so much more than I did for the Cause. I never fought."

"How old were you when the hostilities began?"

"I was twelve when Mississippi seceded. I dreamed of serving—"

"Serving? But you were only a child!"

He met her gaze earnestly. "I could have become a drummer or bugle boy. Hell, I would have been delighted to tend horses, gather wood, dig latrines, anything to make a contribution. But my parents were adamantly opposed.''

"Thank goodness for that. I bet the war was very hard on your family.''

He nodded somberly. "The minute the fighting began, my father shipped my two older sisters off to stay with relatives in San Francisco, and thank heaven both girls later found husbands there. My father and older brother immediately enlisted in the Cause. Papa distinguished himself with Beauregard at Bull Run.'' He sighed heavily. "Pierre was killed at Shiloh.''

A sharp breath escaped Stephanie. "That's right, you mentioned a brother the other night. Then Pierre was—''

"Yes. He was ten years my senior.''

She touched his arm, felt his muscles rippling as he worked the oars. "I'm sorry, Andre.''

He smiled sadly. "I'll never forget how my mother cried when she got the news, how she hugged me and made me promise I'd never enlist, no matter how long the war lasted. Thank God, our home was spared when the Yanks occupied Natchez in '63. But we still saw relatives and friends lose so much. And not just soldiers in battle. People died from displacement and deprivation.'' He paused. "I was never in total agreement with Abe Lincoln, but he made an apt point at Gettysburg. Our country must never again endure such a war. Life deals us enough tragic blows. I've lost a child, a wife, and this does not even begin to count what I, what all of us, lost in that damned war. I want a world where my children can grow up healthy, happy, and free.''

"You'll have it, Andre,'' Stephanie replied feelingly. "We're actually in the middle of one of the most peaceful periods in our country's history, and this will continue into the next century.''

He raised a brow. "You are a seer, madame?''

She laughed. "Of sorts, I am.''

Abruptly all conversation ceased as the boat lurched. Startled, Stephanie cried out and gripped the sides. Propelled by strong currents, the boat sailed past an overhang of trees and splashed into a wide river.

Stephanie gaped about her. "My God, we're in the Mississippi."

"Yes," he replied, struggling with the oars. "And here begins the best part of our adventure. The current is strong, but at least it's taking us in the right direction."

"And what direction is that—New Orleans?"

He chuckled. "Don't worry, I won't be taking you quite that far." He used his oar to shove them away from a gray hulk protruding from the water. "Indeed, we may not get far at all if I split us apart on a dead tree."

"Are you sure you know what you're doing?" she asked skeptically.

"Quit fretting and enjoy the ride."

Enjoy the ride, Stephanie thought. In his own inimitable way, Andre Goddard was forcing her to savor the moment, truly to appreciate the world surrounding them. Whatever the eventual denouement of her adventure in time, she had to thank him for that.

She had been on the Mississippi before, but never *in* it, as they were now. Connecting with the river in this primal way was deeply exciting to her. She felt powerful currents propelling the craft, smelled the river's unique essence— mud, water, vegetation—as if it were the wet root of all life. In wonder her gaze swept from the immense, glittering waterway to the imposing tree-lined bluff. Suddenly she felt small and insignificant, a bit of flotsam in this vast sea.

As they curved around a bend, a slight indentation in the bluff caught her attention.

As if reading her mind, Andre explained, "Yonder beyond the bank lies the old Devil's Punchbowl."

"Devil's Punchbowl? I think I've heard of it."

"Some of it is filled in now, by vegetation and silt. But a century ago, the ravine was quite deep and large, and river pirates used to hide there."

"River pirates! How exciting."

"And deadly for those they victimized. Villains like Sam Mason and his cohorts used to disguise themselves as farmers and tempt passing flatboatmen with carrots, potatoes, or melons. Or, they'd bribe a woman into pretending she was being raped by one of the gang. The whole purpose was to get the poor fools in the rafts to pull ashore. As soon as the flatboatmen complied, they were robbed, murdered, and their bodies were tossed down the ravine.''

Stephanie shuddered. ''How gruesome.''

Andre crossed himself. ''The days of the Punchbowl are long gone, thank God.''

The two fell silent as he guided the rowboat around another bend. Stephanie went wide-eyed, spotting in the distance the hulk of a giant, majestic vessel, lit up and resplendent.

''What is that?'' she cried.

He grinned. ''My dear, behold the steamboat *Natchez*. The next part of our journey is into Natchez Under-the-Hill.''

Chapter 30

~~~⌒◯◯⌒~~~

Stephanie stared ahead, captivated, at the magnificent side-wheeler *Natchez*, moored at the Under-the-Hill landing. Steam whistle shrieking, massive twins stacks billowing black smoke into the night, the riverboat was an imposing yet whimsical presence with its cotton-crammed lower deck and graceful promenade above, where elegant couples strolled. With flags flying, name proudly emblazoned on its side, and layer upon layer of lacy white railings, the riverboat loomed especially majestic against the backdrop of Water Street with its weatherbeaten warehouses sagging on stilts in the mud.

As they glided closer, Stephanie heard a jazz band blaring out the strains of "Dixie." "Oh, this is enchanting!"

"Good, I want to enchant you," Andre replied. "I want to loosen up some of those inhibitions, show you how to enjoy life."

"You think we are on this earth only to have fun," she accused.

"And you think having fun is a sin," he retorted.

She fell silent. He did have a point.

They drifted downriver a bit, with Andre struggling to maneuver them toward the landing. At last the rowboat skidded ashore on a sandbar. Andre hopped out and helped Stephanie disembark, then pulled the vessel securely onto the muddy shelf.

"Come on, let's go get a closer look at the *Natchez*."

Stephanie touched her cap. "But what if people speak to me?"

He playfully tugged down her visor. "I'd lower my voice if I were you."

"Oh." She batted his arm. "How did I let you talk me into this madness, anyway?"

"Come on, quit complaining," he scolded, taking her hand.

They walked down a wide, muddy sandbar, passing darkened, ramshackle warehouses, a stable, and a saloon. Spotting a railway trestle climbing up the bluff, Stephanie asked, "What is that?"

"The Bluff City Railway," he replied. "In the morning, the cars will come down from the Hill to pick up freight and take it back up to town, along with any passengers who want an excursion."

Stephanie glanced askance at the steep angle of ascent. "It looks like a dizzying ride."

"This whole area will come alive in the morning—with drays and carts bringing in cotton and hauling off freight."

Stephanie pointed out what appeared to be a gigantic houseboat, bobbing in the waters not far from the *Natchez*, its gangplank extended. "And what is that?"

"That's the wharfboat, sort of a floating reception area with offices. This one was built from the wrecked hull of the *Belle Lee*."

"You're a real wealth of information tonight," she remarked. "Something tells me you know this area well."

"Shall I start describing the gambling parlors and pleasure dens?" he teased.

She shot him a mock-scolding glance. Then, as they moved closer to the steamboat, she shook loose his fingers. "Watch yourself, or people will think we're really odd."

He threw back his head and laughed. "And we're not?"

She didn't reply as they joined a small group of people—several gamblers accompanied by shady ladies—who stood listening to the concert. The band moved from the spirited finale of "Dixie" to the more somber strains of "My Old Kentucky Home." Stephanie glanced from the uniformed black musicians with their trumpets, trombones, drums, and banjos, to the gentlemen passengers removing their hats in apparent homage to a bygone way of life, the ladies delicately dabbing at tears with their lacy handkerchiefs. With the rolling river a gleaming backdrop to the stately steamer, and silver-tinged clouds floating past overhead, the atmosphere seemed dreamy, almost surreal.

"I'm so glad you brought me here," she whispered.

"Are you?"

Before she could reply, a booming voice inquired from above, "Andre Goddard, you scamp, what are you doing loitering on my landing?"

Andre and Stephanie turned as a towering man in a white suit and white panama hat strode down the gangplank toward them. His long white hair curled about his shoulders; his exaggerated mustache twirled at the ends. Puffing on a cheroot, he held himself as a man accustomed to commanding authority.

"Tom Leathers, you old river rat, I heard you'd be at the landing tonight," Andre called.

"That man is Tom Leathers?" Stephanie gasped. "*The* Tom Leathers?"

Andre didn't reply as Leathers reached their side, shook Andre's hand, then motioned with his cheroot toward Stephanie. "Who's the lad?"

"This is—er—Steven, our stableboy," Andre replied. "I thought it was about time the lad got a taste of sin."

"Out sowing the wild oats, are we, young man?" Leathers asked, eyes twinkling at Stephanie.

She struggled to make her voice deep, but the words came out hoarse instead. "Yessir."

Leathers raised a brow at Andre. "Is the lad ailing?"

"No, he's simply a late bloomer," replied Andre. "His voice is only now changing."

Leathers didn't comment further, though he appeared bemused. "And how is the family, Andre?"

"We're all thriving. And Mrs. Leathers and the children?"

"All well, and as full of spit as ever."

Unable to contain her curiosity any longer, Stephanie asked, "Tell, me, sir, are you the famous Captain Tom

Leathers, whose *Natchez* raced the *Robert E. Lee* to St. Louis?''

To Stephanie's surprise, Andre groaned, and Leathers glared. ''Does the lad covet the next spot in the Natchez Cemetery?''

As Stephanie shuddered, Andre said sternly, ''Steph—er, Steven, that particular steamboat race is a rather sore subject with the captain here.''

''But why?'' she asked.

''Because I lost!'' bellowed Leathers.

''Oh.'' Extremely embarrassed, Stephanie stammered, ''I—I didn't mean to insult you, sir. I just wanted to tell you how honored I am to be in the presence of a living legend such as yourself.''

Leathers grinned, his massive face lighting with pride. ''Living legend, eh?''

''Of course. You are surely the most famous Mississippi steamboat captain in history—except for Samuel Clemens, and he was a pilot, of course.''

Leathers nudged Andre with his elbow. ''I'm liking this boy more by the minute.'' Stepping closer to Stephanie, he added, ''I'll have you know, son, that my opponent, John Cannon of the *Lee*, was a contemptible coward and a cheat. Why, in Europe, most bets were declared null and void because Cannon stripped the *Lee* down to the barest skeleton and accepted help from another vessel while loading.''

''Why, I had no idea,'' cried Stephanie, irate.

Leathers puffed on his cheroot. ''I gave Cannon a good run without stooping to his tactics, and I lost fair and square!''

''Yes, sir.''

Appearing satisfied, Leathers paused. The band finished its selection and several negro singers came forward, crooning ''Swing Low, Sweet Chariot.''

''It's a fine concert, Tom,'' remarked Andre.

Nodding, Leathers gazed about him. ''God, how I miss this place.''

''We miss you, Tom,'' said Andre. ''Natchez isn't the same without you.''

Leathers gave a bitter laugh. ''The whole South isn't the

same, man. How often I remember our little cottage at Myrtle Terrace, and the happy years we spent there. I miss the days when men like John Quitman and Adam Bingaman knew how to serve up the best mint juleps, to hunt till the hounds were dragging their tongues, or deal a smart hand of poker." He sighed. "But alas, Mrs. Leathers said 'twas to New Orleans we would go, and my Charlotte's word is law in our household."

Andre laughed. "That little slip of a woman? Why, I bet you all but blow her down every time you blaspheme."

Leathers smiled wistfully. "She may be delicate as a lilac, but she managed to tame this old river dog." He waved his cheroot. "Well, lads, I was heading over to Silver Street to hunt up a game of poker. Care to join me?"

"Of course," answered Andre.

Leathers waited until the spiritual ended, then cupped a hand around his mouth and bellowed out, "Reuben? Where in blue blazes are you with that bucket? Don't you know Miss Beatrice likes her French champagne?"

In a flash, a negro man in steward's garb dashed down the gangplank, a silver ice bucket with champagne in hand, a spare bottle in the other. "Yes sir, Cap'n Tom."

Leathers motioned to the man. "Come along, all. We're off to Beatrice's."

The group trooped down the darkened wharf, then headed for Middle Street. Wrinkling her nose at the odors of garbage and stale beer, Stephanie stepped carefully to avoid puddles and potholes. As they crossed Middle Street, she glanced down a long row of wanly lit saloons and brothels with red lights winking in their windows. She heard a man's exuberant yell, a woman's bawdy laugh, a tinny piano playing "Flow Gently, Sweet Afton." She lurched to avoid a couple staggering out of a corner saloon, a bedraggled sailor and a hefty, cackling woman.

Soon they arrived on Silver Street and headed for a saloon where yellow light glowed behind grimy windowpanes. Tom Leathers shouldered through the double doors first, followed by Andre, Stephanie, and then the steward. Stephanie stared about her at a typical grogshop, like those she'd seen in countless Western movies. Behind the long oak bar, a mustachioed bartender in gartered shirt stood polishing the scarred wood with a dish towel; in the smoky shadows, shabbily dressed roustabouts played cards and nursed bottles of beer.

"Beatrice?" bellowed Leathers. "Get your pretty self out here!"

A woman's throaty laughter preceded the entrance of a middle-aged, painted doll strutting toward them from the shadows. Beatrice possessed a sagging bosom and lined face too heavily rouged; her hair was a garish color, almost orange, accented by an outrageous red feather headpiece. Her low-cut gown was fashioned of bright green satin, heavily sequined. A cigarette dangled between her full red lips.

"Tom Leathers, you river tramp!" she exclaimed, hugging him. "You been away so long, you've plumb broke my heart."

Leathers grinned. "But now I'm here—with company, and the finest French champagne."

Drawing on her smoke, Beatrice looked over Andre with deliberate relish. "So you are."

"Is the back room available?"

"Always for you, sugar."

Tom scowled. "We'll need a fourth for poker." He jerked a thumb toward the steward. "Reuben no longer plays, ever since those foot-washing Baptists got him."

While Beatrice howled with laughter, Reuben grinned sheepishly.

Beatrice looked about, then snapped her fingers. "Why, there's Clarence Johnson yonder. Today that nice lad fixed the brake on my carriage for free, and I insisted he stay and have a beer on the house. He might join in."

"Splendid." Leathers cupped a hand around his mouth. "Clarence, get your lazy bones over here."

Grinning, a handsome young black man in overalls stepped toward them. "Yes, sir, Captain Leathers."

"Clarence, I want you to join in a poker game with myself, Mr. Goddard and his—er—stableboy."

Clarence shook his head bashfully. "Oh, no, sir, Captain. I can't gamble. I'm plain broke."

"The finest blacksmith in all of Natchez is broke?"

mocked Leathers. "Well, I'll just have to grubstake you for rescuing Miss Beatrice here."

Clarence nodded. "If you say so, Captain."

"I say so. Come along, folks. Beatrice, lead the way."

Beatrice led them to a squalid little back room which barely accommodated a pitiful card table and four rickety chairs. Leathers lit another cheroot while Beatrice served everyone champagne.

Leathers passed a deck of cards to Andre. "Deal, Goddard."

"My pleasure."

As he shuffled the cards, Leathers spoke to Clarence. "Young man, I must tell you something. I don't entirely agree with the outcome of the little skirmish our country settled thirteen years ago, but what was done to your father was a sin."

The young man's features tightened. "Much obliged, sir."

Leathers turned to Stephanie. "William Johnson was one of the finest free men of color Natchez ever knew—damned fine barber, too."

"Thank you, sir," acknowledged Clarence.

"And for him to be struck down in such a dastardly manner . . ." Leathers's voice trailed off, and he shook his head.

"How was he struck down?" asked Stephanie.

While Leathers appeared shocked by her question, Andre explained, "The lad is not from here." Turning to Stephanie, he asked, "I take it you've never heard of the murder of William Johnson and the Winn trials?"

She frowned. "The names sound vaguely familiar."

"Well, as Tom was saying, William Johnson was an esteemed citizen of this community," Andre explained, dealing the cards. "Back in '49, he had a dispute with a man named Baylor Winn over some land, a contention which was settled in Johnson's favor. Afterward, Winn murdered him—and the evidence was pretty clear-cut. However, three trials failed to convict Winn, and he became a free man more or less on a technicality."

"What technicality?"

Johnson's son spoke up. "The law, young sir. At the

time, it said a negro couldn't testify against a white man, and the witnesses to my daddy's murder were negroes.''

"You have got to be kidding!" gasped Stephanie.

As Johnson shook his head, Leathers took up the tale. "The true irony is, Winn was almost certainly mulatto himself, so the negroes should have been allowed to testify. Only, he circumvented the law by convincing witnesses to state that he was half-Indian rather than half-colored.''

"How tragic," declared Stephanie. "No wonder the war was fought!''

At this comment, Clarence struggled against amusement, while Andre cast Stephanie a chiding glance and Leathers again glared. "Well, we don't have to go that far, young man. As for myself, I agree with the poet who wrote, 'Bury Me in Confederate Gray.' ''

"Any time you're ready, Captain," offered Clarence softly, and everyone laughed.

The group got down to their cards in earnest, Andre shoving a handful of coins before Stephanie and Leathers likewise staking Clarence. Leathers swore and pounded his fists when he lost the first hand, Andre's full house beating out his two pair.

"Hellfire and abominations!" he cried, throwing in his hand.

"What's going on in here?" asked Beatrice, entering with a tray.

"Goddard means to ruin me!" declared Leathers. "And Clarence here has already indicated his willingness to bury me.''

"Well, go in style, honey," she purred back, placing the tray before Leathers.

Leathers lit up at the sight of the whole strawberries, with sliced lemons on the side. "By the sweet by and by, Beatrice, love! You remembered!''

"How could I forget how you cotton to strawberries, sugar?" she simpered. "But, land, them lemons is hard to find.''

He chuckled and wrapped an arm around her waist. "A woman after my heart.''

She bumped a shapely hip against him. "Come share it with me later, precious?"

Leathers appeared genuinely contrite. "Now you know I mustn't stray from my dear Mrs. Leathers."

"If you ask me, your Mrs. Leathers is the luckiest lady in the South." She turned from Leathers, licking her lips and ogling Andre. "How about you, precious? What do you have a taste for tonight?"

"Only cards and champagne, Beatrice."

"More's the pity." She turned to Stephanie. "And you, sonny?"

Stephanie felt hot color shooting up her face. Leathers roared with laughter. "Now the boy could use some educating, I hear."

Beatrice trailed a finger along Stephanie's jaw, leaving her wishing she could dive beneath the table, and feeling half-nauseated by the madam's smell of tobacco, cheap perfume, and bordello sex.

With a cackle, the fallen angel teased, "Hey, it feels like you ain't even shaved yet, sonny. A bit wet behind the ears, ain't ya? Bet I can lick you dry. And so pretty you are, too—almost like a girl."

Stephanie was mortified. Andre gently pulled Beatrice's fingers away. "Let's not shock the lad too much his first time out. He's led a rather sheltered life."

She shrugged, then regarded Andre suspiciously. "Favor him yourself, do you?"

"Certainly not!" he roared back.

Stephanie had to turn away to hide her laughter, and she could hear Leathers's ribald chuckle, as well. She glanced up to see Andre scowling formidably at his friend.

"Leathers, one more word from you, and it's pistols at dawn," Andre stated.

"Have I said a word?" inquired Leathers.

Andre shoved the deck toward him. "Deal the cards."

The liquor flowed, and smoke curled about Stephanie's head until her eyes burned. But she knew it would not sound manly to complain; indeed, Captain Tom had looked suspicious enough when she refused one of his fine Cuban cigars. Besides, the evening fascinated her—the way Andre and Leathers roared back and forth at each other according to the vagaries of each hand, and especially the stories Tom Leathers told: about the night he sipped whiskey and discussed philosophy with Samuel Clemens; the day he shot a cannonball over the bow of a competitor's steamboat, "just for the pure-dee hell of it"; that awful April in '73, when he ran aground twice and got caught on the snag just below St. Louis, the one that almost sent up his boiler.

By the time they left Leathers in the wee hours, Stephanie was feeling almost giddy. Outside in the shadows of Silver Street, Andre caught her close. "Did you enjoy our little adventure?"

"Oh, yes," she replied. "It was like living another moment of history."

"You say the oddest things, woman."

"Shhh!" she scolded. "I'm a boy tonight."

"Not to me, love."

She slanted him a chiding glance. "Anyway, I was fascinated to see a colorful man like Tom Leathers with a humble man like Clarence Johnson. I gained so much insight into Southern sensibilities, why the war was inevitable, and how, ultimately, we are all just human beings."

"So even when we are out to have fun, we must learn something, subscribe to some nobler purpose?" he asked rather sadly.

"Learning can be fun, too," she countered. "Tonight was a grand adventure. Even being thought of as a man was—well, provocative in its way."

"So I noticed."

She grinned. "I had a good time, Andre."

He backed her into the doorway of a darkened shop. "Then thank me," he teased.

"You rogue."

"Just one kiss. Surely you can't protest that?"

Indeed, she didn't protest when he gathered her close and hungrily claimed her lips. The entire evening had been deliciously illicit, as was his mouth now. The stroke of his tongue was deep, drugging, erotic; his strong hands roved over her body, caressing her back, cupping her hips. She groaned as she felt his warm fingers sliding over her shirt, finding her breasts, squeezing gently. She whimpered and tore her mouth free just to breathe; the ecstasy was almost unbearable.

"Easy, darling," he coaxed. He drew back, and she could just make out his impassioned features in the silvery light. His thumb flicked over her nipple. "Do you like that, Steffie?"

"Too much," she acknowledged achingly. "But we shouldn't."

He leaned over to nibble at her throat. "Why not?"

"You know why, damn it," she whispered miserably.

"Have you kissed Henry yet?"

Caught off guard, she stiffened. "Henry? What has he got to do with this?"

"Just answer me. Have you kissed him?"

"No."

Andre pressed a palm to her breast, caressing her in a circular motion. "Has he touched you like this?"

By now Stephanie's knees were trembling. "N-no."

"Do you want him to?"

Helplessly, she shook her head.

Again he pressed his mouth to hers. "Does he want you like I do?"

"God, no."

This time, Stephanie kissed him, clinging to him, thrusting her pelvis against the aroused manhood that she ached to have pulsing inside her. With equal amounts of shock and titillation, she wondered if Andre would take her right here in this doorway, and doubted she would do anything to stop him. She could even see it in her mind, see herself clinging to him as he passionately claimed her body. Heavens, she could almost *feel* it. There was something so wicked about this place, something treacherous. Tonight she had succumbed to that iniquity, and succumbed totally to Andre's spell.

"Steffie, come with me," he whispered. "Let's climb the back stairs of some dark, illicit place, find a soft bed, and make love in the shadows. Please, darling, I crave you so much.''

"Oh, Andre," she gasped.

She felt his fingers slipping inside her trousers and shuddered in anticipation. Then all at once they both flinched at the sound of a male whistle.

As Andre jumped back and Stephanie hastily tucked in her shirt, a laughing Tom Leathers strode toward them. "So you fancy the lad after all, Goddard?"

Andre bristled. "You snake—now I *will* call you out."

Leathers only chuckled and tugged off Stephanie's cap, sending her blond hair tumbling about her shoulders. "I knew about the 'boy' from the outset—curves in all the wrong places, you see."

Stephanie burst out laughing.

"Why, you old rascal!" accused Andre.

"Why the ruse?" inquired Leathers.

Andre proudly wrapped an arm about Stephanie's shoulders. "Why, her reputation, of course. And if you tell anyone—"

"My lips are sealed," promised Leathers, eyes glittering devilishly. "For a kiss from the—er—*lad*."

"That's out of the question," blustered Andre.

"*Andre*," intoned Stephanie sternly.

"Yes?"

"Cool it." Grinning, she stepped up to Leathers.

He removed his hat and grinned. "Madame, any lady with such an aura of spirit and mystery I simply must kiss."

"Thank you for the compliment, sir."

He cocked a bushy brow at Andre. "May I first know the true identity of this delightful creature?"

"You may not!"

Leathers laughed, and as Stephanie stretched on tiptoe, he leaned over and quickly, chivalrously pecked her lips. He dipped into a elegant bow, then handed back her cap. "You'll be needing this, ma'am."

"Thank you, sir."

Stephanie chuckled as she watched Leathers stride off

into the night. Then she turned and saw the ardor once again burning in Andre's eyes, and she felt weak.

"Steffie," he whispered, starting toward her.

Thank God, Leathers's interruption had given her a moment to regain some self-control. She pressed a hand to his chest and spoke shakily. "Please—it's time to go home."

Chapter 31

By the time they met George at the base of the bluff, reclaimed their trotter and gig, and drove home, the night had waned considerably. Stephanie slept late, awakening half in a panic. She threw on her clothes, tore a comb through her hair and raced downstairs, only to find the family concluding breakfast.

"You're late!" greeted Gwen.

"I know—I'm sorry," replied Stephanie, taking her seat.

"Gwen, it's not polite to comment when someone is tardy for a meal," put in Ebbie as, smiling, she passed Stephanie a plate containing a stack of pancakes.

"You always do when I am," answered the child.

While Ebbie appeared at a loss, Andre chuckled, eyeing Stephanie with amusement as he dabbed a napkin to his mouth. "I'm sure that if Madame Sergeant slept late, it was because she needed the rest."

Stephanie cleared her throat and avoided his devilish gaze. "I think it's just the change of weather."

"Oh, I agree," said Ebbie. "These crisp autumn breezes make me drowsy, too."

"Perhaps Madame Sergeant needs to spend more time in bed," mused Andre with feigned innocence.

While Stephanie shot him a withering glance, Beau declared, "Yes, Papa, make her take a nap every day like the rest of us!"

At the suggestion, the older children all clapped and

cheered, even little Amy, who was usually so subdued. Stephanie had to laugh.

"Eat up, madame," urged Andre, passing Stephanie a bowl of fruit. "The cook has outdone herself with these pancakes and strawberries."

"So it seems." Stephanie ladled some of the fruit onto her pancakes.

"For that matter, I have a good friend, Captain Tom Leathers, who has a real passion for strawberries," Andre went on thoughtfully, sipping his coffee. "Have you ever made his acquaintance?"

Stephanie's cheeks were hot. "I've heard of him."

Next to her, Paul tugged at her sleeve and spoke excitedly. "Madame, Papa is taking us on an adventure this morning, to see Captain Tom!"

Stephanie raised a brow. "An adventure? You don't say."

"We're going to ride the train down to the landing!" exclaimed Gwen, her green eyes alight.

"A train ride? Really?"

"We're all going to watch the *Natchez* shove off," Andre added.

"The *Natchez* is in town?" asked Stephanie. "Why, I had no idea."

Andre threw back his head and laughed, and Stephanie quickly turned her attention to her breakfast. Yet it wasn't easy to eat with Andre seated just down the table from her, and her shocking behavior of last night so fresh in her mind. Each time he caught her eye or winked at her, she wanted to crawl under the table; each time Ebbie smiled her way, she felt hellishly guilty. She was supposed to be here matching up Ebbie and Andre, yet last night she had all but given herself to him with all the modesty of a Silver Street floozy. Thank God Tom Leathers had come along when he did, although it had still been a battle royal to convince Andre to take her home.

She hadn't expected to want him so much. In the five years since she'd lost Jim, of course she had missed sex at times; but this was different, an obsession, a craving she simply couldn't satisfy. Just knowing she lusted after Andre made her feel a traitor to Ebbie; and when she found herself almost succumbing to him, her regret was unbearable.

She didn't know how to extricate herself from this mess, how to gain Andre's cooperation without paying his "price." More and more, she suspected the price he really wanted was all of her.

Andre loaded up everyone—Stephanie, Ebbie, the older children, Martha and the baby—in a large double carriage, and Willie drove the group to the edge of the bluff, where an empty flatcar from the Bluff City Railway waited near a puffing steam donkey which powered a drum that rolled the cable. The air smelled acrid from the burning coal and reverberated with the sounds of the engine chugging.

Andre got out, spoke briefly to the brakeman, then returned to the carriage. "All set—we'll take the flatcar down."

Willie and Andre helped the women and children to alight. Approaching the car, Stephanie watched Andre hop up onto it; she studied the platform dubiously. Eyeing the sharp arc of the tracks over the verdant edge of the bluff, she grimaced. "Will we be safe?"

"But of course." Andre grabbed her hand and hauled her up.

"We want to ride the train!" cried Gwen, jumping up and down.

Getting down on his knees, Andre hoisted the child on board. "And you shall, pet. Take care, now."

The entire group was boarded, Andre taking special care with Martha and the baby. He personally held Sarah, while each woman took charge of one of the younger children, the group seating themselves on crates braced by sturdy railings. Paul proudly stationed himself at the rear of the car next to the brakeman.

"Take her down gently now," Andre ordered.

"Yes, sir," replied the brakeman.

A high squeal rang out from the cables, and the little car eased over the embankment and creaked slowly down the bluff. The children clapped and cheered, and were so excited by the ride that it was difficult to make them sit still.

Stephanie, holding Amy, stole a glimpse at Andre with the baby, the proud father pointing at the sights and telling Sarah all about them, even though she couldn't possibly comprehend what he was saying.

Stephanie felt an unexpected lump in her throat, a primal yearning warming her insides. Despite his faults, Andre Goddard was devoted to his children. Watching him so protectively, tenderly holding Sarah, she felt powerless over her own emotions. If only she could have his baby . . .

Horrified by the unbidden thought, Stephanie tried to quash it. For that matter, she didn't even know if she could have children. Yet being with this adorable family, with Andre, had left her feeling both conflicted and very maternal. She did want a child to love. Or did she just very badly want *these* children—and especially their father?

Andre Goddard was impetuous, ungovernable, rash. He was also tender, unpredictable, and great fun. When she had first arrived here, she had decried him as a rogue and denounced his hedonistic lifestyle. Yet gradually, he had seduced her with his charm and that very way of life; he had turned her sober, well-ordered existence into a grand adventure—a very seductive, romantic adventure.

She heard Ebbie's laughter and died a little inside. *Great-aunt Magnolia, help me,* she prayed silently. *Your guardian angel is in big trouble. I want to help Ebbie, but my own feelings keep getting in the way . . .*

"Madame, look!" cried Amy, breaking into Stephanie's thoughts.

"I know, sweetie." Straightening the ribbon on Amy's bonnet, Stephanie gazed down the steep bank lined with gold and scarlet trees that gave way to the squalor of Silver and Water Streets, and the teeming wharf beyond, a beehive of activity as roustabouts loaded cotton bales and unloaded bags and crates. The *Natchez* remained moored at the water's edge, dazzling white in the sunshine, the glittering waters of the Mississippi lapping at its hull; a calliope played "Pop Goes the Weasel."

At last the little car came to rest near the wharfboat. Even as the men helped the ladies and children to disembark, Gwen and Beau raced down the muddy bar toward the steamer, the ribbons on Gwen's hat rippling in the wind. Pausing only to stare at a sailor trooping past with a colorful parrot on his shoulder, the two then tore on toward the steamer's gangplank.

Leaving the baby with Martha, Andre quickly chased down the two, with Stephanie, Ebbie, and the others following on his heels.

Scooping Gwen up, Andre admonished, "Minx, you mustn't run off like that. What if you fell in the river?"

The unabashed child laughed. "I'm not afraid!" She pointed at the *Natchez*. "I want to go for a ride on that big boat!"

Andre glanced up at the deck, recognition dawning in his eyes. "Well, good morning, Captain Tom."

Above them on the main deck, Leathers removed his hat and grinned down at the group. "Andre, what an unexpected pleasure."

Andre gestured toward the ladies. "You know Ebbie Rice, of course."

He bowed. "Miss Rice."

"Good day, Captain," she called. "How is your dear wife?"

"Just fine, thank you, ma'am."

"And this other lovely lady is a newcomer to our home, Madame Stephanie Sergeant," Andre added.

Leathers lifted a bushy brow. "Madame Sergeant, what a pleasure. You wouldn't happen to be kin to a lad named—er—Steven?"

Feeling guilty color shoot up her face, especially as she caught Ebbie's confused glance, Stephanie stammered back, "Er—no, sir. No relation."

Leathers's expression was full of mischief. "How singular. I must say the resemblance is striking."

Andre cleared his throat. "What do you say, Tom, old friend. May my brood see your vessel?"

Leathers took out an ornate gold pocket watch and flipped it open. "We're about to cast off, but if you want to come on board, I can take the lot of you as far as Pine Ridge landing."

At Leathers's offer, all four of the older children began

jumping up and down and pleading with their father.

Andre turned to Willie. "Meet us at the Pine Ridge landing with the carriage?"

He grinned. "Yes, sir."

The group boarded the steamboat, the children cheering as the steam whistle blew and the stacks billowed out smoke. The mighty vessel glided away from the landing, its boilers churning, its massive wheel plodding against the current.

While the captain took Andre and his sons into the wheelhouse so all could try a turn at steering the vessel, Stephanie left Martha and Ebbie to mind the baby and enjoy the sights, and herself took charge of Amy and Gwen as the older girl led them on a spirited tour of the boat. The three explored the massive grand salon, with its linen-draped tables and richly patterned carpet, its dazzling ceiling of delicately sculpted white arches counterbalanced by massive chandeliers; they attracted grins from the stewards setting the table for luncheon. Next, in the smoky men's parlor, they raised frowns from a group of gamblers hunched over a card table; in the adjacent ladies' ordinary, they garnered tolerant smiles from a group of women discussing a Bible passage. The threesome then peeked into the huge kitchen, where the staff was preparing crabmeat crêpes, braised duck, and a massive tiered cake grand enough to grace any wedding; finally they paused on the promenade to hear the jazz band play "Amazing Grace."

By the time they descended to the bow on the main deck, Andre, the boys, and the captain had rejoined Martha and Ebbie at the railing, and the *Natchez* was plowing around a breathtaking bend lined with scarlet sweet gum trees. Stephanie's heart did a new flip-flop as she noted that Andre again held Sarah, his cheek pressed close to hers. The moment was pure enchantment, and again her mind was treacherously drawn to the prospect of sharing life with this charming family in this captivating time.

Gwen rushed up and tugged at her father's coattails. "Papa, we just saw a cake bigger than a Christmas tree! May we stay and eat it?"

As the other children joined in with a chorus of pleas,

Andre held up a hand. "Sorry, pet, but we'll soon be at the Pine Ridge landing, and Captain Tom must continue on to St. Louis."

Gwen's face fell. "Why can't we go to St. Louis?"

"Perhaps we will sometime, dear," put in Ebbie gently. "Just not today."

Gwen fell sullenly silent, and Leathers spoke up. "You know, young lady, we've enough of that cake to serve half of Mississippi. You'd do me a service if you'd take a big chunk of it home with you."

Gwen jumped up and down. "May we, Papa? Pretty please?"

"Tom, you mustn't go to any trouble," scolded Andre.

Leathers winked at Gwen. "Anything for the smile of a pretty lady."

Gwen beamed.

"You're too generous, my friend," added Andre.

"Bah—'tis nothing," Leathers insisted. "And you know we'll be back through on Saturday. Bring your brood back to the landing and they can have the run of the vessel."

The children again hooted their excitement. Andre grinned and shook Tom's hand. "We may take you up on your offer, dear friend—*if* you'll allow me to reciprocate. I must insist you be our guest at the Harvest Ball on Saturday night, and for dinner at Henry Robillard's afterward. My partner has given me leave to invite a few of my own guests, and I'm sure he'd be honored to have you."

"Andre, you have a deal," agreed Leathers. He winked at Stephanie. "And who knows? I may run across that charming young fellow who so resembles Madame Sergeant. I've been hoping I might find him again."

Andre elbowed Leathers, and Stephanie sorely wished she could sink through the deck.

Chapter 32

"**T**here, you look simply lovely," declared Stephanie.

"Do you really think so?" asked Ebbie.

"Of course. You'll be the envy of every woman—and man—at the theater tonight."

On Wednesday evening, Stephanie stood with Ebbie before the pier glass in Ebbie's room. Although her friend was frowning dubiously at her reflection, Stephanie did find Ebbie's appearance much improved, and exulted in having finally persuaded her to abandon her usual drab attire.

She felt rather like a magician who had coaxed a butterfly out of its cocoon. Although in her modest, high-necked gold silk frock Ebbie was hardly a *femme fatale,* her hair was loose, curled becomingly about her face and shoulders, and her pearl necklace and earbobs, the small wreath of tea rosebuds in her hair, along with her elegant cream-colored shawl shot through with gold strands, added dashes of verve and femininity.

Stephanie was pleased to have Ebbie out of her perpetual black at last, and hoped that tonight, Andre might finally take note of this dear little woman who secretly, desperately loved him. Still, she wished she'd been able to coax Ebbie into wearing an ensemble that was a little more daring— perhaps one like her own. She wore an off-the-shoulders frock of vivid green taffeta, with white puffed sleeves, a tight waist, full skirt, and a white underskirt trimmed in lace. A green velvet choker with a cameo accented the boldly dipping neckline; her hair was pulled back, with a small wreath of silk violets on the crown of her head, and a cascade of sausage curls spilling down her nape. She did look feminine and provocative, all right, like a woman out to catch the eye of a man. If only her spirits did not sink whenever she realized that man would be Henry Robillard.

"I feel so awkward in this bright color, and with my hair down," Ebbie was fretting. "As if I'll be drawing attention to myself."

"But that is precisely what we want," Stephanie assured her, reaching out to straighten a curl. "Next time, we'll get you into something—well, with a little more *oomph* in the bosom."

Ebbie flushed deeply. "Why, I could never be so immodest." Watching Stephanie blanch, she touched her arm. "Not that you don't look divine in that low-necked frock. Mrs. Hodge was right that the new style suits you to perfection, and Henry will surely be entranced."

"As Andre will be when he sees you."

Ebbie lowered her gaze. "I hope so. He might prefer me in a flashier frock, but I seem to lack your—er—attributes. I suppose I'm just not the type."

Stephanie laughed. "Honey, *every* woman is the type."

Ebbie actually giggled.

Stephanie grabbed her friend's fan and reticule and stuffed them into her hands. "Come on, we're both ready, and Henry should be calling for me any time. Let's go show you off to Andre."

Although Ebbie blushed again at the mention of his name, she dutifully headed for the door. Stephanie grabbed her own reticule and also draped a shawl about her bosom, so as not to offer the rogue any undue encouragement.

Even as two women glided down the stairs in their lavish gowns, Andre stepped out of the parlor to watch them. Stephanie found her heart quickening at the sight of him in his breathtaking black cutaway and pleated linen shirt. How his dark hair caught the light, and his blue eyes gleamed; yet that dazzling gaze was focused on her, when it should be on Ebbie.

"Well, ladies." At last Andre took note of Ebbie, clasped

her gloved hand, and kissed the back of it. "My dear, you look lovely."

Ebbie's eyelashes fluttered. "Thank you, Andre."

"Yes, isn't she simply divine?" Stephanie encouraged.

Without responding to her prompt, Andre turned to her and kissed her hand, as well. "Stephanie, what a stunning gown. That emerald green is definitely your color."

"Thank you, Andre."

"May we drive you to the theater?" he continued solicitously.

"Henry is coming for me."

Even as she made the announcement, a rap sounded at the door. Stephanie noted Andre's chagrined expression as he turned and opened the panel to face a smiling Henry in top hat, gloves, and formal cutaway. "Well, Robillard, what a pleasant surprise."

Stepping inside, Henry removed his hat and shook Andre's hand. "Surely you knew I was escorting Stephanie tonight."

"Alas, it skipped my mind," Andre drawled.

Henry bowed to her and grinned. "My dear, you look ravishing. You, too, Miss Ebbie."

Both woman murmured thank-yous.

Andre was gazing intently at Stephanie. "Indeed, she looks so fetching, I'm not sure Ebbie and I should let her loose. See you treat her well, Robillard, or you'll have me to contend with."

While Stephanie gritted her teeth at Andre's arrogance, Henry visibly bristled. "Why would I not treat her well? I'll have you know my aunt is waiting in the carriage to act as chaperon."

Andre tapped Henry's arm. "Splendid, Robillard. Just splendid."

Clearly irritated, Henry extended his arm toward Stephanie. "Shall we go, my dear?"

"Certainly." Pointedly ignoring Andre, she added, "Have a good time, Ebbie."

Shooting Andre a frosty glance over her shoulder, Stephanie sailed out the front door with Henry.

*   *   *

"Andre, is something wrong?"

Half an hour later, sitting with Ebbie near the front of the Natchez Theatre, Andre was feeling less than serene. The theater was rapidly filling, the air was redolent with the scents of perfume and pomade, and the orchestra was tuning up.

He pulled out his pocket watch, flipped it open, and scowled at the dial. "I'm wondering where in blazes Stephanie and Robillard are. The curtain is bound to rise at any moment."

Ebbie glanced about at row after row of posh red velvet seats, many of which were already filled with ladies and gentlemen in formal attire, as additional theatergoers moved down the aisles. Eyes lighting with recognition, she smiled and waved. "Ah, there is Peter Dearborn with Judge Shields and his family. As for Stephanie and Henry, perhaps they're here and we just haven't spotted them yet."

Andre gestured toward a section to their left. "Henry's season tickets are on the aisle two rows up from us, and as you can see, his seats are still vacant."

"Ah . . . I hadn't noticed. Perhaps they went for a drive first. Sunsets along the bluff can be so spectacular this time of year."

Andre grumbled an unintelligible reply, snapped his watch shut, and replaced it in his vest pocket. He was furious at the very idea of Henry's romancing Stephanie with a sunset ride—even with Katie Banks along.

"Stephanie does seem taken with Henry," Ebbie remarked.

"She does?" he inquired tensely.

Ebbie turned a page in her program. "She speaks of him highly."

He glowered.

Ebbie flashed him an apologetic look. "I'm sorry. Did I say something wrong?"

"No, not at all, dear."

Solemnly, Ebbie continued, "You know, if Stephanie marries Henry—"

"*Marries* Henry?" he cut in sharply. "Since when is she marrying Robillard?"

Ebbie had gone pale at his sharp tone. "Well, she's not, I mean as far as I know. I'm just saying that if things should—er—proceed in the direction of matrimony, Stephanie might not leave us."

"Leave us?" he repeated, brow knitted.

"You're aware of her plans to return to her own people?"

"Ah, yes."

"However, if she took a husband in Natchez, then we wouldn't lose her, would we? At least she'd remain in the same town."

Andre made a sound of contempt. "Henry Robillard is not a fitting husband for our Stephanie."

"He's not?" Ebbie asked, clearly shocked. "And why not? He seems perfectly upstanding, well-to-do—"

"He's a bloody bore," Andre cut in, hastily adding, "even if I do love him like a brother."

Ebbie studied him in puzzlement. "Andre, if I didn't know better, I'd swear that you were . . ."

"What?"

She blushed and buried her nose in her program. "Never mind."

"What?" he demanded. "Jealous of Robillard?"

Flinching at his harsh tone, Ebbie stammered, "W-Well, what I mean is, how could I not take note of the fact that—"

"Yes?"

Bravely, she finished, "Well, that you strongly objected to Henry's escorting Stephanie tonight."

His expression was dark. "The woman lives under my roof. Of course I must act as her protector."

"I see," Ebbie murmured, though she appeared confused.

Andre frowned and drummed his fingers on his armrest.

Ebbie gazed about the theater again. "Ah—there they are now."

At once, Andre twisted about to see Katie Banks strolling down the aisle in a glittering silver dress, followed by Stephanie on Henry's arm. "At least Robillard was not so rude as to miss the first act."

"And you were fretting over nothing."

He turned to her contritely. "You're right, and I'm sorry, dear. Again, I must tell you how wonderful you look in that fine color. I do hope you'll have done with the black now."

She nodded shyly. "Thank you, but I must confess I feel disloyal to Linnea."

He touched her hand, and spoke with uncharacteristic emotion. "You mustn't, Ebbie. Linnea would want us all to put our grief behind us and carry on."

Ebbie fell quiet, eyes moist as she obviously struggled with her feelings. "Yes, perhaps you're right."

Andre regarded her with keen compassion, then leaned over and kissed her cheek. "You poor heart."

Ebbie colored deeply, a hand fluttering to her cheek. "Andre, I . . ."

"Sorry, I didn't mean to embarrass you," he added with a gentle smile, glancing at Stephanie again. "I just want you to cheer up."

Following his gaze, Ebbie spoke in a small voice. "Or perhaps you wanted Stephanie to see us?"

For a moment Andre was stunned speechless, and could only stare back at Ebbie.

"You think I haven't noticed the way you look at her?" she added with obvious turmoil.

At last Andre was able to speak. "Ebbie, please don't jump to conclusions. Stephanie is a lovely woman, of course. But that doesn't change what you mean to me. I'm so very grateful to you for all you've done for my family."

"Are you?" She stared at her lap. "Is gratitude the reason you keep—er—asking me out?"

"Why . . ." He gestured in resignation. "It seemed the proper thing to do."

"I don't want you to feel obligated—"

"But I do," he cut in feelingly. "You've given up everything for my family. If only there were some way I could repay you."

Ebbie was silent for a long moment. "Perhaps there is," she murmured at last.

"Really? What?"

She nervously smoothed her skirt. "This is not the time to speak of—well, so delicate a matter."

"Come now, Ebbie, don't be coy," he scolded. "Tell me what you're thinking."

Yet she shook her head. "Andre, when the time is right, perhaps we should have a long, serious talk. I think you'll be surprised at how alike our thinking is."

Andre was left mystified. Tonight Ebbie had at last spoken out, the reticent little mouse saying more to him in just a few moments than she'd revealed the entire time he'd known her. But she'd spoken in riddles, voicing questions, doubts. What had she meant when she'd said he might be able to repay her?

He shifted uneasily in his chair.

He'd gone along with this charade to have a chance with Stephanie; he'd assumed, perhaps foolishly, that Ebbie couldn't *really* be in love with him. He'd even enjoyed the masquerade and the prospect of winning over Stephanie.

He'd felt so smug, so safe playing this little game. But what if he'd been dead wrong all along and Stephanie was right? What if he really *was* the love of Ebbie's life, and she was destined toward heartache at his hands? The prospect of actually hurting Ebbie wasn't funny at all; that possibility turned the "game" into something insidious. Even if he didn't love Ebbie, he was quite fond of her, and he owed her so much. Having her experience heartache at his hands was unthinkable.

Andre Goddard had never been a man with a particularly troublesome conscience. Thus he found it supremely ironic that Stephanie might ultimately win, and win by virtue of his own belated sense of honor. . . .

Across the aisle, Stephanie saw Andre and Ebbie with their heads together, then watched Andre kiss Ebbie. She churned with longing and jealousy.

Why was she so upset? Wasn't this exactly what she had wanted, to see signs of Andre and Ebbie drawing closer to each other?

Then Andre glanced her way and their gazes locked for a brief, meaningful moment. Stephanie turned hastily away—and came face-to-face with a grinning Henry.

He lifted her hand and kissed it. "Did you enjoy the ride along the bluff?"

"Oh, it was wonderful," Stephanie assured him. "The way the setting sun hit those red and gold leaves—the light was simply spectacular."

Henry's gaze darkened. "No more spectacular than you look tonight, my dear." He leaned over her toward Katie. "Isn't Stephanie a vision, aunt?"

"Why, she's the most shining jewel in this theater," Katie declared. "I'm expecting an elopement to Vidalia any day now."

Stephanie and Henry laughed—Stephanie rather nervously.

As the lights went down and the orchestra launched into a Rossini overture, Katie clapped her hands. "Oh, wonderful, the curtain is about to go up. I've heard this troupe does a smashing *Camille*."

Stephanie nodded bravely to Katie, though inwardly she felt about as cheerful as Dumas's weepy heroine. . . .

Chapter 33

Late the following afternoon, Stephanie returned to her room to freshen up for dinner and was surprised to find a beautiful lady's silk-and-ivory fan spread out on her dresser. Smiling, she traced her fingers over the lovely images of red roses painted on a shiny black background.

Another gift from Andre? Picking up the fan, she was bemused to spot a folded note beneath it. She opened it to see Andre's distinctive handwriting:

> Stephanie,
>
> *We must talk regarding an urgent matter. Meet me in the attic at midnight. Be there . . . or there will be consequences.*
>
> A.

With a groan, Stephanie tossed the note aside. Oh, he could be exasperating—charming her with the fan, then blackmailing her into meeting him again. If she failed to show up, the "consequence" would obviously be that he wouldn't escort Ebbie to the Harvest Ball on Saturday night.

Stephanie considered standing him up, reasoning that surely he would not be so cruel as to refuse to take Ebbie out at the last minute. Ultimately, though, she decided she couldn't afford to risk it, even though the greatest risk of all was that Andre would come closer to decimating her own defenses every time they were alone.

She smiled as another possibility dawned, though an admittedly less likely one. Could Andre want to talk because he was finally coming around to her point of view, or even beginning to care for Ebbie? After all, hadn't he complimented Ebbie's appearance last night? Hadn't she spotted the two of them with their heads together at the theater, even spied Andre kissing Ebbie's cheek?

Perhaps the two were finally becoming an item—and she dared not give vent to the jealous feelings this possibility stirred.

"Come in, my dear," Andre called.

At midnight, after climbing a flight of narrow, twisting stairs, Stephanie creaked open the door to the Harmony House attic. Hoping to hold Andre at bay, she'd deliberately worn a modest, high-necked blue muslin gown and a navy shawl.

The air in the attic was cool and smelled of must. In a pool of soft light at the center of the vast chamber, Andre lounged on a magnificent blue tapestry, depicting Venetian boating scenes, that had been spread out on the floor. With his dark trousers pulling at the muscles of his thighs, his shirt half-unbuttoned to reveal the mat of dark curls on his chest, his hair slightly rumpled, and the line of whiskers along his jaw, he appeared sexy and decadent. Around him were artfully arranged an ice bucket with champagne, two crystal goblets, and a picnic basket. Beside him lay a single, perfect red rose.

Remembering his gift of the fan, Stephanie felt herself softening treacherously toward him, her pulse quickening and her stomach knotting. The setting could not have been more intimate or provocative. Nonetheless, she balled her hands on her hips and faced him down.

"So *this* was the urgent matter you spoke of—a midnight picnic?"

He grinned. "Stop arguing and come closer."

Starting toward him, Stephanie almost tripped over a grime-encrusted brass andiron.

"Careful," he scolded. "This place is crammed with junk."

"Crammed is the word," she agreed, "but I wouldn't call any of this junk."

Indeed, by now Stephanie was gaping at the vast collection of priceless antiques cluttering the huge expanse. Gorgeous Hepplewhite side chairs hung carelessly from the rafters; a magnificent black-and-gold Oriental sideboard gathered dust in a corner. A quaint Gothic cabinet, whose stained-glass front was shaped like an ancient cathedral, dazzled the eye despite a heavy coating of grit.

Stephanie paused by a gilded writing table with elegant carved legs. Running her fingertips over a breathtaking marquetry panel, she declared, "My God, this piece looks like Louis XIV!"

Andre gave a shrug. "It likely is."

Her mouth fell open. "You've shoved a Louis XIV piece into your attic to gather dust?" She twisted about to scowl at a gilt-framed painting propped against the desk, a landscape of an English countryside. "This can't be a Turner!"

"You mean the English landscape painter?" he inquired with an air of boredom. "I believe my mother met him on her and Papa's honeymoon to Europe, many years ago."

Stephanie could only shake her head. She continued about the room, perusing and touching various items with an air of reverence. "Heavens, this is a Baccarat paperweight—I don't even want to think about what it's worth. That striped settee must be Sheraton, that harp from the Regency period. And just look at this japanned box, plus a whole roll of Chinese wallpaper—"

"Stephanie!" Andre cut in.

"Yes?" Holding a harlequin clown figurine, she glanced at him.

"Put down that toy and come over here."

"Toy?" she repeated indignantly, carefully setting down the brightly colored figurine. "Why, this is priceless Meissen porcelain!"

"Yes, and we've scads more of it downstairs."

She gestured around them. "How can you allow all of these treasures simply to rot up here?"

"If we tried to fit them all downstairs, Harmony House would look like a rummage sale. This attic is filled with furnishings my grandparents brought over from France, and many other items my family and I accumulated in our travels.''

"Ah, yes—all those spur-of-the-moment trips to Europe," she mocked.

"Precisely."

"Furnishings so fabulous should be used—or placed in a museum."

He chuckled. "Stephanie, you may have anything in this room that you covet." He grinned devilishly. "Including me."

"You rogue! Trying to bribe me again, are you?"

But she dutifully crossed over and sat down beside him. He regarded her with amusement and admiration, and all at once she became intensely conscious of his scent, the sexy length of his black lashes, the bright blue of his eyes, the ardor burning there. Reclined on one arm, he rather reminded her of an exotic leopard about to pounce—with this fabulously cluttered attic his jungle.

He solemnly handed her the rose. "Stephanie, I'm entirely serious."

She took a whiff of the bloom. "More and more, I think you must have money to burn."

"A novel-sounding pleasure, and one I haven't tried, as yet. Do you want to?"

"Heavens, no!"

"You're too sensible, my dear."

"And you're such a profligate."

His expression turned serious. "I do not apologize for being what I am. I enjoy life, and I intend to see you doing the same."

"There's a difference between enjoying life and being a wastrel, having no purpose."

With a sigh, he turned to open the champagne, and she flinched slightly as the cork popped. He handed her a glass of the bubbling brew. "You persist in thinking rather badly of me. In our times together, haven't you found any redeeming qualities in me?"

Stephanie lowered her lashes and sipped the champagne,

which tasted cool, sweet, and wonderful. "I'd best not comment there."

He nudged her slipper with his boot. "I must insist you do."

She regarded him with grudging admiration. "Well, you're a charming rogue—though I'm not sure that recommends you."

"And?"

Stephanie couldn't repress a smile. "You do have a certain passion for life. I must admit I admire that."

"Then we're making progress." He raised her hand and kissed it. "However, at the moment, my passion is for a certain lady."

Fighting excitement, she forged on. "And you know I think you're a good father—if much too indulgent."

He raised his glass. "Then we'll toast to my passion for life—and my being a good father."

Stephanie solemnly clicked her glass against his and took another sip. She was surprised to watch his expression turn solemn as he set down his drink.

"Is something wrong?" she asked.

He gazed up at her frankly. "Well, yes, I think we do need to talk."

She nodded. "Are you coming to your senses?"

"About what?"

"About Ebbie."

He appeared highly perturbed. "Actually, it's Ebbie I want to talk about."

"Really?" she questioned with a superior smile. "And break your own rule?"

He glowered. "You have brought us to this pass."

"Me?" she asked piously.

"Of course, you!"

"Go on," she encouraged, smoothing her skirts.

He brow grew deeply furrowed. "Well, last night at the theater, I was somewhat taken aback when Ebbie began to question things—like, why I'm taking her out, why I seem so interested in you."

Stephanie tensed. "I do hope you reassured her. I mean—I saw you kissing her."

He reached out to stroke her cheek. "Did that make you jealous, darling?"

"None of that!" she scolded.

"I had hoped it would," he admitted. "I mean, I kissed Ebbie to comfort her, as she was feeling low about Linnea. But afterward . . ." He grinned. "I rather savored the prospect that I might have stirred you up, especially since you had gone to the theater with Henry. You made me quite mad with jealousy, you know."

"Oh!" She wagged a finger at him. "Andre, this is not a game!"

He groaned. "I'm beginning to realize that."

"What do you mean?"

He thoughtfully sipped his champagne. "Despite your claims to the contrary, I think I've been assuming all along that Ebbie couldn't really love me. But after last night, I'm not so sure."

"See?" She waved a hand. "What have I been telling you? She loves you. And, like the rest of Natchez, she's assuming the two of you will marry."

His visage grew grim. "Then I think it's time to call a halt to it."

"A halt to what? To you and me?"

"No, to me and Ebbie."

"*What*?" she cried, sitting up.

He touched her arm. "Stephanie, I could actually hurt her, and that's the last thing I'd ever want. And you're just as responsible for pushing me toward her—"

"I'm responsible?"

"I think we should abandon this charade before real harm is done. Why don't I take Ebbie to the ball on Saturday, and after that . . . I'll, well, let her down gently."

Stephanie's fist pounded the floor. "No, Andre, you can't. You must marry her."

"Why?"

"Because she loves you, damn it."

"But I don't love her," he retorted.

"Must you always think of yourself?"

"What about you?" he countered aggressively. "What's your true motive in this demented matchmaker business?

Why are you so determined to force me to marry a woman who will never be right for me, nor me for her?''

Stephanie was quiet for a long moment, agonizing over his questions. How could she tell him what she actually knew of Ebbie's fate, and reveal where she really came from, without his assuming she was nuts?

She bravely met his gaze. ''Andre, what if Ebbie's life depended on your marrying her?''

He rolled his eyes. ''Stephanie, you're being absurd.''

''Assume for the sake of argument that I'm telling the truth. If it were a matter of life and death, would you marry her?''

''Of course I would.''

She drew a convulsive breath and met his eye. ''Andre, it's a matter of life and death.''

He threw up his hands. ''There you go again. I'm beginning to doubt your sanity.''

''But if I could convince you I'm telling the truth, you'd marry her, wouldn't you?'' she argued passionately. ''You wouldn't want her to die, would you?''

''Stephanie, you're starting to scare me.''

''Answer my question. You would marry her?''

''Yes.'' He gazed at her starkly. ''Especially if I could also have you.''

''Andre!''

''Well, if you're determined to spin such ludicrous fantasies, why can't I have a few of my own?'' he demanded. ''If I must marry a woman I don't love, can't I have any joy in my life?''

Stephanie could only gaze at him frustration and anguish, his words turning her inside out emotionally.

He cupped her chin in his hand and spoke intensely. ''Ebbie loves you, too, you know. She might even forgive me for wanting you.''

Stephanie reeled at his words, *Ebbie loves you, too* . . . Was he hinting that *he* loved her? His expression, his tone, seemed utterly sincere.

With a shudder, she pulled away from his titillating touch. What could she say to reach him? Telling him the truth would only further convince him she was off her rocker. At the moment, all she could think of was appealing to his more devious side.

She proudly tilted her chin. "You know, Andre, if you stop taking Ebbie out, you won't be able to bribe me into seeing you anymore."

He only smiled, leaning over to kiss her cheek. "Then I must take advantage of tonight to change your mind, eh?"

"You rascal. I think it's time for me to leave."

He caught her hand. "You're not going anywhere."

"You're going to stop me?"

"If necessary. You're going to share this picnic with me—and no more arguments."

She glowered.

Chuckling, he opened the picket basket and drew out several small plates covered with napkins. One held blackberries and grapes, another several kinds of cheeses, a third caviar on crackers.

"Have some caviar?" he offered.

She chewed her bottom lip. "Andre, we still haven't—"

"Hush. I promise I'll give it more thought, but we'll not change each other's minds tonight."

You're probably right, she acknowledged with a sigh. She wrinkled her nose at the cracker he had raised toward her mouth. "Thanks, but I've never cared for caviar."

"I intend to see that you develop a taste for many of life's finer pleasures."

"A loaded comment if I've ever heard one," she muttered.

"Quit balking and take a bite."

Stephanie nibbled at the cracker, finding the fish eggs less bitter than memory served. "Not bad."

He plopped the rest of the cracker in her mouth. "It's Russian, from the Caspian Sea. The finest."

"Of course. What else would you have?"

He grinned and proceeded to hand-feed her several blackberries, as well as tidbits of cheese. She wondered at the change in him, from verbal jouster to debonair debaucher of women. She fought a building excitement as his fingertips lingered on her lips, as he sensuously brushed a crumb from her chin, as all the while his bright eyes and seductive smile seduced her. They were entering dangerous territory, and she should try to leave again, but she wasn't ready to tussle with him physically, knowing all too well how it might end. . . .

After a moment, he murmured, "Stephanie, I'm wondering something . . ."

"Yes?"

"Why are you so determined never to love again?"

Knocked off guard by the question, she drew a slow breath. "I suppose I feel it's expecting too much to assume something so special will come along more than once in a lifetime. Besides, I think that what you're referring to is not love but lust."

"Are you so sure?"

She laughed. "Andre, your entire life is a testimony to your excesses. Look at this room, this decadent little love pit you've designed."

"Love pit?" he repeated with a devilish wiggle of his eyebrows. "Now there's an interesting term."

"Oh, hush. My point is, you're pampered and spoiled, and you've raised your children the same way. I was brought up in a much more modest environment, and I've had to work for much of what I've had. The same was true for my husband. Excess and waste bother me a lot."

"I've surmised as much, and I like and admire that unspoiled quality in you. It makes me want to give you all the things you've lacked."

"So you can turn me into you?"

"Not at all. So I can appreciate life more through your eyes."

She waved a hand in frustration. "You just don't understand, do you?"

"What don't I understand?"

"We're totally different. You've never had to work for anything, have you?"

"Well, I have been given a lot. Am I supposed to feel guilty about it?"

"My point is, you're a libertine, while I'm totally grounded in the Protestant work ethic. If I were ever to love again, he would have to be someone like me, with similar values and interests. A blind man can see that we're exact opposites.''

"But opposites can complement each other," he argued, "as we do. You bring me down to earth a bit, and I help your spirit break free—don't I?"

Stephanie gazed at him in mingled joy and anguish. "Yes, you have a point."

"And if it will make you feel better," he went on teasingly, "we'll have a go at being industrious. We'll march about the grounds at least twice daily."

Despite herself, Stephanie giggled. "You're an impossible scamp. I suspect you only want me because you've had to work at it."

A self-deprecating chuckle escaped him as he reached out to toy with a blond curl on her shoulder. "I'll admit I've become rather jaded, and accustomed to women who throw themselves at my feet. Finding a woman who scoffs at what I have to offer is refreshing, to say the least."

"Then you want me because I'm a challenge."

His hands clasped her shoulders, and his voice took on a debilitating, husky note. "Stephanie, darling, I want you because you set me on fire."

Oh, he was devastating! Stephanie tried to pull away, but her own whimper of desire gave her away. Andre's lips moved over hers in soft, fleeting caresses, until she could bear no more and eagerly captured his mouth with her own. A sound of triumph rumbling from his throat, he gently pushed her shoulders to the floor. His solid body rolled over hers, holding her his willing prisoner. He kissed her long, druggingly, his hand cupped over her breast. Helplessly, she responded in kind, tracing her tongue over his lips, sinking her fingers into the rich silk of his hair. He was hot and he tasted so good; they were both on fire. It seemed forever since she'd been alone with him, and she was starved for him. Her mind told her this was wrong, so wrong; yet her body craved this man fiercely—and at the moment her body was winning.

He pulled back and gazed starkly into her eyes. "Now we shall have the truth. You want me, Stephanie. Admit it."

Her anguished face met his. "I do, Andre, but this isn't right. Oh, I'm so confused!"

He arched against her, letting her feel his hard erection. "You're confused? I'm in agony." He planted tiny kisses on her face, and began undoing the small buttons at her throat. "Do you know how much I burn for you? Do you know how good I can make this? I can make you beg for more."

"Oh, God," she gasped. She was on the verge of begging now!

With his lips again coaxing hers, he unbuttoned her bodice, his fingers slipping inside her camisole to caress her bare breast. She was moaning incoherently as his lips slid down her throat, to her breast, her taut nipple. Tremors of rapture shuddered down her spine. His hand slid slowly up her leg, his touch teasing the smooth contours of her knee, her thigh, then moving treacherously higher. At last he found the slit in her drawers, and pressing his fingers inside, touched her intimately. She gasped and tossed her head.

"Stephanie, open your eyes and look at me."

She gazed up to see his eyes burning with passion. "Andre, we must stop—"

"Let yourself feel the pleasure . . . trust me, darling."

She blinked at tears. "I can't."

"Why? Because of him?"

"Because of—heavens, I can't even count the reasons—"

He stroked her with infinite skill and gazed soulfully into her eyes. "You say that as you move against my fingers, as you grow wet for me, as the tender little bud between your thighs threatens to burst against my thumb. You say that even as I can see only one truth—that you want me as much as I want you."

Stephanie was in an agony of need, writhing deliriously. "Please, you must stop this—"

"You cannot stop what's happening between us. You cannot stop what we both are feeling. And such feelings will never materialize between Ebbie and me. Do you understand? *Never!* You can bargain with me, bribe me into seeing her. But you will never negotiate this."

With these fierce words, Andre's mouth closed over hers again, his tongue penetrating, even as he pushed two fingers inside her. Stephanie reeled, tearing her lips from his, panting. The pressure was shocking, delicious, unbearable. When his hungry lips seized hers again, she thought she would drown in hot pleasure. She lost control, arching wantonly against his touch, moving with frenzied need as he pressed deeper. She reached down to stroke him through his trousers, and just feeling him, his size and hardness, sent her over the edge. With a rough cry, she climaxed against his hand. She trembled with the intensity of it; he held and comforted her.

A long moment later, he rolled off her. Stephanie sat up and pressed a hand to her forehead, still half-dizzy, stunned by the storm of desire that had consumed them both. Andre sat up beside her, touching her shoulder.

"Darling," he pleaded, "take off your clothes and lie with me."

Overwhelmed by what she'd done, Stephanie stumbled to her feet. Andre regarded her questioningly. She stared back, her gaze wild and desperate. She turned to leave.

"Stephanie, wait."

She faced him, tears falling. "You just had to prove your point, didn't you? You had to make me lose control. You don't think about anything but your own needs, do you, Andre?"

Pride hardened his features. "Not true. I just gave you your pleasure without taking mine. I'd say I was generous, under the circumstances."

Stephanie felt so torn she could have screamed at him. She left while she could still trust herself to do so.

Chapter 34

⌒ↄↄↄ⌒

The jaunty strains of a Strauss polka swelled from the grand ballroom of the Jefferson Hotel on this, the night of the annual Harvest Ball. Gaslight sputtered in brilliant crystal chandeliers, spilling a sea of bright light down upon Natchez's most esteemed citizens—gentlemen in striking formal black cutaways and ladies in lavish ball gowns painted in enough vibrant hues to fill a rose garden. Conversation sparkled amid the glitter of diamond tiaras, the dazzle of emeralds, rubies, and sapphires, the clink of champagne goblets and punch cups.

While the bulk of the attendees lingered at the sidelines, several prominent couples, including the Rufus Learneds and the Allison Fosters, led an elegant quadrille on the dance floor. Along one entire wall of the vast hall, stewards wearing white gloves served up sumptuous delicacies ranging from mounds of iced shrimp and vast trays of crawfish balls and raw oysters, to enormous Virginia hams and sides of rare roast beef, to blancmange and petits fours. Delicious aromas filled the air, mingling with the unique mixture of smells from the gentry, pomade and talc and shaving soap from the gentlemen, perfume, flowers and sachet from the ladies.

Stephanie stood near the buffet table with Henry. Dressed in one of Mrs. Hodge's finest creations, a dusky rose ball gown of rich velvet, with a full, bustled skirt, a deeply cut neckline, and puffed sleeves, she was struggling to take in everything. She judged there must be at least a hundred celebrants crowding the ballroom, many of them from Natchez's Old Guard. The resplendent occasion seemed a glowing tribute to the elite's recovery from the great war and lengthy reconstruction that had rocked the very foundations of the South.

Stephanie spotted many families she knew—the Bislands, the Stantons, the Waverlys. She spied Captain Tom Leathers towering over several gentlemen near the punch bowl. She chuckled at the sight of Katie, who sat in a corner intently gossiping with several other dowagers. Sweeping her gaze back across the ballroom, she spotted Andre with Ebbie, the two visiting with Mr. Trumble, while Mr. Fortier and Mr. Wister stood nearby quietly conversing. Ebbie looked lovelier than ever in an apricot-colored silk gown, and Andre was splendid in his formal black and white ruffled shirt. Longing swept her at the sight of him.

As the quadrille ended and the orchestra launched into Strauss's "The Lorelei," Stephanie watched Andre lead Ebbie out onto the dance floor and begin waltzing with her. Yet the two moved awkwardly together, timid little Ebbie struggling to keep up with the elegant sweep of Andre's dancing.

Unlike when she'd waltzed with Andre . . . Stephanie quashed the traitorous thought at once.

"Shall we dance?"

Stephanie turned to see Henry smiling and offering his arm. He looked quite debonair, with his hair pomaded and diamond studs twinkling on his linen shirtfront. She just wished his handsomeness stirred more of a response in her.

Nonetheless, she murmured, "Mr. Robillard, I'd be honored."

Guiding her onto the floor and pulling her into his arms, he looked her over admiringly. "Have I told you how beautiful you look in that pink gown?"

Troubled by the fervent note in his voice, the intensity of his stare, she replied, "Only a dozen times."

He grinned sheepishly. "Every time we're together, I realize what a lucky man I am. Why, Aunt Katie already has us eloping to Louisiana."

Stephanie laughed nervously. "Katie is such fun. I'm

sure neither of us would ever do anything so rash.''

He drew her slightly closer. ''Wouldn't we?''

Stephanie fought a grimace. She didn't like the marriage hints Henry had been dropping on their last two dates. Guilt also needled her, because she couldn't help but feel she was leading him on—although the true irony was that she hardly knew the man. She supposed in this time of exaggerated decorum and frequent division of the sexes, courtships rarely probed beneath the surface—unless one was talking about Andre Goddard, of course. Still, for the average man living in an age when the next yellow fever epidemic might shovel under half the town, there was doubtless little motivation to hesitate in asking for the hand of an available female. The fact that the two were virtual strangers was surely no impediment to most marriages among the gentry. . . .

As the music ended, a familiar voice drawled, ''How ravishing you look, Stephanie, dear.''

At the sound of Andre's voice, a scowling Henry and a tense Stephanie turned to watch his approach. Stephanie felt her cheeks heating as his bright gaze swept over her, missing nothing, from the fullness of her skirts, to her tight waist, to the daring plunge of her decolletage. Much as she could have shaken him for his brazen stare, as always, he made his mark, and her insides again twisted with unassuaged desire.

''Good evening, Andre,'' Henry greeted him stiffly.

''Andre,'' Stephanie acknowledged.

''I've been meaning to have a word with you, Robillard,'' Andre remarked. ''The other day, I invited Tom Leathers to join us at the ball, and for dinner at your house afterward. I do hope my last-minute addition will not cause a burden.''

''Certainly not,'' Henry answered. ''Katie is always thrilled to see Captain Tom. I'm sure she'll invite him herself if their paths cross tonight.''

''Good. However, I think a word from you might be in order.'' Andre inclined his head toward the buffet tables. ''As might be expected, Tom's getting well acquainted with the punch bowl.''

Glancing in the same direction, Henry hesitated, frowning.

"I'll keep Stephanie company while you're away," suggested Andre.

Tossing Andre a resentful look, Henry turned to Stephanie. "My dear, if you'll excuse me for just a moment . . ."

"Of course," she replied.

As he strode off, she heard Andre murmur, "And while he's gone, I'll steal your next dance."

Stephanie regarded him reproachfully. "What about Ebbie?"

He chuckled, and gestured toward the orchestra dais. "The Philharmonic Club has finished its set, and the Natchez Quartet will be next. So, Ebbie's amply occupied."

Stephanie watched the quartet members take seats on the dais and start tuning their instruments. She grimaced at the off-key squeak of a violin, the cello's sawing groan.

"Is that a pained look I see?" Andre teased. "Does it arise at the thought of dancing with me, or from the clamor emanating from the dais?"

She shot him a chiding glance.

"Tell the truth now."

"Well, they are quite awful," she whispered.

"Yes, but they're so enthusiastic about it."

Stephanie couldn't help herself; she burst out laughing, and so did Andre.

"*We're* awful!" she scolded.

He pulled her close as the discordant intro to "Roses from the South" droned out. "Are we?" A husky note entered his voice. "I'd say we're wonderful together."

Stephanie could have died from the poignant yearning his words stirred. They *were* wonderful together, she had to admit it. Andre was a brilliant dancer, and being so close to him was bittersweet torture. Shocking memories of her own scandalous conduct in the attic rose to taunt her. She wanted him so—but she couldn't have him.

"Thinking about it, Stephanie?" he murmured.

She stiffened. "About what?"

He laughed, his devilish expression leaving no doubt as

to what he meant. "What a little liar you are, and that innocent look on your face is almost perfect. But you don't fool me. I know what you're really thinking, Stephanie."

"You're a mind reader?"

"I can certainly read *your* mind. You're thinking what I'm thinking—that you're dying to finish what we started the other night."

Of course she was thinking precisely that, her flaming face giving her away. "Your arrogance knows no bounds."

"But I'm telling the truth. Aren't I, Stephanie?" Leaning close to her ear, he whispered, "When are you going to give up and come to me, love? I'm dying for you."

Though her heart hammered and her face burned, she managed to push him back. "Stop that! People are staring at us."

"To hell with them. Answer my question."

"You already know my answer."

He raised an eyebrow. "Are you holding out for marriage? You know, you're making me almost that desperate."

Though his words treacherously excited her, she slanted him a skeptical look. "Save me your desperation. I'm not holding out for anything from you."

He pulled back to gaze into her eyes. "Lord, what a little tease you are. You tempt me, then you pull away. Do you have any idea what seeing you like this—so beautiful— does to me? Do you know how much I want you? Do you know what I'd do if we were alone?"

Stephanie was drowning in those very decadent images. "Please, I don't need the details."

"I'd take off that glorious gown and—"

"Andre, don't torture me," she pleaded.

"You think you aren't torturing me?"

"I'm not going to come to your bed!" she whispered adamantly.

"Not even if I fall down on my knee—before everyone?" he teased.

Surely he wouldn't—not here! "No, not even then," she replied in trembling tones. "However, *if* you were a gentleman, you'd hardly equate falling down on your knee with—er, seduction.''

He appeared intrigued. "Is this another oblique reference to matrimony? I wasn't aware you were so inclined, madame.''

She shrugged. "Oh, I can be full of surprises. For instance, Henry is already hinting at marriage.''

"He's *what*?" Andre appeared thunderstruck.

"You heard me. He's looking for a wife, and it seems Aunt Katie is thoroughly taken with me.''

"But—your marrying Henry is out of the question!" he blazed.

"Why?" she shot back. "Why is it unacceptable for me to become Henry's wife but acceptable for me to become your—" She lowered her voice and finished fiercely, "*paramour.*"

With equal passion, he whispered back, "Because I *want* you, Stephanie, dear.''

"And you think Henry does not?''

"Not like I do. Don't tell me you're seriously considering his proposal?''

"Well, I'm certainly not seriously considering yours!''

The two were glaring at each other when Andre was tapped on the shoulder. He whirled and all but snarled, "*What*?''

Captain Tom Leathers loomed before them, looking dapper in formal attire. Roaring with laughter, he winked at Stephanie. "Goddard is a bit touchy tonight, eh?''

"Indeed," she answered archly.

Leathers offered Stephanie his arm. "Then it seems I must rescue the lady by asking her to dance.''

"My pleasure.''

While Andre stood glowering, Leathers waltzed Stephanie away. Stephanie was pleased to see the rogue brooding. Good! Let him know that she was hardly his possession.

"Enjoying yourself tonight—er, is it Steven?''

Leathers's sardonic voice brought Stephanie's attention back to his amused face. "Captain Tom, surely that is still our little secret.''

"Of course, young lady, though I might have to demand another kiss," he teased.

"Oh!" Feigning outrage, she scolded, "Sir, you have already demanded your due once. Any further blackmail, and I shall notify your wife."

Leathers threw back his head and laughed. "You're a feisty one, all right. But why is Goddard in such a temper? Did you box his ears?"

She smiled. "I suppose in a manner of speaking, I did."

"Why didn't you attend this affair with him?"

She raised an eyebrow. "Captain Tom, I think you're overstepping your bounds."

"Am I?" He scowled. "Well, I don't know why Andre steps out with that mousy little governess. It's obvious she'll never capture his heart."

"And why not?" Stephanie demanded. "I think they make a splendid couple."

"Bah!" He waved her off. "Does a meek little donkey break a wild stallion to the harness? No, the stallion must have a mare of spirit and strong will. It's plain to see you're the one who's going to tame Andre Goddard."

Stephanie's hopes sank. She wasn't supposed to be the one to tame the rogue!

Scowling, Andre strode back through the crowd. So Henry Robillard was talking marriage to Stephanie. The miscreant. Never had he dreamed that his vapid friend might beat him to the punch. Well, he would never stand for this, even if he had to marry Stephanie himself!

Marry her himself. Now that was a novel prospect.

How long had this nonsense been going on? Did Ebbie know?

All at once, Andre realized that several old women, including Katie Banks, were staring at him as he paced to and fro and muttered to himself. Realizing he was becoming a spectacle, he bowed to the ladies, who waved back and tittered. He hastily strode away to the buffet table and grabbed a cup of punch. He started toward Ebbie just as the quartet was finishing the waltz, and watched Peter Dearborn step up to speak with her.

"Here you are, my dear," Andre greeted gruffly, handing Ebbie the cup. "Peter, good to see you."

"And you, Andre." Shaking Andre's hand, Peter remarked, "I was just telling Ebbie and the others how wonderful their music is. I'm such a fan of Strauss."

"Indeed," Andre muttered, thinking to himself that the younger Strauss should consider himself lucky to be in his bed in Vienna tonight.

Peter turned to Ebbie. "We must get together soon to discuss the church's annual Christmas charity drive."

"Oh, yes, Peter, that will be such fun!" she agreed, touching his hand. "And do give your mother our best."

As Dearborn strode away, Andre flashed Ebbie a stiff smile. "Drink up, dear."

She raised the cup. "It was thoughtful of you to bring me the punch."

"I thought all the playing might make you thirsty." Noticing that the misters were watching them with an air of expectation, Andre grinned, and called, "Splendid music, gentlemen. Splendid."

The misters waved and murmured thank-yous.

"Was there anything else, Andre?" Ebbie asked. "The misters and I do need to continue with our scheduled repertoire."

"Of course." Clearing his throat, he leaned toward her and whispered, "Were you aware that Henry is talking marriage to Stephanie?"

Eyes widening, she shook her head. "No, though I must say I'm not surprised. How does Stephanie feel about this turn?"

"I'm not sure . . ." He made a growling sound. "As you're aware, I'm totally opposed to Henry's marrying her."

"But why?"

"Why? The man is completely unsuitable. He's—*dull*."

Ebbie giggled.

"Why are you laughing?" he demanded.

She blushed and lowered her gaze. "Forgive me, Andre, but you know what they say."

"No. What, pray tell, do they say?"

"Why, that dull men make the best husbands."

As Andre turned and strode wordlessly away, he looked about ready to eat a dozen dull men for dinner.

Chapter 35

"**M**y dear, you look simply ravishing in that gown. Tell me, is it one of Mrs. Hodge's creations?"

"Why, thank you, yes it is, Miss Elizabeth," answered Stephanie. "And that burgundy is just the color for you— so perfect for fall."

At Henry Robillard's Greek Revival mansion on Myrtle Street, Stephanie stood in the dining room chatting with Miss Elizabeth Stanton; at Katie's request, she was doing a last-minute check of the superbly set Empire table. Soft light gleamed in cut-glass candlelabra dripping with crystal prisms, in the popular brilliant style. Vast yards of the finest Irish linen covered the long table, each place set with ornate Gorham silver and Old Paris china in the Rose Pompadour design. A centerpiece of calla lilies in an enameled crystal vase stole the scene.

As the succulent aromas of bouillabaisse and okra gumbo drifted out from the kitchen, couples visited, laughed, and sipped aperitifs. Stephanie spotted George Marshall and Colonel Balfour talking quietly together in a corner; she caught a wink from Tom Leathers as he strode past with a bourbon. And over near the mahogany breakfront, she spied Andre and Ebbie chatting with Rufus Learned and his wife.

"What an odd little couple they make," said Elizabeth.

Stephanie turned to her. "I beg your pardon?"

"I never thought Andre would pursue little Ebbie," Elizabeth explained. "Especially when the rest of us Natchez belles want him so badly."

Stephanie demurely sipped her drink. "He does have a certain charm about him."

"My dear, that man is pure lady-killer," Elizabeth confided. "I'm surprised he hasn't turned his talents on you."

Feigning an innocent look, Stephanie didn't comment.

"I suppose the die was cast for those two after Linnea passed on," Elizabeth continued. "Andre likely feels duty-bound to wed her, after she gave up whatever life she had for him and his children."

"Well, if they do marry, Andre couldn't ask for a finer person," Stephanie put in.

"Oh, my dear, there's no doubt about that," Elizabeth agreed at once. "It's just that they're so ill suited. She won't be able to hold his attention any more than did poor Linnea."

Stephanie was dismayed to hear a second person tonight declare that Andre and Ebbie were poorly matched. "There are other reasons for people to marry, besides entertainment value."

"I suppose . . . But just imagine if those two wed. She'll want to attend church all the time, while he'll frequent the grogshops and the racetrack. And what if she takes along her squeaky fiddle on the honeymoon?"

Stephanie struggled to repress a smile. "I doubt many brides pack along their violins."

"But they're not Ebbie, are they?" Leaning closer, Elizabeth confided, "And I'd imagine most grooms are hardly in the mood for Mozart."

Stephanie was fighting giggles as Henry stepped up. "So, there you are, Stephanie." He bowed. "Miss Stanton, as always, you are a vision. Aunt and I are so thrilled to have you and your lovely sisters here tonight."

In queenly fashion, Elizabeth extended her hand to Henry, and he gallantly kissed the back. "Our pleasure, Mr. Robillard."

He cleared his throat. "If you'll excuse us, I'd like a word with Stephanie . . ."

Elizabeth winked at him. "Romance on the mind, eh, Henry?"

Grinning, he took Stephanie by the arm. "Well, one never knows . . ."

"What did you need, Henry?" Stephanie asked as they headed for the French doors.

He opened them and led her outside onto the terrace. "A moment alone with you."

As he turned to shut the doors, she felt uneasy, and shivered in the coolness of the night. This small courtyard divided the main house from the bedroom wing. Potted begonias, blooming roses, and trellises fragrant with jasmine locked them away from the rest of the world. With only the soft light spilling out through the French doors, the setting was dark, cozy, and very romantic.

"Henry, why did you want to speak with me?" she pressed. Straining to peek through the French doors, she added, "It looks as if folks are already gathering at the table."

"This will take only a moment." He stepped closer and touched her bare arm. "Are you cold?"

She shook her head. "The night is mild."

He took her hands, and gazed at her earnestly. "Stephanie, there's something I must ask you."

Oh, brother, she thought, *here it comes.* Aloud, she cautioned, "Henry, I wish you wouldn't."

"But I must." He drew a deep breath. "Stephanie, I realize we haven't known each other long, but already you have captured my affections. Will you do me the honor of becoming my wife?"

Although the question was hardly unexpected, Stephanie felt rattled nonetheless, her face heating. "Henry—you know I think you're a good man," she began haltingly. "But as you've already stated, we're hardly more than acquaintances—"

He raised a hand. "I knew from the moment we first met that you'd make me a wonderful wife. And Aunt Katie agrees. As a matter of fact, we'd like to make the announcement tonight—"

"Tonight?" she gasped. "That's out of the question!"

"Why?"

"Because we're still strangers, and because I think you're really only interested in me because Katie wants us to marry."

"That's not true," he insisted, reaching out to touch her cheek. "I want you, Stephanie. I knew I wanted you the first time I laid eyes on you. And won't our match be all the more special because my aunt has blessed it?"

Stephanie turned away from him, struggling to gather her thoughts. "Henry, I'm deeply honored by your proposal, but I'm afraid the answer must be no."

He touched her shoulder. "Why? Is it because you're in love with Andre?"

A sharp breath escaped her, and she whirled to face him. "Why would you ask that?"

His visage darkened. "You think I haven't noticed the way you look at him, and he at you?"

She raised her chin. "Well, you're mistaken."

"Indeed?"

"Yes."

"Then why won't you marry me?" he demanded.

"Because I'll never feel the same way about you that you feel about me."

"Surely such feelings will come in time."

She sadly shook her head. "Henry, you've misread my intentions. I've enjoyed our outings together, but I never meant to encourage you regarding marriage, nor to offer you more than friendship. I know we haven't discussed this, but the truth is, my loyalty remains with my first husband. I—I don't plan ever to marry again. What's more, once I'm finished helping Ebbie—er—get on her feet, I want to return to my own people."

He appeared crestfallen. "You can't mean that."

"I absolutely do."

"There's no chance you'll change your mind?"

"I'm afraid not."

She heard him groan, and, glimpsing his face, found he appeared devastated. She'd had no idea she'd come to mean so much to him in such a short time. Yet weren't her feelings for Andre, feelings that had taken root in such a brief time span, equally strong, even against her own will and better judgment? The daunting realization made her feel keen sympathy for Henry.

"I suppose that's it, then," he muttered.

"Henry, I'm very sorry." Impulsively, she stretched on tiptoe to kiss his cheek.

At that very moment, the doors to the house burst open, and a deep male voice announced, "Henry, Stephanie, it's time for—"

Henry and Stephanie sprang apart, their faces aflame with embarrassment and guilt as Andre joined them in the court-yard. His gaze, burning with jealousy, moved from Henry to Stephanie, and she felt her heart thudding ominously.

"Have I interrupted something?" he asked mildly.

"That's none of your damn business," Henry replied.

"Oh, isn't it?" Andre countered. "I'll have you know that as Mrs. Sergeant's employer, I'm bound to uphold her reputation."

While Stephanie rolled her eyes at Andre's insufferable comment, Henry drawled back, "You're a fine one to ex-pound on reputations, Goddard, and I was hardly damaging Stephanie's. I was asking this woman to marry me!"

"Were you?" Andre took an aggressive step toward Henry, his dark, accusatory gaze flashing on Stephanie. "And what did the lady say?"

"That," she responded, "is also none of your damned business!"

"And what about your kissing him?"

Furious, she retorted, "You can go to hell."

Andre grabbed her wrist. "If I'm going, you're coming with me."

Henry stepped between them. "Unhand Stephanie this instant, or I'll call you out."

"I'll meet you with pleasure!" Andre thundered back.

"Stop it, you two!" Stephanie cried, pushing the men apart. "I'll not have you overgrown schoolboys fighting a duel over me."

"Then you'll come with me?" Andre demanded.

Glimpsing the barely repressed violence on both men's faces, Stephanie realized she had little choice but to break up the confrontation any way she could. She turned contritely to Henry. "I'm sorry, but I have—some matters to settle with Andre."

"No!" He appeared incredulous. "You're not going to bow to his bullying. I'll not allow it!"

She placed her hand on his arm. "Please, Henry, I don't want your death on my conscience. Go back to your guests."

"Stephanie—"

"*Please*. I—I'll be all right."

He expelled an exasperated sigh. "Very well. But I think you're making a big mistake."

Andre said no more, only grabbing Stephanie's arm and pulling her back into the dining room. To her horror, she noted that everyone else, including Ebbie, was seated. Without a word, he tugged her out of the room beneath the diners' scandalized eyes.

Chapter 36

❧❧❧

"Are you going to marry Henry or not?"

Stephanie seethed at Andre's question as she sat with him in the covered cab of his carriage. She could hear Willie shouting to the team as he propelled the carriage toward Harmony House, and a reckoning she already dreaded.

"I told you before—that's none of your business."

"It is absolutely my business how a member of my household comports herself."

His arrogant words spiked her anger. "If you're concerned about appearances, look to yourself first."

"You're the one who was disgracing herself tonight—"

"I disgraced myself? You're the one who humiliated me, dragging me out of Henry's house in the presence of two dozen of Natchez's most esteemed citizens. Not to mention the shabby way you treated Ebbie, abandoning her."

"I'll see that Willie returns for her."

"Oh, that fixes everything," she mocked. "You disgraced her, and for all your pious concern over my reputation, you have no doubt single-handedly ruined me."

"Don't play the innocent with me, after I caught you and Henry at your tryst—"

"Tryst?" she all but screamed. "I'll have you know, sir, that there is nothing improper about a gentleman asking a lady to marry him!"

"After you've known him for, what? Two weeks?"

"How long did it take you to proposition me? Two days?"

Something dangerous flared in his eyes. "Have you shared his bed?"

"*What*? You arrogant son of a—"

"Have you shared his bed?" His voice was like ice.

"No!" she choked out.

"Then why did you just refer to *my* propositioning you?"

"To demonstrate that when a man wants something, he rarely hesitates," she retorted, then at once regretted her words.

He smiled. "Well put, Stephanie. Perhaps *I'm* finished hesitating."

Before she could respond, he hauled her close, and arrogantly kissed her.

"No!" She shoved him away. "Stop it! Don't you dare kiss me—"

He seized her face in his large hands, and the look in his eyes held her pinned. "Stephanie, you are going to tell me—*right now*—if you've accepted his proposal, or I shan't be responsible for what I'll do next."

She groaned. "I declined."

He smiled.

"Don't look so smug, you snake. I didn't say no because of you. As you're aware, I plan never to marry again."

He stared at her, his gaze passionate. Then he brushed his thumb over her soft underlip, and she gasped. She was furious at him, but being alone with this man she wanted so badly was also an unbearable torment.

"That's right," he murmured. "You're never going to forget your first love, are you?"

Stephanie felt a stab of guilt. Actually, despite her bravado to both Henry and Andre, she'd thought of Jim less and less as her days had passed here.

"You've made me mad with jealousy, you know," he continued.

"I'm aware of that. One marriage proposal, and you go ballistic."

"Ballistic? What is that?"

Realizing her faux pas, she smiled to herself. "It may

have something to do with an overabundance of balls.''

He actually flinched. ''Bite your tongue, woman! I thought you were a lady.''

''You'd never know it by the way you treat me.''

He succumbed to a self-deprecating smile. ''And have I treated you so horribly?''

''Yes! At least Henry has offered me marriage, whereas you have only offered . . .''

''Yes?''

''To take me to bed.''

He trailed his mouth over her cheek, and she couldn't summon the will to push him away. ''Perhaps because from the moment I laid eyes on you, I couldn't resist you.''

''Well, it's not going to happen,'' she asserted, if in trembling tones.

His sensual lips were sliding down her throat, raising gooseflesh. ''And what if I did offer marriage?''

''You?'' she protested with a squeak. ''The Lothario of the county? Be serious.''

''I am serious.'' He pulled back to gaze into her eyes. ''Stephanie, you've utterly bewitched me. Perhaps I will marry you if it's the only way to make you behave—and make you mine.''

Anguish and frustration threatened to burst within her. ''Andre, you know that's impossible.''

''Why?''

''Because wanting me in your bed isn't a good enough reason for a marriage, and because—''

''Yes?''

''Because you have an obligation to Ebbie—''

''An obligation?'' he cut in angrily. ''What about my obligation to myself?''

She laughed bitterly. ''I might have known you would say that. All you ever think about is yourself.''

His answer was a stony scowl, and they continued the rest of their journey in silence.

Stephanie had just finished changing into her nightgown when the door separating her room from Andre's burst open and he strode in. She turned in shock, intently conscious that she was naked except for the thin gown.

Her hand fluttered to her throat. Although Andre still wore his trousers, his shirt was unbuttoned and askew, giving her a glimpse of his muscular chest. His jaw was hard, and his eyes held a predatory gleam. He looked rakish, dangerous—and much too sexy.

"Andre!" she cried. "What in hell are you doing, barging in on me this way? I could have been undressing, or—"

"Naked?" he provided, approaching her with brisk, angry steps.

He paused before her, and she stood riveted by shock. Utterly shameless, he raked his hot gaze over her. To her mortification, her nipples hardened under his fiery perusal and her face burned.

His gaze flashed triumphantly to hers. "Just look at what the thought of being naked with me does to you."

"You cad!"

His fingers seized her shoulders. "Don't play coy maiden with me, Stephanie. I know better. I have touched you— *quite intimately*—and felt your surrender. It's too late to play the blushing virgin."

His words so infuriated her that she would have slapped him, yet she feared his reaction, his certain retaliation, especially given the pent-up passion in him. "I'm not listening to this. Get out of here right this instant."

He crossed his arms over his chest. "I'm not going anywhere until we have this out."

"Have what out?"

"I've come to tell you I've made a decision—"

"Oh? And what is that?"

Bitterly, he announced, "I've come to tell you you've won. I'm going to give you what you want. I'm going to marry Ebbie."

For a moment, Stephanie was too flabbergasted to speak. Then she stammered, "B-but, what brought about this change of heart?"

He shot her a heated look. "I'm a man of strong passions, and my children need a mother. If I can't have you, I may as well marry Ebbie. It's what you want, isn't it?"

Wasn't it? In truth, the prospect of his actually marrying

Ebbie devastated Stephanie—and for very selfish reasons.

Aloud, she managed, "Yes, of course it's what I want."

"Is it?" He smiled. "Think about it carefully, my dear. You know I'll make her life miserable."

Stephanie stared at him, then her eyes widened in horror as realization dawned. "You scoundrel! This is blackmail! You're saying that unless I give in to you, you'll marry Ebbie and *deliberately* make her pay for my sins!"

"No, I'm telling you I'm *incapable* of making Ebbie happy," he replied vehemently. "If you'll just think about it, you'll realize I'm right. Perhaps I deserve to suffer, but she doesn't."

"You just want to pursue your own gratification," Stephanie accused.

She was tossing out reckless words again, and soon reaped the consequences. "Maybe I do."

He pulled Stephanie close and kissed her ardently, the wicked thrust of his tongue making clear how out-of-control he was. His hands roved over her back, her bottom; he crushed her closer and claimed her mouth almost desperately.

He released her abruptly and she staggered, breathless and weak, regarding him with yearning and confusion.

"Make your choice," he drawled, and left her, slamming the door.

Stephanie stood dumbfounded. For weeks she had been fighting Andre, insisting he must marry Ebbie. Now he had taken away all her ammunition by declaring she had won. But had she really? God, she was so bewildered! Was there truly any way she *could* win, or was her mission simply a cruel joke—a joke ultimately played on herself?

She began pacing the room, overwrought, unable to sleep. A light glowed under the door to Andre's room. She knew he was awake; she sensed he was waiting for her—in bed— and the prospect of joining him there tempted her. She was shameless, a traitor to Ebbie, to Great-aunt Magnolia, to her entire mission. She could barely breathe or think, she wanted him so badly.

Yet after endless moments agonizing, trying to look at their dilemma from all angles, Stephanie realized at last that

Andre had spoken the truth. He *would* make Ebbie a wretched husband; he *would* make her miserable. A blind man could have seen how terribly matched the two of them were. The problem was, Ebbie couldn't see that she was in love with the wrong man—she went on blithely assuming she and Andre would wed. How could Stephanie save Ebbie from herself, save her from heartache and possible suicide?

And how could she stay away from Andre even one more night when she wanted him so desperately? She could understand his frustration, for she was every bit as frustrated herself.

Overcome with turmoil, she closed her eyes and whispered, "Great-aunt Magnolia, help me. I don't know what to do anymore. Please, help me!"

The woman who had not even been born yet did not magically appear before Stephanie. But all at once, an image flashed into her mind, the memory of herself and Sam as children, romping in their great-aunt's garden, and words Magnolia had spoken to her, words she would never forget . . .

In that moment, Stephanie had her answer—or at least, an answer of sorts. Tears burned her eyes, and her throat ached. She slipped off her wedding ring, kissed it, and laid it on the dresser.

She crossed to the door between her and Andre's rooms, opened it, and slipped inside his domain. He glanced up at her in delight and surprise. He was reclined on his bed, naked except for the burgundy counterpane that covered his muscled body from the waist down and did nothing to hide the outline of his arousal. That, and the ardent look in his eyes set her reeling.

"Why are you here?" he whispered.

She flashed him a tentative smile and moved a step closer. "I've given you a pretty rough time, haven't I?"

"Yes, you have."

"But you've been relentless, you know."

"So I have, but what can I say?" he asked intensely. "You've captivated me, darling."

She couldn't contain a wince of longing. "Andre, I'm so

tired of fighting. Perhaps—perhaps we both need to get this attraction out of our system.''

She thought she spotted disappointment in his eyes. ''Do we? Come closer.''

Gulping, she tiptoed over to the bed.

''Why are you really here, Stephanie?''

She twisted her fingers together and regarded him helplessly. ''I'm not sure. I thought I was sent here to help Ebbie, but now I see that you're right, that it will never work between you. You would make her miserable, even if you tried not to. I don't know what to do anymore, or even why I'm here.'' Her voice broke. ''I just know I want you so . . .''

He took mercy on her then. With a groan, he pulled her onto the bed with him, drawing her body beneath his. His warm naked chest pressed into her breasts, and only two layers of flimsy cloth separated their heated loins. He kissed her, long and lingeringly.

''Oh, Steffie,'' he breathed, eyes bright with emotion, ''I'm so glad you've come to me. It'll be all right, sweetheart—I promise.'' He sank his fingers into her hair, and leaned over to nibble at her chin. ''You're so damn lovely.''

She gazed up at his fervent face, the dark curl resting on his forehead. ''You're pretty cute yourself.''

''So you intend to get me out of your system, eh, darling?'' he teased.

''I'm not sure,'' she answered unsteadily. ''I was thinking about that just now—thinking about us.''

''Yes?''

''Well, maybe we're like butterflies—''

''Butterflies?'' he repeated with a soft laugh.

''Some varieties only live about ten days, you know. I was remembering when I was a small child, and caught a Monarch in my great-aunt's garden. It was so beautiful, and I didn't want to let it go. But my great-aunt said, 'Release it, child, or it will die. A butterfly only visits this world briefly. It's a sin to cut short its flight.' ''

''A touching story,'' he murmured. ''But what is the point?''

She gazed at him with her heart in her eyes. ''Perhaps

what we have will bloom only for a moment, but I can't pass it by.''

He was slowly shaking his head. "You say the oddest things, darling. Sweet, but odd.''

"You don't understand.''

"Oh, but I do,'' he replied soberly, drawing a finger over her underlip. "You're saying you won't make a commitment to me.''

"I'm saying I can't,'' she acknowledged miserably. "I wish I could, but it's impossible.''

He smiled at her tenderly. "And what if I make you fall in love with me?''

"I'll try not to.''

"That's right,'' he said with an air of hurt. "Why should a woman who swears never to love again concern herself with such perilous feelings?''

Stabbed by guilt, Stephanie said, "I am fond of you, Andre, but we are so different.''

"You're here, darling.'' He buried his lips in her hair. "And maybe I'll make love to you until I change your mind.''

Breathless, she said, "Just promise me you won't tell Ebbie anything about us, until we—''

"Just kiss me,'' he interrupted.

She complied, pressing her mouth to his, surrendering to the thrust of his tongue, and such sweet emotion burst within her that she couldn't bear it. It was as if she'd waited an eternity for this one, glorious moment of surrender— surrender to him, to her own feelings. She wanted him so badly she trembled with the intensity of it. She sank her fingers into his hair, massaged the muscles at his nape, roved her hands over his sinewy back. Oh, he was so strong and warm and smelled so good, and he was hers, all hers— if only for tonight.

"Ah, *ma chérie,* you make me mad with wanting you,'' he murmured.

He pulled her gown off over her head and took a moment to admire the swell of her breasts, the gentle curve of her belly. He drew a teasing fingertip over a tight nipple. She closed her eyes and writhed in ecstasy.

"You're magnificent," he murmured. "My beautiful butterfly."

His mouth moved to her breast, his lips caressing the smooth flesh. Her breath came in sharp little pants, especially when he stroked her bare thigh. His teeth playfully tweaked her nipple and then he sucked hard.

"Andre, Andre," she cried, half-panicked by the sensations consuming her, the wet heat of his mouth, the torment of his tongue. "This is so intense—"

"That's what I want," he murmured back. "I want you desperate, insane, wild, and wanton—"

"Oh, God." She drew his face up to hers and kissed him feverishly.

Soon, his lips moved down her body again, licking, teasing, tormenting. She squirmed in delight as his hand slipped between her thighs. He parted her feminine folds and stroked the center of her with the lightest caress of a fingertip.

She lost control, arching her hips sharply. She heard his throaty chuckle.

"Easy, sweetheart. I don't want to injure you and bring this delightful encounter to a premature end."

"Not a chance," came her fierce reply. She kissed his throat, his chin, his mouth, and drew his palm to her aching desire, unashamed of the wetness his caresses stirred. She felt his fingers pushing inside her and cried out in delight. He drew the moment out until she begged him to take her, whispering wantonly at his ear.

He rolled onto her, and she gloried to the crushing weight of his powerful body, the roughness of his thighs against her soft flesh. Feeling his maleness against her pelvis, she couldn't resist. She had to touch it. She reached down and curled her fingers around him, felt his throbbing response as he surged and hardened to her touch.

"Impatient, are we?" he teased, but in a voice that shook.

She gently rolled him off her, leaned over and kissed the satiny tip of him, then tasted him with light flicks of her tongue.

"*Mon Dieu*," he groaned. "You're a tigress."

Almost roughly, he pressed her onto her back beneath

him. He spread her thighs and began pushing against her. He was hot, smooth, so hard; the pressure of him made her throb, melt, and then she began to take *him*. She moaned, feeling the tip of him penetrating her snugness. She struggled against unexpected emotion, the burning of tears.

He stopped, reaching down to stroke her cheek. "What's wrong? Does it hurt?"

She shook her head. "No, it feels wonderful, it's just . . . been so long. I never thought I'd feel this way with a man again."

He raised her hand to his mouth and kissed it. His gaze was solemn. "Stephanie, I'll never ask you to give up your memories of him. But you're mine tonight. Is that understood?"

She nodded.

"And I insist—no, demand—that you give yourself to me completely."

In answer, she caught his face in her trembling hands and pulled his mouth down to hers. Groaning, he claimed her body with near-savage possessiveness. Heat, ecstasy, and searing tension stormed her simultaneously. She stiffened at the overwhelming sensation of him fully inside her, then relaxed and began to enjoy the warm, delicious friction, the riveting feel of him.

"Oh, yes, you feel wonderful, love, so warm and velvety," he murmured, covering her face with kisses.

Slowly, tantalizingly, he began moving within her, until she moaned and moved with him. Both of them gradually accelerated the fervor, the rhythm, all the while kissing, caressing, holding each other tightly until their passions surged free.

Andre gave a groan of ecstasy, then his taut face loomed above her. "Wrap your legs around me, darling. Let me show you how good this can feel."

His words alone were driving her over the edge. She wrapped her legs about his waist. She felt his hands grasp her hips, holding her a willing prisoner to his loving until her own desires carried her away with him and they moved as one body, devouring each other with an aching sweetness.

She had never felt anything like him. At the moment of her climax, she wrenched her mouth away from his and cried out with a pleasure more intense than she'd ever known.

Then his mouth covered hers again as he took his own pleasure and held her with such fierce tenderness that she felt lost in him . . .

Andre watched Stephanie sleep with emotion burning his throat. She looked so beautiful lying beneath him, her shining hair spread out on the pillow, her face still flushed from passion, her long lashes resting on her cheeks. He leaned over and brushed his lips over the sweet heaven of her mouth.

At last she had come to him, and such bliss she'd brought him. Even now, their bodies were still joined, and he could feel himself swelling to life again inside her. Ah, his sleeping beauty was glorious, but he'd grant her little rest tonight. How long would he be able to resist such potent temptation? How long before he awakened her and devoured her once more?

Ah, this woman, she intrigued and delighted him. She excited him on every level—physical, emotional, spiritual. Every moment they spent together was pure enchantment. Even when they argued, he felt so alive, so passionate. Never had he thought he could feel this way about a woman, craving not just her body, but her heart and soul, as well. He could hardly believe she was finally here with him.

Thank God she had at last abandoned her insane scheme to pair him up with Ebbie. But was she really his? Would she be here for him tomorrow? Or was the love she offered a fleeting thing, like the butterflies she spoke of? His heart ached with these tormenting questions, and even this astounded him, for never before had he wanted a woman with an intensity that brought such pain.

One thing he knew. One taste of her was not enough—would never be enough. Now he wanted her forever.

Chapter 37

❦ ⟨◦◦⟩ ❦

Stephanie stirred to the scents of cinnamon, chocolate, and coffee. Moaning at the delectable aromas, she blinked at the soft light flooding the room, then awakened to see Andre smiling down at her. Propped on an elbow, he looked incredibly sexy, with the heavy line of whiskers along his jaw and the ardent gleam in his eyes. Memories of their lovemaking last night brought a bloom to her cheeks and heat to her blood. She had given herself to him with a boldness and passion she'd never quite known before, not even with Jim. She felt confused and uncertain, but she wasn't sorry—not a bit.

Then, becoming fully aware of their scandalous proximity, she gasped. "Heavens, it's morning. And Sunday, no less. I'd best get back to my room before someone catches us—"

"Not so fast," he admonished, kissing her tenderly.

His mouth on hers was warm and drugging, but she managed to nudge him away. "Andre, please—"

"Hush," he scolded. "You're not dashing off anywhere—especially not after I went to the trouble of fetching breakfast for us."

Stephanie couldn't resist a grin. "You got us breakfast?"

He nodded toward the night table.

Following his gaze, Stephanie licked her lips as she observed the charming tray, with small china coffeepot, two demitasse cups, and buns in a basket. "Mmmmm. So that's where all those delicious smells are coming from."

310

Andre wrapped a roll in a napkin and raised it toward Stephanie's mouth. "The cook made her famous cinnamon buns with chocolate sauce. They're the best in the South."

Stephanie sighed in delight. "You're going to make me fat."

"I wouldn't mind fattening you up a bit," he teased back.

Unable to resist, Stephanie stole a lick of the chocolate glaze. "Oh, it's scrumptious."

Andre raised an eyebrow in mock reproach. "What's this? You are sampling the icing without eating the bun? What would you say to my children if they wanted dessert before their meal?"

Stephanie wrinkled her nose at him and sneaked another taste. "I have a weakness for chocolate."

"Ah." His eyes went wide. "The perfect Madame Sergeant has a vice?"

She ran her fingertips over his bare chest. "Looks like I have several."

Grinning, Andre leaned over and kissed her, then tore off a bite of the roll and popped it into her mouth. Stephanie shut her eyes in ecstasy as she savored the rich morsel. Soon Andre was kissing her again.

"You're so delicious," he murmured. "Now *I* want dessert."

They succumbed to several decadent moments nibbling the rolls, kissing, and sipping coffee. At last Stephanie flashed him a look of regret. "Andre, this has been delightful, but we mustn't risk being discovered—"

"And why not?" he countered. "That would get us wed with due haste, wouldn't it?"

"Wed?" She drew the sheet up to her neck. "You should not joke about such matters."

With a frown, he sat aside the tray and placed an arm around her shoulders. "I'm not jesting, Stephanie. I'm asking you to become my wife."

"Your wife? B-but why?"

"Why?" he repeated, pushing aside the covers and leaning over to playfully bite her shoulder. "Didn't last night make that abundantly clear—you little wanton?"

She groaned in mingled frustration and desire. "You

would ask me to marry you simply because of sex—"

"That's not the only reason, and you know it," he retorted. "We're good together, Stephanie. And not just in bed."

There, she had to smile. "I agree that we seem to balance each other in some ways. But can you honestly say you're ready to settle down again?"

"Yes," he answered without hesitation. "You'll make a great mother for my children—and a wonderful lover for me."

Although the prospect was tempting, Stephanie couldn't accept it. "Andre, I suspect you're just overwhelmed with the emotion of the moment. And you're asking the impossible."

"Why?"

"Why? Because I'm not planning to marry again. And we are still so different in a number of ways. Plus, there's—"

"Ebbie?"

"Yes. I agree that a marriage between the two of you won't work, but think how betrayed she'll feel if she learns about you and me—"

He held up a hand. "I know, and I've already thought about her. If you're so set on playing matchmaker for her, well, we'll have to find her someone else, won't we?"

"Wh-what?" Stephanie gasped.

He laughed. "You mean it's never occurred to you that she might marry someone besides me? What about those three nincompoops in her string quartet, the ones who keep drooling all over her? Doesn't she have much more in common with them than with me? And there's always Reverend Dearborn—"

"No, no," Stephanie interrupted. "None of them are suitable."

"Why?" he demanded.

"Because she's in love with you."

"That's absurd."

"I *know* it's the truth."

"How?" he demanded. "How can you know? Has she told you?"

"Not in so many words, but—"

"Then how can you know?"

She regarded his tense, impassioned face. How could she explain to him what she knew of Ebbie's fate without telling him the full truth about her journey through time?

On the other hand, maybe it was time to risk leveling with him. She'd tried just about everything else and he still couldn't understand her concern for Ebbie. What did she have to lose?

She took a deep breath. "All right, I'll tell you, but you'd better hang on to your hat because this is going to sound pretty damn wild."

He rolled his eyes. "Stephanie, as you can see, I'm not wearing a hat—or anything else."

"Don't remind me," she scolded. "Then hold onto the bedpost, because you're about to experience a massive shock."

"Woman, what on earth are you babbling about?"

Gritting her teeth, she forged on. "I know this is going to sound insane, Andre, but I know Ebbie's in love with you because I come from another time—the future, actually—and I've . . . well, I've met Ebbie's ghost."

For a moment, he regarded her in stupefaction. Then he burst out laughing. "A clever attempt, Stephanie, but I don't believe you for a moment. You'll never win me over to your point of view by acting battier than Reverend Dearborn's mother—"

"I'm telling you the truth. Will you listen to me?"

"Not as long as you're making no sense."

She balled a fist in frustration. "Perhaps I can't make sense—not to you. But you're going to have to try to listen, anyway."

He crossed his arms over his chest. "Very well. I've always found fairy tales entertaining."

She gritted her teeth. "Andre, all this time you've been wondering who I really am, where I really come from, why I keep insisting there can never be a future for us. Well, the reason I know these things is because I'm actually from the year 1996, and I've traveled back in time to help Ebbie."

Thunderstruck, he pressed his palm to her brow. "My God, you must be feverish!"

"Damn it, I'm telling the truth."

"That you've actually come from the year 1996?" he scoffed. "That's impossible."

"Andre, will you at least try to hear me out, if only for the sake of argument?"

"I suppose one must humor a lunatic."

"I'm telling you I have lived in this very house, only over a hundred years from now. My sister Samantha and I inherited the place from our great-aunt, Magnolia. Only I found out the house was haunted, by my aunt, and—others."

"Others?"

"Mainly Ebbie. She was known to play her woeful violin at sunset—"

"You mean, like Miss Percy with her harp, over at Dunleith?"

"Precisely. Anyway, after I moved into the house with Sam, I could get no rest. Then one night, I encountered Ebbie's ghost on the stairwell—"

"You didn't!"

"I did. She looked at me with her sad eyes and said, 'He never loved me. What are you going to do about it?' "

Scratching his jaw in perplexity, Andre didn't comment.

"So, I did some research on Harmony House, and learned of its legend: That Ebbie had fallen hopelessly in love with you, and had died of a broken heart, lingering to haunt the house with her violin."

"And you believed that?"

"What choice did I have? My sleep kept being interrupted, my possessions were disappearing, and strange gifts appearing on my dresser. Then there were the conversations with Great-aunt Magnolia's ghost—"

"Great-aunt Magnolia's ghost?" he repeated, eyeing her askance.

"She could get no peace due to all the restless spirits. Your children were involved, too, you see. They were the wraiths."

He was speechless.

Gesturing nervously, she forged on. "Anyway, eventually Great-aunt Magnolia's ghost told me I must come back in time and straighten out this mess. She told me there would be a sign when my journey began, and another sign when it ended. Soon after, I had a horrible fight with Sam. That night I drank some wine . . . and here I am."

Again, he was dumbstruck.

"If I can only make Ebbie happy," she rushed on, "that will ensure she will never haunt Harmony House, and hopefully I can return to my own time." She heaved a great sigh. "There—so I've said it. Do you believe me?"

He was quiet for a long moment, then raised her hand and solemnly kissed the back. "I believe you're hopelessly mad—but I want you, anyway. Don't worry, darling. We'll find you the best doctors money can buy—even if we must travel to Europe."

"Andre!" she cried, pounding a fist on the mattress. "You haven't been listening to me at all!"

"Oh, I've been listening, all right. And I've had much more intelligent conversations with sage hens."

Exasperated, Stephanie gathered her determination. She repeated her entire account, trying to explain to Andre, in excruciating detail, exactly where she had come from and why she was here. At last he pressed two fingers to her mouth.

"Stop it, Stephanie. I don't believe you—and you're starting to scare me."

With a groan, she gave up.

He clutched her hand. "Darling, you don't have to invent wild stories to sway me. Why don't we talk about the things we can agree on?"

"Such as?"

He ran a teasing finger down her shoulder, to her breast. "Such as how wonderful we are in bed together?"

She fought a smile. "How about the need to secure Ebbie's happiness?"

He gave a shrug. "Very well, we'll find her someone. And in the meantime, I'll have time to convince you that you and I are perfect for each other, and meant to be together."

"Andre . . ." Hopelessly torn, she said, "God, I wish it could be so, but you must understand that I'm only here temporarily, to help Ebbie. Once her future is secured, I'm leaving."

"You're not giving me much incentive to help you," he returned irritably.

Contritely, she met his gaze. "I'm sorry, but my destiny is already set. There's another world—another life—waiting for me. That's where I belong."

He drew her beneath him on the bed, spread her thighs, and spoke passionately. "You're wrong, Stephanie, my darling. Deranged or not, you belong with me."

And he proceeded to prove it.

Chapter 38

⌒◯◯⌒

His conversation with Stephanie haunted Andre all morning, throughout breakfast and church with the family. He found it hard to keep his eyes, or his mind, off her. Watching her nibble at a biscuit at breakfast, he wanted to grab her and kiss her senseless; observing her visiting with the Joseph Carpenters outside the Episcopal church, he wanted to rush to her side and announce to the world that she was *his*. When Stephanie glanced his way, her gaze quickly shied away and her cheeks bloomed. Did she fear he would drag her away again as he had last night? Oh, he was tempted!

When he escorted her, Ebbie, and the children down the aisle of the sanctuary, he could hear hushed whispers from the churchgoers, and sensed the many eyes watching them. Was gossip already spreading regarding his rash conduct last night? How he yearned to shout out to one and all that there was no need for silly rumors, that he would soon make Stephanie his bride, even though he was beginning to question her sanity.

He remained bewildered by all the outlandish things she'd said this morning. Had she truly taken leave of her senses? Or did she feel compelled to invent crazy stories to gain his cooperation with Ebbie—and to keep distance between the two of them?

Why did things have to be so confused and complicated, when all he wanted was to make her his? Last night had convinced him of that. But it did seem that Ebbie held the key to much of this—and he knew he must speak with her at once.

As he escorted his family out of church, he observed Ebbie on the steps conversing with the Reverend Dearborn in her shy, smiling way, and afterward in the churchyard laughing with her misters. Stephanie wanted Ebbie happily wed; yet, as soon as this was accomplished, she would leave him. Damn, but he was confused—and caught in one devil of a quandary. By helping Stephanie, would he lose her?

At home that afternoon, he ran across Ebbie in the hallway. "My dear, I must have a word with you—"

She lowered her gaze. "Certainly, Andre."

He ushered her inside his office and shut the door. "Do have a seat."

"Thank you." She perched herself on the edge of a chair near his desk.

He began to pace. "Ebbie . . . First of all, I must apologize for last night—"

"It did cause quite a stir when you left with Stephanie," she scolded gently. "What happened?"

He groaned. "I caught Henry making—improper advances toward her—although she didn't much appreciate my intervention."

"I'd imagine not," concurred Ebbie. "Stephanie does know how to stand up for herself."

"At any rate, I felt someone needed to lecture her on—well, her reputation and such."

"Ah. So you thought you aided her reputation by dragging her out in the presence of Henry's guests?"

"I . . . lost my head." He paused before her, and grasped her hands. "Ebbie, she intends to leave us."

Ebbie released a shuddering sigh. "I know, and it breaks my heart. I've come to count on her—"

"As have I."

"But—does she plan to marry Henry?"

Releasing her hands, he straightened and pulled his fingers through his hair. "No, she plans to wed no one. She insists she'll return to her own people once she feels you can carry on without her."

"Yes, that's pretty much my understanding. And I was so hoping she'd change her mind—"

"As was I."

"But she keeps telling me she's planning to leave as soon as . . ." Her voice trailed off in embarrassment.

"We marry?" he provided.

Ebbie nodded, blushing furiously.

He smiled gently. "I know we've sashayed all around this, but I think the time has come for us to be frank."

She bravely raised her chin. "I agree."

"So how do you feel about it, Ebbie?"

She stammered, "Y-you mean about—"

"You and me marrying."

Her expression grew uncertain and wistful. "It would have made Linnea very happy."

"Of course it would have, but what about you?" he pressed, his expression anxious. "Would it make you very happy?"

She smiled. "Andre, what woman would not be honored to have you?"

He clenched his fists at his sides. "Ebbie . . . God, I feel so helpless . . ."

"Andre, please speak your mind."

He drew a deep, bracing breath. "I . . . I've come to re-alize that our marrying would be a terrible blunder."

She tensed. "Have I displeased you?"

"No, not at all. It's just that—we're so different. You know how ungovernable I am, whereas you—you're so like Linnea, and my marriage to her was such a mistake."

Ebbie blanched. "A mistake, given the blessing of five beautiful children?"

"Of course I'd trade nothing for my children," he hastily reassured her. "I'm speaking of how ill matched she and I were as husband and wife, how I never made her happy."

"I know she took great joy from the children."

"Thank heaven for that," he said feelingly. "But my point is, I never loved Linnea, and you're so like her, so good and earnest. I cannot bear the prospect of ruining your life, as well—"

"What about your life, Andre?" she asked ironically.

Miserably, he admitted, "I think I, too, would be better off if we didn't proceed with matrimony."

"I see."

Contrite, he clasped her hands. "Please don't be devastated."

Shocking him, she laughed. "Wouldn't any woman be devastated to lose Andre Goddard?"

He glowered. "Woman, are you teasing me?"

She glanced away. "Certainly not."

He straightened and spoke soberly. "Ebbie, Stephanie is determined to see you settled—with me, or, er, with someone."

"I know," Ebbie acknowledged.

"But we're caught in quite a dilemma, for once your future is secured, Stephanie intends to leave us."

"I understand that, as well."

"Do you? How can we convince her to stay?"

Ebbie considered this for a long moment, then smiled. "Andre, remember what I said at the theater?"

"Yes, I do."

She touched his arm, and for once met his gaze without shying away. "Well, my dear, I think it's time for the two of us to have that long, long talk. There are some matters you aren't aware of, and I think it's time for me to speak my heart . . ."

Chapter 39

Later that afternoon, Andre was lost in thought as he rode Prince Albert home from the Reverend Dearborn's cottage. Already he was putting into motion the plan of action he had firmly in mind.

Remembering his earlier conversation with Ebbie, he shook his head. She was amazing, he had to admit it. Their talk had been both emotional and a revelation; he'd come away feeling new respect and sympathy for her. He realized now that he'd failed all along to give Ebbie enough credit.

Galloping toward the house, Andre spotted Stephanie seated on the front veranda. Dismounting and tethering his horse, he sprinted toward the steps.

Ah, she looked a vision sitting on the porch bench in that ivory muslin gown flocked with small red roses; he admired the swell of her bosom accentuated by the ruffled decolletage, the way the lace-trimmed half-sleeves emphasized her lovely forearms. She looked good enough to take a bite out of. He couldn't wait to get her alone again.

Stopping to pluck a daisy from a flower bed, he sprinted up the steps, leaned over to kiss her cheek, and stuck the flower behind her ear.

"Were you waiting for me, darling?" he asked, sitting down and taking her hand.

Although she demurely blushed, she pulled her fingers free. "Of course not, and please don't kiss me publicly this way."

"Publicly? This is my house, damn it, woman!"

In a scandalized whisper, she scolded, "We're on the porch and anyone could see us."

"I still say you were waiting for me," he teased.

She smoothed down her full skirts. "I was catching the afternoon breezes. Haven't you pointed out that I don't spend nearly enough time admiring these beautiful grounds?"

Andre was not fooled. "You must have missed me terribly."

"Not at all. And, by the way, where *have* you been?"

He roared with laughter. "Well, I spoke with Ebbie and apologized about last night."

"Really? How did it go?"

"Oh, it went fine." He coughed and continued casually, "Then I decided to ride over to Peter Dearborn's cottage to invite him for supper tonight—and the good reverend accepted."

"Tonight?" she exclaimed, whistling. "That's fast."

"Well, if we're both going to play matchmaker for Ebbie, we may as well get started, and Peter seems an excellent potential suitor for her."

"Do you really think we can find her someone else?" she asked skeptically.

"Of course we can. And I also think it best that we both nudge her away from the notion that she and I will ever wed, and try to open her eyes regarding other prospects."

She eyed him askance. "So you've got this all plotted out, have you?"

"I'll have to count on your help to lead her in the right direction."

"While you lead *me* further down the path of sin?"

"Why, my dear, what a wonderfully decadent possibility." He leaned over and kissed her again.

She pressed him away and cast him a scolding look. "Andre, please. Haven't you subjected us to enough potential scandal?"

"You're referring to last night?"

"I am, indeed. You were terribly rude to Henry and Katie."

He nodded. "I know. I intend to apologize to Henry tomorrow, and will stop off and make amends with Katie, as well.''

''Well, I'm shocked,'' she quipped back. ''Such humility coming from Andre Goddard.''

''I'm not claiming to have been an angel last night,'' he muttered.

Irresistibly, she looked him over. ''You sure weren't.''

He grinned in obvious pride, then his expression turned sober. ''But Henry is my best friend, and I was very rude to disrupt Katie's dinner party as I did.''

''I'm glad you realize that,'' she replied sincerely. ''But you know, I need to apologize to both of them myself.''

''You?'' He scowled. ''Why must you apologize if I do? Besides, I hate the thought of you being alone with Henry again.''

''But Henry has done nothing improper,'' she protested.

''Except proposing to you,'' he grumbled back.

''*That* was improper?''

He grinned sheepishly. ''You have a point.''

''Can't you at least trust me a little?''

He hesitated a long moment, then nodded. ''I'll trust you . . . but you're going to pay.''

As he kissed her passionately again, she pressed him away. ''I'm going inside, before you ruin us both.''

But as she rose he caught her hand and his gaze swept over her meaningfully. ''Later, Stephanie,'' he murmured.

Just the way Andre said the words made Stephanie weak-kneed. Nonetheless, she managed to go inside and went searching for Ebbie. Finding the other woman's bedroom door ajar, she ducked her head inside. Ebbie was seated at her dressing table brushing her hair.

''Oh, there you are,'' she called brightly.

''Stephanie, do come in. I left the door open so that I might hear the children stirring.''

''Good thinking.'' Stephanie stepped inside. ''I'm surprised they're still napping, but I suppose church and that big meal did them in.''

Ebbie set down her hairbrush and turned on her stool. ''How are you, Stephanie? Andre told me that the two of you had something of a spat last night.''

Stephanie felt guilty color stealing up her cheeks. "Did we ever! Andre took issue with my behavior, totally without cause, I might add. He behaved abominably, and I'm so sorry for any embarrassment you may have suffered—"

"Please don't apologize, Stephanie," Ebbie assured her. "Andre has already done so."

"Good," she murmured. "Did he tell you Reverend Dearborn is coming for supper tonight?"

Ebbie paled. "Why, no."

"I think it's rather spur-of-the-moment. Andre just informed me down on the veranda."

Ebbie's brow was wrinkled. "Did he give a reason for inviting Peter?"

"Oh, paying our respects, I suppose."

Ebbie appeared to be even more perplexed.

Stephanie drew a deep breath. "Ebbie, have you ever considered that you might marry someone besides Andre?"

She laughed nervously. "What an odd question. Why do you ask it?"

Stephanie began to pace. "Well, you know what Andre's like—brash and full of mischief, his eye always on other women."

"Oh, Stephanie, I'm sure you exaggerate."

"What I'm asking is, do you think you could find happiness with someone else?"

Her countenance pale, Ebbie turned away. "I'm afraid that's quite impossible."

Crestfallen, Stephanie rushed to her friend's side, touching Ebbie's shoulder. "Ebbie, I'm sorry. I didn't mean to cause you pain. But I know a little of the world, and I honestly feel that you'd find only heartache with Andre."

Ebbie gazed up in confusion. "Are you so certain?"

"Oh, yes. He's like some force of nature—volatile and unpredictable."

"But I thought you wanted to see the two of us together."

"I wanted it because *you* want Andre," Stephanie replied gently. "But I'm beginning to see that perhaps what you want is not really in your best interests."

Ebbie lifted her chin proudly. "Perhaps there are other

considerations involved besides my best interests. There are the children, and there are matters of honor and decency . . ." Her voice trembled and trailed off. "Matters too heartfelt and profound to speak of . . ."

Stephanie felt keen sympathy at Ebbie's obvious turmoil. "I know how difficult it is when you're caught up emotionally with someone like Andre. But please don't allow your fascination with him to blind you to other possibilities—"

"Other possibilities?"

"Andre is hardly the only eligible bachelor in Natchez. Why, there are three available gentlemen in your string quartet, and there's Reverend Dearborn—"

Ebbie frowned. "Is that what tonight is about? Are you—or Andre—trying to match me up with Peter?"

"Oh, heavens, no!" Stephanie blustered. "Still . . ." She reached out and toyed with a curl at the side of Ebbie's face. "Won't you let me help you with your hair tonight?"

Now Ebbie appeared extremely perplexed.

Several hours later, Stephanie was coming downstairs when she heard the sounds of voices. Recoiling slightly to peer around the newel post, she spotted Andre and Ebbie standing outside the door to his office, chatting together. Wide-eyed, she noted Ebbie's hand placed casually on his arm. Although she felt like an interloper, she couldn't resist listening from her vantage point of relative safety.

"Andre, I think things are proceeding just splendidly," Ebbie was saying.

"I quite agree," he replied. "I'm so glad we've come to a meeting of the minds."

Ebbie nodded. "Me too."

He raised her hand and kissed it. "Thank you for being so understanding."

"How could I do less?" she replied graciously.

"And you're comfortable keeping all this just our little secret?"

"Of course." Earnestly, she added, "Only, I must be true to my promise."

He smiled. "That goes without saying. If we're both patient, I think we'll soon have exactly what we want.''

"I quite agree."

He opened the door to his office and gestured for her to proceed him inside. "If you'll come in for a moment, there are a few more details we must discuss in private."

"Certainly, dear."

Stephanie watched in a state of shock as the two slipped into Andre's office. A moment later, she heard them laughing behind the closed door.

What on earth was going on here? What "secret" did the two share? What "promise" had Ebbie alluded to? A promise to Andre, or to someone else? Why had Andre said they'd both soon get what they wanted? And why had Ebbie looked so uncharacteristically happy and comfortable with him? If she didn't know better, she'd swear the two were more intimately acquainted than she'd ever previously assumed. Even the possibility left her choked with jealousy.

What were Andre and Ebbie up to? The prospect that Andre might have betrayed her was keenly disappointing to Stephanie, but not totally unexpected; yet the very idea that she might have misjudged Ebbie—the possibility that there might be *another* Ebbie whom she didn't really know at all—was devastating to her.

Chapter 40

"**W**ell, Reverend Dearborn, won't you sit down right here, next to Ebbie?"

In the dining room that evening, Stephanie watched in amazement as Andre busied himself seating everyone with all the skill of a majordomo. He placed Ebbie and Peter Dearborn together at the center of one side of the table, wedging the couple between Gwen and Beau.

"There, just look at these two with the children," he declared shamelessly. "What a cozy scene."

The children giggled, Peter appeared confused, and Ebbie blushed crimson.

Andre clapped his hands and took Stephanie by the arm. "Stephanie, we'll put you across from Ebbie and Peter, where you can keep an eye on these two and mind Amy. And Paul, kindly take your seat at the other end of the table . . ."

As Andre seated Stephanie, she muttered under her breath, "Aren't you overplaying your hand a bit?"

Pushing in her chair, he whispered at her ear, "I want this settled so that you're mine."

Watching him take his seat, she felt her heart fluttering at his possessive words. Yet her primary emotion remained embarrassment over his brazen shenanigans.

Andre glanced about the table. "Well, this is so cozy."

"Papa, you've already said that," pointed out Gwen.

He laughed. "So I have, pet." He turned to watch Lilac walk in with a huge silver tray with steaming roast beef, whole carrots, and potatoes. "Do you like pot roast, Reverend?"

"It's my favorite," answered Dearborn gallantly.

As Andre began carving the meat and serving everyone, an awkward silence fell, though Ebbie and Peter exchanged a furtive glance.

Passing Peter his plate, Andre cleared his throat. "Quite some drama over President Hayes last year, wasn't it, Peter? Put in office by electoral commission, by George. Those Republicans are a bunch of sneaky rascals, but I must give Hayes credit for purging the South of the remaining Federal troops."

"Indeed, I think 'tis high time for this nation's wounds to be healed," agreed Peter.

With the conversation lapsing again, Stephanie remarked pleasantly, "I enjoyed your sermon this morning, Reverend. I'm sure I don't think about eternal damnation nearly as much as I should."

"What's damnation?" Gwen asked her father.

He winked. "It's that nasty place we're all bound to, if we don't behave ourselves, pet."

"Oh," she muttered, gulping. She tugged at Dearborn's sleeve. "Are you going to damnation?"

He chuckled. "I shall hope not, my dear."

"What about me and Beau?"

"Well, if you're good children, you have nothing to fear."

"Oh." Biting her lip, Gwen appeared less than encouraged. "My mother didn't go to damnation . . . she went to heaven."

"Of course she did, dear," Ebbie reassured the child.

Gwen slanted a suspicious glance at Dearborn. "Is your mother crazy?"

"Gwen!" gasped Stephanie.

"But I heard Papa saying his mother is crazy."

Even Andre colored. "Peter, I'm sorry, I meant no harm."

"Don't apologize, Andre." To Gwen, he said, "My mother has a rather tenuous grip on reality."

"Oh." Gwen fell silent, appearing baffled.

Beau took up the discussion. "If your mother loses her reality, will she go to damnation?"

All of the adults burst out laughing. "No, no," Peter assured the boy. "If losing our hold on reality were enough to send us to perdition, then we'd all be in a bit of trouble, eh?"

Now it was Beau's turn to appear bewildered.

Gwen spoke up again. "Reverend, are you going to marry Miss Ebbie?"

"Young lady, please!" scolded Ebbie, her face scarlet.

Peter gave a shrill laugh. "Why, I hadn't planned on it."

"Then why are you sitting by her?" asked Beau with a suspicious frown.

"Because your father placed me here," replied the reverend.

Beau turned to his father. "Papa, do you want the reverend to marry Miss Ebbie?"

Andre held up a hand. "Enough! Stop tormenting our guest, all of you, and let the poor man eat his supper in peace."

The remainder of the meal did not pass much better, Stephanie observed. Andre tried to engage Peter in a conversation about next year's cotton forecast, while the children frequently interrupted with more quaint questions that were about as well received as grenades exploding. Peter and Ebbie hardly took note of each other except to exchange an occasional pleasantry about the food.

Finishing his pecan pie, Peter flashed a stiff smile at Andre. "This was excellent. Thank you so much for inviting me."

"But you can't run off just yet. You'll want to stay so that Ebbie can play us some after-dinner music on her violin."

As Peter glanced at Ebbie, she flushed and raised a hand to her throat. "B-but Andre, I have nothing prepared—"

"After all those rehearsals with your quartet? Why, Peter will be devastated if you don't play for us, won't you, Peter?"

"Some music would be nice," he replied tactfully.

"See—what did I tell you?" Not giving Ebbie an opportunity to protest further, he turned to Stephanie. "Stephanie, won't you take the children up, then come back down and join us?"

"Of course, Andre."

While Andre, Ebbie and Peter departed for the parlor, Stephanie took the older children upstairs. Dispatching Paul and Beau to their room, she took charge of Gwen and Amy. As she helped Gwen take off her dress, she could hear the discordant strains of Massenet's doleful "Elegy" drifting up from downstairs.

Grimacing, Gwen whispered at Stephanie's ear. "She's awful."

"Who's awful?" asked Stephanie.

"Miss Ebbie. She plays so bad, she makes poor Amy cry."

Stephanie glanced at Amy, who nodded solemnly. Fighting to keep a straight face, she admonished, "Now, Gwen, that's not a very nice thing to say."

"Well, it's true."

Stephanie turned back to Amy, who did appear very doleful, her lower lip curled under. "You're not going to cry, are you, baby?"

"No," replied Amy, sniffling and cuddling her stuffed bear.

Stephanie hugged both girls to quash a smile.

She tucked the two into bed, and checked on the boys. By the time she returned downstairs, Ebbie had finished with Massenet and moved on to an off-key version of "Drink to Me Only with Thine Eyes." She walked inside the parlor to find both men listening with pained smiles as Ebbie sat beyond them, dutifully sawing away. Stephanie sat down on the settee beside Andre and forced her own pleasant expression.

"Bravo!" cried Andre, clapping when Ebbie finished. "We simply must hear more! Isn't she wonderful, Peter?"

"Quite," he agreed, taking out his pocket watch. "But regretfully, I must get home to Mother. Tomorrow I've promised the ladies of the Missionary Society that I'll meet them bright and early. We're taking baskets to the poor. In fact, I'll be seeing Ebbie there, right, dear?"

"Oh, that's right, I'm glad you reminded me, Peter," Ebbie piped in. "We're meeting at the church at eight, aren't we?"

"Indeed."

"Then you two will see each other again tomorrow," Andre remarked eagerly. "How nice. Ebbie, won't you see Peter out?"

"Of course." Awkwardly, she stood.

Dearborn followed suit. "Thanks again for dinner, Andre. Good to see you, Stephanie."

"You too." Watching them step out of the parlor, she pulled a face at Andre. "Thank God that's over!"

"What do you mean? I thought it went well."

"Well? I can't remember when I've spent a more wretched evening. Peter and Ebbie seemed miserable together, and there's no doubt why."

"Why?"

"My God, you can be dense!" she declared. "Because it was so obvious you were pushing them toward each other."

"Obvious? I thought I was quite subtle."

"You were about as subtle as Norman Schwarzkopf with Saddam Hussein."

"*What*?"

"Never mind," she muttered, exasperated. "Look, why don't you leave the matchmaking to me?"

"Left to you, it will never get done."

"Left to you, it will get horribly bungled." Forcing a silly grin, she mimicked, " 'Gee, don't you two look great with the children.' And they looked about as happy as two kiwis about to be sacrificed to a fruit compote."

He laughed. "You're such a silly woman. Very well, you can help next time if you're so determined."

"Believe me, I will." She took a bracing breath and regarded him sternly. "And there's something else—"

"Are you determined to catalog all my faults?"

"Are you and Ebbie up to something?" she demanded with a suspicious scowl.

"What do you mean?"

"Earlier, I overheard you talking outside your office—"

"You eavesdropped?"

"Don't try to turn the tables on me," she retorted, shaking a finger at him. "Why were the two of you talking?"

"We do live in the same house."

"Well, there seemed to be some funny nuances in the air," she commented archly.

"Funny nuances," he muttered. "Stephanie, you're making no sense."

"Are you trying to seduce her?"

He shouted a laugh. "Isn't that what you wanted?"

"Not now!"

Patting her hand, he replied, "Stephanie, my darling, I'm trying my best to romance you, and to find a husband for Ebbie. Why in God's name would I try to seduce her?"

She waved a hand. "Because you have to seduce every woman, don't you?"

"What a suspicious creature you are," he retorted, then grinned wickedly. "Well, my dear, you may be certain I shall put your doubts to bed tonight."

"Oh, you're impossible!"

Andre laughed and hugged her.

Chapter 41

Undressing for bed, Stephanie could hear Andre moving around in the next room. Excitement danced along her nerve endings as she wondered what he was doing, thinking. Did he expect her to come to him? Much as she wanted to, she held back. How could she go to him when she was convinced there might never be a future for them, that she might at some point be forced to leave him? And after overhearing him with Ebbie, she couldn't help but doubt anew whether he was even capable of committing to one woman.

Still, she wanted him desperately. And when she found herself locking her door to the hallway, she knew it wasn't just because she needed privacy to finish undressing, but because she secretly yearned for him to come to her.

He'd been almost silly tonight, yet so endearing, in his efforts to match up Ebbie with the Reverend Dearborn. If there was ever a hope of getting those two together, Andre had doubtless quashed it with his brazen machinations. She had to give him an A for effort and enthusiasm, yet an F in finesse.

But so much was at stake here—Ebbie's happiness, her very life. Would they be able to find the right man for the shy little spinster? If only Ebbie would confide in her more . . .

Stephanie had just extinguished the lamp and gotten into bed when the door separating her room from Andre's swung open. Her heart pounded as she spied him standing there,

so tall and magnificent, the light behind him outlining his
muscled body, and revealing that he was naked from the
waist up.

"Who gave you permission to sleep apart from me?" he
demanded.

"Do you think you own me now?" she countered.

Grinning, he advanced toward her. "Do you think you're
going to stop me?"

"Rogue."

With a chuckle, he strode across the room, swept her up
into his arms, and carried her back to his room, claiming
her lips along the way. Stephanie moaned in ecstasy and
curled her arms around his neck. Oh, what joy to be held
by him again, crushed against his strength. To feel his
mouth on hers, to taste his tongue claiming her passionately!
Much as she knew she should have protested, she was delighted he had come for her.

By the bed he paused, his blue eyes blazing into hers.
"You're mine, Stephanie," he whispered hoarsely against
her mouth. "God, how I want you."

She pressed her hands to his face. "Andre, we really
shouldn't. What if someone discovers us? I mean, don't
your children ever—"

"Sometimes. But my door is locked tonight—except to
you. And you're not going anywhere, madame—except to
my bed."

He laid her down and joined her there, curling a hand
possessively around her breast.

She drew an unsteady breath. "You say that, but I fear
at heart you're really a scamp, Andre Goddard."

He took her hand and nibbled playfully at her fingers. "If
you must think of me as a scoundrel, you'll only find it
easier to abandon me later on, no? Enjoy me while you can,
darling."

"You rascal."

His expression grew fervent. "Stephanie, I must warn
you that I'm playing for keeps—whether you are or not."

"Are you really?" she asked with an edge of sadness.

He pressed his lips to her hair. "*Oui*. And I can be a
persuasive fellow."

"I know," she acknowledged breathlessly.

He drew back and raked his heated gaze over her, taking in every detail of her body beneath the thin handkerchief linen gown, tempting her to squirm in delight. Then he caught the hem of her gown and began slowly raising it. The anticipation left her gasping.

He hiked her gown above her waist and touched between her thighs, exploring intimately with his rough thumb. Stephanie moaned, her legs automatically clenching. Andre pressed his knees along her thighs, gently holding her open to him.

"There, darling, lie still," he coaxed, still stroking her, and smiling into her eyes. "Do you know how beautiful you look, lying on my bed, with your glorious hair spread out on my pillow, your lips wet from my kisses, your nipples bursting against that thin gown—"

"Oh, Andre, please," she pleaded, awash in delirious sensation.

"—your beautiful legs spread as you open yourself to my touch," he continued hoarsely. "Open yourself to me, Stephanie. Let me see the pleasure in your eyes. Don't shy away."

Already, Stephanie was drowning. She gazed up at him starkly, showing him everything she felt, even the tears that welled as she panted and moved boldly against his hand. His touch was skilled and relentless, raising her to one tantalizing peak of rapture after another. At last the moment grew too intense for both of them and she pulled him down on top of her and kissed him with wild abandon. Her hands slipped inside his trousers, her fingers digging into his firm buttocks. He groaned and arched against her, bruising her sweetly with his hard heat.

Rolling her onto her stomach, he trailed his hot tongue over her shoulders and down her bare spine. She gasped in ecstasy. He burnt a trail over her bottom, nibbling at the firm flesh.

"Oh, you're wicked." She groaned, her hands helplessly clawing the pillow.

"You have a delectable backside," he murmured, caressing her hip.

His teasing tongue blazed down one thigh, tracing circles at the sensitive back of her knee. With a gasp, she rolled over and pulled him close, kissing his face, his ear, his neck, stroking the strong muscles of his arms, his chest.

"Good," he murmured. "Yes, touch me, that is so good, *ma chère.*"

He pulled her on top of him, slid her up his body, and tugged at her breasts with his teeth. She cried out and reached down to unbutton his trousers. She freed him, stroking him. He sucked ravenously at her breast, intensifying the primal hunger throbbing at her core. A moment later she straddled him, rubbing herself sensually against his manhood.

He was at her mercy. "My God, Stephanie, you're a temptress. So slick and wet. Take me, love, please."

Quivering with need, she sank herself upon him. She shuddered as he filled her with his lusty power. Their eyes met, and the ecstasy of their joining was devastating for them both.

"Oh, Steffie, darling."

His trembling fingers gripped her nape, pulling her lips down to his for a deep, heartfelt kiss. His finger slid through her hair. For a long moment, they rocked together, enjoying the delirious, soul-stirring sensations of their melding, heightening the friction and stoking the heat.

Soon the urge to move together grew irresistible. She arched backward and smiled down at him. He caught her waist in his large hands, slowly rolling her about on his phallus until low sobs escaped her at the exquisite pressures ebbing and flowing within her. Never had Stephanie felt such a ravenous pleasure, strong enough to devour her, and yet she was so eager to succumb. . . .

Andre caught her breasts in his hands, kneading almost roughly as she began to ride him with unrestrained passion. After she climaxed with a hoarse moan, he caught her to him tightly and pressed home with a vigor that peaked her pleasure once more.

For long moments they lay entwined, almost limp, tenderly kissing. "You're staying here with me from now on," he murmured. "And you won't need a thing."

*   *   *

Much later, they sat together in the darkness sipping champagne, both still naked. A cool breeze ruffled the lace panels at the window, the moonlight casting glimmering patterns on the floor. In the distance, Stephanie heard an owl hooting.

Andre nudged her ear with his lips. "Stephanie, I want you to marry me."

She sighed, reality returning with a painful thud. "Andre, you haven't been listening to me. I come from another world, and my life is already set there. And there's my sister—we had a terrible fight before I left—"

"You may visit your sister, but your place is here with me," he cut in vehemently. "Didn't tonight convince you of that?"

Miserably, she replied, "Tonight was incredible, but you just don't understand the forces I'm up against. Besides, you're talking about a lifetime commitment to only one woman. Are you certain you're ready for that?"

"I am, darling," he replied, lifting her hand and kissing her fingers. "As they say in the marriage ceremony, 'forsaking all others.' "

Forsaking all others . . . The sweet words brought a lump to Stephanie's throat. Oh, Andre could be so persuasive! Feeling his warm mouth caressing her cheek, she doubted she could ever find another man who would mean as much to her as he did.

As if reading her thoughts, he continued soulfully, "What you must understand, Stephanie, is that we are meant to be. I've never felt like this with a woman. You're my destiny—don't you know that?"

"God, how I wish that could be true," she whispered back fiercely. "I wish I could even know what my true destiny is."

He clutched her closer. "Do you have any idea what it's like to want someone so desperately?"

She gazed at him starkly. "Oh, yes, I do."

Andre set aside their glasses, kissed Stephanie with lingering tenderness, then cradled her against him. She caressed him lovingly, buried her face against his throat, and gloried in his nearness and warmth. Oh, how she did wish she and Andre could be together always. But she knew better, for both destiny and time stood in their way. . . .

Chapter 42

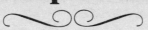

Late the following morning, Stephanie met Ebbie as she returned from her outing with the Missionary Society, and asked to speak with her in the parlor.

Once both women were seated, Ebbie asked, "Is something wrong, Stephanie? Where are the children?"

"They're fine—Martha is watching them." Stephanie toyed with a flower arrangement on the tea table. "Ebbie, I just wanted to apologize for last night. Andre was—well, rather obvious in trying to get you and Peter Dearborn together."

Ebbie breathed a sigh. "Yes, that did seem to be his intention. But you must know something—"

"Yes?"

Soberly, she related, "Peter will never marry, because of his mother."

"I see."

"So you can tell Andre there's no further need to try to match us up."

Taken aback by Ebbie's bluntness, Stephanie said tactfully, "Andre wants—well, we both want—to see you happy and settled."

Ebbie tilted her head to regard Stephanie quizzically. "Is that so? And do you want to see me settled so you can leave us, Stephanie?"

Stephanie felt a twinge of conscience. "Ebbie, you've known all along that I'm only here to help you for a time, until you can be—well—contented with things on your own.''

"You don't have to concern yourself so much with my happiness," Ebbie continued. "I'm sure I'll be just fine. I wish you would stay because . . ."

"Yes?"

Ebbie's expression grew wistful, and somehow reproachful, too. "Because you want to be my friend."

"Oh, Ebbie." Stephanie touched her hand. "Of course I want to be your friend."

Blinking rapidly, Ebbie gathered her bonnet and reticule. "Sometimes it doesn't seem that way."

As Ebbie got up and left the room, Stephanie was confused. What had Ebbie meant by *that* comment?

Following luncheon, Andre insisted Stephanie go with him for a walk on the grounds behind the house. They strolled beneath the tall trees near the fishpond, autumn leaves swirling about them. Although Stephanie worried that they might be seen alone together, she found the cool, blustery day totally invigorating, especially with him by her side.

Not far from a large tree, he laughed and pointed ahead. "Steffie, look at the squirrels."

She craned her neck, watching two squirrels with fluffy tails spring about, doing battle with one another. "Why do you suppose they're fighting?"

"Just watch," he directed. "The little fellow is trying to bury his pecans, and the bigger one wants to steal them."

She stared for another moment, then laughed. "You're right." Feeling a lump in her throat, she squeezed his hand. "You know, over the past five years, I haven't much noticed the world around me. Now I see life through the eyes of you and your children, and everything is new and alive, filled with wonder." Impulsively, she hugged him. "I have to thank you for that."

He leaned over and kissed her. "You're most welcome, my love. But you know I want much more."

"I know," she whispered back tenderly. "It's just that I'm still not sure what's in store for us, Andre. But one thing you have taught me is to enjoy life in the moment. Can't we savor what we have now?''

He groaned. ''Ah, so my own words come back to haunt me?''

She kissed him quickly, and they strolled for a few moments in silence.

Stephanie cleared her throat. ''About Ebbie and Peter . . .''

He sighed. ''Things aren't going to work out for them, eh?''

''No, because of his mother. She told me this morning.''

''Then perhaps we must give this one more try,'' he suggested. ''You know, Abner Trumble keeps begging me to go hunting with him. Maybe I'll go soon, and see if I can set something up for him and Ebbie—perhaps include him in a family outing.''

''Hey, that's a great idea. I think of the three men in her quartet, Ebbie likes him best.''

With a devilish grin, Andre pulled Stephanie behind a tree and kissed her eagerly. ''And of all the women under God's earth, I want *you* the most.''

Stephanie hugged him tight. ''Oh, Andre, that's so sweet.''

The next week passed blissfully for Stephanie. By day, she and the children decorated the house for Halloween, which was now less than a week away, and planned a small family party to celebrate the holiday. She also read to the youngsters by the fire or watched them romp outside in the crisp fall weather.

By night, she found heaven on earth in Andre's arms. She felt relieved when he didn't press her as much about marriage, and both of them enjoyed their beautiful, intimate times together.

On several more occasions, she spied Andre and Ebbie with their heads together, and again wondered what the two were up to. But as the days passed, Stephanie found the prospect of Andre and Ebbie actually being secret lovers to be outlandish. Still, she was puzzled by the unusual bond she sensed building between them—a connection neither seemed willing to discuss with her.

On Thursday afternoon, Andre went hunting with Abner Trumble, and Stephanie left the children with Ebbie while Willie drove her into town. She dropped in at Katie Robillard's cottage and had a long, heart-to-heart talk with her friend, apologizing for Andre's rude conduct at the dinner party, and tactfully explaining why she felt she could never marry Henry. When the cagey old woman guessed that Stephanie was becoming enamored of Andre, Stephanie admitted it was true, but made her friend promise not to tell a soul.

Afterward, Stephanie stopped by the Franklin Street office where Andre and Henry based their cotton brokerage firm. She stepped inside the dusty front room to see Henry seated at a desk cluttered with documents. He glanced up with an abstracted scowl, then smiled and stood.

"Stephanie, what a pleasant surprise."

She shook his hand. "Good to see you, Henry. So this is where you and Andre work."

"Yes, our offices are here, and our warehouses down on Water Street."

She smiled. "I'm sorry to disturb you, but—"

"You were not disturbing me. Please, have a seat."

She sat down, and he followed suit. Earnestly, she began. "Henry, I've already been by to see Katie, to tell her how sorry I am about last Saturday night. But I also had to drop by here, because I owe you an apology, as well."

He smiled tightly. "It's Andre who owed me an apology, not you, and he has already done so, as well as explaining the situation."

She blanched. "Explaining the situation?"

He nodded grimly. "Is it true the two of you are planning to marry?"

Stephanie felt her cheeks burning. "Is that what Andre told you?"

"Yes."

"Well, it's not true," she replied. "I mean, I haven't accepted his proposal."

Henry gave a cynical laugh. "Well, he sure acts like a man who's ready to settle down."

Stephanie frowned, her interest piqued. "What do you mean?"

"Aside from going hunting this afternoon, Andre has actually been at the office all week, helping me grade cotton and work on the books. When I remarked on his new zeal for our enterprise, he shrugged and said he's going to have to behave himself from now on because he'll have new responsibilities. I was stunned—usually the man spends at least half his time gambling or at the racetrack."

Stephanie was also pleasantly surprised. "I'm glad he's helping out more."

"We'll see if it lasts," Henry added. Leaning toward her, he spoke intently. "If you're not planning to marry him, won't you give us another chance?"

She flashed him a regretful smile. "I'm afraid that's impossible. As I said last Saturday night, I do like you, but I'll never feel about you as a wife should."

He sighed. "Then I guess it is over between us."

She touched his hand. "I'm sorry."

Stephanie was pleased to have learned that Andre was settling down somewhat, but annoyed with him for announcing their engagement before she'd given her consent. She was ready to scold him over that.

However, she didn't even see him until dinnertime. She, Ebbie, and the children were already seated, eating soup, when he finally strode in. He was still in his riding clothes, his color high from his ride. As he passed by Stephanie's chair, she noted he smelled of the rugged, woodsy outdoors. He looked incredible—vigorous, handsome, so full of life. But Stephanie remained miffed over his presumptuous announcement to Henry.

"Sorry to be late, ladies," he said, striding quickly to his chair, "but I had a great time hunting with Abner Trumble. I've already dropped off several plump quail with the cook."

"How wonderful," said Ebbie. "And how is Abner?"

"Just splendid. As always, he speaks so highly of you."

Ebbie demurely rolled her eyes. "That man! Such a flirt."

Andre unfolded his napkin. "By the way, we'll be seeing Abner again on Monday. He mentioned that on All Souls' Day, he always decorates his mother's grave at the cemetery, and I suggested we all make an outing of it."

"That's right, " Ebbie said, "we must take the children, for Linnea's sake."

"Will we get to see Mama?" Gwen asked raptly.

Her father gazed at her tenderly. "In our hearts, we always will, pet."

Gwen beamed back, evidently satisfied.

With bemusement, Andre glanced at Stephanie. "You've been quiet, Madame Sergeant. What do you think about our planned outing?"

She flashed him a stiff smile. "Sounds great."

Ebbie turned excitedly to Stephanie. "We'll have to bake soul cakes for the children, won't we?"

"Yes, indeed."

"Can we help?" asked Beau, eyes alight. "Paul and I will be happy to lick the bowl!"

Cheers and laughter reigned at the table as all of the children joined in on the planning.

Stephanie soon had even greater cause to feel perplexed with Andre. Later that evening, she was in the playroom reading the four older children a Halloween tale when Paul interrupted her. "Are you going to try to find Miss Ebbie a husband so you can marry my father?"

Paling, stunned by the child's query, Stephanie set down her book. "Paul, what an odd question."

Paul raised his chin and continued forthrightly. "The other day, my father took me with him to his office, and I heard him tell Mr. Robillard that he's going to marry you as soon as you find Miss Ebbie a husband."

For a moment, Stephanie was rendered dumbstruck as Gwen and Amy giggled and the boys continued to watch her expectantly.

At last she carefully replied, "Paul, whatever you think you heard, it was never meant for your ears."

Grinning, Gwen tugged at her skirt. "Why not, madame? We want you to marry Papa."

"You do?" Stephanie was flabbergasted.

Gwen beamed. "Yes, madame."

"We like you," added Beau. "You're fun."

"We voted, and we all decided we want you for our mother," finished Paul.

Stephanie remained stunned, as well as very touched. "Is this really true?"

She looked in turn at each of the four children, and each, in turn, solemnly nodded.

"Except for Sarah," Paul amended. "She's too young to vote. But she loves you, no?"

Stephanie stared at her lap to hide a rush of tears. Not until this moment had she realized how completely these adorable children had insinuated themselves inside her heart. She was trembling, awash in turmoil and conflicted emotion.

"Well, madame?" nudged Paul.

Sniffling, Stephanie gazed at their four vulnerable, expectant faces. "I—I'm so honored that all of you think of me so highly. However, I'm sorry, but . . ." Clenching her fists helplessly, she finished, "I'm afraid I can't become your mother."

They raised a chorus of disappointed sighs.

"Why?" demanded Gwen.

"Because I have a life elsewhere," Stephanie whispered. "I'm afraid I can't stay here permanently. I'd very much like to, but I don't think I'll be able to."

Gwen's little mouth began to quiver, her eyes gleaming with pride. "Well, I think you're hateful. We don't need you, anyway!"

"Gwen, please—"

The girl sprang to her feet and pulled up little Amy, who also looked close to tears. "Come on, Amy. She doesn't want us."

"No, that's not true!" Reeling, Stephanie watched the girls leave, then turned to see Paul and Beau staring at her with hot, accusing eyes. "Please, let me try to explain."

"No!" cried Beau. "I think you're mean!"

As he too ran out, Stephanie turned to Paul. "Will you listen to me?"

He drew himself up with pride, reminding her strongly of his father. "No, madame, because I think you're selfish. Do you know how hard it was for my brother and sisters to ask you to marry Papa? They lost their real mother, and now you've broken their hearts again."

The way he said the words made Stephanie fear she had broken his heart, as well.

Stephanie barely managed to keep her composure until she stumbled inside her room. Then she collapsed against the closed door and began to sob.

She was so confused, so horribly torn. She had come here to the past to help Ebbie—yet now she wasn't even certain what that meant, what Ebbie really wanted, or how she might improve the woman's life. She felt a miserable failure there.

And she had failed not only in trying to match Ebbie up with Andre, but also in trying to help her bond with Andre's children and become a proper stepmother for the motherless brood. Indeed, the harder she had tried to accomplish her goals, the more the entire family had gravitated to her instead of Ebbie.

She had never intended to become so emotionally caught up with these people. But now Andre and his children had captured her heart, and they all seemed to want her to remain here. But how could she, when she had no guarantees about how long her sojourn here might last, when indeed, she'd been warned her "mission" would end, when her real life lay elsewhere, and she had nothing permanent to offer these people who wanted her?

"Steffie? What's wrong?"

She didn't even hear the door to Andre's room opening. Suddenly, he was there, closing the distance between them, pulling her into his arms, his tenderness twisting like a knife against her already raw emotions.

"Go away," she said hoarsely. "I need to be alone."

"I'm not going anywhere with you so distraught."

"Please, this is private."

He caught her face in his hands and forced her to look up into his turbulent eyes. "No, Steffie, our lives are joined now, and nothing is private between us anymore. Now tell me what's wrong."

"It's the children," she admitted helplessly.

He paled. "Is one of them ill?"

"No, no nothing like that."

"Then what?"

She regarded him accusingly. "Did you tell Henry we plan to marry?"

"What makes you ask that?"

"Did you?"

"Yes."

"How dare you be so presumptuous!"

"Presumptuous? You share my bed each night, and now I'm presumptuous to assume we'll marry?"

"You're wrong to make such an announcement without my consent."

"Why? Are you still hoping to patch things up with Henry?"

"Of course not."

"Then why?"

"Because Paul overheard you! And tonight, all the children asked me . . ."

"What, Steffie?"

"To become their mother," she wailed.

He lifted her chin, his face revealing both anguish for her and concern for his children. "And what did you say?"

"What could I say?" she asked miserably. "I said no, as gently as I could. Still, they all ran out in tears and—oh, God, how I hate this."

"I see." Andre turned and walked away toward the French doors.

She rushed after him, touching his arm. "Andre, I'm so sorry. The last thing I wanted was to hurt your children. I never expected this to happen. Until last weekend, I was trying to get them to think of Ebbie as their mother—"

"Ebbie?" He whirled on her, his eyes alive with emotion. "But how could they? Have you really thought about my children, Stephanie? Ebbie's not comfortable with them.

Much as she means well, she has never really understood them. But you're wonderful with them and we both know it. I try with them, but they need more. They need love, Stephanie, a mother's love. They need *you*."

"Andre, please don't say these things," she pleaded, wringing her hands.

He was heedless. "Of course they've gravitated to you like a starving man to a feast. We all have. Of course they fell in love with you. Who wouldn't?"

His words tore at her emotions, especially as again, he was hinting that he loved her. "Andre, I didn't intend this. You must understand. I don't belong here. I'm not supposed to be the wife of a cotton broker and his five children, in the year 1878. I'm supposed to be a widow librarian, in a time far in the future. I came here to help someone else, not for me, to seek my own happiness—"

He seized her shoulders. "And what about us, me and my children? What about *our* happiness?"

Stephanie was silent, genuinely stumped by his question.

"You say you're here for Ebbie, but what about the rest of us? Ebbie is going to be Ebbie no matter what—she has her violin and her Bible, her misters and the reverend. She doesn't really need you, me, or anyone. If you're so determined to sacrifice yourself, then do so for *us*, for me and my children. We're the ones who really need you. My God, Stephanie, can't you see what's happening here? You've brought us together as a family. You've brought me to my senses in so many ways, making me happy to settle down and make a new life with you. Now you would abandon us?"

Stephanie felt devastated, and could only hold out her hands beseechingly. "You don't understand. I'm only here on a mission. My life isn't mine to give you."

"Is that what you told my children?" he asked bitterly.

She wiped her cheek with the back of her hand. "Andre, please, you're making me cry again."

With a groan, he pulled her close and spoke against her hair. "My love, I'm sorry if tears are required to make you see the truth. You're mine, do you understand me? I'll make you cry if I must . . . and then I'll make you so very happy."

She clutched him to her feverishly, and her voice broke. "You already do. So very happy."

"Oh, Steffie."

He carried her to his room and made tender love to her, amid her bittersweet tears. . . .

Much later, Stephanie slipped out of bed in the darkness. Putting on her gown and wrapper, she stared down at Andre as he slept, his features peaceful and nobly handsome. She remembered the poignancy and passion of their lovemaking, how tenderly he'd held her, the glory of his mouth on her breast, the heat and strength of him inside her, how they'd moved together, so deeply. But it would never be enough because loving him only made her want more, to truly join her life with his.

She loved him. The realization filled her with an agonizing sweetness. Of course she loved him. She adored him and his precious family, hungered to be a part of their lives with an intensity that was overwhelming.

She didn't know what she should do, if she should or could stay. But she did know she could no longer push this dear family away.

Kissing Andre's brow, she left his room and tiptoed across the hallway into the girls' room. She knelt by their double bed, watching them sleep. Gwen was cuddled with her rag doll, Amy sucking her thumb. Stephanie reached out to pull the coverlet over both girls.

Gwen stirred, sat up and stared at Stephanie warily. "What are you doing here?"

Hearing the hurt in the child's voice, Stephanie smoothed her rumpled hair. "Do you know you have beautiful hair?"

Gwen hesitated. "It's from my mama."

"I know."

"She was beautiful."

"Of course she was, darling."

Gwen gazed at Stephanie in uncertainty, then whispered, "You're pretty, too."

Stephanie struggled not to fall apart again. "I'm sorry," she whispered.

For a moment, the little girl battled with her pride, the

struggle on her face heartrending to see. Then she threw her arms around Stephanie's neck. "Don't leave us, madame."

"I'll try not to, sweetie," Stephanie said hoarsely.

In the night, Andre reached for Stephanie but found her gone. He put on his dressing gown and stumbled into her room. Seeing that her bed was vacant, he tried the children's rooms and soon located her in bed with Gwen and Amy.

The sight of the three of them together twisted his heart. Stephanie slept in the middle of the bed, with a girl cuddled on either side of her. Gwen's little head rested on her arm, while Amy's tiny hand was curled about two of her fingers.

How sweet they looked, as if they all belonged together. Feelings of tenderness made his eyes burn. How long had it been since he'd felt the sting of tears? He'd cried the night Linnea had died. He'd held her, felt the life ebbing out of her, and had known such pain, such devastating regret.

But what he felt now was even more profound. He loved this woman, he realized. Loved her with all his heart. The realization was shattering, deeply humbling, more joyous and painful than anything he'd ever felt. For he had never loved before—not this soul-rending, man-woman sort of love, where the very thought of losing her made him want to die.

Somehow, he had to find a way to keep her here. He needed her. His children needed her.

Tenderly, he pulled a quilt over his three sleeping beauties, kissed them all, and left them there together.

Chapter 43

O n Monday afternoon, Stephanie sat with Andre on a blanket on a high, grassy knoll at the cemetery, the spot shaded by the breathtaking canopy of a moss-hung oak, with a spectacular view of the river in the distance. Baby Sarah, pink-cheeked and absolutely adorable in a long, lacy white dress, matching bonnet, and crocheted booties, sat between them, happily drinking from a nursing bottle and cooing to herself. Nearby, Amy was picking late-blooming wildflowers, and placing the blooms on her mother's gravestone, and on the smaller grave of her infant brother next to it. In a clump of bushes a few yards away, Gwen, Paul, and Beau were playing hide-and-seek with several other youngsters whose families were also visiting the cemetery. The children had already gobbled down their lunch of fruit, sandwiches, and soul cakes, and seemed in a festive mood.

In the distance, Ebbie and Mr. Trumble were attending his mother's grave marker. He was pulling weeds from the surrounding ground, while she arranged fresh flowers in an urn before the headstone.

Gazing about the many terraced levels of the lovely old cemetery, Stephanie was surprised to see so many Natchez families present today. While the children played, the adults scrubbed or painted headstones, cleaned up the plots, and laid out wreaths and flowers. Several Civil War widows were present, draping their husband's graves with Confederate flags. And although the mood in the memorial garden was thoughtful, it was far from somber, since the family members seemed to be here more to honor the dead than to mourn them.

She glanced at Andre, and found his expression was both tender and pensive as he watched Amy dump a skirtful of blooms on her mother's headstone.

"Are you thinking about her?" Stephanie asked.

He nodded. "Of course I am."

"Do you miss her?"

He cleared his throat. "She was a fine lady, devoted to us all. I deeply regret that her life was so brief." He gazed down at the baby, arranging a curl on her forehead, and she gurgled up at him, blowing milk bubbles. His gaze shifted to the grave of his infant son, and he sighed. "At least we didn't lose another child." He stared off in the distance. "Unlike the Sweeneys, who've lost four of theirs in epidemics."

Stephanie looked in the same direction. Not far from the pond, a young couple in black stood before a long row of small headstones. The wife was holding a baby, while the husband removed his hat and crossed himself.

The scene tore at Stephanie's heartstrings. "Yes, what could be more devastating?"

Andre took out his handkerchief, wiping milk from the baby's chin. "The night Linnea died, she took such joy from knowing Sarah had survived. My wife was an unselfish creature. I'll never forget her final words: 'If one of us must go, I'm glad it's me.' "

Stephanie nodded. "I think if it were me, I would have felt the same way."

He flashed her a contrite smile. "I'm sorry. I didn't mean to turn morbid."

"You're not. It is a day of reflection."

He reached out to stroke her cheek. "And what are you reflecting on, Stephanie? You don't have anyone here, do you?"

She fell silent, keenly missing her own family. No, she had no ancestors in this cemetery, not yet; her family would not even move to Natchez until the turn of the century. She remained a displaced soul; in a sense, she hadn't been born yet. Each time she contemplated her odd station in life, it boggled her mind.

"I suppose I'm thinking of those I've lost," she said at last.

"Your husband?"

"Yes. And my sister, my parents. I haven't really lost them, but they're so far away." She laughed mirthlessly. "In another world."

He slowly shook his head. "Darling, I wish I could understand what you mean by such comments, but I just can't."

"I know," she acknowledged sadly.

"But I am glad you're here."

She smiled into his ardent eyes. "I'm glad I'm here, too." *For however long,* she added to herself.

He gestured toward the river. "Today is a day not just of reflection, but also of hope. Take a look, Stephanie."

She craned her neck and spotted Ebbie and Mr. Trumble strolling along the bluff hand in hand, even as the wind carried over the sounds of their shared laughter. "Yes, perhaps there is hope. I think she really likes him."

"And perhaps we're that much closer to being together."

They were regarding each other wistfully when Amy skipped up, a clump of blossoms in her hand. Shoving the blooms at the baby, she pointed toward the headstone and said meaningfully, "Mama."

Dropping her bottle and grinning, Sarah grabbed a handful of the blooms and crawled over to fling the blossoms at the headstone.

"Mama!" she chortled, waving her plump arms.

Stephanie felt stirrings of tenderness. "Oh, Andre, that's so sweet."

"I know."

Both of them watched in awe as the baby pulled herself up on the headstone. "Oh, Andre—do you think she's really going to walk today?" Stephanie asked. "I've noticed her trying several times lately, but she usually falls after a step or two."

He clucked to the baby. "Come to Papa, minx."

The child giggled, let go of the headstone, and toddled

awkwardly toward her father. Just as she was about to fall, Andre scooped her up into his arms.

"You did it, minx!" he declared with pride, lifting Sarah high into the air, as she kicked her feet and squealed. Settling her in his arms and kissing her cheek, he turned to regard Stephanie, who was wiping away tears. "What's wrong, love?"

"Nothing," she said hoarsely, smiling at him. "It's just all so endearing. It's as if Sarah let go of her mother—and went to you."

"To *us*, darling," Andre whispered. "To us. We need you, Stephanie."

She clutched his hand. "I know."

We need you. As Andre leaned over and kissed Stephanie, the words reverberated through her heart, and the last vestiges of her doubts about him began to melt away.

Funny, how she'd always thought of Andre's world as being without purpose, a world where she didn't really belong, but now she knew better. She *was* needed here, by Andre and his children. She did have a purpose—to love and care for them all. What higher goal could any human being aspire to? She would leave her other life for them—gladly.

But *could* she? Or would she end up hurting them all?

Toward sunset, the group parted, Mr. Trumble riding off for his plantation, and Andre driving his family home in the carriage. Swirls of red-gold leaves and shards of golden light showered the conveyance as they proceeded along the bluff in the rarified beauty of late afternoon.

In the backseat, Ebbie whispered to Stephanie. "Mr. Trumble asked if he may sit with me at the church covered-dish supper on Thursday night."

"He did?" she asked, thrilled. "I do hope you said yes."

Ebbie nodded, smoothing down her skirts. "I think that will be lovely."

Stephanie playfully nudged Ebbie. "You like him, don't you? And I think he'll make you a wonderful beau. You have so much in common."

Ebbie blushed. "Yes, we do share our music. And today

he spoke so highly of his deceased mother.''

"Wonderful! I can't wait to help you dress for the church supper.''

At last she and Andre were making some progress, Stephanie thought excitedly. She couldn't wait to tell him.

But if Ebbie's situation were resolved, what would this mean for her and Andre? Would Fate allow them to find their own happy ending?

Over the next weeks, Andre and Stephanie were encouraged to see Abner Trumble join Ebbie and the family for a number of activities, including several holiday parties and teas. Ebbie even announced she would likely invite Abner to spend Thanksgiving dinner with the family.

Stephanie continued to share Andre's bed at night, and she felt closer to him with each passing day. When her period was late, she found it odd but, given her history with Jim, dared not hope she might actually be carrying Andre's child. She figured the tardiness could be due to the stress of her current situation, and, especially, trying to find the enigmatic Ebbie a husband. She kept hoping the robust Mr. Trumble would be the one.

Andre and Stephanie felt elated when Ebbie announced that Abner had invited her over to his Vidalia plantation, to meet a cousin and his wife who were visiting from Washington. On the morning of the outing, Andre and Stephanie stood on the lawn, Gwen and Pompom between them as they waved at Ebbie and Trumble driving away in his buggy.

Andre squeezed Stephanie's hand and whispered at her ear. ''Think he'll propose to her today?''

"Well, Ebbie does speak highly of him," Stephanie replied. "And he's introducing her to his relatives. She's been talking all week about meeting Gaylord and Constance.''

Gwen tugged at Stephanie's skirt. ''Who are Gaylord and Constance?''

Stephanie chuckled. "The people Miss Ebbie is going to meet.''

"Oh." Gwen grinned up at her father. ''Is Miss Ebbie going to marry Mr. Bumble?''

Laughing, Andre lifted the child into his arms. "We'll hope so, pet." He ruffled her hair. "Now didn't I promise you and your brothers and sister that we'd fly a kite this morning? Let's go find the others."

"Yippee!" cried Gwen, as they all hurried off for the house.

Stephanie had great fun that morning romping with Andre and the children. Yet she also wondered about Ebbie, and hoped her friend was faring well with Abner in Vidalia.

Her hopes were dashed during luncheon. She was sitting with Andre and the children in the dining room when she heard the front door bang open and caught a glimpse of a very disheveled-looking Ebbie limping in and heading for the stairs.

Alarmed, Stephanie tossed down her napkin. "Excuse me," she said and dashed into the hallway. She spotted Ebbie hobbling up the stairs. Her dress was torn in several places, and a heel was missing from one of her shoes.

"Ebbie!" Stephanie cried hoarsely. "All you all right? What on earth has happened to you?"

Ebbie whirled, drawing a finger to her mouth. Her hair was mussed and her hat tilted at a rakish angle, with several flowers ripped off.

"Please, Stephanie, let me get upstairs before someone sees me in this disgraceful state," she implored.

"Not until you explain," Stephanie retorted.

Andre hurried out of the dining room, trailed by Beau. Wild-eyed, he confronted Ebbie. "*Mon Dieu,* woman, what has become of you? Did that cad Trumble try to assault you?"

Ebbie laughed dryly. "Heavens, no."

"Then explain this to us."

She heaved a sigh. "Very well. If you must know, Mr. Trumble and I have decided not to see each other again. You see, Abner asked me out today under false pretenses—"

"I knew it! I'll call out the scoundrel!" declared Andre.

"No, you don't understand," Ebbie replied in frustration. "You see, I thought Abner wanted me to go to his plantation to meet Gaylord and Constance, but we never even got as far as the front door. I soon learned that the real reason he took me to his property was to introduce me to his six hunting dogs."

"His dogs?" inquired Andre.

"Yes—er, to see if I'd pass muster with the bird dogs and the hounds. And suffice it to say, the seven of us don't get along. Not at all. The dogs had the run of the place—and of me."

"But—what about Gaylord and Constance?" asked Stephanie. "Didn't they try to help?"

Ebbie made a sound of mingled amusement and contempt. "I'm sure they were cowering in the house. Can you blame them?"

As Stephanie and Andre looked on, flabbergasted, Ebbie turned and continued limping up the stairs. Beau raced back into the dining room, yelling, "Miss Ebbie has gone to the dogs!"

Neither Stephanie nor Andre laughed, both standing for a moment in stunned silence.

"What next?" Andre asked with an exasperated wave of his hand. "First we're thwarted by a crazy mother, now by a pack of deranged dogs."

Stephanie was shaking her head. "I'm surprised the beasts didn't attack you when you went hunting with Abner."

"Well, they did seem rambunctious." He sighed. "Stephanie, I think it's time to tell Ebbie the truth about us. We can't continue with this charade."

She mulled this over, then nodded. "I suppose you're right. But should we just give up on finding Ebbie a husband? There's still Mr. Fortier—or Mr. Wister."

Andre rolled his eyes. "Stephanie, I think we both need to admit that we've been dismal failures at matchmaking."

She laughed bitterly. "And how."

He gave her a quick hug. "Come on, dear, let's rejoin the children."

Reentering the dining room with him, Stephanie remained troubled. She wanted to find her happiness with Andre—wanted it desperately. She prayed that things could somehow work out for them and the children. But she felt a failure for not having resolved Ebbie's future. She very much feared her friend would be left with nothing.

Nothing, that is, except heartache . . . and death.

Chapter 44

The next day dawned cold and wet, and Stephanie awakened feeling out of sorts. She picked at her breakfast, and even grew nauseous at the smell of the baked catfish served for lunch.

Ebbie was mysteriously gone for a good portion of the day. In the afternoon while the children were napping, Stephanie spotted her friend in the dining room. She was intrigued to note that Ebbie was arranging a bouquet of red roses in a crystal vase. She stepped inside; the room was chill, and rain pounded at the windows.

"Why, Ebbie, what a lovely arrangement," she said. "Who sent them?"

With a frown, Ebbie glanced up. "Oh, hello, Stephanie. A friend just sent these, hoping to cheer me up over the bad news."

Moving closer, Stephanie nodded. "Bless your heart. You mean the bad news about Abner?"

Ebbie waved her off. "Not that. You see, while I was out, I had a terrible shock."

"Oh, no. What has happened now?"

"It's about the quartet."

"Yes?"

Fretfully, Ebbie related, "Well, I met Mr. Fortier and Mr. Wister for brunch, and . . . Do you remember Charles talking about how the men in his family always join the French Foreign Legion?"

"Yes."

"Well, I'm afraid Charles has decided to accept his own commission."

Stephanie was stunned. "You're joking."

"I wish I were, but the man is packing even as we speak."

Stephanie struggled to make sense of this. "But, I thought Charles was different from the others, such a high-brow."

"I know, but the men in his family believe they must serve in order to build character, even though Charles's father got lost somewhere in the Sahara, and his life ended rather badly, I'm afraid."

"My heavens."

"At any rate, I understand it was an inspirational letter from Charles's uncle Maurice that ultimately compelled him to enlist."

"But what about the quartet?"

Ebbie gave a great sigh. "I'm in quite a dither about it. You see, it gets worse."

"Worse?"

"Mr. Wister has decided he can't bear to part with Charles, so he's joining the French Foreign Legion, as well. Of course, he can't become an officer like Charles, but he doesn't seem to care."

Stephanie had gone wide-eyed. "You can't be serious!"

"I am." Ebbie paused in apparent perplexity. "Though I can't imagine why two men would run off together."

Stephanie had to smother a laugh. "Then your string quartet is down to—"

"Two members, and I'm not even speaking to that black-guard Abner," Ebbie continued grimly. "The consequences are going to be simply devastating. We're going to disappoint so many who were expecting us to perform at all the Christmas functions."

"Yes, I'm sure the entire community will be distraught," Stephanie muttered.

Ebbie frowned critically at her handiwork, rearranging a couple of blooms. "I stopped by to discuss our predicament with Peter, and he has generously offered to fill in. But 'string trio' doesn't sound quite right, does it?"

Stephanie sighed. "I'm so sorry, Ebbie—and particularly about the fiasco with Abner."

Ebbie flashed Stephanie a brave smile. "Stephanie, you needn't fret so much over my happiness. I know you mean well, but I do think that sometimes if we just leave things well enough alone, everything works out in time."

"Sure, Ebbie."

Puzzled, Stephanie left the room. Ebbie was certainly one odd duck. Had her parting words been a hint that she was still in love with Andre? In any event, she and Andre were all out of potential suitors, and she'd reached a dead end in her efforts to help her friend.

Shivering at the sound of a thunderclap, Stephanie rubbed her arms. The house had definitely grown colder.

She went up to her room and wrapped a shawl around her shoulders. Feeling at loose ends, she wandered into Andre's room and opened the French doors to the veranda. Although a chill wind swept in cold droplets, she was entranced to watch the rain slashing against the stately oaks, to hear the sound of the thunder and smell the cold freshness.

At moments like this, she felt lost, so far removed from the world she'd once known, not understanding why she was here. She couldn't seem to help Ebbie or understand her. And each day, she became more emotionally enmeshed with Andre and his family. If she eventually was wrenched away, as she sensed she might be, she was in danger of breaking too many hearts—her own, the children's, even Andre's. How she wished there were someone to guide her—but all she had was that one, brief dream in another life, in which she'd been charged with her mission.

She heard the door swing open, and Andre's voice. "Stephanie, what are you doing here alone?"

She turned to him. "Hello. I was just watching the rain."

Closing the door, Andre stepped inside his room. He frowned worriedly at the sight of her, shivering beyond him, features forlorn. "My God. It's freezing in here." He rushed over to close the French doors, then pulled her into his arms, alarmed at how cold she felt. "Darling, you're shaking like a leaf. Are you ill?"

"No, I don't think so."

"You hardly touched your lunch."

She shuddered. "Well, I have been feeling queasy all day, and now—guess I'm just down."

"Down? You mean in low spirits?"

She nodded.

"What's wrong?"

She gazed up at him in uncertainty. "I can't make sense of anything, Andre."

"What do you mean?"

"Ebbie, the children, us. I'm so confused. I keep asking myself why I'm here. Sometimes I'm afraid I may be doing all of you more harm than good." She sniffed. "Maybe you'd be better off without me."

"Perish the thought, woman." Andre began rubbing her arms. "What inspired this crazy talk? Just because Ebbie got attacked by dogs—"

"It's not just that, Andre. As you aptly pointed out, we're not helping her." She laughed. "Indeed, Mr. Fortier and Mr. Wister are running off together, so we are completely out of suitors."

"What?" he cried.

"You heard me."

His expression bemused, Andre pulled Stephanie to a wing chair, sat down, and settled her on his lap. Wrapping his arms around her and pressing his lips to her temple, he murmured, "Come on, darling, matters can't be so very dire. We're together and we'll find a way through all this."

She stared up at him. "I'm glad we're together—at least for today."

Stephanie's words gave Andre pause. His heart struggled with a painful paradox, that even though she was here with him now, he might be losing her. How could he convince her they were meant to stay together always?

He cuddled her closer and whispered at her ear. "You know, a few nights ago, I spied you in bed with my daughters. Never have I seen anything so dear. Steffie, surely you must know you belong with us now, that you and I are meant to become husband and wife."

She pulled back, her emotions stark on her face. "I want

to belong with you. Lord, how I want it, especially with the children growing so attached to me. But you don't seem to understand that I may not have a choice. And I hate the thought that you and the children could suffer when I leave.''

''Leave? Why do you keep saying you must leave?''

''Because I'm from another time, and I've been warned that my days here will be limited.''

''Warned by whom?''

''Great-aunt Magnolia.''

He could only shake his head. ''Stephanie, I don't understand at all.''

''I know you don't,'' she replied with a sad laugh. ''I really don't, either. If only I could have some sort of sign—a sign that I'm meant to stay here—then maybe I wouldn't be so terrified that I'm going to hurt all of you.''

He kissed her cheek. ''Darling, you'd never hurt us. And don't be afraid. I'll protect you.''

Cuddled against Andre's strength, Stephanie was tempted to believe him. But could he protect her from time itself?

The following morning, as soon as Stephanie awakened and sat up, she was beset by dizziness, quickly followed by nausea. Within seconds, she was compelled to make a dash for the dresser. At the basin, she gagged and retched.

She felt Andre handing her a towel, then slipping her wrapper around her shoulders. ''*Chérie*, what is wrong? You were queasy yesterday—now this.''

She wiped off her face and turned to him, thinking about the last few weeks, and how funny she'd felt yesterday. ''My God, I wonder . . .''

''What, darling?''

Eyes aglow, she continued, ''Well, I knew I was late but I thought . . . Heavens, could I be pregnant?''

Andre's face lit with delight and he pulled her close. ''But of course you are.''

''Oh, my God.'' Stephanie reeled with emotion—wonderment, fear, blinding joy. ''But I didn't think I could conceive—''

Andre caressed her cheek. ''I did. I always had faith in

you. And every time we made love, I said a little prayer, just to be sure.''

She regarded him in awe. ''You wanted a baby with me?''

He gazed at her poignantly. ''To tell you the truth, it did scare me a little, the thought of you enduring childbirth, after what happened to poor Linnea. Still, I knew how much you wanted a child, and thus I wanted it for both our sakes.''

Exultant tears burned her eyes, and she hugged him tight. ''Oh, Andre.''

He pressed his lips to her brow. ''Are you happy, darling?''

''Of course I am.''

He drew back. ''You know we'll have to marry now. There's no longer a choice.''

Considering his words, Stephanie was overwhelmed with emotion, filled with love for him, and deeply thrilled to know that his child was growing inside her, a miracle she had never expected. Was her pregnancy a sign that she was meant to remain here with him? But what about Great-aunt Magnolia's warning that her mission would end? What of Sam, and her own life back in the present? What of Ebbie's fate if she and Andre should wed?

Gazing up at him in uncertainty, she asked, ''Andre, do you really think this can work?''

''Of course it can, darling.''

''And you'll have no regrets?''

He lifted her chin and stared solemnly into her eyes. ''*Chérie*, you must know something. I want to marry you because I love you. I think I've loved you from the moment you stepped inside my parlor wearing that dowdy gown. But I dared not tell you of my feelings, for you were afraid to love me in return.''

Her heart warmed by his admission, she threw her arms around his neck. ''I'm not afraid now, Andre. I love you, too. I think I've known it for a long time, but I dared not hope I could stay with you. I kept looking for an answer somewhere, and I think we may have been given that answer, straight from heaven. Perhaps our child is a sign that

I am meant to be here, that we can make it together—''

"Of course we can," he whispered.

With a catch in her voice, she finished, "But I'm really scared for Ebbie's sake."

His smile was supremely confident. "Don't worry, we'll get through it darling . . . together. We'll figure out something for her soon. You'll see."

She gazed at him with love and doubt. "But what if I'm wrong? What if you still lose me?"

Reaching down to stroke her belly, Andre whispered, "You're a part of me now, my love. You're not going anywhere. Marry me, Stephanie?"

"Yes," she whispered, kissing him amid more blissful tears. "Oh, yes."

Chapter 45

Later that morning, two couples faced each other in the parlor of Harmony House. Stephanie and Andre sat close together on wing chairs, with Ebbie and Peter Dearborn across from them on the settee. The small talk had been exhausted, and an awkward lapse in the conversation had stretched out to an excruciating tautness.

Glancing at Andre, Stephanie was stunned at how tense he looked; a worried scowl gripped his handsome visage, and he kept shifting uneasily in his chair.

For that matter, he'd been a nervous wreck ever since they'd decided they would tell Ebbie the truth; indeed, he was the one who had insisted they summon Peter Dearborn here to help prop up Ebbie emotionally, arguing that Peter had been a good friend to her, if not a suitor.

Andre cleared his throat. "Well, Ebbie, I guess you're wondering why we've gathered everyone here . . ."

She smiled. "It does seem a trifle odd to have Peter here so early."

"Yes, I know. I thought you might need his counsel and moral support."

"Did you?" Ebbie appeared puzzled.

Andre flashed her a stiff smile. "The truth is, Stephanie and I have hidden something from you."

"You have?" she asked blankly.

Andre groaned. "There's no easy way to put his. Stephanie and I . . . Well, we're in love."

Stephanie watched her friend closely, only to have her

worst fears confirmed. For a moment Ebbie appeared uncertain as she glanced from Andre to Stephanie; then her lower lip began to quiver; then she burst into tears and fell into Peter's arms. Looking helpless, Peter held her and patted her back.

Stephanie wrung her hands. "I knew it!" she cried to Andre. "We've devastated poor Ebbie."

"We're really sorry, dear," he muttered.

Then, Stephanie was flabbergasted to watch Ebbie lift her head from Peter's shoulder and begin to laugh! "No, no, Stephanie. You're so wrong."

For a moment, Stephanie was too taken aback to speak. "What do you mean, I'm wrong?"

Wiping away her tears, Ebbie flashed Stephanie an ironic smile. "I'm far from destroyed, only relieved, so very relieved."

"*Relieved*? You're relieved?"

Turning to Peter with a look of sublime joy, Ebbie declared, "Now Peter and I can marry!"

Even as Stephanie gaped at the other couple, Peter gazed lovingly back at Ebbie. "Yes, darling, didn't I tell you all would work out in time?"

Dumbfounded, Stephanie watched the two fall into each others' arms again, blissfully hugging and kissing. She glanced at Andre, and he merely gave her a look of bafflement.

Stephanie looked back at the other couple to see Peter with an idiotic grin on his face and his arm around Ebbie's shoulders. "Isn't this wonderful?" he asked.

There was another moment of mystified silence, then Stephanie sprang to her feet to confront the two. "Now, wait just a darned minute! I demand an explanation here. Ebbie, you've told me all along that you will marry Andre! You've all but admitted that you love him. Now you're saying you're really in love with Peter?"

"Oh, yes, I am," Ebbie declared, gazing radiantly at him.

Stephanie waved a hand. "You can't just drop a bombshell like this, then sit there cooing like a couple of lovebirds. How did this happen?"

Ebbie regarded Stephanie apologetically. "You're right,

we do owe you an explanation. Actually, Peter and I have been in love for ages. But you see, I made a deathbed promise to Linnea that I would care for her children . . . and wed Andre.''

''You did?'' Stephanie asked, eyes widening as she remembered Ebbie mentioning a ''promise'' to Andre.

''Yes, indeed,'' affirmed Ebbie.

Stephanie glanced suspiciously at Andre. ''Did you know about this?''

He looked rather guilty. ''Well, not for some time.''

''So that's why you kept alluding to obligations and such,'' Stephanie said to Ebbie.

She nodded soberly.

''Ebbie's vow was a sacred duty,'' Peter explained, squeezing her hand. ''Much as I loved her, I knew she could never marry me—or anyone else, for that matter—as long as she remained obligated to Andre and his children.''

''Okay,'' Stephanie muttered, still struggling to absorb everything. ''So, Ebbie, was your promise the reason you resisted all our matchmaking attempts, even with Peter?''

''Yes,'' Ebbie confirmed. ''I knew I had to save myself for Andre unless he found someone else first—which was, of course, the only way I might be released from my obligation.'' She sighed. ''I must confess I wasn't very happy about my fate, but I was determined to do my duty.''

''My God!'' Stephanie cried. ''At last it's all beginning to make sense to me. You sometimes seemed so sad and mopey *not* because Andre didn't love you, but because you were bound by a promise that kept you from marrying Peter!''

''Precisely,'' agreed Ebbie.

''Then Peter was the mysterious person who sent you those love letters and the roses?'' she pressed.

Ebbie beamed at him. ''Indeed he was.''

''But when I first arrived here, why were you so befuddled around Andre, blushing and even dropping things?''

Glancing at Andre, Ebbie's cheeks grew warm once again. ''Forgive me, Andre, but I was never very comfortable around you back then, given my promise to Linnea, and its—implications.''

Smiling magnanimously, Andre got up and moved over to place an arm around Stephanie. "I understand entirely, Ebbie. Don't give it a thought."

Ebbie glanced sheepishly at Stephanie. "I must also admit to being a trifle perverse in resisting your help, Stephanie, since I really was hoping you and Andre might become sweethearts, which would be a godsend for me, leaving me free to marry Peter."

Stephanie laughed. "This is too rich! Are you actually telling me that, while I was playing matchmaker with you, you were playing matchmaker with me?"

"Precisely," Ebbie admitted with a guilty smile.

"Then the joke is actually on me?"

Appearing utterly sincere, Ebbie got up and went to touch Stephanie's arm. "Stephanie, dear, I want you to know I didn't just maneuver you so I could be with Peter. I sensed all along that you and Andre were perfect for each other. And I also wanted you to stay, because . . ." She sniffed at happy tears. "Because I wanted you as a sister."

"Oh, Ebbie!" Stephanie hugged her friend, feeling deeply touched that Ebbie had resorted to such desperate machinations to keep her here. Moving back, she slanted Ebbie a look of gentle reproach. "Of course I want you as a sister, too. But still you put me through hell, frustrating me at every turn."

Ebbie stole a glance at Andre. "Well, you made it clear to both Andre and me that you intended to leave as soon as my happiness was secured. So of course I couldn't actually commit to *any* suitor—and there I include Andre— or you would have left us. Moreover, Andre and I knew that we had to keep you guessing, keep you around long enough so that you'd realize you really loved him." She winked at Andre. "Isn't that right, dear?"

He winked back. "Indeed. Ebbie and I agreed that we must thwart your goals however we could so you couldn't leave us."

Listening to the two, Stephanie was astounded. "Now, wait just a cotton-pickin' minute! This is beginning to go beyond the pale! Do you honestly mean you and Andre got together and plotted against me?"

Ebbie pressed a hand to her chest in mock indignation. "Me and Andre plotting?"

Piously, he added, "Why, perish the thought, woman! Would either of us ever stoop to anything so underhanded?"

Stephanie faced down Andre with hands balled on her hips. "I don't know about Ebbie, but you'd manipulate me in a New York minute! Oh, of all the tricky, underhanded . . . ! I knew you two were up to something!"

Andre pressed a finger to Stephanie's lips, tender amusement glinting in his eyes. "Hush, darling. You may have lost to us, but you've also won. When are you ever going to find a family who loves you so much that they'd go to such lengths to keep you with them?"

Stephanie's outrage dissolved in a welling of heartfelt emotion. For Andre had spoken the truth. She had lost—but had won so much more!

"Andre Goddard, for once you're absolutely right," she admitted, her love for him shining in her eyes. "I'm lucky to have you both."

With a contented sigh, he held her close.

"Oh, this is so wonderful!" declared Ebbie. "Do you suppose the four of us can have a double wedding?"

"Yes, Ebbie and I can't wait to marry," added Peter.

"Ooops!" Stephanie exclaimed. "We've all forgotten one problem—and it's a doozy."

"Yes?" inquired Peter with a frown.

"What about—pardon my bluntness, Reverend—your crazy mother?"

He chuckled. "She's going to go live with the General in Charleston. He finally got released from the asylum, and his daughter, Millicent, has promised to act as caretaker to them both after their wedding."

Stephanie's mouth dropped open.

Ebbie clapped her hands ecstatically. "Do you suppose we can all get married at Christmas? Wouldn't that be fun?"

As Ebbie and Peter again embraced, Stephanie shook her head, while Andre whispered, "I *told* you she never cared for me."

Chapter 46

O n Christmas day, two radiant brides walked down
the aisle of the Episcopal church, heading toward
two smiling grooms who awaited them at the altar graced
by flowers and backlit by glorious stained glass panels. Stephanie was escorted by Henry Robillard, while Ebbie was
on the arm of Abner Trumble. Just ahead of the brides were
the flower girls, Amy and Gwen, adorable in pink velvet
dresses as they dispensed giggles and rose petals along the
way.

Ebbie looked beautiful in a white silk gown embellished
with seed pearls, Stephanie glorious in a dress of beige satin
trimmed with the finest Valenciennes lace. Both brides carried corsages of white camellia blossoms, wore veils of
wispy tulle, and sported long trains appliquéd with orange
blossoms and edged with lace and ruffles.

The congregation was filled to capacity, with Beau and
Paul sitting proudly in the first pew, next to Katie Banks
and Martha, who held little Sarah. Since one of the grooms
was the rector of the Episcopal church, the white-haired
bishop of Mississippi, William Mercer Green, was offici-
ating today.

As Stephanie arrived at the altar and Andre moved out
to join her, he smiled solemnly at her, and her heart fluttered
with excitement. How dashing and incredibly handsome
both grooms looked in their formal cutaways—especially
her groom! Stephanie noted Ebbie's look of radiant bliss as
Peter joined her. Over the past weeks, the mousey little

371

spinster had become transformed into a beautiful, vivacious bride-to-be, whose eyes were gleaming with love as she prepared to marry the man of her dreams. Stephanie took such pride in knowing she had managed to secure Ebbie's happiness, after all. Completing her mission had brought her such blessings—she'd found a new sister, as well as a new family for herself.

The past month had been filled with Christmas soirées and engagement parties; both Andre and Stephanie had been thrilled when the children had accepted their upcoming marriage so well. Yet even as Stephanie's heart was overflowing with joy that she would get to marry the man she loved, even as she felt his tiny baby beginning to swell within her, doubt still nagged at her. She continued fervently to hope that her pregnancy was a sign that she was destined to remain here. But Great-aunt Magnolia's warning that her mission would end still troubled her, making her fear she might yet return to the present.

Oh, she didn't want to return now. She did miss Sam; indeed, her biggest regret was never having made peace with her sister, and never seeing her family again. But she sensed her place was here, where she was needed by Andre and his children. Andre had not only turned her life into a grand adventure, he'd given her a love she'd never thought she would know again—a love more precious because she might yet lose it.

Every time she thought about leaving him and the children, the possible impact on them devastated her. How could she take away Andre's unborn child? How could she rob the children of a new stepmother, when they'd lost their real mother only a year ago? How could she bear to leave this family whom she loved, who loved her so much, even if, ultimately, she might be wrenched away against her will?

She had discussed these doubts with Andre, arguing that he could be inviting heartache for himself and his children if they proceeded with the marriage. Yet he'd insisted that they must wed, and that of course she'd be allowed to stay. Stephanie knew he was so confident because he'd never really believed in her time-travel experience. But she knew better.

Nonetheless, as Bishop Green began the wedding service, Stephanie listened with joy and lovingly repeated her vows. She smiled radiantly at her husband-to-be, and he grinned back.

She also noted the look of exquisite happiness on Ebbie's face as she and Peter said their vows. When Andre placed the ring on Stephanie's finger, when he gazed at her with such incredible tenderness and deep love, she felt tears welling. At last the minister said proudly, "You may kiss the brides." As Andre drew back her veil, took her in his arms, and ardently claimed her lips, her happiness was complete.

"Are you my mama now?" asked a grinning Gwen.

Back home in the parlor, Stephanie was touched when Gwen rushed up to ask this question. All around her, guests were milling, eating cake and sipping champagne. In one corner, a festive Christmas tree gleamed with candles and brightened the room with its sugarplums, toy ornaments, and popcorn strings. At the base of the tree, Beau and Paul were playing with a wrought-iron train. Nearby, a lady from the church sat at the piano, playing "Beautiful Dreamer."

Stephanie reached down to squeeze Gwen's hand. "Of course I am, darling—but only if you want me to be your mother."

"I do," announced Gwen, and nearby, several guests chuckled.

Amy rushed up and hugged Stephanie's legs. "Mama!" she announced gleefully.

Stephanie patted the child's head and wiped away a tear.

As the girls dashed away, Andre joined Stephanie, handing his bride a glass of champagne. "Darling, this is a joyous occasion. You shouldn't be crying."

"But that's why I'm crying."

"You've stolen all our hearts, Stephanie," he murmured with deep emotion.

She squeezed his hand. "You've stolen mine."

The two were sharing a smile as Katie Banks stepped up. "Congratulations, dear," she said, hugging Stephanie. "I wish my Henry could have had you, but I'm thrilled to see you so happy."

"Thanks, Katie," Stephanie said.

Katie wagged a finger at Andre. "You take care of this fine girl, now, or you'll have me to reckon with."

"You may count on my cooperation," he replied with a proud grin.

As she moved away, Henry Robillard stepped to the center of the room and held up his champagne goblet. "A toast, everyone! To Andre and Stephanie, Peter and Ebbie."

As everyone toasted and cheered the newlyweds, Stephanie smiled at her dear friend, Ebbie, and she smiled back. When she noticed Peter had moved away to a refreshment table, she stole over to her friend's side.

"Ebbie, you look so beautiful," she said.

Ebbie touched her arm. "As do you."

"But you've truly become transformed these past weeks."

"If I have, it's thanks to your help."

"Are you truly happy now?"

Face aglow, Ebbie hugged her. "I'm all but mad with happiness!"

"Speaking of being out of one's mind . . ." Stephanie nodded toward Peter, who was in the corner handing his mother a cup of punch and a plate of cake. "I don't envy you your honeymoon, taking Mrs. Dearborn to Charleston."

Ebbie laughed. "Actually, Mother Dearborn's delusions seem harmless enough and can even be fun. Ever since Peter and I informed her we would take her to be with the General, all she's been talking about is how the South is going to rise again."

Stephanie shook her head. "I still don't envy you . . ." She touched her friend's arm. "But I know you and Peter will find the greatest joy together. Take care, my friend."

Ebbie hugged her again, and her voice came choked. "I will. And I can't wait to get back, so we can be friends and sisters always." She moved back to eye Stephanie solemnly. "Is that agreed?"

Stephanie fought back the lump in her throat. "I'll try my best."

"Good. You know, Andre invited Peter and me to join you on your wedding trip to Venice in the spring. He says

Katie and Henry have already volunteered to keep the children. What do you think?''

"I think that would be simply divine."

All at once, Stephanie smiled wistfully as the strains of "The Last Rose of Summer" drifted over from the piano. As if on cue, Andre arrived before her and handed her a dusky pink rose.

"May I have the honor of this dance, Madame Goddard?''

Overwhelming love filled Stephanie's heart as she accepted the rose and smiled back at her husband. "Of course you may, Mr. Goddard."

Tenderly Andre pulled his bride into his arms. With eyes only for each other, the newlyweds waltzed. Peter and Ebbie joined in, and everyone else looked on joyously.

By the time Ebbie, Peter, and Mrs. Dearborn departed, Stephanie was exhausted. As Andre was bidding the final few guests farewell, she took the children up to bed, then went to Andre's room to undress for their wedding night. Even though she'd had only a couple sips of champagne, she could barely keep her eyes open. After brushing out her hair and donning her lacy white nightgown, she slipped between the covers . . . and found herself dozing immediately.

Sometime later, she was awakened with a kiss. Andre sat beside her, handsome and sexy in his dressing gown. As she sat up in bed, he handed her a small glass half-filled with wine.

"Happy, Mrs. Goddard?" he asked.

"Never happier, Mr. Goddard." Recklessly, Stephanie gulped down the wine.

"Hey, take it easy," Andre chided. "I don't want you falling asleep again tonight."

"You rascal," Stephanie teased back. "You know you brought me the wine to make it easier to have your wicked way with me."

He scowled. "But darling, I didn't bring you the wine. It was already poured on the dresser. One of the servants must have left it there."

All at once Stephanie gasped as she gazed down at a

hauntingly familiar crystal goblet—the one etched with a rose, the very same wineglass that had mysteriously disappeared on the night she'd arrived back in time! It didn't take her long to make the connection and realize the significance of what she'd just done. Panic overwhelmed her, and her crazed eyes met Andre's.

"Oh, no!" she wailed. "What have I done? This must be the sign, the one Great-aunt Magnolia warned me about! My mission here has been accomplished, Ebbie is happy, and now I'm about to leave you, Andre! Oh, God, I don't want to go!"

"Silly girl, what are you ranting about?" Andre scolded, taking the empty glass and setting it on the bedside table. "No more wine for you, my pet. And you aren't going anywhere."

"But you don't understand—it's the sign, the very glass I drank from before!" she cried, wringing her hands. "Oh, how could I have been so stupid! This is terrible!"

Andre pulled her close. "Stephanie, hush, now. Darling, it's all right."

"It's not! Oh, Lord, it's not." Clinging to him, Stephanie felt near-hysterical, certain she was about to be wrenched away from the man, the family, she had come to love so much.

He stroked her back and spoke soothingly. "Sweetheart, I'm here, and I'm not going to let anyone take you away from me. Do you understand?"

Even as she tried to protest again, Andre silenced her with a tender kiss. Stephanie responded with heartfelt passion, terrified she was about to lose him forever.

He pushed her back against the pillows, and his gaze burned into hers. "You're mine, darling, mine," he murmured, his lips trailing fire down her throat. "We belong together—you'll see."

"Oh, Andre, I hope so," she whispered back, burying her face in his hair. "With all my heart, I hope so."

She moaned in ecstasy as his wet mouth found her swollen nipple, as his hands caressed her intimately. She gave herself to her husband eagerly, welcoming his deep, drugging kisses, the heat of his naked body on hers, the rapture of his devouring thrusts, the blinding sweetness of their shared climax. Tears spilled from her eyes as Andre clutched her hands tightly in his and whispered at her ear, "We're truly one now, darling . . . for always."

"For always," she whispered back, kissing him tenderly.

Afterward, Stephanie clung to him and fought to stay awake, fearing she might indeed awaken back in the present, that she'd find her arms cruelly empty, forever. Eventually, however, the warmth and strength of Andre's body drugged her, and slumber overcame her . . .

Stephanie found herself in a lovely, brilliantly lit church, where the atmosphere was brightly surreal. She was sitting in a pew in her nightgown, watching a bride stroll down the aisle . . . it was her sister, Sam, and she looked beautiful, radiant!

Sam turned and smiled at Stephanie, handing her a long-stemmed white rose. Stephanie took the flower, enchanted to see a Monarch butterfly feeding on its nectar. In awe, she watched the butterfly flutter its wings, then soar off toward the lovely soft light of the stain-glassed windows. She gazed up at Sam questioningly.

"It's all right, Stef," Sam whispered. "I know you're okay now. After you disappeared, I went to your office to get your things, and found your journal in your desk drawer. I know all about your life with Andre. You even left me a picture of the two of you with your darling baby boy."

Awed, Stephanie glanced at the front of the church, where she spotted Chester smiling and waving at Sam. "You're really okay?" she asked Sam with a catch in her voice.

Sam quickly hugged Stephanie. "Yes. And you were right, Stef. I told Chester he must choose between me and Mama, and he chose me. Don't worry about me, I'll be all right. Good-bye now. All is well."

Stephanie wiped away joyous tears and watched her sister glide down the aisle toward the man she loved. . . .

Stephanie awakened with a gasp, terrified she might be back in the present. When she twisted about, she was overjoyed to see Andre smiling tenderly at her. It was morning and she was still in bed with her beloved bridegroom.

"Darling! Thank God, I didn't leave you!" she cried, kissing him.

"Of course you didn't leave me, silly goose," he scolded.

"You won't believe what just happened," she continued. "I had a dream in which I saw my sister. Sam is happy now. She gave me a white rose—with a butterfly that flew away. She married Chester. And I can stay here with you now . . . forever!"

"Why, I'd lock all the doors if you ever tried to leave," he declared with a feigned scowl.

"I suppose I really did accomplish my mission," she continued with wonderment. "And part of it must have been coming here—and loving you."

"Darling," he murmured, kissing her cheek, "you've only just begun loving me."

"Indeed I have." She frowned thoughtfully. "But I must start keeping a journal—and knitting blue booties. Then later, we must have a picture made—you, me and the baby. And find a way to leave it all for Sam . . ."

As Stephanie continued thinking aloud, Andre eyed her in bemusement, then scowled as he glanced down at the covers. "What's this? There's a drop of blood on the coverlet."

Andre drew back the bedspread, and both of them stared, awestruck, at a long-stemmed white rose clutched tightly in Stephanie's hand.

Andre glanced at his bride in amazement. "What does this mean?"

For a moment Stephanie was too moved to speak, tears burning her eyes and overwhelming emotion filling her heart. Then she gazed up at him starkly. "Andre, there's much I have to tell you, and one of these days you *will* believe me."

"I'll try, darling," he promised.

Tears spilling down her cheeks, she caressed his face with her free hand. "But for now, just know I love you so much."

"No more than I love you."

Andre set aside the rose and tenderly kissed the small wound on Stephanie's palm. With a sob of joy, she slipped into her husband's arms . . .